Vallamont

The massive stone castle built by Abel Cottor high above the vast domain he ruled like a king.

Vallamont

Symbol of the savage battle fought by two generations of Cottor and McKay men for control of the rich Pennsylvania timberlands—and for the possession of a beautiful woman.

Vallamont

The setting of a divided love, a consuming rage, and a dark vow of vengeance!

Pamela Gayle

Vallamont

PUBLISHED BY POCKET BOOKS NEW YORK

Another *Original* publication of POCKET BOOKS

POCKET BOOKS, a Simon & Schuster division of
GULF & WESTERN CORPORATION
1230 Avenue of the Americas, New York, N.Y. 10020

ISBN: 0-671-81486-9

First Pocket Books printing January, 1979

10 9 8 7 6 5 4 3 2 1

Trademarks registered in the United States and other countries.

Printed in the U.S.A.

CONTENTS

PROLOGUE

1862–1875

I fell in love with the mountain called Vallamont when I was a little girl, just as surely as I fell in love with Steven Cottor the first time I saw him there.

The mountain was my special place. During the days when we owned it, my parents would bring me with them when they rode for picnics to the wide, grassy clearing at the top. Up there the war the grown-ups talked about seemed far away. Vallamont was peaceful and grand, especially in that high meadow. There my father would pick me a little bouquet of wildflowers and sometimes tickle my chin, and mother's, too, with the soft petals of a buttercup. Then he and I would walk through the tall grass, my child's pinafore swishing in the cattails and Queen Anne's lace as I tried to keep up with Father in his shiny black high-topped shoes. And when we reached the spot where we could see out over the pine forests to view the whole valley, Father would scoop me up in his arms and hold me so I could see what he saw.

Together we would look down at the tiny buildings

3

of Grampian, spread out like children's blocks along the edge of the blue Susquehanna River far below us, and at the hundreds of tiny logs, some of them floating free, others stacked up on rafts, that were coming down-river with the current to the Grampian lumber mills. We would find Father's mill first, barn-shaped, painted white, way off to the left with the other mills and down-stream from our big new house. Then I would point out our old house, which Father now rented, and the other buildings in town that we owned, repeating in my little girl's voice, "That's ours, and that one . . ."

Sometimes then Father would point out something we owned that I had missed, or point to another place —some land, a house—and ask whether I thought we should get that one, too. And I would always answer yes, and he would give me a brisk hug and a squeeze, the skin of his ample cheeks cool and smelling clean with the fresh air. "Someday, young lady, you'll have bought the whole of it, eh? And what then? Want to buy Ohio?"

A laugh, another squeeze, and we would start back for the shade of an oak tree at the edge of the clearing, where Mother had laid out the picnic lunch from the big wicker hamper we had carefully strapped behind the saddle of Father's horse. I loved those times as much as anything else I can remember in my childhood, especially the moment when Father, having carried me all the way back on his broad shoulders, would stand before Mother and announce, "It's official, then. We'll buy it. Catherine says we should go ahead!"

But the year of my eleventh birthday the picnics stopped. A man named Cottor was making trouble for Father. I was too young to understand it all then; I only knew that Father had done something called "over-extending," and that he had to sell some of the build-ings he had bought even though he did not want to. A short while later he came home in a very bad temper one night and I learned he had lost yet more buildings. And a few months after that, after remaining withdrawn and silent all through dinner with us, Father grimly announced that as of today we no longer owned Vallamont.

I was too big to cry, even though I felt like it. I only said, "We'll buy it back someday, won't we, Daddy?"

He gave me a little nod, a warm look that said he was glad I had spoken up. And then his voice was hard. We would get Abel Cottor for what he had done. We would see him dragged down from Vallamont and ruined. Abel Cottor was not going to hold on to Vallamont for even another year.

But Abel Cottor did. Even as Father, working harder than ever, gradually built back his holdings, so, too, Abel grew stronger along with many other lumbermen in Grampian. A year passed, and then another, until it was late August, just before I was to leave for my first year away from home at a school in Boston.

I was fourteen. I had come up to the clearing on Vallamont by myself, as I had done whenever I could for the past two years. Partly I wanted to defy Abel Cottor, the man I had never seen who was the hated enemy of our family. Vallamont belonged to me; I still felt that, and I still hungered to stand on its summit and look down. I could see the buildings myself now, for I was tall enough. And I would go up there and point to them one by one, in my child's fantasy, those my father owned now, and those we had lost but would get back, and those I would someday, somehow, buy on my own.

But today when I reached the clearing someone else was there ahead of me. I had walked up through the pines and so had he, for there was no horse feeding in the grasses nearby and no one else in sight. He had his back to me, standing with hands on hips, naked to the waist and well-muscled. He stood on my lookout spot at the crest.

The red stripes of a lash showed harshly across his back and shoulders.

He turned and saw me as I approached. His face grew more handsome with every step I took. Dark eyes, large and expressive, studied me as I walked through the open field. A full mouth was set in a well-poised half-smile. Wavy black hair, dampened at the edges with perspiration, framed a fresh, smooth face that showed only slightly the pain he must have been feeling from the red welts on his back. I judged him to be about seventeen.

Mindful of the dangers of meeting a strange man alone, even one so good looking and young, I told him that I was from a farm over in the next valley and that my brothers and I were hunting squirrels here on the south slope of the mountain. He told me that his name was Steven. This was his favorite spot, he said, when he had something troublesome to think about.

"Like those marks on your back?" I asked. "They must hurt." A few years earlier Mother had cared for a painful scrape on my knee when I had fallen up here. Now, just as she had done then, I took water from the canteen I had brought along, and with a few strips of cloth from his shirt and a sprig from one of the aloe plants that still grew nearby, I tended to the wounds.

He smiled at me when I was done. "You're beautiful. Do you know that?"

I gave a matter-of-fact nod, partly because I did know it. They had always told me I was a beautiful child, and now my breasts were beginning to fill out, slowly, softly, so that when people made comments now they said I was getting to be a lovely young lady. But when he said the words then, I felt something different, something that by instinct I thought I should not let show.

He would not talk about who had whipped him or even who he was; he just said that he lived in Grampian and liked to come up here. We watched the view together, the river and the mountains beyond. His speech was as well educated as his manner was authoritative, and he was knowledgeable about the lumber yards and the mills and the rafts. He spoke as if he knew the men who owned the vast array of stock and equipment that lay before us, mentioning names of Gibson and Rawles and Sprague with a carelessness that indicated he held little esteem for any of their dealings, or for the whole of the lumber industry, for that matter. As I watched him, I wondered who he was. He seemed the very image of the dreams we girls at school whispered about during unguarded moments.

I felt an urge to tease him, to get through that air of casual bravado and see what lay beneath. "Well, I think I should be going," I said with a smile. "Maybe you should, too. Will they beat you again if you're late? I wouldn't want them to do that on my account."

His face darkened for only a moment. Then he arched his eyebrows in mock surprise. "So soon? A busy young lady. When can you come back? I'll be here tomorrow."

He was talking down to me as if I were just another silly little fourteen-year-old! "Well, I won't," I said. "I won't be back until . . . until next Christmas." I was not sure of my school vacation calendar, but I could not imagine them keeping us away from home during the Christmas holiday. "Do you think you'll still be in town then?"

"I might. I might even stop over at your . . . ah . . . farmhouse in the meantime to say hello, if you're so sure you won't be over this way for that long."

He was watching me closely, as if he did not believe my story any longer and wanted to see how I reacted.

"You needn't bother. I'm leaving for school tomorrow. Christmas is the first time I'll be back."

"Oh, really? I had no idea farmers around here believed so strongly in education for their daughters." He was smiling now, sure that he had caught me.

"My father does," I said, my voice firm. "If you want to see me again, you'll have to wait until Christmas. Now, I do have to go."

He put out a hand, lightly, touching my arm. "Ah, now, just one moment. What *time* at Christmas? You

7

don't expect me to wait up here in the snow for a week, do you?"

"Well, perhaps I could send you a note, when I . . . when I have more of my plans decided. Just tell me your name and where to send it."

He laughed. "You're clever, aren't you? I like that. No, I'll tell you what I'll do. I'll send *you* the note. Then perhaps we'll meet somewhere else, somewhere not quite so hard to get to in the winter."

"But I haven't told you . . ."

He held up his hand. "You're clever. Perhaps you'll be able to think how I'll do it. But since it's to be such a long time, and since I may not even be able to manage it and never see you again, I think it would be appropriate just to have one quick kiss. . . ."

He pulled me into his arms then, with such an easy, swift movement that I scarcely realized what had happened. As I began to say "No," he covered my lips with his, warm and full, and though I struggled, he held me too strongly for me to break away. No one had kissed me on the mouth before. I had never felt such a heady, dizzying warmth as the feeling that swept through me then. But then he released me and smiled, pleased with himself, though I felt dazed and strangely excited, I pulled myself up and slapped him suddenly across the face.

Then I turned and ran, his laughter from behind me ringing in my ears.

But all that fall I wondered who "Steven" had been. And as the time for vacation in December approached, I wondered more often whether when I got home there would be a note from him waiting for me.

His note, though, arrived before I went home. One December noon I had collected my mail before going into the dormitory dining room for lunch, when the matron held up before me an envelope bearing the shield of Harvard College. "This came for you, too," she said, her plump face set in a stern expression. "A young man brought it by the school this morning.

Said he was a relative of yours. As you know, our regulations prohibit your seeing anyone but a relative while you are in our charge."

As she held the envelope, I could see where atop the Harvard insignia had been printed plainly: STEVEN RAWLES. Steven! Hoping that I did not show any surprise, I explained casually that my cousin Steven was taking a degree at Harvard and that he was likely dropping me a note to see if I wanted to share transportation expenses on the trip home for vacation.

She studied the name on the envelope for a moment or two and then handed it over. "Be so good as to tell me if there's any reply," she said. "And if you change *any* of the arrangements your father has already made, be certain to let me know so that I can advise him."

And with a look that made me feel like a criminal trying to escape from prison, she dismissed me.

The note said:

Will call upon you this afternoon at four, if I may. My back has healed quite well.

Steven

It was fortunate he had not said more, I thought, looking at the envelope. Plainly, the letter had been steamed open and then resealed.

When he called, dressed in elegant tweeds, he stayed only a short time. Under the watchful eye of the chaperone in the reception lounge, he asked what train I would be taking back to Grampian, and when I told him the train and the compartment number, he put on a disappointed look. "Ah, well, I'm afraid I'll have to be back sooner than that. Promised 'em faithfully. But don't fret, I'll give the folks your regards and tell 'em you're still alive. Don't study too hard till they let you out."

He met me at my compartment on the train a week later. That day I found out that he had known who I was even before I had met him, for he had seen me with my father downtown in Grampian.

I found out also that I was in love with him, for when he took me in his arms and kissed me once more, the way he had kissed me on Vallamont, I did not protest —not even though he had told me that his father had been the one who had whipped him that summer morning, and that his father's name was Abel Cottor.

Of course, I could not see Steven again while we were in Grampian. But we did manage to meet that spring, coming home for Easter. Also, for a short while that summer, until our family sailed for Europe, we met sometimes on Vallamont, where there was no one to see us.

By the end of the following school year we had become lovers. It was not terribly difficult, even though I was still in the same school and under the same stern regulations. By then I was seventeen, and, like the other senior girls, I knew who on the staff needed money in exchange for looking the other way on the particular nights when they were on duty. We thought it was a great lark to smuggle a young man to our rooms without the matron being the wiser.

The first time there was a little pain. But after that it was only a delicious wildness that left me feeling full, glowing inside.

That summer Mother and I were in Europe again. And in the fall I was in college, along the Hudson River, and Steven, having graduated from Harvard, was in Grampian working for his father. During the next four years we saw each other rarely, only on those occasions when he had some excuse to travel to New York on business. Those times we did share were best when I could go into the city with Lisa, a school friend who lived there, for a weekend visit with her parents. That would give us a free afternoon Saturday for "shopping," and while Lisa shopped for both of us, Steven and I would make slow, wonderful love in his room at the Astor, where again money had ensured that none of the staff would ask any embarrassing questions.

I lived for those times, though I was busy with my studies and with the usual round of supervised callers and dances that were part of the college's social life. Many nights I lay awake wondering when next I would see him again. Many other nights, as my time came around each month, I worried about the consequences of our lovemaking and wondered whether I would soon be sent home in disgrace. But that never happened. Whether it was because of precautions on Steven's part or simply by chance, I did not know.

Naturally, I never gave myself to another man. Though I had many suitors, many very attractive, I did not take any of them seriously. I was saving myself for Steven.

And, yet, as my college years began to come to an end, a change came over our relationship. It began one Saturday in October when Steven told me of the great stone castle his father was building for himself on Vallamont, just in the center of the clearing where the two of us had first met. Steven spoke of it lightly, the way he always did on those rare occasions when either of us mentioned our parents. My father remained Abel Cottor's outspoken enemy, and his hatred, from what I could gather from Steven, was returned in kind.

Steven described the plans for the building, quite ornate, and then he said, "I suppose you'll want to marry me just so you can be mistress of the place someday when Abel gets tired of it."

His flippant tone stung something inside me and I flared back. "You'd be wiser to marry me. Then my father might let you set foot on Vallamont someday, provided I ask him to."

The intensity of my reply surprised him. It even surprised me. But there it was. Even though five years had gone by and I was a child no longer, I still clung to the belief that one day Vallamont would belong to our family again.

He glossed over it, but that afternoon was the beginning of the end for the idyllic love Steven and I had shared, the end of the time when the two of us, young and clever, could laugh at the rest of the world, with its poor, misguided foolish wrangling. Oh, we kept up the pretense that day, together in the soft double bed of his hotel room, where the roar of the New York City trains and the endless carriage traffic filtered through the shuttered window only dimly. But even as I shook with ecstasy in his arms, at the back of my mind I knew that when I returned home things could never be the same. He was Steven Cottor, and I Catherine Rawles, and once we were both back in Grampian there would be no convenient way around that fact.

I cried that night, silently, so as not to awaken Lisa or her family. And when the day finally arrived for me to graduate under the proud gaze of my parents, the tears I wept were not all tears of happiness.

And then it was back to Grampian, where within a few weeks the world my parents had so carefully prepared for me, and that other world, the one I had built for myself so happily with Steven, were to collide and change my life forever.

PART ONE

GRAMPIAN

ONE

May, *1875*

When I heard a cry coming through the dark pines from somewhere to my right, I had already slowed my horse to a walk. I had been about to swallow my pride and wait for Steven Cottor to catch up with me, for riding here on the unfamiliar north side of Vallamont had confused my sense of direction.

The voice came again, still from too far away to distinguish the words, although I could plainly hear the anguish in the tone. Was it Steven's voice? No, definitely not. I was certain I had never heard a cry like this before.

I reined in my horse, stopped, and listened. The cry seemed to come again, fainter this time, a moaning mixed with the wind in the pine boughs above me. Was it my imagination, or did the voice cry out "No more!"? I brushed a few wisps of my auburn hair back away from my eyes and tried to see what was over that way. But all I could see was the dark gloom of a pine forest, the great trunks with their dead lower branches, the green boughs high overhead that blocked out the sun, and the sweet-smelling dark carpet of brown pine needles that covered the forest floor and gave it an eerie stillness.

Should I go and see what the trouble was? I hesitated. It was late afternoon, and I really ought to have been on my way back some time ago. Unless I returned home soon, I would have to explain why I had stayed so long at the Saturday afternoon riding lesson that was to be the usual thing for me now that I had finished school. And if Father had the least notion that my story required checking, he would soon find out that I had missed my lesson and had instead gone riding with Steven Cottor.

I could not face the thought of that battle now. Even though I knew it would have to come sooner or later, I wanted to keep Father from learning about Steven for as long as I could.

Father and I had fought enough as it was during the past week. Ever since I had been home we had quarreled about his plans for me. He wanted to have me marry someone, of course—some wealthy prospect whose capital would fit in with Father's business empire. And, naturally, I refused to listen to his talk of a "practical" marriage.

"I'll choose my own husband when I'm ready for one," I had said, "and not before!"

"You'll do as you're told!"

He glared at me, but I would not be intimidated. If he was a fighter, so was I.

"You'll not tell me to sit around idle here in Grampian for single rich men to look at! I'm not going to! You've not brought me up as some . . . display creature, and I'm not about to begin now. If I'm going to stay here, I want to work!"

Yet Father refused to let me have anything to do with his business affairs, just as I refused to discuss any suitors. Even though there were hundreds of things I could have done to help, even though I had worked on his account books before, during summers home from school, and even though I had been the only woman in my class at college to receive top honors in a business course, Father still turned a deaf ear. All week long we had been in an angry stalemate. Neither of us would give in.

But I could *not* give in. If Steven thought that I was seeing someone else, even to please my father . . . it was impossible! Only this afternoon Steven had tried to force me to tell Father that we were engaged, and I had ridden off in tears. . . .

I did not want to think about that. I shook my head, trying to clear my mind. I was here on the north slope of Vallamont, with no one in sight. Steven had not caught up with me. After the quarrel we had just had, he might very well have decided to let me ride off and spend the rest of the afternoon alone.

The moaning up ahead had grown fainter. Perhaps someone had been hurt. I peered in the direction where the sound had come from. Was I mistaken, or were the woods less shadowy over there?

I turned my horse that way and went forward at a walk between the quiet, tall trees. Soon I had reached the crest of the mountain. Up ahead I could see a thick row of blue spruce, and above them I could see the bright afternoon sky. Beyond that row of spruce trees there was a wide clearing.

The stone mansion! There was only one clearing on Vallamont—the clearing I had known since I was a little girl. And that was the land where Abel Cottor had built his mansion last year.

I had never seen it, of course, but Steven had told me about the huge stone building that the people in town called "Cottor's Castle." Inside, the mansion was said to be even more extravagant than the homes on "millionaires' row" in Grampian. Abel had bought old-world oil paintings by the square foot, they said, and stained glass and sculptures by the hundredweight.

Wood-carvers had worked for months on the ornamentation alone. After out-spending everyone, Abel now could look down on the rooftops of the other millionaires' mansions along the river, as though they were so many little insects far below him. And even though I could scoff at such a transparent attempt to buy status, it was hard not to be fascinated by what Abel had done. Twice since I had been back in Grampian I had climbed the flights of stairs to our fourth-floor cupola and looked out, trying to see the outlines of the "castle" at the top of Vallamont. But I had not been able to find it among the trees.

My pulse quickened as I dismounted and walked ahead of my horse between the last of the tall pines. The castle had to be behind the wall of spruce, even though I could not see it. The spruce had been planted so close together that they scarcely had room to grow. But my horse smelled something. It snorted and jerked at the bridle, nearly tearing the reins out of my hand. Whatever it was afraid of was not far away.

I steadied my horse and looked again at the wall of trees. Should I go in there? Of course, I was trespassing on Abel Cottor's land, but someone might be in danger. Then, even as I hesitated the voice came again, this time louder and more frightened.

I made up my mind, walking up to the trees and parting the boughs of the nearest one. Instinctively, I crouched low, as close to the trunk as I could get, while I peered between the limbs and the stiff blue-green needles.

I could see clearly. On the other side of a wide green lawn stood what could only be Cottor's Castle. The high walls were smooth, shaped in the graceful lines of an Italian villa, and covered with that heavy yellow stucco they said Abel had brought in by railroad. On the far side I could see one of the two stone towers that gave the mansion its medieval quality. This turret rose a full sixty feet into the air, and its companion piece around at the front rose even higher. I could see the top of the front tower over the pink-tiled roof, the stone blocks with the open spaces between them calling to mind a shadowy host of defenders who might be hidden there, ready to hurl down missiles and arrows at any attackers. Amidst the green of the lawn and the darker green of the surrounding forest, the castle seemed richly elegant, even from this distance. And, yet, though the afternoon sun flooded over the pink roof and the high walls of the castle's western side, the building looked strangely cold. Breathtaking, imposing, but cold.

Then I saw two men on horseback coming around to the lawn from the other side of the mansion, about a hundred yards away. Behind the two horses were ropes. The riders were dragging something along the ground.

In a moment I realized that what they were dragging was a man.

As I tried to reason through what had happened, another man, gray-haired and wearing a white shirt, came out of the mansion's rear entrance and walked toward the two riders while they dismounted. Soon they all stood together on the lawn, in the shadow of the stone walls.

What should I do? At this distance I could not recognize any of the men. I thought of riding out there with a story about being lost. Maybe that would stop them from whatever they had been doing to make that poor fellow scream so. But that would only be temporary. They might just give me directions and send me away and then go on with what they were doing after I was out of sight.

On the other hand, I could not ride out there and order them to stop. I had not seen them do anything. I did not even know who they were, except I was fairly certain that the gray-haired man who had come from the house was Abel Cottor. I was trespassing to boot, which hardly put me in a position to give them orders.

I decided to go around the edge of the clearing closer to where they stood, keeping out of their line of sight behind the spruce trees. If I saw something I couldn't prevent, my father would be only too happy to see that Abel Cottor received just punishment. I made certain my horse was comfortable where he stood, and then I walked around behind the spruces in the direction of the house, wishing with every step that the expensive riding boots Father had bought me didn't have such thin leather soles.

I stopped where I could hear a harsh voice.

"A name, Warren, give me a name."

I bent down behind a big blue spruce and found that the afternoon sun was directly in my eyes, coming from just over the treetops. Squinting, I shaded my eyes with one hand until I could see clearly. I was not twenty yards away from where the men were standing.

The man I was certain was Abel Cottor stood over the man who had been dragged as though he were about to kick him. The man lay prone. I could see the ropes tied to his wrists; the other ends were still attached to the saddles of the two horses. The two riders had mounted up again.

Abel was a big man, with a spreading waistline and a tall, long face, craggy and leathery, almost like an Indian's. He wore a crisp white shirt, well-creased black trousers, and black shoes as well shined as if he had just been at a formal dance. I knew that the Cottor mansion entertained frequently, even though Abel was a widower, but it struck me as unusual to see him dressed so well out here on his lawn astride a man in torn work clothes. For a moment I thought of Abel's ball next Saturday and the invitations that had set off such a stir in our family this morning. Then Abel bent over the man and my attention was riveted.

"You didn't think of it yourself, did you, Warren?" He took a good handful of the man's hair in his grip and yanked the head up straight. Warren had a thin, weak-jawed farmboy's face. He looked to be perhaps twenty-five, thin and gangly.

A trickle of blood came from one corner of his open mouth. "I . . . dunno what ya mean."

Abel looked him straight in the eye for a minute, the way a man does while he holds the head of a dog or a horse. Then he twisted Warren's head around away from him toward the big oak tree midway between the house and the edge of the back clearing.

"Who was it, Warren? You wouldn't just spike the logs in your own mill. Someone outside gave you those spikes. Someone wanted to slow us down. Isn't that right, Warren?"

"I dunno what this is. Lemme go out of these ropes."

Abel brought the man's head up higher, nearly lifting him up off his knees and onto his feet. Then he let Warren settle back down again, taking care to keep the face pointed at the oak tree.

"Warren, we don't have any use for you if you can't give us a name. You know that?"

"Lemme go, I tell ya. I ain't done nothin'."

"You, Garth." Abel looked at one of the men on horseback, a fat man with reddish hair. "Anybody see you bring Warren up here with you?"

"No, sir. Brought him in the carriage, just like you said."

The other man, dark and wiry, steadied his horse as it snorted and took a few steps, stretching one rope taut and pulling Warren's arm up by the wrist.

"All right, now, Warren. I'm going to give you one more chance to make yourself useful. I want you to look at that big, hard oak tree out there in the middle of the lawn, all by itself. And now I want you to tell me who gave you those spikes. Don't be afraid of him, whoever he is. We'll see to it that he doesn't harm you. Just tell us his name."

A moment went by. Then: "I can't tell ya nothin'."

Abel let go of the man's hair and examined the ropes on Warren's wrists, checking to see that they still were tied securely. Then he stepped back. "All right, then." He dusted off his hands. "You, Parsons, ride for the left side of the oak out there. Garth, you ride for the right side. Ride hard now, but keep even, just side by side, with Warren, here, right in the middle. When you get up to the tree, keep right on riding, hard and fast, so he hits the tree just face-on."

Parsons sucked in his breath. The man called Garth only nodded.

Abel continued. "Then if his arms are still attached, you bring him on back and try it again."

I stared in horror at the man called Warren, who had slumped over, one cheek on the warm earth. His mouth hung open while he tried to comprehend what they were going to do with him. The big calf eyes looked up at Abel, then around at the house, as if he hoped someone would come to rescue him. The horses pulled him around, straightening the ropes, until he was flat on his belly with his arms stretched out toward the tree. They waited, and he hauled himself up onto his knees. Then he sat back on his haunches.

I tried to cry out, but words would not come. My mouth was dry with fear. I struggled to stand up, to distract them, but I could not move. I was frozen as Abel nodded to the men, and then the two horses started to move forward.

Then Warren began to scream, and I struggled again to rise and somehow stop them. Instead, I felt myself falling. The ground, darkening, rushed up at me, but before I landed I lost consciousness.

I awoke in the same place to the pain of the stiff spruce needles on my cheeks. My hands were clutching the tree's rough bark for support. The sticky resin was all over my fingers. I looked out onto the lawn, and saw the man called Warren kneeling on the ground, thoroughly drenched with what must have been water from the bucket Parsons was now holding. Warren was soaked and shivering, but his face appeared unhurt. They must have stopped, I thought. They must have frightened him into telling them the truth.

I strained to hear what they were saying. The wind made the branches overhead rustle and sing, though, and I was still dazed, so it was hard to concentrate.

"Give me the name, Ruch," I heard Abel say. "Or do I tell Parsons to get back on his horse?"

Warren Ruch shook himself and wiped water from his eyes before he looked up. "I don't know who you are, mister," he said, "but I'll tell you what you want to know."

"Go ahead, then."

"I was workin' the feeder bin one afternoon when this guy I never seen before comes over near me and says my name."

"What did he look like? Who was he working for?"

"Didn't say. Tall, had a real orange head of hair, brighter'n any I ever seen before. He didn't say his name."

Abel looked at the other two. "Mean anything?"

Garth spoke. "Man like that works for Rawles, up by the long reach—when he works. Most times he don't. Name's Campbell. Could be him, but he don't come into town much, 'cept to get drunk."

"Rawles!" There was a fury in Abel's voice that made me wince. "All right, then, Warren, what did he tell you?"

Ruch began to whimper. "He said I could have two hundred dollars if I just put fifty spikes in the stock we had waitin' last night. Two hundred dollars if I did, but if I didn't, or if I told, he said they'd come for Alice . . ." His voice broke off for a moment, and then he said, "You wouldn't let 'em do nothin' to Alice, would ya, mister? I ain't goin' to tell no one, I swear. I don't even know what your name is."

"Nobody's going to do anything to Alice," Abel said. "Now, tell me, did this man give you the two hundred dollars yet?"

"He said he'd give it to me later, after he saw the repair crew come into the mill." Ruch wiped his nose on his sleeve, getting his face dirty again.

"Where's he going to meet you?"

"He didn't tell me that." Ruch looked up at Abel as if he were afraid of being struck across the mouth.

Abel shook his head, seemingly disgusted. "Well, we'll keep an eye on the both of you in the meantime. Maybe we'll even put on a little repair show down at the mill." He turned to Parsons. "All right, then. Get some whiskey in him and make it look like he got drunk and fell down and messed up his clothes. Dose him up good and lead him down the mountain to town. When you get to the edge of the woods, you can turn him loose."

He nodded once to the three of them, and then he turned and headed for the house, his long strides swift and authoritative.

As I watched him go inside and heard the door close tight, the anger boiled up inside me. How could they connect my father with this cowardly sabotage based only on a man's red hair? And how could they go on tormenting this Warren Ruch? They were struggling with him on the ground, trying to force whiskey from a bottle down his throat.

It was foolish of me, but I was not going to stand idly by for another moment. I forgot that I should have been back at the stables by now. I forgot that I was trespassing, and for the moment I forgot that these two men had been prepared to carry out a cold-blooded murder.

I stood up and pushed between the trees, the boughs catching on my jacket. The thin dark man saw me first as I stepped out onto the lawn. His face took on an astonished look for a moment. Then he was up and running toward me. Before I could speak or move another step, he had grabbed my wrist and twisted it painfully behind my back. His chin dug into my shoulder from behind, and his voice rasped horribly close to my ear. "Trespassin', ain't you? The boss likes to find out about trespassers."

He gave me a rough shove forward, but I would not

go another step. "You take your hands off me if you know what's good for you," I said. "And release that man."

He twisted me around to face him, his thin mouth in a crooked smile. "What is he, some friend of yours? How long you been up here?"

I looked him straight in the eye, for I was as tall as he was. "I said to release that man."

The one called Garth spoke up. "Hey, Parsons, why don't you hold her there a minute? See if she talks to me like that. Looks to me like she needs those teeth of hers loosened up some."

Suddenly I realized what an insanely foolish thing I had done. These men would not hesitate to hurt me. And if they found out who my father was, they would probably expect Abel to reward them. . . .

". . . not too quick with that," Parsons was saying. "Just pitch me over that whiskey. Let's see if we can't *persuade* her to tell us what she's doin' up here."

He grabbed my arm again, hard, making me wince, while Garth prepared to throw the whiskey bottle.

What happened next occurred so swiftly that I remember it only as a blur of events. Suddenly the man called Ruch lashed out at Garth with a kick that took him by surprise. Garth staggered, and then Ruch kicked him in the belly, knocking him down. Ruch made a running leap into the saddle of one of the horses. As Ruch struggled with the ropes on his wrists, Parsons pushed me down in the grass and dashed after him.

Now, I thought. Now was the time for me to get to my own horse and ride away from here!

I picked myself up and stumbled back behind the cover of the spruce trees. The needles hurt my face, but I pressed on, running through the forest as fast as I could, through the slippery pine needles on the forest floor. If I got to my horse, I could circle around to the road that I knew led up to Abel's mansion from Grampian. Once I was on that road I could head straight into town, then head for home.

No. I would have to take the horse back to the stable first. Otherwise, there would have to be explanations. Would I see Steven at the stables?

My toe caught on a root and I nearly fell flat. As it was, I stumbled against a tree, and one of the stubby, bare branches around the lower part of the trunk poked into my side and made me gasp with pain. Watch where you're going!, I thought angrily. Get to the horse first and then away from here. Then you'll have plenty of time to think.

I got my bearings again and set off. Up ahead I could see my horse's silhouette through the trees. It was right where I'd left it. Just a few steps more and then I had the reins in my hands and was steadying the horse to mount.

But I panicked when I heard someone ride through the trees close behind me. I gave a little cry and began to run, even though my lungs ached and I knew I didn't have the strength to get very far.

Then behind me I heard a voice, and suddenly everything changed. "Hey, hold on there, Catherine! Hold on there! Where do you think you're off to?"

I turned and looked up into the dark, handsome eyes of Steven Cottor. Quickly he had dismounted and was at my side, supporting me as I began to grow faint again. Suddenly I realized how disheveled I must look by now. I could feel my cheeks grow warm with the flush of embarrassment. He was asking me what had happened.

"I . . . need to catch my breath. One of your father's men attacked me back there, and I had to run away."

I leaned against Steven and told him about Warren Ruch. Slowly I began to feel that I was safe again. Surely Steven would protect me, even though we had quarreled, even though I could not do what he had demanded.

When I had finished speaking, Steven's brown eyes

hardened as he looked off in the direction of the castle. For a moment he seemed lost in another world far away from the woods where the two of us were standing.

"That bastard Abel." Steven called his father by his first name, behind his back and to his face, as well. "I swear he'll pay for it."

When he looked back at me, his eyes were warm with feeling. "Why do they have to drag us down with them? If only they weren't so damned foolish, we could . . ."

I knew he was talking about my father and his, and about the feud that still kept Steven and me apart. "Let's not quarrel again, Steven," I interrupted. "It's just going to take time."

As I turned my face up to his, I realized how much I wanted to reach out and touch the smooth contours of his face, as I might run my fingers lightly over the face of a marble statue. I was still fascinated by Steven's easy grace, by the way his boldness shone through his air of unmistakable breeding.

I had never refused him anything, really, until today. This afternoon I had blazed with anger. I would not be bullied into a marriage, I had told him, by my father or anyone else, including him.

Yet, even now, even though we had not yet settled our quarrel, Steven Cottor was difficult to resist. The warmth of his presence stirred feelings deep within me. The little half-smile that played around the corners of his lips seemed charming. I knew he understood the effect he was having.

And I knew, too, how much he wanted me.

His full, sensuous lips were only inches from mine.

"Oh, Steven," I said, "we can't make it hard for each other. What shall we . . . how shall . . ."

He brought his lips close to brush my words away, and in that moment came a glad release of welcoming. I yielded as his kiss came, warm and smooth, and then suddenly hard, urgent, demanding, until those desires we had shared together burned deep within me, and the wind, the afternoon forest, and the smell of the pines around us all were gone and there was only Steven.

All at once I grew frightened. I broke away from him, stepping backward to steady myself, looking around for a few moments until my thoughts cleared. I had been ready to give in to him just then! If he had asked me to promise him . . .

"I'd better be getting back," I said, and I was relieved that my voice did not betray the tumult of emotions that I felt. I could not think that I would give up my freedom and my family for the fascination of Steven's lovemaking. And I certainly could not have him thinking so!

Yet, I saw the confidence in his dark eyes. I found myself agreeing to meet him late that night in the rose arbor at the far end of our garden. And as we rode quietly down to the trail that led to the stables, the thought crossed my mind that beneath the surface of the proud millionaire's daughter I had been brought up to be might lie something or someone entirely different.

TWO

After I returned my horse to the stables and made sure that it would be properly attended to, I had Jared, Father's coachman, drive me home along the river road. This wasn't the quickest way home, but I knew that I needed time to think. Besides, I liked to watch the mountains and the river as we drove along. There was a range of mountains called the Bald Eagles across the Susquehanna River, rising up from its southern bank. These mountains were not as high as Vallamont, but they gave me a feeling of peace, with the new green of fresh spring leaves showing on them like a mist above the waters of the wide river. Since it was late Saturday, the river was nearly quiet. Only a log raft or two, each with its two polemen, floated along on the way down to the mills in Grampian from the "boom," the floating corral where branded logs from every lumber camp were stored upstream. Here and there on the banks were the fishermen: shantytown boys with fishing poles, or solitary men in ragged work clothes, still hoping to catch a trout or a bass for the night's dinner.

From my seat in Father's open summer carriage, I watched the river and tried to put my thoughts in order. I was safe now. I would be seeing Steven later. But what should I do about that man I had seen so cruelly treated this afternoon? Had he escaped? I could not be certain that he had ridden away from Vallamont without being caught. He might have run into other men who worked for Abel Cottor. What would they do to him?

What could I do about what I had seen? If I told Father that I had been to Vallamont, he would be furious! And would it help anyone to tell him that Abel Cottor had caught Warren Ruch? This would mean that Warren would never get his two hundred dollars, certainly—if he had indeed been working for Father— for Father would never pay if he knew Ruch had been discovered. But hadn't Abel Cottor said that he was going to have Warren followed, that he was going to try to trap the man called Campbell when Warren asked for his payment? That might prove Father was behind it.

It was all so confusing!

And as I watched the late-afternoon sun shimmer on the peaceful waters of the Susquehanna, my confusion grew. Why would Abel Cottor come within a hair's breath of murdering a man and then tell him that he was free to go—and, moreover, that he would use him to get legal evidence against Father? All that Warren Ruch needed to do was to tell the authorities what kind of treatment he had received, and Abel would be in worse trouble. But Warren couldn't tell about the treatment he'd received, at least not in court. Warren Ruch had no witnesses to corroborate his story.

Except for me.

I had seen it all. Again it struck me how foolish I had been to show myself up there on Vallamont. Now I was a threat to Abel. As soon as he learned that there had been a witness, he would know that Warren Ruch and I together could bring him into court. And, of course, they would soon learn who I was. I had told

Steven, and Steven would be certain to tell them. And then they would know that they had to keep me quiet.

I was suddenly very much afraid. I should have kept out of sight. I never should have tried to interfere. I never should have told Steven. . . .

But now, if I told Father, that would only make matters worse.

I felt boxed in. To tell Father would bring me swift punishment for disobedience; I could be sure of that. But to say nothing might keep me in danger if the Cottors thought I would speak out. Unless I could convince Steven that I meant them no harm, that I was not going to get involved in the struggle our families were waging against each other . . .

But *could* I do that? Could I stand by and watch my father taken to court? Was this what Steven had meant when he said they would drag the two of us down with them?

I wished I never had met Steven Cottor. Yet, even as I thought of him, I felt a warmth returning to my body as I remembered his touch, his kiss, the magic he had awakened within me. And I would be seeing him tonight! I told myself that tonight I would find a way out. Steven would tell me how things stood, and we could plan what to do. Neither of us wanted to be enemies. I could trust him, just as he could trust me. I would enjoy the mountains and the river and the rest of the ride home.

After our dinner guests had gone, after everyone in the house had gone to bed, then I would see Steven.

I had just begun to relax and grow absorbed with the view when I heard horses behind me, and my father's voice, loud and vigorous, called out: "Hey-yo, Jared! Whoa up there! Pull over!"

We stopped on the grass at the roadside, under a clump of tall elm trees, just as Father galloped up alongside, his big bay stallion snorting as he reigned it in. Father, bulky, red-faced, and energetic, looked in good spirits. He carried his large frame well, sitting tall and in complete control of his horse. Without even looking at his tailored gray wool jacket or his hand-tooled polished leather saddle, one could tell that Sam Rawles was a man of authority and means. His wide face, his broad smile, his tufts of soft, thinning blond hair—all had that sleek look of the man who has been well cared for. And his quick gray eyes, constantly alert, marked him as a man completely accustomed to having his own way.

"Well, who've we got here?" he sang out as he saw me. Then over his shoulder: "Come on over here, Nathan! Want you to meet m'daughter!"

Another man, younger and not as heavyset as Father, rode up in a swirl of hoofbeats, his light brown hair tousled by the wind. He was dressed in a tan riding suit, shiny tan boots, and a white shirt open at the collar. Both he and my father carried rifles slung across their backs. I noticed they both had full game bags.

"Catherine, say hello to Dr. Nathan McKay. Nathan, this is my daughter, Catherine."

So this was Nathan McKay, the young Philadelphia doctor who had amazed the town by making a fortune from a small lumber mill! Mother had spoken of him often, for he was the despair of society women in Grampian. Remote and standoffish, he never had time for social occasions. His every waking moment, they said, was spent at his work. He had brought in European machinery and scientific equipment, and with methods no one quite understood, he had turned his initial small investment into one of the town's most efficient properties, which he never ceased to improve. He even worked on Sundays. If the town had not been grateful to him for the charity clinic he had built for the men of the mill, their families, and for the town's poor, Dr. McKay would have come in for even more criticism in the town's drawing rooms than he now received for his unsocial ways, and that was no small amount.

"How do you do, Dr. McKay? You've been hunting, I see."

Just then Father noticed the marks on my face that I had received from the Vallamont spruce trees. "What the devil's happened to you, young lady?" he asked. "What happened to your cheek there? Looks like you've been in a fight, and lost! Let me tell you, Nate," he said before I could answer him, "she usually looks a sight better than this. You reckon it's anything serious? Want to have a look at her?"

From the expression on Father's face, I could not tell whether he was really concerned or whether he was only joking, but I could feel my temper starting to flare. My cheeks burned with embarrassment as I sat there in the carriage while these two men stared at me and the third, Jared, deliberately affected a disinterested air.

Without moving from his horse, Dr. McKay appraised me, his penetrating blue eyes lofty and amused, as though they saw through my deception.

"Nothing serious, I'd imagine," he said easily. "Ride too close to a branch, did you?"

"As a matter of fact, yes." How blue his eyes were! For a moment I forgot to be angry with Father. This man appeared to be enjoying himself, and his lean, square-jawed face was almost smiling. Could this be the cold, humorless scientist whom Mother had spoken of?

Then those eyes turned inward, no longer seeing me, and the lean face became a mask. I turned to Father.

"I don't see that there's any need to make a fuss over a few small scratches." I wished I could have said more, but with others present I wanted to be polite. So I changed the subject. "What have you got in your game bag?"

"Couple of pheasant," said Father, eyeing me quizzically. "You sure you're all right?"

"I told you I was, Father! Now, please!" I was really growing quite irritated.

"Well, all right." The broad smile appeared again on

Father's face. "Got good news. Nathan, here, is going to sell us that little beauty of a mill he's got!"

I raised my eyebrows politely and nodded. "Oh, indeed . . ."

Dr. McKay interrupted, his tone easygoing, yet crisp, and I thought I noticed a slight Southern accent. "I'd better correct that, young lady, before your father gets to believing his own words. You see, he's made me an offer. It's an offer I'm considering, and that's all there is to it just now. It'll take some time to study the whole matter and see if that's the way we want to go."

He turned to my father with an even smile. "Right, Sam?"

Father tugged at the curly blond hair of one sideburn. "Well, that's right for today, maybe. In a day or two, you'll see it looks even better than today—and you'll sell. Mark my words. But we'll not talk about that. What do you think of my daughter, eh? You two have never met before, have you? Big city we're getting here, people not knowing each other, eh?"

"It's not that," said the doctor, still in that easy, level tone. "There's just no time, that's all. With the business property to attend to and a clinic—people's lives come first before I take any time to socialize, I'll guarantee you."

And as if the conversation had reminded him, he glanced at his pocket watch. "It's been a pleasure," he said, giving me a slight nod and then looking at Father, "but I've some things to take care of."

"Busy man," said Father, turning to me. "Had a devil of a time gettin' him even to take an afternoon off for huntin'! Well, Nate, you just go on ahead. But, remember, Claire's expectin' you tonight, too."

"I think I'll be there. I've cleared the evening. So, unless something comes up, I'll see you both tonight." He gave another slight nod, then turned his horse and dug his heels into its flanks as it went galloping off.

Father walked his horse up just beside the carriage. His hands showed white as he gripped the reins. "What did you think, daughter?" He scrutinized my face, clearly looking for some reaction, and I realized what he had been doing. Dr. McKay was one of the town's most eligible men, and Father had been showing me off! The thought made my blood boil, but I strove to contain my indignation. My temper had gotten me into enough of a predicament already today without my adding to my troubles by antagonizing Father.

Nevertheless, I could not resist a bit of sarcasm. "I think he might have been favorably impressed, Father" —I brushed back my hair, just slightly touching the marks on my right cheek—"even though the goods were a trifle damaged. I hope I didn't disappoint you."

He was stern. "You know perfectly well what I meant, young lady. What did you think of him?"

"Oh? I wasn't aware that my opinion mattered. As long as you think the doctor's mill is worth having? Or do you suppose someone with even more desirable property might also find me attractive?" I could see the muscles in his face tighten with anger, so I hastily added, "But I've never thought that first impressions counted for much. Let's just say it's too soon for me to have made up my mind, shall we?"

The anger gradually faded from Father's gray eyes as he brought it under control. Finally, he said, "Well, see that you keep an open mind on the subject, young lady. And keep a civil tongue in your head!"

He turned his horse around, and in a moment or two he had ridden away.

For the rest of the way into town I fumed at Father. How could he be so insensitive by putting his daughter on display and then calling attention to marks and scratches? Had he no idea at all how I must have felt? And then to hint so broadly that I should find myself attracted to this doctor who thought of nothing but work, just so Father could have a new mill! It was really too much for me to have borne in silence. I was glad I had spoken up, even if it had provoked him. Perhaps that would teach him to use a little tact in the future, especially if he had any more ideas about selecting a prospective suitor for me.

I smiled grimly to myself then at the thought of what a surprise Father would have if he learned how well I was doing on my own in that regard. Steven Cottor was certainly wealthy enough! Father, I could say, I can now offer you the valuable opportunity to bring a huge estate into the fortune of our family!

But Father would sooner die. He hated Abel Cottor with a bitterness I never saw in him at any other time. He had hated Abel ever since the days when the two of them were partners in starting the lumber boom upriver. Something had happened back in those years, nearly two decades ago. Neither of my parents would discuss it with me, but it clearly must have been something dreadful to keep the fires of hatred burning all this time.

When I arrived home, I found Mother waiting for me in the entrance hall. To find her here like this, practically at the door, was unusual. Mother had an easy, open disposition that rarely showed any signs of worry. She adored Father, yet she stood up to him, too, without betraying the slightest hint of fear. "You're just wrong, Sam," she would say, with hands on her slender hips and with a matter-of-fact tone, "and if you'd quit chasing your tail, round and round, you'd wake up to what you're really doing soon enough." How I wished I could follow her example and keep calm when I had to face Father in a disagreement! But, no, I could not. He would flare up and so would I.

Her brown hair pinned up in a bun, mother eyed my reddened cheek. Her green eyes, behind silvery half-spectacles, showed relief.

"A riding accident! Your father said you had a riding accident, and all you come home with is a pair of pink cheeks! Pshaw!" And after giving me a hug, Mother marched me back to the wide stairs of polished walnut at the end of the hall. "You've three dresses laid out for tonight," she said. "I'm partial to the blue, but you take your choice. Emily's drawn the bath. Remember, we serve at eight, and I shall want you downstairs to make charming conversation by seven. The Scotts are certain to arrive early, and it is likely the judge will, too—I fancy he's taken a shine to Amanda Scott's red hair. Now, are you all right? Good. I've got to tend to my own business now, so off with you!"

So I marched upstairs to my three rooms on the third floor, cheered by Mother's usual good humor and grateful that she had not asked any questions. I wanted nothing so much as a quiet, warm bath and a chance to be alone for a time. On my bed I found the three dresses—two of them in rose-colored faille, and the third a blue chambray gauze with gold-colored stripes woven lightly through the fabric. All three, I reflected wryly, had been warmly praised by Mother's dress-maker for what their fascinatingly low necklines would do to captivate any man. That was the last thing I wanted tonight, I thought. Father had set me on display once today, and once was enough. I would choose something more modest.

The bath was already drawn, with soap bubbles piled high over the polished mahogany frame that surrounded the long copper tub. I had no sooner undressed and stepped in than there came a knock at my door.

"It's Emily, Miss Catherine. Your father says he wants to speak with you in the library."

Oh, did he? Well, he could certainly wait until I had finished my bath. "Tell him I'll be with him shortly, Emily. And lay out my gray silk, would you? The basque, with the velvet trim."

It seemed only a few moments until Emily was back. "Your father says he wants to see you now, Miss Catherine."

Really! "Well, you tell him, Emily, that I am taking my bath, and that I shall be with him as soon as I am properly dressed."

I sank down in the tub, luxuriating in the soft warmth of its perfumed waters. Then I began gingerly to apply a washcloth to my face. There was no stinging, only tenderness, which meant I had no real scratches from the afternoon's adventure. I breathed a sigh of relief and wished my other troubles would go away as easily.

Then, on the wall above me, the speaking tube burst forth with a loud roar. "Catherine!" It was Father's voice, echoing through one of the hollow tubes that connected our home's thirty-three rooms. Even through the tube I could hear the hoarse fury in his voice. "Catherine! You get down here this instant!"

I stood up, wrapped myself in a towel, and reached for the tube. "I am in the bath, Father." I kept my voice maddeningly polite. "I do not wish to keep you waiting, but I should like to finish bathing and dressing."

"This instant, I said!"

"Don't shout at me!"

Shaking with anger, I thrust the cap of the speaking tube back into place, blocking whatever reply he might have made. I was not going to be bullied! Carefully, I stepped out of the tub and dried myself with a fresh towel. There was steam from the tub over the mirror in my bathroom, so I took my hair brush into the dressing room and sat down before the vanity mirror and unpinned my hair, letting it fall down in shining auburn waves around my bare shoulders. Then I began to brush it carefully, deliberately, refusing to hurry just because Father thought he could demand my presence at a moment's whim.

As I brushed my hair, I examined my face critically. My complexion was flushed from the heat of the bath and my tirade with Father, but there were scarcely any marks visible now. A few touches of powder and no one would notice tonight. There were no marks on my long, slender neck, or on my shoulders, so if I wished I could certainly wear one of the three dresses Mother had selected—but I would not. The gray silk, with its smooth fit, was equally attractive in its own way, though since it had a high neckline the appeal was not quite so direct. A subdued effect—that was what I wanted tonight. I was not going to advertise myself for Father's doctor friend, and I certainly did not want to go out in bare décolletage tonight to meet Steven!

I studied my blue eyes, trying to imagine for a moment or two that I was Dr. McKay. How would I find this woman's face that looked at me so steadily? Would I see it as empty, or sincere? Would I discern an intelligence behind that gaze? Probably, I thought, Dr. McKay would not even notice. He would be thinking of some piece of scientific equipment or about a new way to improve the processing at his lumber mill, and not about a woman's eyes. Besides, his own were even bluer than mine. Idly, I wondered if there might be some way to darken the lashes. Hadn't I read somewhere that the Egyptians . . .

Suddenly the bedroom door behind me flew open with a crash, and I could see Father's outline in the mirror. His face was a crimson mask of anger and I was suddenly very frightened—I had never seen him so furious.

"Cover yourself, young lady!"

He had changed into his evening clothes—crisp black trousers and the formal starched shirt front—but he had not yet put on his necktie. I could see the veins and muscles at the sides of his neck bulging outward with tension as he glared at me, or, rather, at my reflection in the mirror.

I trembled with fright, but I got up as steadily as I could, and without looking around I got my yellow dressing gown from my wardrobe cabinet and put it on. Drawing the silken cord tightly around my waist, I turned to face him. I wanted to berate him for bursting in upon me like this, but I was afraid to trust my voice just then. I simply looked at him, still holding my hairbrush and thinking vaguely that I ought to set it back down on the dressing table.

"By God, haven't you anything to say for yourself?"

That startled me and changed my fear to indignation.

"I told you I would come down when I was ready. But if there is something so important to you that it makes you forget all notions of a lady's privacy, I suggest you say it now and be done with it!"

"Oh, it's a lady's privacy, is it? A lady!" His voice was mocking and cruel as he came toward me. "You call yourself a lady? Tell me, what *were* you doing this afternoon?"

I said nothing. Surely he could not know where I had been. It was a trap, a trick to get me to tell him what he did not know.

His big hands grasped my shoulders and he shook me so that the room spun around and I stumbled. "You go riding with Steven Cottor and you call yourself a lady? Answer me!"

A horrible emptiness and dread seized me, as I now realized that he indeed did know. But how? And the answer came instantly: Jared had told him. Of course! What a fool I had been! Jared had seen Steven Cottor ride up to the stables, and he would even have seen the two of us talking in the exercise grounds. Possibly he might also have seen Steven ride back from Vallamont with me until we had come within sight of the stables. And, of course, he would have had his instructions from Father to report immediately on anything like that. And now, because I had kept him waiting so long, Father had grown even more incensed, and I would have to face the consequences!

"Wait a moment," I said, and as I spoke I found myself gaining confidence. "There is absolutely nothing for you to worry about. I could not avoid Steven Cottor this afternoon; he sought me out at the stables. I rode away from him, into the woods, and it was there I received the marks on my face, from a tree. Steven did not catch up with me until I was well on my way back to the stables, and even then I spoke to him but slightly. And that is the truth!"

Thank God at least part of it was the truth, for I

was never able to lie with conviction. I looked Father in the eye, determined to make him believe me.

I could see that my words had at least some impact, for he released his grip on my shoulders, though his expression did not soften. "By God, if you've been lying to me, young lady . . ."

"I haven't, Father! Why must you be so . . ."

"Haven't I ordered you to keep away from that . . ."

"I *did* keep away! He rode right up to me!"

"And you spoke with him! By God, if you think I'm going to have my daughter consorting with a damned whoremonger . . ."

Without thinking, furious, I swung my open palm at his face and slapped him as hard as I could, so hard that my hand turned numb with the pain. He stared at me, shocked, surprised, and then enraged, and I grew frightened again, horrified at what I had just done. With my hand throbbing, I looked at him transfixed with fear, instinctively raising my arms to protect myself.

He tore the hairbrush out of my hands and pushed me roughly across the room so that I nearly fell across the dressing table. "By God, I'm going to take you across my knee, young lady! I'm going to teach you who your father is! You're going to learn some obedience here and now!"

And as I struggled, terrified, burning with shame, he brought the back of the hairbrush down hard across my buttocks, harder and harder, so that I cried out at the shock of the stinging, brutal hurt. The thin silk of my dressing robe was scarcely any protection, and the pain was real, undeniable, making me sob nearly as much as did the fear, the anger, and the humiliation of such treatment.

When he finished, I had no voice left, no words. There was only stunned numbness as he stood me upon my feet again, and then he made me sit back at the vanity mirror, as if by so doing he could pretend that nothing had happened, that he had not mistreated his daughter so badly.

"There," he said, "that should even things up a bit. And you'd better learn to keep a leash on that tongue of yours, or there'll be worse things ahead for you until you learn what it means to respect your father."

Tears rolled down my cheeks as I nodded, still frozen with shame.

"And if that Cottor animal ever comes close enough to you to talk again, if he so much as touches you, he's a dead man. Dead! Do you understand me?"

My voice sounded empty. "I understand you, Father."

"Now, get dressed. And don't think for one minute you can make me feel sorry for you. You've had this coming for a long time. Now, stop sniveling and get dressed!"

I stood up. But when the door closed behind him, I threw myself on my bed and sobbed, soundlessly, wordlessly, until I thought I could cry no more. "Even things up," he had said. But we were not "even," not yet, and I would never forgive him!

By the time I had finished dressing I had composed myself, drawing a temporary curtain over the great wound I now felt inside. I had thought I had known my father, thought that he loved me, but now here was the proof of how he really felt. I was nothing to him— only another piece of property, an animal that was to be beaten brutally whenever I gave him the slightest trouble.

But I was not going to let him stop me. Oh, no! I was not going to give way to hurt, to surrender meekly and obey this man Sam Rawles, this stranger I had never really seen before. Now I realized for the first time what a man like my father really must be like inside, the kind of man who drives everyone around him relentlessly, determined to break them to his own selfish will. That was what my father had done here in Grampian, wasn't it? And wasn't that just what he was still trying to do to Abel Cottor, who was likely the one man who had stood up to him, who wouldn't give him what he wanted?

I coldly examined my reflection as I applied just a trace of lipstick to my lips and a bit of powder to my cheeks. Was it my imagination, or were the outlines of my mouth harder, firmer, more determined? And my eyes—did they look as if I had been weeping? I thought not. These were not the eyes of Sam Rawles's obedient and contrite little daughter. For I knew with an icy certainty that today my father had lost me. I would not play the coy, bashful maiden for his millionaire friends, letting myself be used as live bait, as a pawn in his empire-building! Before my full-length mirror, I smoothed the gray silk dress that clung to my breasts and tapered in a neat line down to my waist. I had pinned up my hair in a French knot, and I had foregone flowers, either for a corsage or for my hair. I had only a single strand of pearls wrapped tightly around my neck for ornamentation. Yet the effect was exactly as I wanted it—restrained, attractive, but clearly nothing I had taken a great deal of trouble to produce. Father's guests would know that his daughter was certainly not overly concerned with the impression she was making tonight.

Yet they would have a surprise or two coming to them, I thought with a sudden resolve that gave me a cool satisfaction. The conversation at the dinner table tonight might be a bit more lively than Father had intended!

It was seven o'clock. Not more than an hour and a half had gone by since I had come into this house, where I had once felt so much at home.

I found Mother waiting for me when I descended the stairs and walked between the huge oak sliding doors into the drawing room. Father had built this room on a grand scale: the ceilings, all ornamented with "wedding cake" white plasterwork, were twenty feet high, and nearly the entire east wall consisted of narrow French windows, gracefully arched at the top. With the evening sunset coming from between the trees out on our western grounds, the room was filled with light that caused its furnishings, especially the sleek marble and the enamel tiles of the fireplace mantel, to shine with a special brilliance.

Mother must be feeling pleased with what she had done here, I thought to myself as I came into the room. The soft whites and grays of the furniture and the carpet, the touches of red in the occasional cushions and drapes, and in the small Oriental rug before the hearth, gave the feeling of lightness and warmth. So much nicer, I thought, than the heavy, dark parlors of so many of our friends. The room, I supposed, was more or less a tribute to Mother's good taste, a triumph of her Philadelphia upbringing over the rough, new-moneyed Grampian society that her love for my father had led her into just after I had been born. He had come out here to the new territory, had seen its promise, and had persuaded Mother that our family would one day live a grander life than even a well-to-do Philadelphia lawyer could dream of.

And Mother had followed him here, to the Susquehanna valley, and had watched him make good on that promise. Perhaps the first years had been difficult, though I certainly remembered them only as happy ones. She had told me that there was little money back then, since Father had put it all into his lumber investments, and she had to do all her own work—the cooking, the baking, the cleaning, and even tending to the poultry we had in those days. But it had been good; she never ceased to remind me of that. She had been busy, and happy, and the work had led to greater things. She never said so, but I suspected that her keeping so busy also helped her get over the disappointment she must have felt when she nearly died after a second pregnancy. The baby, a little boy, had been lost, and the doctors had told Mother that she could bear no more children.

And now she was a grand lady, who could spend

summers in Europe and winters in Florida if she chose, but who often as not preferred to stay at home. Tonight, she, too, had dressed with tasteful simplicity, in a dress of very dark green velvet and gauze, with a single white camellia as a corsage.

As I came into the room she looked up, her eyes full of concern.

"You've had another quarrel with your father."

"Oh, did he tell you?" I sat beside her on the settee closest to the window and folded my hands in my lap. I was determined to keep up my cold resolve and to make this evening one that Father would not soon forget.

But I had not reckoned on Mother's influence. "You must be feeling terrible, child. He's not been himself lately at all." She told me of the strain Father was under, with huge investments in new projects that would take time to earn a profit, with loans coming due, and with larger and larger payrolls to meet every week.

I found my bitterness losing a little of its force as I began to understand that Father did not really have things his way all the time. And then Mother said something else that softened me even further.

"You're troubling him, too. I can see it in him since you've come back. He hadn't really noticed you so much these past years, with you away at school and traveling in the summertime. But now here you are, finished with school, back in his house, and all grown up, and he just wasn't ready for it! He just . . ."

We were interrupted by the too eager bright voice of Amanda Scott, who was announcing herself to the butler and greeting him as if he were a long-lost friend.

Mother turned to me and patted my hand. "I hope you understand, dear. He's wrong, but I hope you can forgive him anyway."

She rose and went forward to greet the Scotts, Amanda and her father, Reverend Scott, the rector of our Episcopal church.

As I waited behind, I felt the pain of uncertainty once again. I knew I could not find it in my heart to forgive Father. As much as Mother would have liked me to forgive him, he had hurt me too deeply. He had deliberately denied me the respect I was entitled to, and I was too proud to let that pass. Still, I told myself, I could find other ways to get even with him instead of spoiling his dinner party tonight. After all, it was Mother's company here, as well as Father's, and she was likely to be just as hurt as he by anything I might do that would publicly embarrass him. So I greeted Reverend Scott and then made small talk with his freckle-faced daughter Amanda as if tonight were just another night, and as if I were glad to see them. I admired Amanda's new paisley shawl and said how I thought the green of the material went well with her red hair. I examined the mother-of-pearl calling-card box that one of the women of the church had given her. I chatted about our new silver napkin rings, each of which had a tiny silver vase on its top that held a fresh red rosebud.

But I vowed that Father would get no help from me in his battle with the Cottors. I would not tell him what I had seen on Vallamont, not even if *ten* of Father's paid men were going to get caught for trying to wreck Abel Cottor's mill!

At dinner I was to be seated beside Nathan McKay, as I had guessed I would be. We had fourteen persons, not counting our family, at the table, but, to my delight, Dr. McKay was not yet there. During the first course I could not resist giving a frosty smile to Father, down at the end of the table, as my eyes took in the empty seat beside me. The best-laid plans!

But then the doctor's lean figure appeared at the dining room doorway, being directed to his seat by our butler. A momentary hush fell over the group as Nathan sat down while Father greeted him. Nathan waved their attentions aside with a few quick words of explanation and bade everyone not to mind his being late. After he had seated himself, at my right, the others at the table returned to their conversations and he began talking with me in a casual, easy manner that put me surprisingly off my guard.

"I suppose you're done with school now for the summertime," he remarked. "What do you read now on your own time?" He cocked his head and looked at me out of the corner of his eye as he applied his spoon to the fruit cup. His blue eyes had a twinkle to them up close, and there were little lines at the corner of his eyelids when he smiled. Was this the snobbish know-it-all we had heard about?

"Oh, nothing much." I was wondering how old he was—thirty-two, perhaps?—and the words just came out by themselves. "Just a cheap novel I bought to read on the train coming home." As soon as I said the words I winced inwardly, but then I told myself that it did not matter. I *wanted* to make a bad impression on Nathan McKay. It would serve Father right!

"That so?" he continued amiably. "I thought you'd say you'd been reading poetry. Don't you read poetry? I thought all the well-off young ladies read poetry."

"I didn't say I didn't—just not now." I found myself smiling.

"Haven't unpacked those slender little volumes yet, eh? You mean you like to read poetry?"

I allowed that I did, occasionally. Then I asked him if he read poetry, too, and he laughed.

"Only to fall asleep—wasn't that what you were expecting? No? Well, to tell you the truth, I've been known to read a verse or two in my time. In fact, I've even seen it do some good." He went on, lightly. "Actually, that's why I asked you in the first place about what you liked to read."

"I don't understand."

"Have to let me finish first," he admonished, his eyes still laughing. "Now, you see, down at the clinic we have quite a few people who appreciate a good story or a bit of poetry to take their minds off their troubles—and they've got troubles aplenty, I'll guarantee you. But the problem is that most of them can't read."

"So you need someone to read to them."

"We *had* someone. Nice lady, but she moved West last week and the patients miss her fiercely. Do you think you'd have time? They'd appreciate it. You can depend on that. Just an hour or two every day."

I hesitated.

"Oh, come on, you can do it. The hard part will be getting away *after* just an hour or two. Come on, you'll do them a lot of good."

"Well, I guess I could try it and see if . . ."

From across the table Amanda Scott interrupted. "Excuse me, Dr. McKay." She leaned toward him, her green eyes bright, her thin face and mouth set in a determined smile. "You know, I'm Amanda Scott, Reverend Scott's daughter, and I couldn't *help* overhearin'—about the poor people at your clinic, I mean."

He nodded politely. "I'm delighted to meet you."

"Well," she continued, and suddenly I realized that Amanda was subtly copying Dr. McKay's slight Southern drawl as she spoke, "I *have* had some experience with elocution and all, and I'd be delighted to come to your clinic an' read"—she looked at me before she finished, and then back to him—"*if* there's a need."

He raised his eyebrows and smiled slightly. "Well, we'd be most happy to have you, both of you. Perhaps you'll want to come on alternate days, or even work out a schedule of readings."

"Oh, yes," said Amanda, "we'll have to talk about that, won't we, Catherine?"

"I'll be pleased to read to your patients, Dr. McKay," I said. "What time would you like . . . us to be there?"

We soon agreed to meet tomorrow afternoon after church, for the first day, and to take turns in the mornings thereafter. Then Amanda's attention was drawn away by Judge Hawthorne, whom mother had purposely seated on her left. The judge, in his fifties, nonetheless came alive in the presence of a young lady, and especially, it seemed, in the presence of Amanda. She had all she could do to maintain a polite smile on her face. As I watched her struggling with the judge's droning witticisms, I felt amusement but also sympathy. There was nothing really wrong with Amanda. She had a good heart, from all I knew of her, and she was continually doing favors for people in connection with the church. Since her mother had died, she had become more or less the mainstay of social events there, which was quite a responsibility at her age. She was only two years older than I. Why not let her have her chance at a bit of happiness? She was working hard at being good, perhaps too hard. Maybe that was the only thing about her that I didn't like.

Certainly I was not jealous because she had invited herself to share Dr. McKay's invitation to read to his patients. Dr. McKay was nothing to me. He was distant. He was a perfectionist. He was Father's idea.

Suddenly I was seized with a thought that nearly made me laugh aloud. What if Dr. McKay wasn't interested in a wife at all? What if he had only been looking for someone to read at his clinic? Wouldn't that be a wonderful joke on Father?

I wondered if that were the case. Dr. McKay was now talking with the woman on his right. I looked around the table. Above us the huge crystal-tiered chandelier glittered brilliantly. Around us the white linen glowed, and the gold filigree on the wine goblets shone. Those at the table were enjoying themselves. There were two ministers, three mill owners, including Father and Dr. McKay, two lawyers, a judge, and their womenfolk. The net worth of this table was probably somewhere close to ten million dollars. Much of it was now in stocks and bonds and real estate, but it had all started with lumber, and that had all started with Father's idea for a lumber "boom." Once he had built the huge floating log corral upriver,

branded logs could be kept secure until they were
needed by the mills. Fewer were lost or stolen, and
expenses decreased accordingly. But at the same time,
with the war in the South, there was a huge rise in
demand and the mills couldn't turn out enough boards
to begin to satisfy the need. And so new mills had been
built, and prices had gone up, and more logs were
cut and branded and stored in the boom. . . .

And Father, instead of being a farmer or a lawyer,
was now at the head of a table of millionaires. I looked
at him again, and I was forced to admit that he did
carry it off well. He enjoyed himself, and he made
others around the table feel a part of his excitement
as he planned more great deeds. I could hear him
talking about the hotel he had opened last year in
the middle of the oak park near our house: two hundred rooms, four stories, an enclosed park with six
white-tailed deer, and a Continental chef. Also, there
was a ninety-nine-year agreement with the Pennsylvania Railroad that their passenger trains between
Philadelphia and Pittsburgh would stop here for meals.
And they would never move the station from where
it now stood, only a hundred feet from the hotel's
real entrance, even though the downtown section of
Grampian was more than two miles away, farther down
the river. Was that an inconvenience for railway passengers who wanted to come to Grampian? Perhaps,
but Father was just completing a trolley line into town
for them. He had thought of everything.

But he had not thought well enough for his daughter,
I told myself. He might have sent me to school and
taught me to keep an account book, and even let me
balance some of his own books during my vacations,
but that was not enough for him to own me. Now,
even if he had another plan, I had Steven Cottor!

Across the table, Reverend Scott raised his glass in
an elaborate toast to praise the new cathedral Father
had just given the Episcopal church. When he was

done, Father glowed with pride, but he shook his head modestly.

"That's enough said about that, Reverend. Next thing you know, these Baptists and these Methodists"—he indicated the judge, and lawyer Clay Anderson—"will be wantin' me to build one for them, too!"

There was appreciative laughter around the table. On my right, Nathan McKay asked me if the tall stone Gothic structure had really cost all of eighty thousands dollars to build, the way the papers had reported.

"That's how much he paid the contractors," I said, for I had seen Father's books on the matter just after I had come home from school last Easter. "They estimated twenty-five thousand, but they charged him eighty."

"That's quite a fortune. Your father must be very generous."

"He can afford it," was all I said. But as I spoke I remembered Mother's words, and I wondered.

"Hey, Sam," Judge Hawthorne was saying, "you goin' to let Abel Cottor come down to your church now that he's asked you up to his place next week?" He spoke with a good-natured laugh, obviously intending to make fun of the invitations that Abel had sent to all of the town's wealthy residents this morning. I could still picture ours, a large envelope of thick cream-colored paper, with an elaborate red wax seal. Father had torn it in half without even opening it. Now he remained silent.

"They say he's bringing in a famous orchestra from New York," one of the other women, Clay Anderson's wife, added. "And my baker tells me he'll be busy all week with the pastries. And there are more people coming up by train from Harrisburg."

"Cottor's spending a lot of money," remarked Reverend Scott.

And the unasked question hung in the air: Would Father take it unkindly, be really offended, if someone who was at his table this Saturday night went up to Abel Cottor's next Saturday?

"And I suppose there'll be those who go up there to see what he's bought with it all," said my mother, her calm voice causing heads to turn from Father's end of the table down to hers. She, in turn, looked directly at Father, as if reminding him that he ought to give his opinion on the subject and get it over with so that his guests would at least know where they stood.

Father took the hint. "I suppose there will be, too," he said. "But I happen to know old Abel's got another purpose in mind besides just showing the good people of Grampian a good time. Isn't that right, Judge?"

The older man looked surprised, as if his mind had been wandering. "What say? Another purpose?"

"Evidently the folks in the county clerk's office don't keep you as well informed as they do me. It hasn't been a week that's gone by since Abel registered surveys of the bottom third of that mountain of his— all subdivided into nice, neat lots. Folks who go up there are going to be treated to a real estate sales pitch along with that New York orchestra."

"Oh, I can't believe he'd sell Vallamont, can you?" asked Mrs. Anderson. "He could never bring himself to part with an inch of it. Everyone knows that the Cottors are both half crazy about that mountain of theirs."

"The Cottors are going broke," said Father, without even flicking an eyelash. "I happen to know he's in debt quite heavily for that new mill of his and for that famous stone castle everyone seems so fascinated with. And some other notes are coming due not long from now. He needs to raise the cash, and quickly."

Amanda Scott spoke up. "But what good would it do anyone to buy a lot up there? There's no gas line, no road to speak of."

"That's right," said Father. Father had control of

the gas company. "And there won't be any, either, as long as Abel owns that mountain."

Eyebrows went up. Ah, so this was the message Father wanted to send out! People could go up to Vallamont and drink Abel's champagne if they wanted to, but if they bought any of his mountain lots and expected to build on them, they'd be wasting their money.

"Well, I wasn't interested in any land up there, anyway," said Mrs. Anderson. "But I thought we might just go up and see the party for a while. I always did like a ball."

"You won't see me there," Father said abruptly, "or any of my family. Isn't that right, Claire?"

I waited to see if Mother would go along with this commanded display of obedience, though I really had not much doubt that she would. What I worried about was my own response. I had vowed to stand up to Father, but I did owe it to Mother not to make a scene.

"Oh, I see enough New York orchestras when I go to New York," said Mother. "I can't say that finding one in Abel Cottor's ballroom would be any great attraction."

"Catherine?" I could feel the tension in Father's voice.

I spoke to the others at the table instead of to him. "I'm sure you all can see that we make up our own minds in our family," I said briskly. "I just haven't made mine up yet."

"Well, you'd better. No one in my family is going to that affair—no one." His color had deepened, and he was staring directly down the table at me, as if the others in the room did not exist. For a long moment we faced one another. I could feel my own temper rising. My mind raced. I wanted to hurt, to humiliate, him. How dare he bait me publicly like this! I wanted to smash that determined glare from his face, to hurl my glass of wine full in his eyes!

But, no, I thought. Imagine the way tongues would wag about Catherine Rawles and her passionate outburst at the table! Poor Catherine, she must be head over heels in love with that Steven Cottor! She just lost her head completely as soon as her father wouldn't let her see him at Abel's ball!

I could just hear Amanda Scott spreading the word now, a satisfied tone of pity in her voice. Poor Catherine! Poor Sam, with a daughter who's just out of control like that!

Well, I was not going to give them the satisfaction of seeing me lose my temper. Certain now that I could contain my fury, I raised my glass and addressed the guests again. "Why don't we all drink to that, then? Father's wish is his family's command!"

"Hear, hear," said the judge, and some of the people raised their wineglasses and drank, not sure of what else to do. Father, of course, did not touch his wine. He sat silent, and for a moment he looked as if he could have broken me in half.

But then he began to talk to the lady on his right as if nothing had happened.

THREE

I still felt the glow of triumph late that night as I slowly opened the door of my bedroom and looked out into the hallway. The whole house was silent. It had been two hours since the last guest had departed and only a few minutes less than that since Father had given me another curt warning to tell me that he meant what he said. I had checked my temper then, too, and felt proud of myself for doing so. Then I had come up to my room, but instead of getting undressed for bed, I had changed into another riding costume, this one with a hooded jacket, leaving my hair pinned up.

Now the thick red wool of the hall carpet deadened the sound of my boots as I stepped outside my room and locked the door behind me. I came down the carpeted stairs, with their glistening walnut newel posts casting shadows in the gaslight of the hall, past the second floor, where my parents slept and where Father had his library, and down through the dining room and quietly out the French doors and into the night sounds and cool air of the garden.

I had done it! My heart racing with excitement, I walked through the garden and then looked back at our house. No lights appeared, and there was no movement at the windows. There was not a sound, except for the chirp of a cricket and the solitary cooing of a pigeon. There was a crescent moon tonight, but the stars shone clear overhead and I could see fairly well by the glow of the streetlamp that burned out in front of our house, for some of the light filtered through the trees and came back to where I stood on the lawn behind our home's rear entrance.

I pulled my hood up over my head and turned toward the rose arbor, where Steven was to meet me. The night air smelled wonderfully clean, and I felt splendidly alive and confident.

Then from behind me I heard the click of our back door being opened.

Panic seized me as I stood there in the center of the open lawn, ten yards at least from the nearest tree. I did not stop to think. I took to my heels and ran for the shadows of the tree, and then, without turning around to see what was behind me, I raced on for the next one, which lay just a short distance from the rose arbor. Then I stopped and leaned against the tree, trying to catch my breath without making any noise. I was afraid to look. Perhaps, I told myself, it was only one of the servants out for a midnight stroll.

But it was not. Standing now at the back of the house, a few feet from the door that led down the stairs to the kitchen, was my father. He had a dark lantern with him, partially open at the top, and I could see his face clearly. He was wearing a rough woolen shirt over his evening trousers, which he had tucked into a pair of hunting boots.

And he was carrying a pistol in his hand.

Had he seen me? I could not be sure, for the expression on his face told me nothing. Was he going somewhere? I thought not. He was standing quite calmly, motionless, as if he were waiting for someone to arrive.

I tried to think clearly. If I had made some noise, done anything to alert him as I was coming down the stairs, then he would have come out like this, and probably with a gun. But it would have taken him longer to dress than the few moments that had elapsed from my leaving the house until I first heard him opening the back door latch.

Well, then, he was waiting for someone. And even if he had seen me, running quickly for the shadows with my hood up, it was unlikely that he had recognized me. Otherwise, he would be out here at the back of the lawn, looking to drag me in. As long as I stayed quiet here, I was safe . . . unless whoever Father was waiting for had seen me.

At that moment I felt a hand at my elbow, and I gasped, but then I quickly realized that it was Steven. He had come up behind me quietly in the darkness. "Be still," he said in a low undertone I could barely understand, even with his lips nearly touching my ear. "I saw you come out. There's a way through the back to my place. We can be there in a minute or two. Or do you want to wait here?"

I gave a quick glance back to where Father was still standing. No, I could not stay. I did not want to know what Father was doing, and neither did I want Steven to know. "Lead the way," I said softly.

Within a short space of time we had dashed quietly through the shadows to an open spot in the fence at the back of our arbor and were in the yard of the house behind ours. From there it was only a short walk to the front porch of Steven's mansion, a huge, rambling, gabled affair that I always found dark and foreboding. Even after Abel had moved out to Vallamont with his mistress and left Steven as the only occupant here, I still did not care for that house.

But the spring air was sweet and cool. We stopped on the porch to catch our breath, watching the lights and the silent trees. He took my hand. We heard the church tower clock—Father's gift, too—strike twelve. The deep brass notes echoed slowly in the soft air.

"Chimes at midnight," said Steven, drawing me closer to him.

Then as the lantern glow of a night policeman approached us from the direction of the church, Steven's house offered shelter. Inside we went, and in the large, dark entrance hallway I let my hood fall back with a sigh of relief.

"Very attractive, I must say." He was looking at me after having lit the lamp beside the sofa in the parlor. From where I stood, his face appeared softer now than it had seemed that afternoon. Oddly enough, he looked older, too. Still his eyes had that same faintly mocking glint, and there was still that little half-smile when he spoke.

"You weren't meant to see me this well," I said. "I don't know how you managed to get me here. I only agreed to a few moments of talk in the garden."

I tried to sound firm. I had missed his lovemaking. We had not been together that way since February. But I did not want to let myself go, especially when we had been quarreling about marriage. Somehow what had seemed so beautiful and innocent before had taken on serious, even threatening, overtones. I could not afford to lose control, or I might find myself making promises I could not keep. . . .

"Ah, well, then," he was saying, "shall I turn down the light? You can pretend that we're still outdoors."

"I think not," I said, coming into the parlor, "definitely not." I stood beside the sofa and looked around. This was the first time I had been inside Steven's mansion. The room was enormous. Our shadows from the light were gigantic on the high ceiling. Yet the room, aside from the long sofa and two upholstered chairs over here by the unlit fireplace, was totally bare of furniture or decoration. The enormous, thick Oriental rug stretched out along the floor in all directions, empty until it disappeared into the shadows along the empty walls.

"Most people find it odd at first," Steven said as though he had read my thoughts. "But I have no need for more furniture. Actually, I like it better this way." He was wearing a loose-fitting shirt of dark blue silk that was tucked into the wide waistband of his tight-fitting gray trousers.

He crossed over to the mantel, where there were some bottles and glasses. "Some wine? As long as I brought you here, I can at least play the generous host."

"I don't think I'll stay that long," I said.

"Suit yourself." He came back with two filled goblets, anyway, sipping from one of them. "More for me, that's all. You're welcome to stay, or you can go when you like. No one's going to know when you leave. The cook's away for a week and I have no other servants."

He sat down on the sofa and stretched out his legs. His black boots glistened in the lamplight.

"You know, Abel was a bit distressed tonight. When I told him Sam Rawles's daughter had seen what he was doing this afternoon, he . . . ah . . . he took it badly, you might say. Seemed to think that you'd take the story straight to your father."

He waited, looking at me quietly.

"Well, I didn't," I said. "Even when Father found out that I'd seen you today, I didn't. Even when he said he would kill you if he saw us together, I didn't."

Steven raised one eyebrow and sat up a bit straighter. "In that case, I'm just as happy he didn't notice us in his garden tonight. That pistol of his might have been all too convenient."

"Are you frightened of him?"

He nodded, but without losing a bit of his composure. "I'd be a fool to say I wasn't. Sam Rawles has a bad, bad temper, and he has the town's law in his back pocket. Why do you think Abel didn't go to the police when he caught that man spiking his logs? But we won't talk about that business any further."

He swirled his wine and looked at it for a moment. "I said this afternoon that I didn't want those two dragging us down with them."

His eyes met mine. And then the warmth of desire I had felt for him earlier now suddenly returned. I wanted to touch him. My body ached with a longing to be caressed, and for a moment I felt shamelessly, wantonly excited to be alone with this man in this room.

He was watching me. Could he see my excitement? I blushed. "What were we talking about? Something made me forget. I think I'm a bit tired. . . ."

Unsteadily, I came over to the sofa and sat beside him, telling myself that I would only stay for a short while. I would excite him, too, as he had excited me, but then I would surely go. . . .

"Yes, where were we?" he was saying. "I seem to recall a conversation about announcing our engagement at Abel's ball next week. As I recall, you were against the idea, being rather severe about it, too, I might add."

He looked so sure of himself, so confident of his own powers! It would be a pleasure to watch that cool self-assurance turn into passionate longing!

"Oh?" I asked archly as I drew just a little closer to him. "And have you anything to say in your own defense?"

"Well, actually, by now it's all for nothing. Abel says I've got to be in Harrisburg all next week. I probably won't even be back until the morning after. So I couldn't have taken you anyway."

He smiled, reaching out to kiss me, and I let him come near me, let him touch my shoulders with his warm hands and draw me up to him, let him kiss me fully, lingering, savoring my lips like a sweet and heady wine.

"Though God knows we ought to tell both of those old fools just exactly . . ."

"Let's not talk now, Steven, shall we?" My lips moved against the smoothness of his cheek as I whispered. I breathed in the nearness of him, the warm, masculine scent of his body that enfolded me like an intoxicating cloud. Again I felt the longing to touch him, to awaken his passion as he had awakened mine.

He gripped my shoulders, his powerful fingers pressing into my flesh. He covered my mouth with his, and then again came the fierce pressure, the hard, sweet pangs that sent fires racing through me and blotted out all else. I wanted him with a certainty that made me tremble. Oh, I wanted him. The need for his touch, the heat of him, yes, all of him, was suddenly overpowering.

I pressed him close to me, holding him tighter and tighter as I tried to will him away, wishing to escape somehow from this fierce intensity, but the longing only grew. And then he was lifting me up in his firm embrace, and I opened my eyes to see that his own were lit with the same urgent desire. Oh, and I have won, I thought, but the words came faint and small and I knew that he had won more than I.

Steven made love to me that night, and I thrilled to see him moan with his own pleasure. He brought me again to the brink of ecstasy, holding me helpless, shuddering, and I yearned for him never to release me. I was his, utterly, every fiber open to his touch, his caress, his demand.

Yet something brought me back to my senses several hours before dawn. Silently, under the stars and the setting moon, Steven led me home so that I would awaken in my own bed that Sunday morning.

FOUR

When I did awaken Sunday, I had to wash and dress hurriedly so as not to miss church. I was still in a half-awake daze, still hugging the memory of last night to me in its warm, secret glow. I had time for a sweet roll and coffee in the kitchen. Then it was out to the open carriage to join my parents that lovely spring morning for the ride to the new cathedral.

Fourth Street, the "millionaires' row of houses," looked especially grand in the spring. The cherry blossoms were still pink and white, the dogwoods were in bloom, and everywhere, it seemed, there were azaleas, scattered splashes of red and violet beside the huge houses. The slender flowering trees, spaced apart on the wide lawns, muted the bright azaleas with their cool pastels and reminded me of a Japanese watercolor in their soft tranquility.

I rode to church that Sunday with no feelings of regret, even though I knew what havoc my secret might have caused. Father has sworn to kill Steven, I thought as I looked at him there beside me, so proud and prosperous, smiling and doffing his silk hat to those we passed along the way. Would Father really commit murder? Well, he would not find out about Steven until I was certain he was ready to accept him. That was all. I felt so good that morning, as if I were seeing the world with new eyes. I knew I would be able to arrange things so that there would be no violence between Steven and Father. And as we alighted from our carriage and walked up the wide stone steps of the church, I fantasized that one day the bitter rivalry between our two families might end here, with a wedding.

Throughout the prayers and the lovely ritual of the service I thought of last night and of the future. Was it wrong, what Steven and I had done? The question was familiar, and the answer was the same one I had always known. Nothing that I did out of love for Steven was wrong. I felt certain of that, even when I repeated the prayer that said the remembrance of my sins was grievous unto me and the burden of them was intolerable.

Toward the end of the service, though, I began to think more clearly. I was sitting in our family pew, the third row back from the altar on the right of the aisle, where Reverend Scott was almost directly above us in his marble pulpit. I looked up at him, splendid in his white-and-gold robes, his manner bold and confident, his brown eyes and russet hair shining. I have no idea at all what he was talking about that Sunday morning, but as he spoke it came to me what I would have to do, as clearly as if someone had whispered the message into my ear. It would be difficult and painful, but I would have to stay away from Steven's lovemaking. Everything had changed between the two of us since I had come home. I had wanted Steven to take me last night, but was that love enough? I did not know. I had been strongly attracted, so physically drawn to him that I ached to remember it. But Steven wanted me to give him my life. What would our future be like if we married? Our times with each other had been all secret lovers' meetings. Would the magic fade when our times were no longer secret? We had never talked about the things we would do in the future. I could not risk everything until I knew that I would be happy with Steven outside of the bedroom, as well.

"Are you all right, child?" Mother whispered. I realized that I was standing for the recessional hymn without having my hymnbook open.

But I felt better, having made a choice and set my mind on what I was going to do. That afternoon, as I set out for my carriage ride to Dr. McKay's clinic, I was still in a holiday mood. I came around to the front of the carriage outside our house and looked up at the startled Jared. "I should have been furious with you, Jared," I told the flabbergasted coachman, "but I'm not. You were only doing your job to report on me."

"Yes, 'um," he said, not knowing, I think, whether to smile politely or not. As I stepped up into the carriage, helped up by Perkins, our butler, Jared was still shaking his head in amazement.

We drove away, and passing along the row of mansions for the second time that day, I noticed Steven's —a deep, red-brown frame house with many gables. I noted that it was the only one without flowers or cultivated shrubbery around the lawn. Only a dark green hedge grew around the sides of the property, leaving the front plain and bare.

Where was Steven now? I wondered. Probably on his way to Harrisburg. He would come to me soon enough. I was certain of that. The sight of the house reawakened the memory of last night, but I would have to think of other things now.

As we rode, we swung down closer to the river and drove along the streets where the mill workers lived with their families. These houses were smaller, of course, but almost every one had its own front yard and front porch, where I could see children at play. Fathers, many of them in their Sunday black vests, sat out on the porch rocker awaiting Sunday dinner. Which of these men, I wondered, worked for my father, and which for Abel Cottor? I knew that at least some of them were likely to work for other mill owners such as Nathan McKay, but the mills owned by the Rawles and the Cottor families accounted for three of every four mill jobs in Grampian. That was three thousand jobs during the cutting season, which had now begun. Many of these men counted on making enough in the mills to last through the winter until the next cutting season, though I knew that most would leave their families after work slacked off in the fall and head for the lumber camps, where they would join the gangs of woodsmen in the dangerous work of cutting the logs and skidding them with horses and sledges over the cold, wet ground and down to the river.

Were these the men I would be meeting this afternoon at the clinic, these hard-working family men? Or would most of them be the roughnecks from the barracks of cheap rooms and hotels that lay farther along the river, closer to the mills? These were a rough and brawling lot, most of them dirty and unkempt. We saw them at their worst some Saturday nights if we drove into town to see a play or an opera, for the taprooms were not far away. Hundreds of the "jam-crackers" and "boom-rats" wandered through the muck of the streets when they had drunk so much that no saloon keeper would serve them. Then they would mill about outside, looking for a fight. And when our carriage rolled by we could see them cursing us, their red eyes glaring and their wet mouths gaping. Once from out of the mob someone had thrown a glass at Father just as he was getting out of the carriage and knocked his silk hat to the ground. Father picked the hat up, mud and all, and shouldered into the crowd until he found whoever it was who had thrown the glass. From the carriage I could not see what he did, and Father would not tell me. I only heard a terrible

65

scream and saw a man in torn black overalls, writhing in pain, being carried away to one of the dark clapboard houses.

Today these gray wooden buildings were quiet. Only a few men slouched in doorways, and an occasional woman stood near one of the closed dark taprooms where men drank, even though illegally, on Sundays. So, too, closer to the river, the mills were quiet. Their great fires would not be raging until five A.M. tomorrow. The huge steam saws would not move until a short while after that, when the first log of the day's thousands would be pushed through to be cut apart and added to the huge walls of stacked boards, some fifty feet high, and to the great mountains of sawdust that rose high beside the back of each mill. In the winter this sawdust would give the poor of the town some inexpensive fuel.

Each of the mills and its nearby lumber yard was quiet as I passed by. Yet tomorrow these silent streets would be swarming with activity as men stacked the boards fresh from the mill and prepared thousands of others to be shipped all over the country.

Inside Dr. McKay's clinic there was very little quiet. Some of the men had seen me getting out of the carriage, and I could hear them calling from their windows as I walked into the neat, plain reception area, where there was some sitting-room furniture and a desk.

The voices still came from the rooms upstairs.

"Oooh, will ya look at that!"

"Hey, now, ya just come to the right place, honey!"

"Don't listen to him! He ain't got . . ."

I thought for a moment that perhaps I should have worn a sun bonnet and chosen a jacket that did not show off my figure to such advantage. But it was clearly too late to do anything about that now.

Dr. McKay was not available, so a nurse in dark gray dress showed me the room of the men that I was to read to. Amanda Scott had not arrived yet. I did not wait in the first-floor area for her. The nurse explained that several of the patients in the closed ward nearby might have smallpox. So up the stairs I went and was soon in a large, airy, white-washed room with seventeen beds and as many lumbermen, most of whom were very much awake.

The cries began again as soon as they saw me.

"Oooh, that's appetizin'!" "Over here now, honey . . ."

I cut them off with a wave of my hand and a hard look. "That will be enough of that, or I will walk straight out of here and you'll not see me again. Do I make myself clear?"

Most of them sat back, respect in their eyes. But one burly, broad-shouldered man with a dirty black beard gave me a scowl.

"Don't start none of your goddamned high-toned talk, ya rich bi——"

His words were stopped suddenly by the ham-like fist of an even larger man, with curly blond hair, who swung quickly out of the next bed and delivered a crashing blow all in the same swift motion. Blood showed bright red on the mouth of the bearded man.

"Just watch that tongue o' yours there, Gould," said the young blond-haired giant in an easy tone. He bent back Gould's arm, making him gasp. "Ain't no way to talk to a lady. Now, ya behave yourself, or do ya want me t'take this here arm off your shoulder?"

Gould grunted, shaking his head no. The blood was flowing more freely.

"Has that man lost a tooth?" I asked, ready to call for the nurse.

"Oh, he's all right, ma'am. Just a nosebleed. Ain't that right, Gould?"

Gould winced and nodded yes, and the other man released him, looking at me as he sat back down on his own bed and eased the white plaster cast on his leg into position. His gray eyes were warm and friendly, and his casual, almost boyish, air was very appealing.

"Now, ma'am, it's Billy Joe Walker at your service. Let me welcome ya here and apologize for the fellas gettin' excited. They didn't mean nothing by it. Ya can be sure and certain of that."

He grinned a little sheepishly at me, as if he had just then realized that what he had done to the man named Gould next to him was also not quite up to gentlemanly manners. Though he had the physique, especially the neck and shoulders, of a bull, Billy Joe looked surprisingly gentle. I wondered briefly what had prompted him to come to my defense with such sudden violence.

I smiled at the group. "That's quite all right. As long as we understand each other, I'm sure we'll get along very well."

And so began my afternoons reading to the men at Dr. McKay's clinic. It appeared that I was the only one, because Amanda did not arrive that afternoon. As I got to know the men a bit better the next day, I realized that most of them were dejected and unhappy. After an unexpected injury or illness, they genuinely needed cheering up as much as they needed medicine, and certainly more than they needed the poems I had brought. So the third time I came to the clinic, on a Wednesday afternoon, I came armed with some humorous tales and the novel I had bought for reading on the train.

As luck would have it, this Wednesday was the first time Dr. McKay looked in on us. When the Doctor came by, the men were guffawing loudly over a story from Artemus Ward that I had just finished.

"Why don't you come in and join us?" I called out to him.

He took a step into the room, very tall and dignified in his white coat, but still looking quite young. His blue eyes fairly radiated crisp authority.

"I take it you gentlemen approve of Miss Rawles," he said with a smile.

The room fell oddly silent. I wondered if this was because these men knew my father's name, or simply because they were intimidated by the presence of the doctor, who was, after all, their employer, as well.

Then heads began to nod assent, and there were respectful voicings of "Yes, sir."

"Good. And I take it that you've found it agreeable so far?" He nodded at me, and again came the smile, though not quite as broad this time.

"This is my third time in three days." I said, pressing my book close to my lap. "I should hardly have come back otherwise."

"Very good. I'll see you all later, then." He was gone before anyone could reply.

Yet he was waiting for me downstairs after I had finished. Was it my imagination, or did I see interest as he let his gaze travel over my fitted blue riding coat and then back to look me in the eye? Could it be that I had the power to excite this enigmatic man? I told myself it did not matter. Steven was all I needed for excitement. But I could not deny that I was curious, and, to some degree, even attracted. Nathan McKay radiated a magnetism different from the rough, hearty power of my father, and certainly different from the dark, romantic energy of Steven Cottor. Nathan felt cooler, somehow, and yet very strong. When I saw him there waiting for me, I felt a tightness in my throat and an urge to quicken my steps.

For a moment I was frightened. I knew perfectly well what I had done with Steven Cottor and how I had felt when I was with him. I knew the softness, the vulnerable warmth, and the delight he had awakened in me. Could it be that someone so different could bring about the same feelings after only a few days? I wished I had been alone, for I needed the time to sort out my confused thoughts.

He was looking at the volume of Artemus Ward. "The latest thing from the schools these days, I suppose?" His smile was cool but friendly.

"I understand President Lincoln used to read these

to his cabinet," I said. "So I suppose they'll have them in the schools someday."

"I heard that story, too," he said, "from Stanton, the secretary of war. I think it's a fine choice. But, tell me, why have you come in three times in three days? I thought you and Miss Scott were going to take turns."

"So did I. But I haven't heard from Amanda. I thought you had. When I didn't see her, I just came ahead."

"You don't mind working the extra time?"

"Not for now, no." I flushed slightly. I really didn't mind at all. In fact, I had been glad for the opportunity to keep busy, to keep my mind occupied so that I would not be thinking of Steven Cottor. I had heard nothing from Steven since I had last seen him on Saturday night. I supposed he thought it would be too dangerous to send a note.

Nathan was saying something about the Cottors and Saturday night, and for a moment I had the uncomfortable feeling that he had read my mind. Then I realized that he had just asked me to attend the ball at the Cottors' with him.

"You hesitate. Are you afraid of your father? That's a surprise, from what I remember."

"No, it's just that . . ." I did not know what to say about Steven.

"You don't want to break the family boycott? Sam Rawles stays away, so everyone stays away? Come on, don't be foolish. It's time your two families dropped this war of yours. It doesn't help the rest of us in this town one bit."

Suddenly I felt lighthearted. What a fine joke on Father! If Nathan McKay was taking me, Father would be hard put to make any objection.

I said, "You haven't told Father about the mill yet, have you? Whether you'll sell it or not, I mean."

He nodded, as if he were pleased with the way I recognized his position of strength with Father. "Not yet. Perhaps next week sometime I may make up my mind. I've already told your father that, but you might mention it to him again—if you decide that you're going with me on Saturday."

"I think I shall. Thank you for asking me." I gave him a pleasant smile and a nod as I walked past him and out the door to the waiting carriage.

That night at the supper table I told Father and Mother about Dr. McKay's invitation. Father immediately forbade me to accept. The cold fury in his voice and the blaze of hate in his eyes made me frightened once again, and I shuddered to think of what would have happened had he discovered Steven and me in the garden while he had that pistol.

When Mother tried to stop his tirade, it only seemed to inflame him all the more. "You!" he raged. "I'm not going to listen to a single word from you in defense of the Cottors! You're not going to . . ."

"I'm not going to defend them," said Mother quietly from her end of the table as he shouted at her. "I'm not going to defend them. I'm simply pointing out what a fool you are on the subject after twenty years."

"What did you say?" Father fairly bellowed out the words. His eyes widened in anger and he half-rose in his chair. "I ought to come down there and . . ."

"A fool. Twenty years. A fool." Mother repeated the words in that same quiet tone, and they finally had their effect. Father suddenly was standing over her chair, and as I watched, horrified, he slapped her across the face.

"No!" I cried out at him and tried to pull him away, my chair toppling over and my feet slipping on the carpet. "No!" He seemed barely to notice me. I could not budge him as he stood over her, his hands upraised to strike where already an ugly red flush had appeared on Mother's cheek. I had never seen her frightened before, but now there was cold fear in her green eyes as she gazed up at him, helpless. Father's face had become a mask. I saw his muscles tense for another cruel blow, and without thinking I flung myself against his arm, trying to hold it back. But he only pushed me aside with a force that made me gasp. I stumbled back against the chairs against the wall and sank down sobbing onto the carpet. For a long moment I waited, watching my tears turn tiny circles on the carpet into a deeper crimson.

The blow would fall any second. And I would probably be next.

But there was only silence, and then footsteps on the carpet, and then the doors were shut. I looked up. Father had gone and Mother sat pale and shaken, numbly smoothing one of the silken sleeves of her tan dinner dress.

"Ashamed," she whispered, "he ought to be ashamed."

Later that evening I tried to get Mother to tell me why Father hated the Cottors, but she was as impervious to my questions as usual. "You'll know someday, child," she said with a faraway look. "That'll be soon enough. Meantime, you stay clear of your father when he's wrought up like that."

She was sitting in her dressing gown, a pale yellow that tonight made her look frail. We were in her room. I was helping her brush out her hair.

"But I just don't understand *why*. Father's not usually like this. I've never seen him so . . . I don't know . . . . crazed, as if he weren't really himself!" I watched her face in the vanity mirror as I brushed her hair, but she did not change her expression, except to appear a trace more somber and tired. The flesh under her chin no longer looked firm, and her eyes, bright under heavy lids, looked sadly up at me so that I wished I had not even brought up the subject.

"You'll know soon enough," was all she said. Then she took a deep breath and drew herself up before the mirror, visibly brightening.

"Well!" Another deep breath, and then she turned

around to face me. "We're certainly not going to get you ready for Saturday night sitting here this way. What are you going to wear?"

"You mean you think I should go? I thought . . ."

"When your father comes to his senses, he's going to realize that you're too old for him to stand in your way. And Dr. McKay is too valuable a friend to lose— especially as a prospective son-in-law. Have you ever thought about that?"

The question took me by surprise, and I blushed. I felt a sudden impulse to tell her of Steven Cottor, but I quelled it. Even if I never saw Steven again, our days and nights of magic could not be taken away, and to speak of it now would invite sympathy that I did not need or want.

"I can see you have," said Mother knowingly. "Well, it's good to be thinking about these things. You're certainly going to have your share of proposals until you finally say yes—unless Dr. McKay wins you over first. And that might not be a bad thing at all, from what I've heard of him."

"Oh?" I was curious. "I really haven't heard anything, except that he's become quite wealthy here in Grampian."

"Not many have heard anything beyond that," said Mother. "It was only last fall when I was in Philadelphia that I even learned he'd been married before. Naturally, I kept the story to myself, for I don't believe in gossip."

I waited. If Mother wanted to tell me more, she would. If she didn't, no amount of coaxing would get the story out of her.

"From what I heard, it seems that Dr. McKay wasn't always as wealthy as he is now. According to the woman who told me, the McKays lost a fortune in shipping when three of their freighters were lost with all hands and none of the cargo was recovered. They'd put their money into building a steamliner, and, of

73

course, that couldn't be finished properly. It went down in a storm on its second voyage out. And that happened the same year that Dr. McKay, just beginning his practice, married one of the Main Line set—one of those spoiled, headstrong brats I always vowed you'd never become."

She paused and looked at me for a moment before she went on.

"This young lady just took it to heart when she found out that her husband suddenly didn't have all the money she thought he had. Even though there was plenty from her own family, she wanted more. She began to interfere with his medical practice, pressing him to see only her wealthy friends and to raise his fees."

"And, of course, he refused," I said. I knew Nathan McKay at least that well.

Mother gave a tight-lipped smile. "He not only refused, child, but he stopped seeing most of the wealthy patients and opened a clinic for the poor. That's when the real trouble started with his wife. It caused quite a scandal, I'm told. She started carrying on with other men, drinking too much, and telling everyone she met what a mistake she'd made to marry 'beneath herself.' Maybe she thought she could shame him into changing his ways or maybe she was just spiteful, but whatever the reason was, it didn't work."

"What happened?"

"Well, they found her passed out one morning in the guesthouse of one of the Main Line estates. The man who owned it said he'd brought her home with him after a concert because she'd not been feeling well. What he meant was that she'd taken to mixing opium with her alcohol and was afraid to go home to her husband in the condition she was in. When they found her, there were three vials of laudanum in her purse."

She paused a moment, taking the brush from me and setting it on the dresser before she began arranging her hair into braids, as she did every night.

"Well, his wife wasn't dead," she went on, "but she came close to it. When they found her she hadn't taken off her dress, which saved the owner of the house quite a bit of explaining, I gather. They couldn't wake her up. As soon as Nathan McKay found out, he put her in a sanitarium, started divorce proceedings, and left Philadelphia right after that. He sold his house and gave half of the profits for the care of his clinic patients, and then he came up here with the money that was left. You know the rest."

"He's divorced, then?"

Mother shrugged slightly. "Can't see how they'd stop it. She gave him cause many times over, from what this woman said. She wasn't at all particular about her men, as long as they had money. By the time of her accident, most of Philadelphia society was talking about her behind her back. And they invited him to places they didn't invite her—though, the way I heard the story, he didn't often have time to go, anyway."

A sudden whim made me ask what the first Mrs. McKay had looked like.

"Not like you, child, if that's what you're wondering. She had fiery red hair and was thin as a rail."

"Amanda Scott." I said the name without thinking.

"You're right about that," said Mother. "I understand she's been spending her mornings down at the clinic these days, too, helping in the women's ward."

So that was why I hadn't seen Amanda at the clinic! Probably she hadn't wanted the men to make comparisons. . . . I brought my thoughts up short. It would not do to think of Amanda as a rival. I barely knew Nathan McKay, and I was certainly not going to set my cap for him just because he appeared to be such a good match! Steven was just as good. More important, I was my own woman. I would choose when I was ready, not before.

"Not that it's done her any good, I suppose," Mother was saying. "If she's after him, probably her looks are against her. And he did ask you instead of her to go with him Saturday."

"Perhaps he asked both of us." I smiled at the thought of what Amanda would say if she saw me in the carriage when she came out with Nathan.

"Not if he knows what's good for him. Now you run along to bed. Tomorrow we'll have the dressmaker out here with some fabrics and we'll look over your gowns and see what we can do with three days' notice. Honestly! You'd think he'd have more consideration than to ask you this late. But I suppose he's so busy it never entered his mind that a woman can't be seen at one of these affairs in something she's worn before."

Shaking her head in mock dismay, she motioned me to go. But a thought occurred to me then, and I felt the apprehension coming back.

"What about Father? What if . . ."

"No, you leave him to me. I'll manage that part. You can take my word for it that he'll see reason. You're going, and that's that."

Thursday passed, with the dressmaker in the morning and the clinic in the afternoon, and a very subdued conversation at dinner, during which time Father did not mention the Cottors. Friday went much the same, for Madame Peret, mother's dressmaker, wanted to make something completely different for the occasion and required me to stand for fittings nearly all that morning, as well. That afternoon, to my disappointment, the bed where Billy Joe Walker had been had a new occupant, a sallow-faced, thin fellow with a bandage on his head. When I inquired, the patients told me that Billy Joe's leg had healed. His cast had been removed from his leg last night, and he had started back upriver this morning.

"Serves 'im right," said another of the patients, a big man named Pete Brand who had lost an arm in an accident at one of the lumber camps. "He don't get to take it easy down here anymore. That's what he gets for pickin' on poor old Gould all the time, hey, Gould?"

The bearded man made no reply. He just sat there silently glowering under heavy black eyebrows, as he always did. Even when the men were laughing, Gould's expression did not change more than to soften a little.

"Isn't that right, hey, Gould?" Brand was taunting him now. "Bet you're glad old Billy Joe's gone off. Now maybe ya won't be screamin' and hollerin' in your sleep no more . . ."

"You shut up!" Gould's voice was low and level, toneless.

"Oh, now can't take it, eh?"

I interrupted them. There was no reason to begin another fight. "I think that's enough, Mr. Brand. Mr. Gould's pain is his own concern, and I'm sure it does not improve matters any to make jokes about it."

As I turned to my book to begin to read, I thought I saw a flicker of appreciation in Gould's flat, cold stare, but it was only for a moment.

On my way out the nurse at the desk, Mrs. Martin, motioned me over. "Dr. McKay left a message for you," she said, open envy in her eyes as she looked up at me. "He meant to be here to tell you himself, but I was to tell you if he wasn't able to return in time."

"Yes?" I was surprised to find a catch in my voice. What if he weren't going to the ball tomorrow?

"The message is, he'll stop by for you shortly before nine tomorrow evening. He wanted to make it a bit earlier, but there simply wasn't time, he said."

She waited for my response, and I could see just from looking at her that she was in love with him. Mrs. Martin was brisk and efficient, probably as old as Nathan, and with a wedding ring on her finger, but there was no mistaking the luster in those eyes or the vigor with which she pushed back her blonde hair. As I looked at her, I thought how painful it must be to have someone so close, and yet so far out of reach. And yet there was nothing to do for this woman's own inner suffering but ignore it.

"I'll expect him then," I said. "Please tell him that for me when he comes back."

As I went to sleep that night, I thought how fortunate I was not to have suffered over Steven Cottor the way Dr. McKay's nurse must be yearning for Dr. McKay. I still had not heard from Steven, and it had been nearly a full week. He had said that he was going to Harrisburg, but for all I knew he might have disappeared from the face of the earth.

Still, he would come to me. He had said he would return the morning after the ball, and then he would come to me.

FIVE

There was a light rain Saturday morning, but it had stopped by afternoon, leaving the air wonderfully crisp and clean. Mother and Madame Peret had finally finished my gown. I had bathed, serene and quiet, enjoying the smooth feel of a new fragrance oil on my skin. An hour before dinner Emily had come up to arrange my hair, and she had arranged it in soft ringlets with her curling iron. Soon I had brushed the ringlets out into waves that glowed with an auburn sheen and fell lightly around my shoulders. Then after dinner, which Father did not attend, it was time for me to put on the gown that had taken so much time to complete.

"It's too bad Madame Peret couldn't be here to see you now," said Mother after I had come down the stairs and into the front parlor. "I think she's done nobly. Just stand there a moment and let me see the back, now that your hair's down."

While Mother made her inspection, I studied my reflection in the oval wall mirror beside the doorway. The gown had turned out more than just satisfactorily.

It was a light shade of pink silk, cut with a graceful neckline that showed my full breasts to their best advantage while exposing only a hint of the cleavage between them. The waist was also fitted snugly, and the skirt below spread out crisply over the Alaska down bustle and fell in shimmering folds to the floor. With the dress I wore no rings, only a simple ivory cameo held tightly around my neck by very thin golden chains at both top and bottom. I had white shoulder-length gloves. Dr. McKay had sent a single white orchid, which I wore pinned to my gown just below my left shoulder. The effect was striking, and I knew we had done well to trust Madamè Peret's judgment. As I stepped lightly around to face Mother again, I felt bold and lighthearted. Let Nathan McKay try to act the busy man of science tonight!

Suddenly I saw Father standing in the doorway. He was dressed formally, as he usually was for dinner, but dinner had been over for an hour. Could it be that Father was planning to go to the ball?

He saw what I was thinking. To my relief, he smiled slightly. "You look quite splendid, Catherine," he said. "I'm sure they'll be charmed up there at the Cottors'. But they won't have the benefit of seeing Claire, for she's coming with me down to the hotel. I've arranged a little surprise entertainment for the guests—in the ballroom. If things get dull on Vallamont, you might have Dr. McKay bring you down for a waltz or two."

I might have known that he would have done something like this! Father could not rest while there was a victory to be won over the Cottors. I was thankful again that I had not told him what I had seen on Vallamont last week, for he would doubtless have used it against them and brought me no end of trouble.

But I smiled at him, and said that I certainly thought this would be a more enjoyable evening for Mother than staying idly at home. Father's hotel really did have an excellent ballroom, and the food there was always superb. On previous nights when there had been dancing, the midnight suppers given afterward had been the talk of Grampian society for days.

Just then I heard a carriage pull up at the front entrance. I looked at the clock, and it was almost nine. "That must be Dr. McKay now," I said. Mother rang for Emily to bring me my wrap, for the night was cool.

Father looked at me, quietly, as though we had all the time in the world. "I believe you know what I expect of you," he said.

"You have made that clear, Father, yes."

A long moment passed.

"That's all, then. I trust the doctor will be good company."

He dismissed me with a nod and turned to urge Mother to get dressed and come with him.

The first stars had just begun to dot the deepening indigo of the sky as Nathan escorted me out to his waiting carriage. This was a very elegant closed coach, shiny black with gleaming brass trim and curved glass windows at the front. It was drawn by a pair of spirited black horses. The large coach lamps on either side illuminated the red velvet-and-leather interior as the driver, dressed in a dark gray uniform with a military cap, opened the door for us and courteously pointed out where I should step up. Inside, the coach seemed strangely quiet, until Nathan drew back the sliding glass windows on one side to let in the fresh air. As he leaned toward me to reach the other beveled glass panel, the coach light glistened on his slightly tanned face, showing just a trace of lines around the corners of his eyes. With his white tie and crisply starched collar, he looked so glowingly confident, so radiant in his easy self-sufficiency, that I think no woman alive could have resisted him. Certainly I felt a thrill as those blue eyes looked back from the window to flicker over me, and then to meet my gaze, full and vibrant with a clear light. I knew at that moment why he had been so successful here and why his people were willing to work so hard. The magnetism in him called forth something that I had felt before during very private moments, a compelling strength and determination. It was not the same feeling that I had felt for Steven Cottor, yet as Nathan talked with me on the ride through the twilight and up to Vallamont, I began to sense that he might awaken those desires in me, as well.

We spoke of many things during that ride, but I was so caught up in my quiet tumult of emotions that I scarcely remember most of them. What I do remember, though, is what he said as we left the open fields at the foot of Vallamont and entered the gravel road that led through the forest to the top. "It's a good first step, tonight," he said, looking at me and then at the woods ahead.

"Do you think so?" I waited for him to continue. I had no idea what he meant, but I had an idea that he might be talking about the two of us and was surprised at how comfortable that made me feel.

But he was evidently not in a mood to be romantic just then. "What we've got to do," he said, pressing his fingertips together, "is stop this insane war your family has with the Cottors. You don't see much of it, I'm sure, from where you are, but it's poisoning the whole territory. A man's either a friend of the Rawleses or of the Cottors, it seems. He can't be a friend of both. Even *my* men feel the pressure to take sides. Do you have any idea how much time and energy and money is wasted here in this valley just because two men hate each other?"

"I'm glad," I said, somewhat dryly, "that you think my coming along with you tonight serves some useful purpose." As soon as the words were out I regretted them. It really was not fair for me to talk that way. I recovered as smoothly as I could. "But I'm simply glad to be here."

I spoke with a smile, which he returned, though with a momentarily searching glance. "Well, of course, the same is true for me. That goes without saying. I'm not in the habit of spending time where I don't enjoy the company. Too busy for that."

And he began to talk of the territory once more, how President Grant was interested in its lumber wealth, how it could be developed as a great commercial hub if only our wealthy lumbermen would have the foresight to pool their influence and make it be felt in Washington. Together, he said, there was almost nothing that we could not buy from Congress. All it would take would be the courage for each man to put up the money and the political sense to know where to spread it around. The Susquehanna valley could become a perpetual center of wealth if men worked at it now. If they did not, there would be twenty years, perhaps thirty, remaining until the forests were gone, and then Grampian would become no more than any of the other farming towns along the river.

"You'll be forty then, Catherine," he said. "Is that what you want?"

I could feel the pine-cooled air coming through the carriage and hear the low breathing of the horses as the wooden wheels crunched over the gravel. It struck me then that I had never really thought about what I wanted twenty years from now, or even five years from now. I had assumed I would be married, thought I would have a large house to run, as my mother did, and be occupied with important people to entertain and children to raise. But I had never stopped to think whether or not I wanted those things. I only knew that I would not allow myself to be forced into something I did not want—I had the courage and the intelligence to prevent that from happening, I was quite sure.

I said, "I suppose not. I really haven't thought about it."

He smiled slightly. "You haven't had to, I guess. But come over here and look up ahead at Abel Cottor's place. You can just see the outline through the trees."

I moved across the leather seat to sit closer to him, and I looked out the curved glass of the front coach window at the dramatic dark outline of Cottor's Castle. Lights blazed from the windows on all four floors of the building, illuminating parts of the Mediterranean trim that gave it the air of a villa in Nice, or perhaps Spain. But the more striking feature was the tall medieval round tower that served, at the bottom, as an entranceway. The huge double doors were thrown open, sending forth a blaze of light and allowing glimpses of colorful gowns inside. And looming high over this bright wide doorway, high over the entire building, was the shadow of the great turret, in complete darkness except for the glimmerings of light from the other windows. The tower made a somber, almost sinister, contrast to the bright gaiety of the rest of this strange, isolated mansion.

I thought of Steven. When would I see him again? And what would I say to him? It seemed impossible, after the way I had felt only a week ago, to treat him coldly, and yet perhaps in the long run we would have to test our feelings for each other. I knew I had been glad to be with him, to savor the warmth of his lovemaking. But I was glad to be sitting beside Nathan at this moment, though we were barely touching one another. Was it only physical attraction with Steven? I asked myself. And with Nathan McKay . . . what? I could not tell.

The carriage came up the circular driveway and stopped before the wide doorway. No one met us, so Nathan opened the door and helped me to step down. Once inside, we looked for someone to greet us, but again no one seemed to come forward. From the large rooms on either side, people drifted out into the wide hallway, and we saw several couples go up the wide circular staircase at the far end of the hall. But these were guests, evidently too busy admiring the extravagant decor to take notice of us. We could hear music from upstairs, which meant that the ballroom was on the second floor.

Nathan led me inside, past the carved, throne-like

chairs in the entrance hall, across the polished parquet floor patterned in several different woods. In the rooms on either side of us, the bright glow of many well-trimmed oil lamps illuminated the feast Abel Cottor had waiting for his guests. The room on our right held a square of tables crowded with bottles of many shapes and colors, with a man in the center who was busy uncorking champagne and filling the glasses of guests who milled around. In the other room, tables lined the walls and were piled high with foods of every description. I had a glimpse of a man in a chef's hat slicing a tremendous roast, while people with plates in hand helped themselves to portions of huge hams and turkeys, great lobsters, mounds of vegetables and salads, or, on the far side of the room, to a pile of frosted pastries that stood as tall, it seemed, as many of the guests. I had thought some of the displays at dinners given by my parents had been wasteful, but they had not even compared with this!

On every wall there hung huge paintings: green landscapes, huntsmen laden with game, dancers, still-lifes of fruits and flowers. On the newel post at the foot of the stairs, a life-sized brass statue of an Elizabethan shepherd lofted a cornucopia above his upturned mouth as though it were a wineskin. Atop the horn rested the cut-glass globe of what would have been a gasolier—if Abel had had a gas line.

"Are you impressed?" Nathan asked as we walked up the stairs.

"Ridiculous, isn't it? He could feed the whole town here tonight." Even as I spoke, though, I had to admit that the castle was fascinating, for all its ostentatious display of wealth.

Upstairs, perhaps a hundred couples had spread themselves across the wide expanse of a ballroom that seemed to cover the entire second floor. Musicians were playing off to our left as we entered, but I took little notice of them just then. My whole attention at the moment we entered, try as I might to think otherwise, was riveted on the crowd of dancers. Was Steven among them? I stood as if in a trance, oblivious to everyone for several moments as I searched the room.

But Steven was not there. Even though I had not expected to see him, I still felt suddenly tired.

"You look pale. Are you all right?"

Nathan touched my arm, supporting me briefly, and I felt my strength return. "I must have climbed the stairs too rapidly. I feel fine now."

"Good. Here comes our host at last."

And it was Abel Cottor, coming toward us with a practiced smile of welcome. His leathery, almost Indian-like face and his iron-gray hair were just as I remembered them. In fact, his whole appearance was the same, except that he had put on a formal white tie and a cutaway jacket. I felt exposed, for he knew of my eavesdropping last Saturday. Yet I steeled myself. I knew something that was dangerous to him, and I had done him a favor by keeping that a secret. It was he who should be afraid of me, not the other way around.

He greeted Nathan warmly, but when he turned to me his manner changed. "Surprised to see you here. You're Sam Rawles's daughter, aren't you?" It was not a question the way he said it. I felt vaguely uncomfortable with the way his cold black eyes appraised me, as if the gown I had been so pleased with not long ago were not even there. But I pushed that feeling aside.

"I am. And you did send us an invitation, so I don't see why you act surprised. I remember getting it last Saturday morning, as a matter of fact."

My tone was pleasant. I watched his face to see if the mention of Saturday would have any effect. It did not. If anything, he seemed more sure of himself.

"So I did. Hope you like it up here. Nice view from the balconies over in the front, if you want some air. And if you don't like the music, there's gaming upstairs on the third floor. Just go up the steps in the tower there."

He indicated a doorway across the room, between

the two French windows that opened out onto the two balconies.

Then he added casually, "Steven's up on the fourth floor, getting dressed. Just arrived back from Harrisburg a few minutes ago. When he's ready I expect he'll take over greeting folks, and then maybe I'll have a chance to talk with you, Doctor, about a little business proposition I've . . ."

"It can wait till Monday, I expect, don't you think, Abel?" While Nathan smoothly went on putting aside Abel Cottor's invitation, my own thoughts whirled swiftly. Steven was here! He had just come back from Harrisburg, the better part of a day's trip away. What would he say if he found me here? The questions raced through my mind, more disturbing now than the feelings I had kept carefully controlled all week. Had he been waiting to see me tonight, missing me, looking for the chance to come back to Grampian earlier?

I pulled myself up short, brought back to reality by Nathan's firmly even voice.

"Why don't we have a look at this view of Abel's? Give us an idea of whether he's going to have any luck selling those lots of his."

And I was moving with him across the well-lit dance floor, nodding automatically to the people I knew. Some of them had been at Father's dinner last week and seemed surprised to see me, but the surprise changed to a knowing smile when they recognized Nathan. Nathan, too, was nodding at people he recognized, repeating the names of the prominent ones he thought I might not know. "Well, there's Garrison, the congressman from up North, and Farber, building the new tannery downriver, and, well—Senator Vandemeer himself! Quite a display Abel has managed to gather in his behalf. Your father's going to be interested to know, I'd expect."

We reached the open doorway to one of the terraces, where the air was cooler. I felt as if I had to prove I had been listening. "Likely they'll be down at Father's hotel later on in the evening," I said. "Father has his own orchestra for the night, and no doubt he's sent the word around that he's looking forward to seeing all his friends there."

"Really? He hadn't told me. But then I suppose he left that up to you."

Then we were out on the balcony, looking out over a view that made my reply come out almost in a whisper. Far off toward the horizon, the Bald Eagle mountain range and the wide Susquehanna River shone silvery under the rising moon. Before them, on the near side of the glittering river, were the lights of Grampian: small windows glowing yellow amid the cool moonlight on the trees and the rooftops. And out beyond the mountains were more mountains, and beyond them were the stars.

At that moment I knew, felt with an irreversible sureness, that this mansion and I were bound up with one another. The strange feelings from past years when I had looked up at the forbidden Vallamont all came flooding back over me now. I understood perfectly how Abel Cottor must feel about selling parts of his mountain, for, if it had been mine, I knew I would gladly have fought long and hard to keep from giving up a single acre. I wanted this mountain, wanted to stand here and look down on this valley any time I chose, to watch the seasons turn from here, to see the trees change from green to golden red and then to white with the winter snows, and then to the fresh yellow-green of spring. . . .

Suddenly I realized that Nathan was no longer looking at the view, but at me. His skin looked darker somehow in the moonlight, and his eyes more brilliantly cool and penetrating.

"If they all like it as well as you do," he said, "your father's going to lose his fight."

He gestured out to the edge of the lights in Grampian, where Father's Deer Park Hotel, at this distance a small, brilliant rectangle of gas-lit elegance, glowed with quiet rivalry against Cottor's Castle.

"Do you suppose your father can see us from down there?"

"I doubt that he'd be looking," I said. For some reason I longed terribly for Nathan McKay to kiss me just at that moment and then to take me away somewhere that was safe. I drew closer to him and looked up, hoping he would . . . and then there were voices behind us, and two other couples were making their way out onto the balcony to see the view.

We went inside to dance. Nathan moved smoothly, as we waltzed at arm's length. I knew he was enjoying himself. I knew that I was, too. Yet, beneath that feeling of quiet happiness was foreboding, for I knew that any minute Steven would be here, would see me, would ask me to dance with him, and then the turbulence would begin. Twice I was on the verge of suggesting that we leave, but both times Nathan began to talk of something else, and the moment passed.

Now the musicians had finished playing. We applauded politely, and I turned to Nathan for a third time. "Why don't we say our good-byes now and go down to Father's for an hour or so? I'm sure he'd appreciate it."

But Nathan's eyes were fixed on something or someone behind me. Then I heard a voice, and with a sinking heart I knew that I had been too late.

"Good evening." It was Steven, dark and sleek and moving quickly, with that trace of irritability one finds in a person who is long accustomed to getting his own way. "Dr. McKay, I believe. I'm Steven Cottor. My father's sent me to look after the lady while he talks with you downstairs in the library. Would you mind? Abel hates to be kept waiting."

Nathan looked at him, cool and unmoved. "I've already told your father I have nothing to say to him until Monday. As a matter of fact, the lady and I were just leaving."

"Oh, so soon? And I had looked forward to at least a waltz with her, and perhaps a tour of the gaming rooms upstairs. Are you sure you have to leave?"

He looked directly at me as he spoke, and the dark power in his gaze set me immediately on my guard. I wanted to face this power of Steven Cottor's. Yet I longed not to have to go through with it.

And as I hesitated, a chance encounter made my choice for me. Amanda Scott, her red hair pinned up rather elegantly, I thought, and with a not unattractive gown of forest-green silk, joined our group and began to monopolize "Dr. M." with talk of his clinic and what she had been doing there. Nathan was being polite, and as the musicians began again Amanda practically insinuated herself into his arms and began to pull him out onto the dance floor with her. He acquiesced with a tolerant smile for a step or two. Then he excused himself for a moment and came back to me and took me aside.

"She's worked hard at the clinic," he said. "And she came with her father, so she really hasn't danced at all. Why don't you take Cottor up on his offer and see the place? You're interested in the house. I could tell that when we first drove up. I'll meet you back here in a half hour or so, and then we'll drive down to the hotel party. All right?"

I nodded. It all seemed so reasonable. It was foolish of me to be afraid. I smiled at Nathan, and then I turned to Steven to say hello for the first time since he had made love to me a week ago.

"We have a half hour," I said.

"I must talk to you. If it's just a half hour, then let's not waste it dancing."

And he led me to the door of the tower staircase, a narrow spiral of wrought iron. We walked up one flight, then another. "Wasn't that the gaming-room floor we just passed?" I asked.

"That's right—green felt tables, a roulette wheel, dice, cards. You can say you've seen it." Already he was opening the door to the fourth floor and leading me through. The hallway was lit by only one wall lamp, and the dark red carpet seemed somehow harsh. There was wallpaper, a matching striped pattern that I found looked rather tawdry, and said so.

"Abel's taste," said Steven. "He decorated this floor like a whorehouse. It's where he keeps his woman. She's just down the hall at the end, the last door on the left. Did you wonder why you didn't see her downstairs? It's Abel's way of being respectable tonight, so he can please all the guests and make land customers out of them."

He walked as quickly as he spoke, and by the time he had finished he had stopped, taken a key from his pocket, and unlocked a door on the right side of the hall—the only door that I could see. "Come on in before anyone sees us."

He closed the door and turned the key before I quite realized what he had done, for I was staring at the room before me. It was lit by moonlight streaming down over a huge bed, several sofas, and a large, cold fireplace from a high ceiling that was made entirely of glass panes. The cascade of cool light transformed everything: the furniture, the bed, Steven, and me. I felt like a statue one moment to see the glow it made on my dress and the smooth flesh of my arms as Steven gently slid off my glove. Then I felt the warm surge of passion that I knew I had kept hidden for seven days and nights. I had to fight it off, had to contain it with all the strength I had. I pressed my lips together tightly and made my voice hard as I drew away from him.

"So, you intend to see me regularly, once a week without so much as speaking to me the rest of the time? That's rather an unrealistic fantasy on your part, I must say."

"Let's not waste time with games. I left for Harrisburg early Sunday morning, on Abel's orders. I've seen no one all week but greedy, tedious legislators, each one certain his vote will be more valuable to what we want than the next. I've been haggling over land grants and rights of way and charters, and doling out petty bribes and favors and jobs until I'm sick of the entire business. All week. All for a pack of votes that will . . . well, never mind that. Just call it something Abel wants, all right?" His voice softened. "I did think about you."

He moved closer to me. The little cleft in the center of his chin, where I had kissed him a week ago, appeared deeper in the moonlight. His eyes had a silvered haze over their dark surface. Suddenly I was frightened again.

He took me gently but firmly by the hand. "You don't fool me at all, Catherine. I saw you last week and I see you now, and I can tell that you're mine. You didn't expect me to send a messenger to your house with a note from Harrisburg last week, did you, now?"

Still I resisted him. "What was it you wanted to talk about?"

"All in due time," he said. "First I want you."

My eyes widened, in shocked surprise. "You can't be serious—not here." I was astonished, but I was doubly shocked when I felt how the idea excited me.

His hands were at my waist, unyielding, and he looked down at my breasts, unabashed, openly admiring them. "That's a nice dress, Catherine. I wouldn't want to spoil it. Take it off."

"You're insane," I said. "I'm expected downstairs any minute." Frantic by now, I tried to still my hidden desire for him.

"We've been away from your doctor escort not quite five minutes so far. There's plenty of time. Take off the dress."

"I will not."

"You will. You belong to me. Even if you won't admit it in public, you're going to show me now that we're alone."

He drew me to him and covered my mouth with his, and I struggled to break free, desperate to keep back the response he demanded. But he parted my lips and I gave way, and suddenly I could contain myself no longer. He kissed me fully, satisfyingly, knowing well the effect he was having as I clung to him. I was helpless, longing, unable to stop myself.

Time seemed to halt until he finally released me. Holding me at arm's length, he looked deep into my eyes. "I want you, I said. And you want me. Isn't that right, Catherine?"

I could not speak. I burned with shame and desire, and I could feel my body trembling.

"You want me," he said. "Say it. You want me. You belong to me."

"I . . . want you. I belong to you."

His hands were at the back of my dress, loosening the clasps. I wanted to stop him, but I could not. Soon the dress lay on the carpet, a silver-pink cloud. Then off came my petticoat. Before I knew it, I stood naked before him.

"Say it again—you want me."

With silent tears spilling over my eyelids, I said it.

Steven used me then, as though he thought of nothing but his own lust. He did not even bother to undress, or even to come under the covers of the bed. I felt ashamed, even as he made me cry out with pleasure.

But underneath the pain was the hard, sweet torment of desire that built and built, until at last, as I felt him shudder and moan, I, too, found release.

I could not look at him as I dressed, though I felt his eyes on me all the while. I hated what he had made me do, hated the way he had forced me to yield and to want him, even as I hated myself for responding. I had made such plans, and where were they now? I had betrayed myself. Yes, came a voice from within me, but I had also done what I wanted, had I not? I shook my head. There was no way for me to sort out my feelings just then. I dressed swiftly, a little surprised to find that, though I felt weak all over, my hands still worked with skill and speed.

He was looking at his watch when I finished, an amused half-smile on his face. "I'm afraid we have used up our time." Irony was heavy in his voice. "But I still want to show you the other reason I brought you up here."

"I hate you," I said. "I never want to see you again."

"You don't mean that. You can no more stay away from me than I can from you. Neither of us wanted to stop, and you know it. I've wanted you all week. If I'd had my way, you'd have spent the night here with me. But, no, you come up here with another man and you give me a half hour of your time. And I'm supposed to be grateful to waltz you around and then pat the other man on the back and wish the two of you a good night? Don't talk to me about that. Here, look at this. Abel said I should show it to you."

"I don't want to look at anything. I only want to go downstairs and get away from here." Suddenly the room, with its strange, cold light, was making me very upset.

He shrugged. "As you wish. But you really should read it. It explains a number of things."

He had an envelope in his hand, the paper faded and yellow.

I shook my head, unable to cope with whatever it was. I wanted only to leave. I moved to the door.

"I'm not going to see you again, Steven," I said at last. "You've . . ."

He cut me off. "I don't want to hear any more of your objections. You'll change your mind soon enough. Now, if you want to go, I suggest we leave."

Too overwrought to give him the retort he deserved, I simply turned and opened the door.

When I reentered the ballroom, I saw Nathan still dancing with Amanda Scott. Both were smiling and engaged in animated conversation. I felt as if I were fifty years older than either of them.

SIX

I was still shaking inside as Nathan led me out to the carriage and helped me climb up into that quiet, softly padded compartment where such a short while ago I had felt so strong, so confident. Now I was forced to confront my own weakness and, more frightening, the power of another over me. Steven had proven to be stronger than I had the will to resist. I had tried to conquer him, but I had failed.

Worse yet, I had to admit there was another desire I felt that was very nearly as strong. I wanted Vallamont. Before he had taken me back to the dance floor, Steven had insisted on leading me through other rooms of the house, and I could not help feeling once again the powerful urge to call this mansion my own. We had walked quickly though the huge portrait gallery and the several sitting rooms, which were now being used for gaming on the third floor. Then on the first floor we had glanced in at the huge baronial library, with its great enameled fireplace, large enough to stand inside. Abel Cottor had been holding forth on the desirability of the land up here to the rapt attention of several guests. Distraught as I was over what Steven had just done to me, I felt a rightness about this mansion, a need to own it, to mold its grand but rustic splendor into the center of a fine and spirited social circle that would dazzle even the jaded Grampian millionaires.

Steven had asked me, as we hesitated for a moment alone in the portrait gallery before going downstairs, how I would like to be mistress of the mansion. I had replied sharply, hurting him, I had hoped. "Since this mansion is hardly yours to bestow, I fail to see any use in pursuing that question. And I meant what I said—I won't be seeing you again."

"But you will," he repeated. "You can't change it any more than I can."

I had ignored him then. He was so damnably arrogant!

Now, in the carriage with Nathan, I tried to clear my mind of this whirlwind of emotions. All right, I did want Vallamont. And Steven Cottor still had a hold on me. I could admit that. But I had vowed not to see him again. Couldn't I keep that vow? I stole a glance at Nathan out of the corner of my eye as I pretended to look out the darkened window. He seemed relaxed, self-assured, as though he were perfectly willing just to ride down the hill in silence. He had been through fire, or so Mother had said, with his first marriage, and yet he sat perfectly composed and in control now. How had *he* done it?

I remembered his question during our ride earlier that evening. Was Vallamont, and Steven Cottor, really what I wanted in twenty years? Steven would use me without regard for my feelings. Did I want that? I knew I was worth more than the treatment I had received tonight.

I felt an inner strength and determination returning. Come what may, I vowed I would never allow Steven Cottor to degrade me as he had done tonight. I would certainly not allow him to be alone with me until I was absolutely sure I had somehow broken his hold over my feelings.

I rested my feet on the bolster of tufted velour that nearly covered the floor of the carriage. Turning from the window, I took a deep breath of the fresh night air of the forest. I glanced again at Nathan. Perhaps I really could stay away from Steven Cottor altogether. Certainly my father would make that decision easier to abide by!

Nathan saw that I had now come out of my daydream. Soon he was asking me about the patients at the clinic, and then about school, and about Europe, until almost before I knew it we were back among the houses of Grampian and on our way to Father's hotel.

Behind the oak trees of the park we could see the hotel's white arched porticos ahead of us, lit by Father's party. Then I heard the sound of another carriage and voices. We stopped and Nathan got out, only to return almost immediately. His face was grim.

"There's been a serious accident. They want me to look in. We'll meet your father there."

"Where?" The carriage had turned around and was gathering speed.

"It's at your father's mill. They think one man's dead, and there may be others."

"But the mill's shut down tonight. I don't understand. There's no one even supposed to be near there except for the night watchman."

"Exactly. No one working for your father was supposed to be there." He grimaced, and I recalled the way he had looked when he had warned that the insane rivalry between our family and the Cottors would have poisonous results.

A crowd had gathered outside the mill entrance, but the big planked doors, large enough for a wagon to pass through, had been kept shut and there were two constables standing guard. As soon as they saw Nathan, they waved their lanterns and called for the crowd to stand aside so that we could get through.

"Out of the way, you! Doctor's here, can't you see? Give him room, give him room!"

But as we passed I heard one of them say in a lowered voice, "No rush with that one in there, Doc. Likely he's cold by now."

The doors clattered shut behind us and we were surrounded by the huge interior of the mill. The walls and the wide, sloping roof, with piles of lumber stacked on the rafters, were all in shadow, lit only dimly with the lamps held by three men some thirty feet away from us in the center of the mill floor. I recognized Father among them. They were standing between two of the large vertical disk saws, one about ten feet behind them. The teeth of the other saw blade, which was closer to us, made pointed black shadows and blocked our view of the figure that lay crumpled at their feet.

Father saw us and took charge immediately. "How do, Nathan. Sorry we had to bring you down here like this. Catherine, you stay with me. I'm taking you home just as soon as we get squared away here. Come stand behind me and don't look."

I did as I was told while Nathan briefly examined the body. A hollow-eyed, thin man named Doebler, who was the watchman for Father's yard across the street, told us what had happened. He had been making his rounds, had heard a terrible scream from within the mill, and he came in to find his friend lying here lifeless, his head smashed by a lumberman's short pike that still lay beside the body. Doebler's untrimmed moustache shook as he finished his tale.

"Then I ran out in the doorway and saw the constable going by, and he went for help. That's all I know, but, by God, I want to get the man what done this to poor Blake. I want to see him hanged!"

"All right, that's enough," said Father. "He's dead, then, I take it?"

Nathan nodded. "But just a moment, Doebler. You say you've been here since you heard the scream? You just went outside the door to call for help?"

"I didn't go nowhere else. Stayed in the doorway and waited until the constable came back with . . . ah . . . Mr. Rawles, here, just a few minutes ago."

Nathan was looking around, silent. Outside we could head the soft rippling of the current as the river flowed past the entry chute and along under the stout wooden beams that held the floor of the mill high above the water.

"Let me have that light," said Father. "I see what you're drivin' at, Doc. The son-of-a-bitch could still be in here."

He held the lamp so as to cast its beam on the far end of the mill, the upriver end, where the wide hatchway doors opened through the floor, leading to the loading chute below. The doors were shut.

"Oh, my God," said Doebler, "that's the only other way he coulda got out, ain't it? And he didn't open them doors, not while I was here."

"He wouldn't have closed them from outside, either," said the constable, taking out his gun.

Father put a hand on my shoulder and began to walk me past the big saw and slowly back to the door to the street, where we had come in. "All right, just easy does it now. Goddamn, I was a fool to let you in here in the first place."

Nathan spoke up, hard and quick. "Up, Sam, he's on the rafters!"

There was a noise in the timber directly above us and we looked up. High overhead on the edge of a pile of timber, the beam from the constable's lantern shone on a lanky, thin figure crouched low, straining to lower himself down into the shadows, where he could not be seen.

"You, there!" The constable's voice quavered slightly as he drew his pistol while trying to keep his light steady. "Get down here before I shoot!"

"It ain't me, I tell you! It ain't me!" The voice echoed hoarsely down to us, and suddenly I knew I had heard that voice somewhere before.

Then the boards overhead rattled with another movement, and the thin, lanky figure, now lit in the glare of Father's lantern, lost his balance and pitched forward off the beam. With a dreadful, drawn-out shriek, he came sailing down head first. The terrified white eyes seemed to stare directly at us, though they were rolled back in fear. Mouth gaping, he spread his long arms apart as if to engulf us in a final embrace before he crushed us to the ground. I screamed, and Father pushed me away so that I nearly fell beside the iron base of the great disk saw. And then I heard a horrible wet crackling sound above me. I looked up. There, impaled lengthwise on the teeth of the circular steel saw blade, was the body of Warren Ruch. The eyes stared lifelessly at me. A little trail of red froth began to issue from his nose and mouth. My hand, as I pushed up from the floor, felt something warm. When I stood up and saw that there was blood on my glove, the room grew suddenly dark and I lost consciousness.

I awoke, sitting up with Father and the constable beside me, aware that I had just been moaning something about Warren Ruch, for I could remember the sound of the words as the faces above me came slowly into focus. "I'm all right," I said, and I took a deep breath.

Then from the far side of the mill came the echoing sound of gunfire. "Look out, Nathan!" yelled Father, and he quickly shielded me with his body. The constable turned. I heard the rattling of a chain pulley suddenly let loose, and then the creaking of the wooden hatchway doors followed by the crash as they fell open. The constable fired once and, cursing, he began to run toward the loading chute. More gunshots followed and then silence, and Father let me sit up.

"There was another one up there," said Father. "Looks like he got away." He helped me to my feet and called out, "Hey, Nathan! You all right? Get a look at him?"

There was no answer from the other side of the room. We could see the glow of a lamp behind some machinery, but we could hear only the voices outside and a scuffling along the stones of the river beneath us, where the constable had gone.

"Nathan!" I broke away and ran to him, with Father close behind. He lay at the edge of the circle of light thrown by his lantern, his face in the shadow. And beside his head I could see a dark stain widening over the floor.

I was shaking with fear for him as I knelt by his side. Then as Father held the lantern over his head, I saw that the bullet had grazed the scalp over his temple, knocking him unconscious and causing the blood to spurt forth, bright red, even as we watched. I knew what I had to do, and quickly, if Nathan was to live. Without hesitating, I took off one of my long cotton gloves and folded it quickly into a pad. Then I pressed it against the wound and held it there with all my strength to stop the flow of blood. The cloth grew wet, and I pressed harder. Father set down his lantern beside me and took out a small silver flask from his pocket. The odor of whiskey mingled with the blood and the night air from the river, and for a moment I thought I would not be able to keep from fainting. Hold on! I bit down hard on my lip and pressed harder, cradling Nathan's head in my lap as I knelt there. I steadied him with my left hand as I kept up the pressure with the pad in my right hand. His thin face looked strangely serene.

Father held the flask up to Nathan's lips again and again, trying to revive him with the smell of the whiskey. For what seemed like an eternity, there was no response. And then he moaned and moved, as if he were trying to get up. Feeling a strange, quiet joy, I held him close to me for only a moment. Then, keeping a firm pressure on the bandage, I gently moved around to one side and lifted him to a sitting position. His breathing came more regularly now, and I thought I saw more color coming back into his face.

When his eyes finally opened, I realized that I had been praying.

The next day I was standing before Father's wide ebony double desk in his library. It was Sunday afternoon. They had allowed me to sleep late, and I had missed church, waking to a haze of recollections. I wondered if they had caught the other man by now. Certainly the constable had missed him last night. He had swum across the river, some said as we came out, though the constable claimed that he had stayed close to the bank on this side and had been lost in the shadows. No one had seen him clearly, not even Nathan, who was well enough to talk now. Father and I had helped him to his house and saw to it that one of the nurses from his clinic stayed at his side all that night after his wound had been properly cleaned and bandaged.

But now Father had called me in, and I knew why. He got up from his desk and went over to the door and shut it. I sat on the chair in front of him, on my side of the desk, and I waited for him to sit down. But he did not. He came and stood at my side.

"I was real proud of you last night," he said, looking at me for a moment and then at the books that lined the walls up to the ceiling. "I want you to know that."

I winced inwardly at what he would have done had he known everything about last night. But I nodded and thanked him, and I waited for what I knew he would say next.

"They told me the name of that man," he said, "the man who died in the mill. Do you want me to tell you what it was?"

I steeled myself. I nodded. I was not going to give anything away.

"It was Ruch . . . Warren Ruch. Just the name you said last night when you were coming awake after he

103

died." Father put his hand under my chin and tilted my face up to meet his gaze. "They didn't mention Vallamont, though, when they identified him. All they said was that he worked at Abel Cottor's mill."

I said nothing, not knowing what to say. I had made up my mind this morning that I would not help Father one bit in continuing the war with Cottor. One of Father's men had been killed and so had one of Cottor's, and I was not going to add to the conflict by telling what Abel Cottor had done last week.

"I want an explanation, Catherine. How did you know his name?"

"I have nothing to say."

"You can't mean that." He pressed my chin harder.

I felt the anger build inside me as I thrust his hand away, pushed back my chair, and stood to face him. But even as the hot resentment grew, I was aware that this time I would stay in control. I knew somehow that Father could not goad me to do what I did not want to. I knew I could keep my presence of mind no matter how he might try to force me to break down.

And then it came to me with a welcome icy certainty just what to say. For the truth, I realized, was as damaging to him as to Abel Cottor.

"Very well, then. I did see Warren Ruch, on Vallamont. Last Saturday I rode up to . . . our special place at the top—and alone, too, I might add."

His eyes softened for only a moment, as perhaps he was remembering the times that I, too, remembered so well. Then he compressed his lips in a thin line and waited for me to continue.

"I saw Warren Ruch in the clearing behind that mansion of Abel Cottor's. I hid behind the spruce trees he's planted and saw Abel and two men of his beating Warren Ruch. They kept saying his name; that's why I knew it."

"By God, that's perfect! You're going to tell Judge Hawthorne all about what you saw, and we'll have old Abel down here in jail just as quick as . . ."

104

"Just a moment. I haven't finished. They were beating Ruch because they had caught him spiking the logs at Abel's mill. They were forcing him to tell who had paid him."

"And?"

"It was one of your men who gave him the spikes. Warren Ruch said as much. I really don't think you'll want Judge Hawthorne to hear about that."

He pressed me for details, and I told him everything I remembered. He tried not to appear concerned. It was all conjecture, he said, and just because Ruch had described a man who looked like Father's man Campbell didn't mean a thing. It could have been anyone.

"That's very true," I said, "but what if they decide to investigate? Suppose they bring Campbell in for questioning? Suppose they check up on what he's been doing this past week and find some evidence?"

"They won't. Judge Hawthorne will see to that."

"Are you sure? There were some powerful men at Abel Cottor's ball last night. I wouldn't underestimate his influence if I were you."

We stared at one another. I could see that Father was weighing the alternatives in his mind. Then he went around to his side of the desk and picked up a small ingot of gold, about the size of a pocketknife, that he used as a paperweight. He hefted this small metal bar in his palm, still thinking.

Finally he said, "We can still do it. You just tell Judge Hawthorne that Warren Ruch was the man you saw up on Vallamont, tied up and beaten by Abel Cottor. Forget what you heard. You can say you were too far away to hear clearly. Let the judge draw his own conclusions." He paused, looking at the ingot. Then he continued. "Likely as not, he'll decide Abel was trying to force Ruch to come set fire to my mill last night. You know they did find two cans of kerosene up there in the rafters where he was hiding."

I said dryly, "I doubt you'd succeed in convicting Abel Cottor with that kind of evidence. Any one could have put that kerosene up there. You'll have to catch the man who ran off last night and make him confess. Unless you do that . . ."

He cut me off. I could see he was growing angry. "You're wrong. Don't tell me what will and won't get him. We don't need to convict him. All we need is enough to bring him to a trial. The newspapers will do the rest."

Of course. Abel Cottor needed money. He had huge loans coming due—that was why he was selling parts of Vallamont! And if he were on trial, his reputation would be harmed, even if he were not convicted. A few discreet words from Father's friends, coupled with the publicity, and most banks would refuse to touch Abel Cottor—just at the time when he would need an extension on his credit.

It was, I supposed, poetic justice. Now it would be Abel Cottor's turn to sell off his holdings, to cut back as Father had been forced to cut back years ago.

We might even be able to recover Vallamont.

It all went through my mind so swiftly—what the newspapers would do with the juicy details of my testimony, the names they would call Abel Cottor for his cruel torture of Warren Ruch, even though it could not be proven. It would set people to talking, and the bankers would listen. And not many would rush to buy a lot on Vallamont from the man about whom such things were said.

Yet I knew, too, in the same moment that this would not end the battle. Abel Cottor would struggle back, just as Father had struggled back. The fighting would go on, even though our side had a temporary advantage.

And we would have gained that advantage only by my testimony, which was not the whole truth.

I made my decision. "I see what you mean, Father."

"Good. Let's get on with it, then." He moved to open the door.

"But I won't testify." It was hard to say those words,

but once I had said them I knew I could stand by them.

"What are you talking about? Of course you will."
He stood there by the door, his mouth clamped tightly shut, his jaw muscles working.

I kept my voice in a reasoning tone. "I won't. I see that it would hurt Abel Cottor. But it would not finish him. It would just be another blow in the fight—and a low blow at that."

I could feel Father's shock at what I was doing. The disappointment, the anger, the pain all shone in his eyes and hung palpably in the air of that library of his. Outside, the afternoon sun streamed through the leaves of the oak tree by the window. I watched those long, shiny green leaves, for I could not look at Father. I knew how he had longed for revenge; I had longed for it, too. It took all my strength to maintain my refusal, knowing so well how deeply I was hurting him. He could see what I was doing only as a betrayal.

When I looked up at him there was a dangerous light in his eyes. He was keeping his voice controlled. "Before we go any further, I want to know one thing. Why? For God's sake, Catherine, why?"

"I told you. Nothing would really change. In a few years the two of you would still be fighting."

"I can't believe that," he said coldly. "I can't believe that a daughter of mine . . ."

"Oh, Father! Can't you see? There's been enough fighting! One of your men died last night. One of Abel Cottor's men died last night. Isn't that enough for you?"

He acted as if he had not heard me. In the same chilling, controlled tone he went on. "No daughter of mine would do Abel Cottor a favor, not after what he did to us. Never. Unless . . ."

He began to come toward me slowly as he spoke.

". . . unless she had some other reason, some other very good reason . . . unless maybe she weren't doing a favor for Abel Cottor at all. . . ."

He tried to grab my wrist then, but I was too quick

for him. Sensing what was coming, I moved quickly behind his desk.

"You keep away from me!" I raised my voice. Someone would hear. Then I would not have to face him alone.

"Last week you went riding with Steven Cottor. Last night you spent quite a bit of time with him. Don't try to deny it. I had to listen to it from that Amanda Scott at church this morning. And that was after I told you specifically . . ."

"I was polite, only being polite. Nathan McKay practically pushed me at him when Amanda . . ."

". . . specifically never so much as to speak to him!"

The door opened. It was Mother, still wearing the yellow dress she had worn to church, trying not to look worried. "Now, what's going on in here?"

When Father saw her, a cruel smile came over his face. "Well, Claire, glad you could come to hear this. It seems that our Catherine, here, has decided she wants to take up with the Cottors. She tells me she thinks too highly of their young Steven to help us give Abel Cottor what he deserves. Isn't that right, Catherine?"

"That's not what I said! You've no right . . ."

"Oh, he must be an attractive young man, this Steven. Amanda Scott said you were away from the dance floor with him for quite some time." I had never heard him speak with such ill-natured rancor.

"He was showing me the . . ."

"You know what I told you I would do if I caught you with him, don't you?" His eyes danced with malice.

Mother tried to stop him, but he spoke right over her words.

"Well, you'll be happy to know that I've changed my mind. I'm scarcely going to put my head in a noose for the likes of him. What I am going to do is to see Judge Hawthorne myself . . . unless, that is, you decide to change *your* mind and come with me to testify."

"I don't see what that would accomplish," I said.

"You don't have anything to say to Judge Hawthorne . . ."

"If I do go see him, and I will, it won't be to talk about Abel Cottor. I intend to make the legal arrangements right then and there to disown you. You'll be out of my will, and out of this house—forever! Do you understand?"

I was too shocked to speak. The room, the books on the walls, Mother's face by the door—they all seemed to spin around me. I leaned against his desk and put out a hand to steady myself.

"Sam," my mother said softly, "how could you . . ."

"And you stay out of this, Claire. Or maybe you'd like me to do the same with you. Then you could go up and depend on the Cottors to take care of you both."

Mother closed her eyes and lowered her head.

Father looked back at me. "I'm going to Judge Hawthorne's now, Catherine. Make your choice. Are you coming with me?"

I stood numb, mute. Had I been able to speak, I would have refused him again. I would never forgive him for the way he had spoken to Mother.

"Then, good-bye, Catherine. When I get back, you had best be packed and away from here, or I'll have you put out."

With that he pushed abruptly past Mother and through the doorway, and then he was gone.

I rushed to Mother and put my arms around her. All the color had drained from her face and she could barely stand up. "Don't listen to him," she whispered. "He doesn't mean it. He's been so worried, he doesn't know . . ." She faltered for a moment, but then determination came into her eyes. She held me close then and told me what we would do.

By the end of the afternoon I was in a suite of rooms at Father's Deer Park Hotel. Many of my clothes still remained at the house, but I had enough with me to get along for weeks, or perhaps months. In my purse

I had nearly a hundred dollars, all the cash Mother had been able to find in the house. But in the hotel safe I had my jewelry and an emerald necklace of Mother's. That would see me through many months, perhaps even a year. I could travel, Mother said. I was free. She would send me money whenever she could. All I need do was to write.

I tried to look at the advantages. I got out a pen and some paper and made little notes, lists of possibilities. I tried to decide what I would do about Steven. I sent for my dinner from room service and forced myself to eat.

But I felt a great, exhausting emptiness inside. It was scarcely dark before I crawled between the cool, smooth sheets of my bed and fell instantly asleep.

SEVEN

That Monday morning I awoke ravenously hungry, and with a plan. I would go to Judge Hawthorne myself and tell him what I knew—that someone working for Father had likely paid Warren Ruch. The judge would see what Father was doing and would force him to revoke whatever legal papers he had drawn up against me. The judge had always liked me, ever since I had been a little girl. He would help. . . .

But in the light of day, as I ate breakfast in the hotel dining room, painted pastel yellow with white trim, I could see that Judge Hawthorne would hardly weigh my word equally with Father's. I had to be realistic, I told myself. I would sound like a spiteful child, trying to get revenge on Father for the loss of my inheritance. Father would say I had made up the story, and who was there to back me up? Abel Cottor and his men were certainly not about to come forward to say I had seen them torturing Warren Ruch!

I would have to make other plans for my future. After the waiter brought me some of the hotel's excellent browned sausage and shirred eggs, I felt my confidence returning. I sipped at the marvelously flavorful hotel coffee, watching the others in the dining room as I thought. Many were obviously salesmen, starting their Monday with breakfast in the hotel before going out to whatever business had brought them to Grampian. Some of these looked at me with undisguised admiration, though they were careful not to stare. The staff, of course, was treating me as one would expect the owner's daughter to be treated. I had spoken briefly with Malory, the hotel manager, when I had arrived Sunday afternoon, and he had seen to it that I was given every courtesy.

While I ate breakfast I began to test out my feelings, imagining myself as one of the people around me who had to work for a living. I could not depend on Steven Cottor for my support; I knew that. He had humiliated me on Saturday, when I was wealthy. What would he be like when he learned that I had lost it all? I could not afford to let him have the upper hand that way. If I were to marry him, it would have to be on my terms, because I wanted to, never because I had to.

Well, then, what would I do? I could go visit friends for a while until I found a man I wanted or a situation that I liked. I had money to travel anywhere I pleased. Perhaps I might find work—where? I had a college degree in arts and sciences, which was certainly more qualification than most women had. I could volunteer, perhaps, while I still had money to live on, and then apply for a salaried position somewhere after I had gained experience. Perhaps an office somewhere. Perhaps a hospital. . . .

And I thought immediately of Nathan McKay. How was he, after his wound from that man's pistol? I had been so caught up in my own problems that I had forgotten him completely.

I finished my coffee, certain now of what I would do—at least for today. I would write to a few of my friends from school and suggest a visit. Then I would go off to the clinic for my regular time with the patients. After that I would see Nathan. At the back of my mind, though I hardly dared think about it, was the possibility that he might take a hand in helping me, even at the risk of offending Father. And, possibly, if the feelings I had begun to sense for him began to grow . . . but I would not think about that. It was wrong to even think that way, for it would put me in the wrong position. I was not going to go to any man like a supplicant looking for help. I had beauty and intelligence enough to make them come to me.

I left the breakfast table feeling stronger than before. And as I walked up the stairs to my room, hotel stationery and envelopes in hand, a vision began to take shape in my mind. I could see myself standing atop Vallamont looking down, just as I had done in my childhood fantasy. But this time I had gained control of Vallamont *myself*.

Not long afterward, my letters written and mailed, I had changed from my gray morning dress to a crisp, fitted blue taffeta dress with a matching jacket. I was on my way out the hotel's front entrance, ready to walk across the park to the trolley and go into town and Nathan's clinic.

Pulling up to the entrance in front of me as I came through the doors was Father's carriage. It stopped. I waited. I watched, wide-eyed, as Father got out and helped Mother step down. Mother looked very tired, but she was smiling. And when Father turned to face me, all the anger was gone. He looked like a different person from yesterday. I saw love in his eyes again, and I nearly wept to see it.

He apologized calmly, with dignity, but it was an apology, all the same. He had already apologized to Mother, he said, but he did so again in front of me, just so that I would know that he had seen reason, as he put it. He had been under too much strain, working too hard and being too wrapped up with his problems. It was time for a rest. We would take a cruise to Europe again, the three of us, with maybe a friend of mine from school if I wanted to bring her along. Mother and I should take the carriage downtown and order some new clothes for wearing on the ship.

It was incredible. I had not seen him like this since those days before his first reversal, when he first had to taste defeat at the hands of Abel Cottor. The old kindliness was back, along with the exuberance I remembered. As he spoke, my eyes filled with happy tears, and my hopes slowly, cautiously, began to rise. Perhaps in time he might unbend, too, in his attitude toward the Cottors. Perhaps Steven Cottor and I might even be able to have a proper courtship and learn how well we would get along in real company, outside the hidden world of secret meetings and passionate bedroom encounters.

Afterward, alone in the carriage with Mother on our way into town, I asked her what had happened.

She was wearing gray, without flowers either on her bonnet or her dress. The lashes of her eyes were moist and the light layer of powder she always used had been disturbed by tears. And even though relief showed clearly in her expression, it was also plain that something still troubled her.

She kept her voice even as she told me that nothing really had happened. She had talked to Father when he had come back, but he had still been overwrought and obviously was not listening. They had slept apart last night. But this morning she had come down to breakfast to find him a changed man. He had apologized, and he had already sent word to Judge Hawthorne to destroy the papers of yesterday. I was his daughter again, and he was going to see to it that I was treated well before I finally decided to marry and settle down. Business could take care of itself for the summer. We were going to Europe, probably for the last time as a family, and we were going to enjoy ourselves.

"That was all," said Mother. But I could see she was keeping something back.

"But you're still worried. I can see that. Why?"

She frowned slightly. "I know him. He's really not been himself for a while. Something's been building up inside him for months now, and to have it just vanish in one night? . . ."

She patted my hand. The red leather upholstery of Father's coach made a squeaking noise that mingled with the hoofbeats of his matched pair of horses. The wheels clattered as we went through a patch of gravel on the packed dirt of the street. The question hung in the air. ....

I thought of Saturday night a week ago, when I had seen Father waiting outside in back of the house.

"Do you suppose he could have . . . it may sound foolish, but might he have met someone last night? Made some secret arrangement that he thinks will somehow take care of his business problems? . . ."

My voice trailed off, because it sounded foolish even to me. If it was a business problem, why couldn't he have met in the morning? But Mother considered the idea.

"I hope you're right," she said finally. "But I think it's something else, something inside him. The weather's changed too quickly, I think. I just don't want it to change back again."

She was thoughtful for a time, as if she were about to say something else. Then her manner became brisk again. "But let's enjoy it while we can, shall we? What do you suppose we should look for at Madame Peret's this morning?"

And the rest of the way we talked of cruise fashions, and she teased me about the effect I would have on the men I met. I did not have the heart to tell her that I still had not made up my mind whether or not I would go with them.

Mother went home after we had picked out several of the designs that Madame Peret and *Harper's Weekly* assured us were the latest in elegance. I had set out on my own for Nathan McKay's clinic. I was walking slowly along the wooden sidewalk, still somewhat caught up in my mood of the morning, before I had been restored to Father's good graces. I watched the women with their canvas shopping bags as they moved about between the shops purchasing the day's groceries. Some of them were shopping for their own husbands and families; others, by their uniforms, I could tell were clearly kitchen maids or cooks' helpers, buying for a family like ours. But their faces were quite the same, most of them, in their concentration. They all knew what they were supposed to do that day, and they were doing it. While I, however, was sure of my afternoon plans, I still had no real certainty about what direction my life would take. Yesterday and today had taught me the hazards of depending on a man, even a father. I really was hesitant about accepting his invitation to travel to Europe. It would be my third summer there, and I had the unmistakable feeling that I ought to begin to plan my own future and build a base that a man's whims or favors would not, could not, affect. What did I want? Well, I did want Vallamont. I knew that much. Perhaps the way to Vallamont was really through Steven, after all. If I could simply get the upper hand with him . . .

My reveries were interrupted rather abruptly. A portly, bald-headed man in a butcher's apron came stumbling backward out of a shop doorway I was passing and nearly knocked me down. From within the shop came a string of oaths, and then another, younger, man in an apron came in a staggering rush backward out the door and collided with the first. Together they fell from the sidewalk onto the dust of the street.

As they picked themselves up, a voice came from inside the shop and then the tall, curly-haired figure of Billy Joe Walker appeared in the doorway. "Next time we get a load of rotten beef up at Long Reach camp," he said, as the two butchers watched him and cringed,

"I'm gonna throw ya sons-of-bitches out from the *roof!*
Ya hear me? From the roof!"

Beaten, they both got to their feet and hesitated, not
certain whether or not to go back toward their shop,
with Billy Joe still in the doorway.

Then Billy Joe caught sight of me. "Oh, my goodness," he said, with a friendly smile that showed he was
not the slightest bit embarrassed. "Now look what I've
gone and done. Howdy, ma'am. Hope I haven't done
nothin' to offend ya!"

He came over and stood beside me while the two
men in their aprons slunk back into the shop. "Sorry
I hadda do that while you were passin' by, Miss Rawles,
but those two had half the camp up sick the other night
with their cheap, no-good . . ."

"That's quite all right, Billy Joe. I understand." I
gave him a smile, tilting my head back to meet his eyes.
He was even bigger than he had seemed in the hospital.
His tight-fitting red wool union shirt was unbuttoned
at the neck and bulging with the powerful muscles of
his chest and arms. But the amiable grin and the
friendly blue eyes made him seem not frightening, really, but something just the opposite—almost the kind
of man a woman wants instinctively to protect.

"Ya know," he said, "I never got to thank you for
comin' in and spendin' time with us like you did. They
just had me up and outta there before I knew it."

"I enjoyed it. No need to thank me. In fact, you
were a big help getting me off to a good start."

"Aw, I was just there, that's all. That Gould is a
bad 'un, just wants to spoil everythin'. We all knew it.
Only a crazy man would try to give a woman like yourself a hard time."

"Well, then let's just say we're even."

I smiled again and he smiled back, momentarily
awkward. Out here, both of us were conscious of the
distance that separated our two lives. Then he found
his tongue again. "Well, it's good seein' ya, ma'am. But
I better be gettin' back up to camp now that I'm done

here. Wouldn't want your pa to find out old Billy Joe was loafin' around town on the company's time!"

"My father? I thought you worked for Nathan McKay."

"I did—till your pa bought the camp last week. I guess you don't keep up with that kind of thing, though. Well, you take care of yourself. Say hello to the boys at the clinic and tell 'em Billy Joe says to get back to work."

Another grin, then he headed off in the direction of Hartman's stables, where I guessed he would pick up a horse for the twenty-mile ride back to his camp.

Later that afternoon I came downstairs from my hour of reading to the men at the clinic and was shown into the small, tastefully decorated office of Nathan McKay. I say tastefully, because the furniture and the paintings on the walls did all go well together, though none was in any style popular at the time. Instead of the massive oak and walnut that most doctors' offices displayed, Nathan had limited his furniture to frail-seeming, thin-doweled pieces that had all been made more than fifty years earlier. Collecting was a hobby of his, he had said, though I suspected he simply did not care for the tastes that called for desks and chairs to be made in so much larger proportions. I did not, either, but I liked the French style, or the Oriental style then coming in from England called Chinoiserie.

Behind his desk Nathan sat upright as usual, his head bound with a narrow white strip of gauze that held a more substantial gauze dressing over the wound he had received. The eyes seemed clear, but without their usual intensity, which was natural, I thought, after the fatigue he must have felt and the loss of blood.

Still, I thought it was odd that he did not get up from his chair and come around to offer me a seat. I took the small cherrywood caned chair that faced his desk and sat down. "How do you feel?" I asked. "I would have thought that you'd still be recuperating."

"Well, needless to say, I *am* still recuperating." He

indicated the bandage with his eyes and went on, very businesslike. "I should thank you. I understand you saved me from losing quite an amount of blood the other night."

"Thanks are quite unnecessary." His tone was beginning to put me off. "Was that why you sent for me? I had intended to stop by on my own and inquire . . ."

"No. I wanted you to come by for another reason. To make it short, and I suppose as painless as possible, I think you should consider today your last one at the clinic."

"I don't understand! What possible reason could you have . . ."

He interrupted. "I said I wanted to keep this short. Let's just say I'm aware that you'd prefer to be spending your time at some other place, shall we? We'll let it go at that."

His eyes met mine. The blue in them seemed harder, opaque.

"What other place? What are you talking about?" I was genuinely bewildered, but growing more angry by the minute. How could he speak that way to me after what I had done for him the other night and since I was at his clinic out of sympathy for his patients? "You sound as though you think you're dismissing one of your employees. What makes you think you can talk to me that way?"

"Not *what*—*who*. I had a visit from Steven Cottor. He tells me the two of you find each other's company quite fascinating. So I think you'll be happier to have more time to spend with him."

I was unable to believe what I was hearing. I found it incredible that Steven could stoop to something like this. To take a woman's reputation and deliberately, willfully . . . it was too much. What he had done to me Saturday did not even compare with this.

I tried to protect myself, though the shock must certainly have shown on my face. "I'm certain Steven was jealous," I said, "when I came to the ball with you. I have seen him in the past, spoken with him. But why would he say something like this to you? And why would you be so quick to believe him?"

The eyes held steady, though his expression softened a little. "Catherine, I knew he was jealous. I could see that. But from what he told me, he has reason to be. From what he says the two of you"—he paused, shaking his head slightly—"well, it's not necessary to talk about it. Just tell me that it isn't true, Catherine."

"Tell you what? How can I tell you something when I don't know what he's said?"

"Don't mince words. Just tell me. If you say it's not true, I'll believe you. Just tell me."

I looked at his face, and in its smooth, narrow lines I could see pain and hurt, as well as selfishness and anger. In that moment I felt, too, the hopes he might have felt, the chance to make a fresh start after his first marriage. . . . It would be so easy to lie.

But the words would not come out. I turned my head aside, away from his gaze. Then I got up from my chair.

As I left I heard his voice, and it sounded almost sympathetic, yet still quick with that brisk professionalism. "I hope you'll excuse me if I don't walk you out to the door, but I'm still not feeling too well, and, needless to say, if I weren't really pressed, I wouldn't even have come in to work. . . ."

He stopped talking as I closed the door softly behind me.

Outside I hailed a carriage to go back to the hotel. I would not admit to myself that Nathan was a loss. Who did he think he was, calling me to account that way? If he thought he could make judgments about my past, then he simply was not the man I wanted, that was all!

But one day, I vowed, I would have my revenge on Steven Cottor. I hated him. I would never speak to him again. Or I would marry him and then humiliate him by tantalizing his friends. I would see his father ruined and his fortune gone. With Father, I would . . .

And then, with a shock that made me suddenly fearful, came the question: What if Steven decided to tell Father? If he had told Nathan, Steven might be capable of doing anything. And I had seen the emotional strain erupt in Father only yesterday. I shuddered to think how quickly only a few arrogant words from Steven would destroy the peace of mind that seemed to have come to Father this morning.

The fear haunted me as I walked past the people in the lobby of Father's hotel, some of them lounging in the wicker chairs reading newspapers, others seeming to just idle away the remaining few minutes until the dining room opened for dinner. At the desk I forced myself to be calm as I arranged for my things to be sent back to the house, though for some reason my hands trembled momentarily as I picked up my jewels and Mother's after the clerk had retrieved them from the hotel safe. I held the emeralds in my hand for a moment or two before I put them back into their box and into my purse. Not long ago I had been depending on these shining green stones to help carry me through. Now I was depending on—what? Father, obviously. And what if Father changed his mind again?

Then, when I entered our house and was told by Emily that Father wanted to see me in the library, the questions began to fly round in my mind so that I had to steel my nerves and think clearly for a few moments before I gave Emily a reply. Finally, I said, "Very well, Emily. Tell him I'll be there within five minutes." Then I went upstairs for a quick word with Mother. As I had thought she would, Mother urged me to keep her emeralds as a small insurance policy against Father's whims. I took them to my room and hid them, and then I walked down the carpeted stairs to the library with a sinking emptiness beneath my heart. I would prevail, I kept telling myself. I would prevail whether Father chose to help me or cast me off. I had friends. . . .

I stood before the heavy oak double doors that walled off Father's library from the rest of the house. I grasped the brass knob firmly, turned it, and pushed the door open, expecting the worst.

Father had a large leather valise open on his desk, into which he was putting his three large green account books: one for the mills and lumber property, one for other investments, and one that he kept for personal accounts. A fourth, for the household expenses, was kept by Mother. I knew, because these were the books that Father had let me "balance" several summers ago. I would add the columns and make the entries in pencil, and he would check my work later when he made the final entries in ink. Why, I wondered, was he taking these books away with him?

He looked up, saw me, and, to my relief, smiled. "Have a seat," he said easily, still appearing as calm as he had this morning. I took one of the red leather chairs near the door and sat down as he told me he was going for a trip upriver. One of his lumber camps had a lot of men laid up from accidents, a string of them, that looked like sabotage. Another camp, one he'd just bought, he said, had half the men sick with food poisoning. It was good business practice to get up there now and take them some good food and a few treats to cheer them up. That way they'd know they weren't working for somebody who just wanted the job done and nothing else. After that, he'd be heading over to the new resort hotel he was about to open at Eagles Mere Lake for a last-minute check.

"I can't afford to take chances nowadays." He gave the valise a pat. "These books in here tell a tale, you know. And they say we can't afford less than a bumper year all around."

"Is that right?" I asked. Mother had said he might be overextended again. It might do him good to talk about it. I smiled. "I thought we always wanted a bumper year all around."

"Well, we do. But this year we've got to have it, or else in fourteen months we could find ourselves in trouble, just like old Abel Cottor is now."

He paused and lifted the silver lid of his cigar humidor and took one out, long and thick. "What I did, you see, last night when I got back from the judge, was take a look at these figures in here. And they tell the tale, all right. When I got done, I realized that it didn't matter whether Abel got rich or was hanged in the next few weeks. I still had to make a high-paying proposition out of what I've got right now. And I can't do that by wasting my time trying to knock off Abel Cottor."

My heart lifted with pride. Father had changed his mind on hard facts and common sense. And from the sound of things, he knew he was going to have to stick by the change. "I'm so happy to hear you say that, Father!" My eyes felt moist.

He puffed smoke and made a joke out of it. Here was his daughter, who'd kept his books and knew about these things, and when he told her he was in debt up to his ears she says she's happy! He'd never understand women, never!

He zipped shut the big brown valise. "Anyway, I'm going to be away for just about a week, which ought to be enough time to get things on the right track. Then not too long after that you and your mother and I will leave for the cruise. Don't worry, we can afford it. What we spend on ourselves this summer won't be enough to make any difference one way or another. We either have a good cash flow come in from the mill and the hotels, or we fold. In fact, if I were to keel over tomorrow, which I have no intention of doing, we'd fold sooner than that."

"I don't want to talk about that," I said. "I'm just glad that we don't have to get bogged down in that business with Abel Cottor and that man who was killed."

Father grinned at his cigar. "Well, I agree with you. We don't have to get involved. In fact, I learned that myself from Judge Hawthorne yesterday. Abel's in enough hot water as it is, without us saying a word."

"I don't understand."

"Seems this Ruch wrote it all down last week what this Abel did to him, and he left it with his wife, Alice. Fortunately, he didn't mention what Abel had caught him doing or who he thought was going to pay him for spiking Abel's mill. Guess he had sense enough not to incriminate himself. This Alice brought in the note paper to the judge just yesterday. Abel's going to have just one hell of a time when it gets into the papers . . . one hell of a time."

I saw the grin on his face, and I knew what must have happened last night. He had come back from the judge knowing Abel was going to be in trouble. He had gotten out the books to see how much money there was to pick up what Abel would be forced to sell. And then he had seen that there was no way he could cash in on Abel's misfortune. He would have to buckle down now to make sure the same thing didn't happen to him later. All he could do was watch while Abel scrambled to salvage what he could of his credit ratings and his property.

So much for the "temporary" part of Father's overnight conversion! He had just finally become aware of the truth: it was better to let Abel hang himself than to get tangled up trying to hurry the process.

"You know what?" Father said. "They've even started trying to make a deal, looks like. That Abel sent his boy Steven around to see me today. Of course I wasn't in, but he left a card and said he'd stop back tomorrow, just as respectful as you please. Wanted to talk about some important business, he said."

I forced myself to stay calm. So Steven *had* tried, after all! It wasn't enough for him to cut me off from

Nathan McKay; he wanted to cut me off from my own father, as well! It was hard for me to keep my voice casual and light, but I managed to do it.

"Do you think you'll see him?"

"Doubt it. I want to get an early start tomorrow. Besides, I've got a natural hate for snakes."

He paused and looked at me meaningfully, the heavy lids of his eyes raised higher. "And I hope you have, too."

An idea came to me suddenly. If I went with Father, there was a chance that I could prepare him for whatever Steven might say. Perhaps I could find the right moment to explain. I could say that I had made a mistake. "Father, let me change the subject," I said. "I can prove I don't want to stay here and see Steven Cottor. Just tell me first, who is managing the new resort at Eagles Mere?"

"I don't follow you," he said, but he told me, anyway. A man from Harrisburg named Gilbert, with twenty years' experience.

"All right," I said. "Then here's my proposition. I want to go with you on your trip."

For a moment or two he was surprised. Lumber camps were no place for a lady, he said, and what did that have to do with the new Eagles Mere hotel? But I explained. He had sick men in the lumber camps, sick and injured men that I could help cheer up, just the way I'd done for Nathan McKay's men the past week. And when we got to Eagles Mere, I could inspect the new hotel from a woman's point of view. The guests weren't going to stay long if the wives didn't like the place, and I could notice things that Father and this Mr. Gilbert might miss.

It took a good deal more convincing than that, but in the end I won out. I could go along. It was a good idea, he said, and he was glad I was taking an interest in the family investments. As if I had not tried to help him earlier!

But I was going. I had my chance.

That night we had a farewell dinner. Mrs. Jennings, our cook, outdid herself with trout done in lightly seasoned butter, a chilled cucumber soup, squab, and Father's favorite, baked Alaska, piled high with the crisp meringue topping. The three of us sat at one end of the long oval table, far from the wide silver centerpiece floral stand with its thick sprays of blue irises and lilacs, punctuated by the round white rhododendron blossoms. The only note of sadness was that Mother did not feel well enough to travel with us tomorrow.

Later, as I packed my valise for an early start, I thought of the things I had heard about lumber camps. Wild places, and in wild country, where a man might die as easily from an accident out in the forest as from one of the all-too-frequent fights back in the camp. The work was hard and dangerous, and it bred that kind of man—from the "choppers," whose axes brought the trees crashing to the ground, to the "sawyers," to the "haulers," who cut the trees into logs and brought them down to the river. In winter they lived in one suit of woolen underwear and wool pants and shirt, never changing or washing. Even after a fall into the icy river, they simply dried off and kept going, certain that this was the best way to stay strong and ward off any fever. In summer, though, there was more time for devilment. That was when Father worried about strikes and "sawdust wars" between the men of the different camps. In winter they were too busy fighting the cold and the river to fight each other very much. In the summertime, there were more fights over women, the prostitutes who set themselves up in tents or in a cabin near the camp. One of the men in McKay's clinic had been recovering from one of those fights, with deep wounds in his chest and shoulder from another man's hunting knife.

As I climbed between the smooth sheets of my soft, four-poster canopied bed, I wondered what the next few days would bring. Would I really have time alone with Father? And how could I find the right way to explain to him about Steven? I knew that in the eyes of many I was wrong not to be married to Steven now, but it was my life, not theirs. Steven had been arrogant, demanding, as if his past with me gave him the right to claim me forever. I felt sad then that my love for Steven had changed so much since I had returned to Grampian.

But that could not be helped. I thought again of the camps and the new hotel. I was bound to help Father make a better impression on his men just by being along. And I felt certain I had seen enough hotels here and in Europe to judge whether Eagles Mere was ready for lively guests and a profitable season.

Outside I could hear the soft, haunting song of the caged nightingale in our garden calling out for its mate. I tried to shut out the song from my mind, quieting the emotions and desires that struggled to break free.

Where was Steven tonight? I vowed that I did not care.

PART TWO

EAGLES MERE

EIGHT

Along the edge of the narrow dirt road, we stood under the tall pines and hemlocks that reared up high to catch the afternoon sun here on the northern side of the mountain. The forest was cool and shady, thick with pine needles and smelling of damp moss and ferns, moist earth and puffy white toadstools. Not far away we could hear the crack of a sledge driver's whip as he cursed at his horse, urging it to drag the heavy load of pine logs a little faster. To my left stood Father, talking with Vince Panella, the foreman of the camp, a dark, swarthy man with a kindly smile and a squared-off chin.

On my right, still looking slightly uncomfortable, stood Nathan McKay. Both of us had been surprised when, very early that morning, we had met on the railroad station platform behind Father's hotel. Father explained that Nathan had agreed to check over the medical facilities of both camps and perhaps the new resort, if there was time. While he told Nathan why I was going, too, I thought how odd it was that Nathan would take a two- or three-day trip so soon after a bullet had nearly killed him. He still wore a bandage over his right temple, yet he was up at six-fifteen to meet the train Father had ordered. There had to be more at stake than just an inspection of medical facilities. Perhaps Father had hinted at something else—a business or political advantage to be gained, or some other return for this favor Nathan was doing for him.

But, whatever the reason, I was not about to speak with Nathan after what he had said yesterday. My pride forbade that, and evidently his did, too, for he made no attempt to talk to me during the entire train ride fifty miles upriver, or when we got off and changed for horses at a small waterfront town after we had first crossed a narrow, swaying footbridge to the south side of the river.

We had ridden far over one mountain and up to the top of the next, where the logging camp had been built some five years before. The rough wood cabins had been gradually expanded to make room for some sixty men. There was now a bunkhouse and a sturdy frame mess hall with an adjoining kitchen shed. We had arrived in time for lunch—huge portions of steaming corn mush, maple syrup, and slabs of ham, which the men at the rough-hewn tables wolfed down in great quantities with pitchers of cold spring water.

This first camp was the one that had recently suffered a series of "accidents." I could see the effects of these past weeks on the fearful, suspicious faces of many of the men. At the dining hall, many looked at each other, as if wondering which one was the killer hidden amongst them. We knew there were now fifteen men in the infirmary-bunkhouse Father had had built this spring. Many of them would likely be crippled for life. Would there be more?

After lunch, which the men of course called "dinner," Nathan inspected the infirmary. We all spoke with the injured men. I succeeded in making a few of them smile with one of my Artemus Ward stories, but the others were in too much pain. Nathan promised to come back later that evening and give their injuries a careful examination as soon as we had come back from the woods.

While it was still daylight, Panella wanted us to see the long downhill skid where they had lost two men in one accident and where three more had been crippled at other times. This was the only spot at which there had been more than one mishap, and the men were beginning to balk when they were told to work even near it.

Yet the skid had to be used. In the warm weather there was no ice to make the mountain roads slick enough for a log sledge to be drawn any appreciable distance. That skid saved over a day's hauling time with each load, and to build another would take more than a week, with no assurance that the new one would be any more safe than the old.

Now, on the side of the mountain just at the top of this two-hundred-foot skid, we waited in the shadows of the pines to watch the sledge being sent down. Father and Nathan each studied the terrain, looking for clues as to what could possibly have gone wrong with three stout ropes to send three different sledges hurtling out of control down the hillside, where their logs had broken loose under the terrific impact at the bottom and crushed whatever stood in the way.

I looked down the steep incline, the wide path, bare of all trees, that plunged sharply down from the logging road. At the other end of the skid two hundred feet below, the logging road reappeared. From the point where we now stood to where the road looped around, hairpin-like, below us, was a day's drive for a loaded sledge, yet to go down the skid would take less than a quarter-hour. Not far from the bottom of this skid, another had been cut to send the logs down yet another level, to yet another hairpin-loop of road, and so on, level by level, until the last skid that sent the logs pouring down into the Susquehanna River. There raftsmen would gather them up with pikes and cant hooks and float them down to the Susquehanna Boom, just northwest of Grampian, where they would be held until Father's mill called for them. And that would likely be soon. Father had used up nearly all of his stock from the winter logging already as his mill pushed ahead overtime to fill new orders. If they ran out, Father would be forced to buy stock from the other mill owners at high prices, unless he could get enough of his own logs down to the mill in time. That was why it was important to have the extra stock from Nathan's camp and to have both camps turning out the logs in good order and on schedule. Every day lost to injury was costing money in delays at the mill and in lost orders from those builders who wanted good board stock shipped out immediately.

At the bottom of this skid where we stood, there was grim evidence of the past. On the left side of the open path, toward the bottom, great trees leaned crazily away from us, battered and cracked at the bases of their trunks, where the heavily loaded sledge had hit them. The earth on the skid was moist, freshly scarred with the marks of horses' hooves and sledge runners. The tracks ran straight here at the top, but down toward the bottom they slashed deep and dark at an angle where one sledge had turned from the trail and veered headlong into a great boulder that lay just at the right edge. A dark stain on the gray face of this huge rock was visible to us from where we stood. Whether it was from the blood of a man or the blood of a horse I did not ask.

Overhead I could hear the cry of a jay, and there came the intermittent drumming of a woodpecker somewhere behind me. The other sounds of the forest were stilled as the horse, a big brown dray that must have been half again as heavy as my riding horse, strained to haul the sledge with its ten thick logs into position for the long drop.

I shivered, even though there was no wind. As if reading my thoughts, Vince Panella remarked, "I think this one's gonna go just as smooth as silk. Whole camp knows you came here to look. Nobody'll try nothin' until you're gone again."

"So we'll all keep a sharp watch while the sledge goes down," said Father. "I want us to look for every possible thing that could go wrong, whether it's with the rope or with the sledge. Then we'll be in a position to warn the other drivers of what to expect."

"Where did the ropes break?" asked Nathan. "Near the sledge?"

Panella said no, that it was up here at the stump. They had all snapped somewhere between fifty and a hundred fifty feet out, when the sledge still had more than half its run to make down the skid. Panella explained to me how the rope, a stout hemp braided two inches thick, was tied firmly to the back frame of the sledge, and then coiled six or seven times around a large tree stump that had been shaped with an axe into a smooth cylinder of wood that was rooted in the ground. These coils served as a brake, checking the downward plunge of the sledge as the driver or his mate at the top paid out the hundreds of feet of rope, foot by foot, as slowly as he could so as never to gain too much speed for the rope to handle. If the sledge went too fast, the friction on the rope as it spun around the stump would grow so intense that the heat would make the rope catch fire and break. Or if a stump had been cut unevenly, a hot spot could develop that would scrape the rope and weaken it so that it would snap later on.

" 'Course, sometimes a man just loses his hold. His gloves might wear through and the rope would tear his skin off to where his hands were too bloody to hang on. Or he might lose his footing, if he's on the rope from up here, and get dragged into the stump, where he'd have to let go. Or, if he didn't like the fella on the sledge, he might lose his hold—accidentally on purpose. That's what some of the fellas claim happened here the first time."

"How can you tell?"

"You can't. So a lot of men like to do it themselves, like you're goin' to see now. Just one driver takes the rope, coils it around the stump, and then climbs back on the sledge with it, so you've got a double length going down. It's a little harder, 'cause you've got to look where you're goin' and handle the rope at the same time. But you don't have to trust nobody but yourself."

Nathan spoke again. "But you've lost two sledges here that way. How many men checked the ropes?"

Panella was slow to reply, brushing one side of his short black hair with the stiff fingers of one hand as he spoke. "Three men check the rope. Firmstone in supply. Me, personally, and the driver, of course. Nothing wrong with a one of those ropes. All five hundred feet are good, sound, two-inch hemp."

Father looked unimpressed, and Nathan bent down again to examine the smooth surface of the stump where the moving rope had polished it to a pale yellow sheen. After a moment or so, Father spoke again. "Of course, all it would take is a little nick with a knife or an axe or a pike that you might have missed. Any little weak spot is going to break up when it's put under this kind of strain. When did the driver check the rope?"

"The ones that die, I can't say. Others, they say they check just before they go down. And they look at the rope all the time it's passing through their hands. Nothing wrong. Then all of a sudden up at the stump something happens and the rope starts to come fast and then smoke, and then they're flyin' down the skid, tryin' to jump clear. Nobody knows what does it."

"It doesn't happen every time on this stump, then?" I asked.

Panella shrugged, turning down the corners of his mouth. "It's three time this week. We been down safe twenty times this week, even twice this morning. Nobody knows what happened the three times we crashed."

"That's more than we had all last year. Isn't that right, Vince?" asked Father.

"You betcha. And the men, they're startin' to worry."

The driver of the sledge, a husky, gray-haired man in denim overalls and a worn shirt of red wool, was going about his business slowly and carefully. Panella had already explained to him why we were there, and he told him that we would be keeping watch to warn him if there was any sign of trouble. The sledge was now poised with its front end facing the edge of the road. It seemed like just a slight push would tilt it over the edge and send it hurtling down the slope. Actually, we knew this was not true: it would take several good strong heaves from the big dray horse to drag it completely down off the road. This horse waited quietly at the front of the sledge, now and then blinking away an insect from one of its bulging round brown eyes. The horse's sides still heaved from the exertion of its last pull. There was foam around the padded leather harness collar that fitted over its neck and across its chest.

To our left, the driver was crouched beside the smooth white stump, carefully straightening each turn of the thick yellow rope as he coiled it, from top to bottom, tightly around the polished wood. He turned the rope in his hands as he worked, looking for weak spots. "New rope," he said to Father, as if he were explaining why he had gone so slowly, "but you don't like to take no chances."

We waited, scarcely hearing the chatter of a squirrel overhead. The moist earth and the brown pine needles clung to our leather boots and to the broad hooves of the horse as it shifted uneasily in the harness.

"Why don't some of us watch from down the hill at the other end?" I asked.

Father reflected a moment. "No reason why not, as long as you're careful. Just make certain you're down on the road, where you can get out of the way if anything happens."

Nathan said something quietly to Father, who

nodded. Then he joined me for the long walk down the steep skid. We kept to the edge of the open stretch, grabbing at trees to keep our footing balanced. It was nearly like descending a cliff. My skirts dragged on the dirt, and more than once I fell and had to stop myself from sliding away by clutching the cool earth with my fingers. When we reached the bottom, my dress was torn in several places and my hands were covered with a layer of the soil, as if I had been sculpting a statue out of clay. But we were safe on the road, Nathan still trim in his black suit and his Western-style black boots, since he had proved a better climber than I had and not fallen once.

It was the first time the two of us had been alone since yesterday in his office. I looked away from him, back to the top of the hill.

Nearly two hundred feet above us the horse and the sledge had already started to come down.

"What did you say to Father up there?"

He was looking at his pistol, turning the cylinder to be sure each chamber was loaded. "I told him to stay away from that coil of rope."

"Why?"

"I'll tell you later." His blue eyes glittered, intent on the slope above us. The sledge was now moving faster, about a hundred fifty feet from where we stood. The horse was walking fast. If it fell it would be crushed under the sledge, for there was no way the driver could bring the load to a halt. His rope acted as a brake, but only to slow, not to stop. As the sledge went on, in fact, a gain in its speed was inevitable from the tremendous forces that built up steadily each moment the load was moving.

We could see dirt and round rocks now tumbling down onto the road from high above, where the runners of the sledge had dug them loose from the earth. They clattered and bounced off tree roots and other rocks, and at first I thought the crackling noises from up above us were part of the din raised by the stones, or perhaps the rattle of a woodpecker drumming on a dry, dead branch.

But then, halfway up the hill and about fifty yards off to the left of the trail, I saw a little tiny flash of light, and then another. Someone was firing a gun up there!

Nathan saw it, too. He cupped his free hand to his mouth and called loudly, "Driver! Jump clear and take cover!" Then he was running up the slope, his pistol at the ready, through the trees in the direction of the shots.

Alone on the road, I watched the driver, waiting for him to jump clear. But he did not change his position, as though he had not heard the warning. Then at the end of the two swaying lines of rope high above him, I saw a white puff of smoke, and then with a frightening swiftness the sledge seemed to leap forward.

Trapped in its collar and harness, the horse must have sensed what had happened, for, before the sledge and its logs were upon it, it began to run, the big front hooves reaching far out and downward, the eyes wide and rolling white with terror as it tried to maintain its balance ahead of the great weight. It took huge, galloping strides, seeming to fly through the air in gigantic bounds. On the back of the sledge I could see the driver's gray hair whipped up by the wind as he tried to climb up over the back railing, where he could jump away from the sledge and its trailing rope to safety. Time seemed to hang suspended as they came on, ever faster, and I remember thinking that I had never known a horse could move at such great speed.

And then they loomed up large, no more than thirty feet away, and I realized with horror that they were coming straight for the spot where I was standing on the road.

My legs felt paralyzed with fear. Above the roar of the sledge there was a sharp metallic snap as the log chain burst. The huge black logs seemed to fly apart.

I found my strength at last and ran up the road to

my left, heading for the cover of the trees as I prayed that the sledge would not veer off in my direction. Behind me came a grinding, splintering crash as the sledge hit the road bottom, and then came the hideous cry of the horse as it tried to turn away from the trees on the other side. The noise seemed so close that I flung myself forward instinctively. I heard the scream of the driver just before I lost my footing and fell, barely missing the thick trunk of a big pine tree. Just in back of me then came the terrible impact as the sledge collided with the doomed horse and bore it crashing against the trees.

And then there was a stillness, broken only by the noise of individual logs as each rolled to a stop on the hillside. From the far edge of the road I heard a moan, and I knew the driver must have jumped clear. From the sledge behind me there was only silence.

I got to my feet, not daring to look back to where I knew the poor horse lay crushed. I had to try to help the driver, even though I was dazed and badly shaken. I stumbled across the road, my head spinning as I forced myself to move. We would have help soon, I told myself. Nathan and Father were just up the slope. They would come down. I heard the gunshots then, but I hardly noticed them. I tried to clear my head, tried to summon up the courage for what I knew awaited me behind the tree ahead, where I could see the driver twisting himself in pain.

The log that had crushed his arm against the rock seemed so huge, so solidly permanent, as he writhed beneath it. His uplifted face bathed in an agonized sweat, he struggled feebly with his other hand to push at the log, but he could scarcely reach it. Barely conscious, he moved with a pitiful weakness that frightened me.

I forced myself to look away from his face and that pathetic arm that waved so softly. I knew I had to get the log away from him. I heard gunshots again, closer, and a crashing in the woods not far above me, but I paid it little mind. The trunk was too big for me to get my arms around it, but I tried, anyway. Bending over it and grasping it with both arms, I tried to straighten up, but I could not budge its rough, weighty mass. I tried again, without success. Finally, I went around to where the upper end of the log jutted up into the air about two feet from the ground. Bending beneath it, I was able to get the log onto my back and shoulder, and then I pushed up with my legs to lift it slightly. My right ankle had started to hurt. I trembled under the weight, but I knew I had to try. I prayed the log would come down clear of the man's arm and put all my strength into a single upward push that lifted the log clear and sent it crashing to the ground a few feet away. For a moment I stood trembling. My shoulder ached where the bark had cut into it, and every joint in my body seemed to throb in reaction to the strain. But the driver was free now.

When I saw his arm where the log had been, my legs weakened under me and I closed my eyes, kneeling down beside him to recover. The world seemed to spin. I could hear his voice, a faint whisper that I could barely understand. "Don't . . ."

I opened my eyes. His mouth was open as he took ragged gasps for air. His eyelids were clenched tightly against the pain.

"We're going to get help," I said as confidently as I could. "There's a doctor here. He's coming right down."

"Don't let him . . . don't let him . . ." He moaned again, and tears spilled from between his closed eyelids. He was deathly pale.

"I can't hear you," I said. "Don't let him do what?"

The words came out in a great sob. "Don't cut it off! For God's sake, don't cut . . ."

And then, as if exhausted by the effort the words had taken, he turned his head to one side and seemed to sink into himself.

Nathan's voice was behind me, and from a distance I heard Father's voice and then horses on the road.

The sound of the gunfire seemed to echo in my memory. I closed my eyes in gratitude that both of them were safe.

Nathan's strong arms were helping me to stand up. "You mustn't amputate," I said as I leaned against him, vaguely conscious of his body warm against my breast. I was tired and wanted to go home, but I felt somehow obligated to speak for this man, who now lay so quietly at my feet. "He told me just before he lost consciousness. That's all he could think about."

"I'll have to be the judge of that," Nathan said quietly, "after I take a look at him. But you've done amazingly well. You mean you got that log off his arm by yourself? Here, now, don't try to walk just yet. Looks like you've twisted that right ankle, haven't you?"

I nodded. Just standing on the ankle made me wince with pain. I also felt slightly dazed. "What happened up there?" I asked. "I heard gunshots."

He tightened his arm around me, holding me closer to him. "I'll tell you in a minute. First try to point your toe up. Not too much pain? Good. It looks as if you've not torn anything loose, then. We'll leave the shoe on for now and keep the swelling down till we get back to camp. Now, can you manage to sit down here on the log while I have a look at this arm here? Don't worry, I'll tell you what happened. We're all safe."

As he examined the arm of the unconscious man, Nathan explained quickly that someone had been firing a rifle at the stump from a distance too far away from the sledge to be heard over the noise it made as it scraped over the rocks and dirt of the skid.

He paused, and I watched Nathan's quick, slender fingers gently feel under the driver's throat for a pulse. He seemed to be encouraged by the result, whatever it was, for he relaxed his tight-lipped concentration somewhat as he snapped shut his thin gold watch and tucked it carefully back into his pocket.

"Is he all right?" I asked. "He was so worried that he might have to lose his arm."

"I'm going to look now. But we may know better after we get him back to camp."

He took out a slender gold pocketknife and clicked open the blade. Deftly, without disturbing the man's arm, he slit through the red wool of the sleeve, now bloodstained. Then he peeled back a flap of the material and the wound lay bare.

"What do you think?" I asked.

"The bone's shattered. By rights we ought to amputate."

"What do you mean by rights? Isn't there something else you can do?"

An edge came into his voice. "I must say, Catherine, you're taking more of an interest in this case than I would have expected."

"That's because you weren't here when he was conscious," I shot back. "His arm was all he wanted, all he could think about. Don't you feel anything of how important that is?"

"This is a textbook case." His own voice was harder, the words more clipped. I could see that Dr. McKay was not accustomed to having his opinions questioned. "Needless to say, this bone is much too fragmented ever to mend. Anything else but amputation would be long and complicated, and I'll thank you to . . ."

"Oh, it would? And you might have to work a little longer and harder?" I could not keep the sarcasm out of my voice.

He looked at me coldly and then turned away. If there was one thing Nathan McKay possessed in more than ordinary amounts, it was the drive and discipline to work more, and more intensely, than ordinary men. He was justifiably proud of his capacity for work, and to call that capacity into question here rankled him immensely.

But that was just what I wanted. He deserved every bit of irritation I could give him, I told myself, after yesterday. I felt proud, too, that now I had found my tongue and stood up to him!

He was checking the driver for other possible injuries, and ignoring me, when Father rode up behind us. Panella had gone for a wagon, he said, after he had made sure that I was all right.

On the way back up the road, Father and I sat at the front of the wagon. The injured logger was stretched out on a pad of folded rough blankets with a third blanket covering him. He had not yet regained consciousness, and every so often Nathan, who sat at his side, would check his pulse, pressing skilled fingertips lightly just underneath the side of the man's jaw. Nathan did not speak often during the ride, maintaining that easy, impenetrable calm that answers questions with only a word or two and conveys the impression that the most sensible thing to do for the moment is simply to wait.

Father, on the other hand, was ready to talk about what had happened on the mountain. They had killed the sniper. Nathan had drawn his fire and flushed him out from his cover, and Father had caught him with two pistol shots as he was trying to reload. There was little doubt that he had been the cause of the accidents on that particular skid. They had found the spot where he had dug himself in sometime ago—a place with a clear view of the stump and the rope that coiled around it.

I didn't understand how he could break a rope that thick with just a bullet or two, and I said so.

"Remember the strain that rope was under," said Father. "He didn't have to break it. Just a nick would weaken it, fray some of the fibers so the others would stretch. Then the heat of the coil and the weight of the sledge would do the rest."

"So all he had to do was shoot at the stump. I see. He waited until there was enough noise from the sledge to cover the shot, and then he just fired away. But why didn't he stop more of the sledges, then? Was he working on one of the crews the rest of the time?"

Father nodded. "Panella recognized him." Then he began to talk of the celebration we would have back in camp. He grinned at me. "Well, you wanted to help cheer 'em up, and now you've gone and given 'em something to cheer up about! Wait till they learn they've got Sam Rawles's daughter to thank for getting that man. They'll cheer so loud that we're gonna need a new roof on the mess hall!"

"Nonsense, Father. I didn't do anything but stand there."

"We'd all o' been up waitin' at the top if it hadn't been for you. And we wouldn't have seen where those shots came from at all. Instead of bein' dead, that son-of-a-bitch with the rifle would have been laughin' up his sleeve back at the camp. We'd likely have had to shut down that skid altogether."

We returned to camp, where I could wash up a bit in the cold spring water and make my hair more presentable. Later the men did cheer, just as Father had predicted. After supper they passed around the rich, aromatic cigars and the half-dozen bottles of imported whiskey Father had brought for this camp, and around the long tables rose clouds of smoke and hearty laughter. There were songs roared out under the high-beamed roof to the accompaniment of a mouth organ, and then one fellow with a Swedish accent stood up and led the men in three rousing cheers for Sam Rawles! Father beamed. When the last echoes had died away, the same man continued. "And now, for the yong lady"—he cupped his mouth in a hoarse stage whisper—"vat's her name? Katrine! Hip, hip!"

And then the other men: "Hurrah!"

I would never have believed that the cheers of those men could have moved me the way they did, but my heart rose within me and I felt a warm, dazed glow as I smiled at them and nodded my appreciation.

And then Nathan McKay entered the room, his tall,

erect figure framed in the doorway across from us in the last soft gold of the setting sun. A hush fell over the group, for everyone in the hall knew that "the doc" had been out in the infirmary shed ever since we had gotten back to camp more than two hours ago, working on Frank Kelso, the gray-haired logger, who had still not regained consciousness when Nathan had ordered us to leave him and the camp orderly to their work.

The man who had led the cheering was still on his feet. "Vat's the news, Doc?" he asked, his voice wavering slightly.

Nathan looked around the room momentarily until he found where we were sitting. Then he said simply, "He's awake. Some of you can go see him, but one at a time. We saved his arm."

A tremendous cheer erupted in the hall, and as Nathan made his way to our table men rose from their seats to shake his hand or clap him on the back.

"He ought to be running for election," I remarked to Father as Nathan came closer.

"He's gonna be," Father said. "I've already talked to some of the right people. They want to send him to Washington in the fall."

Nathan was sliding into his seat, still shaking hands with a few men who had followed him over. When the last of them had gone, Nathan grinned at Father. "Quite a crew you've got here, Sam," he said.

"They know when somebody does right by 'em, that's for sure," Father replied. "Now let's get you some dinner, eh?" He beckoned to one of the men who was waiting tables, and the fellow was soon on his way into the kitchen for some more hot venison and corn bread.

Nathan turned to me, the blue eyes friendlier but still distant. "I think I owe that cheer I just got now to you," he said.

Later that night we were sitting before the small stone fireplace in foreman Panella's cabin, which he had given us for the night. I was to sleep in the bedroom at the back of the cabin, while Father and Nathan would have cots out here, in the area Panella used as an office and sitting room. The chairs, framed of three-inch logs and with backs and seats of varnished wood slats, were surprisingly comfortable. Outside it was dark. A chilly mountain wind had prompted Panella to get a good fire blazing in the hearth before he had bidden us good night and headed for the bunkhouse. The cabin was warm and brightly lit with the kerosene lamp that hung, freshly trimmed, from a peg over the door.

All three of us felt the glow of the day's success, especially Father. I knew how relieved he must have been to have the trouble at the camp settled in such a quick and decisive way. Both of us knew, too, that the men would be working better and harder now at this critical time, when their wood was so badly needed in Father's mill. Father calculated that we could count on a record production from this camp during the next few weeks, at least.

"But, then," he said with a wry smile, "old Cottor'll have some other skunk on his payroll up here and we'll have some more trouble. Just you wait." His face shone in the firelight, but he did not look as if he was getting angry about it, just as if he were stating a fact.

"I thought Cottor wanted to ease up for a while and be friendly," said Nathan. "He's been saying that around town all week."

"Old Cottor's a lying sack of . . ." Father glanced in my direction, hesitating to use the word I knew he had in mind. ". . . manure," he said finally. "And so's that worthless son of his."

I had a flash of inspiration. Here was my chance to spoil Steven's plan to tell Father about our past and to embarrass Nathan McKay in the bargain!

"Oh, I don't know, Father," I said casually. "Dr. McKay seems to have a fairly high opinion of Steven

Cottor. He's prepared to believe practically anything Steven Cottor tells him. Isn't that right, Nathan?"

Nathan McKay looked at me as if he could scarcely believe what he had just heard. I smiled inwardly, pleased to have taken him so completely off his guard.

"What are you talking about?" asked Father when Nathan did not reply right away. "What's she talking about, Nathan?"

"Don't bother to explain," I said to Nathan. "You see, Father, last Saturday Steven Cottor evidently decided that he ought to have my company all to himself. He sought me out at the dance, and then on Monday he came to Nathan with a story that must have been quite scandalous, for Nathan as much as told me he considered me—what?—Steven Cottor's personal property, I suppose."

I gave a disinterested shrug, as if the matter were not worth any further discussion, while I watched to see what Father would do. I was certain that he would not lose control now. The day had gone too well for him, and, besides, he would never allow Nathan to see him in a rage. And I was right. Father simply waited, stone-faced, looking across the small room to where Nathan sat beside the fire.

"Beg your pardon, Catherine," Nathan said evenly. "I never said that."

"But you did ask me to deny that Steven's story was the truth, didn't you? And when I wouldn't, you made it plain that you thought it best for me not to come back to the clinic. It amounts to the same thing."

Nathan began to reply, but Father cut him off with a wave of his hand. He locked his gaze squarely with mine and asked, "Catherine, what did Steven Cottor tell you on Saturday?"

I kept my voice even. "He seemed . . . quite taken with me. He said that he wanted me to . . . be his, I think was the way he phrased it. When I told him that would not be possible, he said he had ways of making me change my mind. I presume that his talk with Dr. McKay was one of those ways."

Father nodded, but he continued to look straight at me. "All right, then, but Nathan asked you to deny it. Why didn't you?"

Without a tremor in my voice, my eyes triumphant, I replied, "Because, Father, there are some things that a lady does not have to stoop to denying."

I got up from my chair before either of them could reply. Looking directly at Nathan, I continued, just as evenly, enjoying his obvious surprise and admiration. "Good night, gentlemen. I understand we are to make an early start in the morning."

And, ignoring the pain from my ankle, I swept into my room and closed the door.

NINE

As I undressed for bed, I could hardly contain my delight. I felt as though I were free, completely free, of the hold Steven Cottor had kept me under. With one single bold stroke I had denied the past—and there was surely no reason why I could not continue denying it if Steven tried to make a claim on me again. I had seen the belief in Father's eyes, and in Nathan's. I was sure I had convinced them that Steven had lied about me, and I probably had convinced Father that Steven would try the same lie after we returned to Grampian. A warm reception he would get if he did!

I drew the curtain on the one window in my room and stepped out of my dress, then my chemise, feeling the cool air around my full breasts. In the next room I could hear Father and Nathan quite clearly, since there was only a planked wall separating us, and even that stopped at a height of about eight feet, leaving an open space all around the center of the cabin and the fireplace chimney, which went up through the peak in the roof. The voices were as plain as if I had been sitting in the same room. They were talking of Abel Cottor's money problems, pointedly avoiding, I supposed, any reference to Steven Cottor or to me.

I sat down on the small hard mattress and finished undressing. For a moment or two I savored the sensations of complete nakedness. I smiled to myself as I heard Nathan's voice, easy, factual, discussing a rumor that Abel Cottor was about to sell all his shares in the Susquehanna Boom Company. If I were to get up now and unlatch the door, would that voice still keep its calm, reasoning tone? Of course I would never have seriously considered doing such a thing, but it was exciting to think about teasing Nathan McKay. There were passions beneath that handsome, efficient surface of his, passions that—why not admit it?—I could easily enjoy arousing. Those cool blue eyes—could I conquer their icy control, make them long for me, make them cloud over with passion, make them . . .

I found myself suddenly flushed at the thought of making love with Nathan. The feeling had crept over me without warning, and when I realized what had happened I was surprised and a little afraid. I had never had this kind of desire for a man before, except for Steven Cottor. But now Steven had proved himself unworthy, and I had vowed never to see him again.

But I was hardly going to leap into the arms of Nathan McKay, either! I brought my thoughts up short. This time I was not going to be drawn into an affair just because of the physical attraction a man could arouse in me. That had happened once before, and once was too often. Steven Cottor had treated me shamefully, and I had let him because I had been too weak to say no to the demands of my body. But now I was no longer a foolish schoolgirl, a virgin who longed for unknown pleasures. I was my own woman now, and I was going to make a choice of a man who would never use me the way Steven Cottor had done!

I drew on my nightdress, feeling the soft cotton of its high collar and buttoning it up all the way to the top.

What did I know of Nathan McKay? He was wealthy, and he had been married before, to be sure. He worked with the energy and intelligence of two or three men, and he had the loyalty and the admiration of his staff. . . .

But what did any of that matter if he were selfish, or domineering, or uncaring to a wife! Or unfaithful! I was not going to allow myself to make a mistake of giving myself to anyone until I was very, very sure of just who that someone was and how he would treat me.

I blew out the table lamp beside my bed and climbed between the rough but clean sheets, doubly pleased with myself. I had triumphed over Steven, and over Father, and I had the strong suspicion that Nathan McKay would soon take the opportunity to apologize to me before the trip was over. But, more importantly, I told myself, I had triumphed over my own heart's passions. I lay quiet, waiting for sleep to come as I listened to the men talking in the next room. They had lowered their voices by now, since they had seen the ceiling over my room go suddenly dark, but I could still make out nearly everything they said.

"So Panella says"—it was Father's voice—"he never came back from Saturday night. And he was a mean son-of-a-bitch. Even I never met him alone without havin' a gun with me."

A gun! The image of Father in the garden, pistol in hand, flashed before my eyes. That moonlit night when I had gone outside to meet Steven . . . Was this Campbell the man Father had been waiting for? I realized what must have happened. Campbell had seen Warren Ruch get caught and had somehow gotten word to Father to meet him. No wonder Father had been in such a stormy temper that night!

Now from the next room I could hear Father still talking about the man called Campbell: "It's my theory that old Abel got to him and paid him to change sides. And that's what he was doing in my mill instead of Abel's."

"It fits, doesn't it?" said Nathan. "Too bad there's no way to get proof."

"Well, just think hard, now. Are you *sure* you didn't get enough of a look at him before he shot you? There was a good moon out that night. Just a look, only for a second, maybe; just the red hair, even."

I realized with a sudden chill that they were talking about the man in Father's mill, the murderer the police were looking for. And Father was saying that the man *had* worked for him!—the red-haired man named Campbell. And he had been working here at this very camp! It was foolish of me, but I began for some reason to be afraid.

Outside, the sounds of the night seemed to grow louder and take on a cold and ominous tone. The friendly song of the crickets seemed to turn ugly, the scraping of scaly insects. The owl that hooted was a merciless silent predator with blood on its beak and claws. There were night animals out there in the darkness, I knew, but I would not think of them. I clenched my fists tightly and concentrated with a fierce urgency on the voices in the next room. There were two men within just a few feet of me, I told myself, and both of them were armed. They had killed one threat to our safety today, and they were perfectly capable of doing the same thing again, should it become necessary.

"Well," said Father, "I'm going to take this bottle over to the bunkhouse and see who's still up. Maybe I can loosen a few tongues about our Mr. Campbell. See you in an hour or so."

"I'll be right here," said Nathan. "Brought some work along with me."

The door closed and I was alone in the small cabin with Nathan McKay. For some reason, knowing that just the two of us were here excited me. I felt the warmth begin to build again, and I could not help thinking what would happen if he came into my bed. . . . But, no! I had made up my mind about that. It was

153

not going to happen. I had latched the door, hadn't I?
He could not get in, even if he wanted to.

Or was the door latched? Suddenly I could not remember. I strained to see in the dim light that came
from the lamp in the next room, but I could not. Oh,
this was foolish. Of course I had latched the door. Or
had I?

Well, I couldn't just lie here wasting time thinking
about it. I would find out for myself. My fingers located
the matches in the drawer of the bedside table. I slid
out of bed, my bare feet chilling the rest of me when
they touched the cold floor. The cotton quilt had been
so warm, and now the night seemed to have lost its
softness. I was tired. What was I doing out of bed,
shivering in the dark, looking for somewhere to strike
a match? Of course the door was latched!

I groped my way over to the door and felt the handle, then the latch. Shut tight. What had I been thinking
of, imagining that I had left it open! I shivered, and
then I started back to bed.

And then I heard a noise under the window. I froze.
Someone was outside the cabin, outside my window! I
listened, trembling, and the noise came again, a soft,
slow scraping. But that was only a tree limb brushing
against the wall, I told myself. Just a leaf or a twig
scraping in the wind. How foolish to be afraid of . . .

But then I felt a draft of cold air on my bare feet,
and as my eyes grew accustomed to the dim light I
could see the window curtains move slightly, touched
by the incoming breeze. The noise came again, and I
realized, horrified, that someone was opening the window!

For a moment I thought I would scream. I closed my
eyes, frozen with fear, and then I gathered my wits. I
went silently to the door, keeping my eyes on the gradually opening window. There could be no doubt of it
now. There really was someone there. I fought off my
panic and very quietly unlatched the door to the other
room and Nathan. He saw me as soon as I opened the

door, but he was silent when he saw I had my finger to my lips. Shaking, I pointed to my bedroom.

Nathan got to his feet and, with a grim look at my fear-stricken face, quietly drew his pistol from the holster he had slung over the back of his wooden chair. Then just as silently he walked the three paces to my doorway.

Behind him, I watched in the dim light from the door as the white curtains flapped like restless spirits. The window continued to move up, inch by inch. We waited, and I thought: Why doesn't he *do* something? Then I realized that Nathan wanted the intruder to commit himself, to try to climb through the window where he would be a clear target without an easy escape.

Had it not been for the wind, we would surely have caught him. But suddenly as we watched, the window went up nearly half a foot and the breeze parted the curtains wide. There in the shadows just outside, we saw the face for an instant that seemed eternal. Cruel, staring eyes flickered with hate as he saw us. Behind the bright red beard, white teeth flashed in an animal snarl—and then the face disappeared. We heard muffled footsteps vanishing into the forest.

The strain was too much. I flung my arms around Nathan and sobbed, silently, fearfully, weeping like a schoolgirl as the reaction to the ordeal set in.

Nathan just held me, quietly waiting for me to get control of myself. "Easy, now," he said softly. "He saw the gun. He won't be back. I think we scared him more than he scared us."

I could not contain my apprehension any longer. "But he had red hair! Don't you see? That was the man who Father was . . ."

His hand tilted my chin. His eyes were clear and unafraid. "It could have been," he said. "But it could have been someone else, too. This Campbell's not the only man in the territory with red hair."

"But he was coming in the window! If I'd been asleep . . ."

"He didn't, though. And he won't." Nathan held me in his arms. His warm, reassuring presence gradually took away the chill of fear. Soon I was able to see that he was right, and I looked up to those blue eyes with some courage of my own. We would be safe. We would close the window and the man would not come back. Then in the morning we would find out who the man was and punish him. Both of us had seen his face. We would give the camp foreman his description. Even out here in the mountains such a man as that would be recognized. I buried my head in the warmth of Nathan's shoulder and closed my eyes.

The heat of the fireplace began to steal up under my gown. After a few moments of quiet, I was suddenly conscious of Nathan's body. I felt so soft against him, my gown so thin. I trembled as the warmth I had felt earlier began to radiate through me. The feeling was so strong, so exquisite in anticipation. I clung to him and hoped he would think I was still afraid. I could not bring myself to move away, though I knew I would have to. Through my mind flashed visions of his kiss, the smooth, hard sleekness that would be his body. I could feel my breasts against his chest. My lips were only inches from his. My fingers were pressed into the firm muscles of his back. I wanted to rouse him, madden him. . . .

His grip tightened on my shoulders as he held me away from him and looked at me, a smile beginning to appear in his eyes. What were those eyes saying? And what was this new trembling sensation that had filled me?

"You're all right?"

"I am. I'm better." I looked up at him, my lips parted, still breathless with the strange passion that gripped me and made my flesh burn with excitement. How I wanted him to kiss me! But if he did, I knew that the last vestiges of control would vanish and I would be utterly helpless.

I summoned all my will and let go of him, stepping

back. I felt suddenly cold, and I moved in front of the fire. "Thank you," I said. "You were very . . ." But the other words would not come, except in a whisper, as I realized what had just happened. He knew. It was impossible that he did not know. All my woman's feeling for him had been there in my eyes, and he could not have failed to see it. And now what would he do? What would he think of me?

I heard him walk to the window and close it. Then he was at my side, taking a fresh log from the wood basket and setting it across the low flames in the hearth. As he straightened up, he looked at me with that same half-serious, half-smiling expression and turned me to him with a touch of his hand. "Why don't you get the quilt and sit out here by the fire till you get sleepy again. You've had quite a day out here."

And then he kissed me, lightly, on the lips, just enough so that I realized what his eyes had been saying all along. In another place, at a better time, when we could be safe and secure and not think of interruptions or of anything but each other . . . "Oh Nathan," I said, "I've been so . . ."

"You don't have to explain." He drew me to him, hard, for a moment, and I knew with a rush of joy that he shared the emotion that had possessed me. And then he had sent me on my way for the quilt, the touch of his hand on my back still lingering on my skin and making my cheeks burn hot.

When I came back, he set me down in the chair before the fire and wrapped the quilt around me. "All right, now you just stay right there," he said with a look that promised wonders to come, that made all the past struggles with Steven and Father simply disappear. Then he grinned. "I hope I don't do something Sam Rawles wouldn't appreciate if he came in. I've always said there are some things a lady shouldn't have to put up with."

In the warmth of his gaze I felt too full to speak. I could scarcely believe what seemed suddenly so clear.

As he picked up his book and settled down in the chair across from me, I wondered how I could have been so close to Steven before, and yet tonight have such feelings for Nathan burst upon me so forcibly with scarcely a kiss! Oh, but they had said I would know it when it happened. How could I be sure? ...

"You're getting sleepy," he said. "Do you want to stretch out on the cot, or can you manage in the other room? I've locked the window."

I wanted to stay, but my pride led me to go back. There was nothing to be afraid of now.

The next morning, though, my anxiety returned as I looked at the rough faces of the men in the dining hall at breakfast, trying to see if one of them had been the intruder of last night. They were a hardened lot, many of them surly and swollen-eyed from last night's drinking. Father himself looked a shade the worse for wear, though he had been all brisk attention and activity since he had heard of the man I had thought was Campbell. He marched with me between the lamp-lit tables, nodding at the somewhat surprised men as we passed by and making certain I got a good look at them all.

None of them was the man from the night before. I told Father that as soon as we reached our table. "He's not here, Father. None of these men even has the same shade of hair, let alone the red beard. It must have been ..."

"We'll talk to Panella," he said quietly. "Maybe someone's stayed away from breakfast."

I looked around the room. There were several vacant places at two of the rough-hewn tables. Outside the open hatches that served as windows, the gray mist of early morning in the mountains was giving way to the rising sun. Nathan had not come in yet. He was seeing to Frank Kelso, his patient with the shattered arm in the infirmary cabin.

I had awaken before dawn that morning to find that Nathan was already up. From my window I could scarcely see him in the mist, but I knew that it was Nathan from the way he stood, straight and slender. He was standing by the little stream that ran behind the cabin. I wanted to call out, but Father was still asleep. So I quickly slipped into my dress and put on my shoes and went out to the stream to join Nathan.

He heard me coming. His face was almost bare of the lather from his shaving mug, which he had set down on a rock alongside the clear, shallow water. "Short night," he said with a smile. "Be right with you."

Shaving without a mirror, he finished the last few strokes and then bent down to the stream and rinsed away the remaining lather, then toweled himself dry.

"Had a talk with your father when he came in."

"Oh? About the man we saw?"

"We mentioned that, yes. And nobody's seen Campbell, or so they said last night. If he's back here, he's hiding somewhere."

I looked down the little slope toward the window where the man had stood, and I shivered. If Nathan had not been there last light, or if I had not been awake . . . but I was not going to be foolishly afraid this morning.

Nathan gave my hand a squeeze. "Don't worry about it. They'll be looking for him. We're putting up some reward money that'll have even his best friend coming over to our side, not that he's all that likely to have any friends. From what your father says, he kept pretty much to himself while he was here."

He paused, and for some inexplicable reason my heart began to beat faster. Why did my feelings have to rise up to the surface when he looked at me that way? With Steven I had been filled with emotion, true, but when we were not making love, at least, I could harden myself and keep him somehow at a distance. With Nathan it seemed to be just the opposite. My heart saw promises in his every move, and it seemed to leap at them.

"Your father and I also talked about you last night," he was saying, and I felt a tightness in my throat. His eyes were steady as he went on. "There are certainly more conventional places and times to say this, but somehow up here and now seems appropriate."

He put his arm around me, glancing up at the mist-filled trees in the cool gray morning air before the sunrise.

I knew then what he was going to say. A hundred thoughts flashed through my mind all at once in the split second before he spoke: my doubts about Steven; my raging battle with Father; this strange new feeling I had known in Nathan's carriage the night of the ball; a vision of the dark interior of the mill, where I had cradled Nathan's head in my arms and stopped his bleeding. How strange, I thought, that he had scarcely courted me at all, and that as recently as last night I had promised myself to keep a well-guarded distance between us. Yet now I felt that it was safe to give myself to him. Why? There might have been innumerable reasons, but none of them mattered. I knew; that was all. As surely as I knew anything, I felt the certainty that my future lay with this graceful, disciplined man.

I listened, knowing he would propose marriage and knowing that I would accept. I wondered if he would first apologize for believing what Steven Cottor had told him, but he did not. It was just as well. I knew I had deliberately misled him, but that was something he did not have to know. I had been protecting myself against Father, that was all, and I refused to believe that would have changed his mind about me. No, what counted was the feeling we shared. That had been plain last night, and before that, and now as he spoke.

"Catherine, I'm in a strange position right now. People in Grampian don't know about my wife, and I don't particularly like talking about her, but before I go on I want you to know the situation."

I nodded, more certain than ever that we were about to become engaged, but wanting him to tell his story his own way. Of course, I remembered what Mother had told me about his wife, so I didn't look at all surprised, I'm sure. I found myself thinking that I must seem terribly worldly, to simply nod my head when the man who has kissed me announces that he is married.

He told me that Elaine, for that was her name, had been placed in a sanitarium near Philadelphia for treatment of opium addiction, and that she had stopped being his wife, in his mind, long ago because of what she had done. In the eyes of the law, she would no longer be his wife within a matter of weeks, when the decree of divorce was awarded to him.

"There has been a delay—from her family. They're quite well off, and for some reason Elaine's been dead set against divorce ever since she first learned what was coming. So her lawyers have thrown up obstacles every step of the way."

"Is she still in the sanitarium?"

He nodded. "Greenmeadow's the name of it. Very few people even know about it, let alone know where it is. They give her good care and a lot of attention. I really don't think she could function outside an environment like that—she certainly couldn't when we were living together, at least."

"I'm sorry to hear that." The words were automatic, so purely a conventional answer that I was almost embarrassed to have said them. Yet I could not very well say I was not a bit sorry that this Elaine was now safely locked away from him.

"Let's not talk of her. I only wanted you to know my background and position. I'll be free of her soon, a matter of one or two weeks at the most. And when that time comes, Catherine, I want you to marry me."

It was so like him: straightforward.

I was caught off guard for a moment, even though I had been expecting the proposal. "That's certainly a direct way of putting it," I said.

"Would it make a difference if I gave you flattering speeches about your eyes or your character or about how lovely you are? Somehow I didn't think it would change your answer."

"You're right," I said, "it wouldn't. I . . . I'll marry you, Nathan."

How smoothly handsome his profile was! Those blue eyes—how they made the spirit rise in me so that I felt bright, lively, as if I could perform wonders! Together, we could accomplish . . . what? Anything seemed possible. Grampian could not be the same again with the two of us together.

And when we kissed, the heady, dizzying glow made all other thoughts disappear, momentarily blotting out even the sound of the rising morning breeze.

Just as he released me, though, an unbidden image floated to the surface of my thoughts and I felt strangely lonely. In my mind I saw the Cottor mansion on Vallamont. I saw it disappear, and then a new mansion took its place, and the mansion was mine. I saw it so vividly: a Federal-style brick house with lights at each of the leaded-glass windows and a garden with tall fruit trees, and I was standing inside, but Nathan was not. The thought sent a chill up my spine.

"Hold me," I whispered, pressing suddenly against him. And soon the chill went away, and it was replaced with the hard, satisfied certainty that one day Vallamont would indeed be mine. Nathan and I together could not fail to defeat the Cottors.

Then the breakfast gong rang, and we had walked hand in hand back to the cabin.

We had told Father then—awakened him with the news, in fact. Asleep, his face looked vulnerable, the features almost swollen. Then it changed as he awoke, from momentarily confused to relief and happiness when he grasped what I was telling him. His reaction was so simple I found myself deeply moved. He gave me a quick hug and then held out his hand to Nathan, smiling, his cheeks and eyes still puffed with sleep.

"Well!" He had pulled himself up and gotten his

feet out from under the bedclothes and onto the floor, his gray eyes blinking but happy. "Well!"

Now Nathan came into the dining hall and walked toward our table. As he walked, he took care, I noticed, to get a good look at the faces of the men.

As Nathan joined us, Vince Panella also had come over and sat down. Father spoke casually to Nathan first. "Anybody look familiar, Doc?"

"Haven't seen any since dinner, if that's what you mean." I wanted to reach out and take his hand, but of course we could not make a show here before the men. We would not even be able to announce our engagement until word came from Philadelphia that Nathan's divorce was final.

Quickly, Father explained to Panella that a man had tried to break into our cabin late last night. Panella nodded as soon as he heard the description.

" 'At's Campbell, I tell you. He started that beard just a week or so ago, just before he went into town for the last time. Some of the men, they say he's trying to hide from somebody with that beard."

Father nodded, his face impassive. "I saw him without it a while back. But, look, might it have been somebody else from the camp? Isn't there anyone else you know around here who's got a red beard?"

Panella's lips came together and his chin dropped, giving him a dour look. "Nobody else like that." He gestured with his hand at the rest of the hall. "You can see."

Nathan asked, "Is everybody here this morning? Nobody stayed away?"

Panella sent his eyes quickly around the room. I could see his lips move as he silently counted the men at the tables. "Okay, that's sixty two in here, and you got how many in the sick house, seven? And that scum we killed yesterday, that makes the seventy. That was all."

"All right," said Father, "then we can assume it's Campbell. Pass the word to the men that whoever puts us onto him gets himself a thousand dollars—after he's in custody alive, though. Dead, he's not worth anything."

Panella nodded, asking no questions.

After Panella had gone, the three of us were alone at the table. It was daylight outside, the sun through the leaves making mottled shadows and glittering patterns on the tables near the windows. Father said to me, "We'll find him. Don't you worry. And then we'll make him talk. I'll give you twenty to one that he killed my watchman, and ten to one that Abel Cottor put him up to it."

A week earlier, I would have been antagonistic, refusing to let Father set up yet another battle line between our two families. Even this morning I was tempted to remind Father that he had resolved to let Abel dig his own grave by himself only yesterday. But part of me was too elated with Nathan and our engagement to get upset over something like that. And the rest of me had come to realize that Father's long war would not, could not, vanish overnight, even with the best of intentions on Father's part. The old hatred was built in by now. It had become a part of him and would always be there while Abel was alive, perhaps even while Steven was alive. The best I could hope for was that Father might become wrapped up in something else that would keep him from immersing himself in his personal vendetta, and that the rest of us could somehow manage to keep ourselves clear.

So I simply nodded and said something noncommittal and then changed the subject by asking Nathan how his patient was getting along this morning.

Nathan shrugged slightly. "He's a strong man and he's in good condition. The worst part is over."

"Will he be able to use the arm?" I asked.

"If it heals properly." Nathan went on to explain how he would fit Frank Kelso with a stiff leather brace, strapped tightly around the upper arm where the bone was missing. Even though three inches of bone were now gone, the brace would give the support he needed to work the arm and to perform most of the tasks he had been doing around the camp.

"Will he be able to skid a sledge?' Father asked.

"It depends." Nathan turned a palm up. "Probably yes, but he might not feel up to it for a few months. If he asks for that assignment, say, anytime after four weeks from now, though, I'd let him try it. Be good for him."

Around us the hall was empty now, with only a single waiter in denim overalls clearing away the remaining plates and utensils from the vacant tables. Inside that quiet, sun-filled hall, I felt for a moment what it would be like for Frank Kelso to get back on that sledge again and the private battle he would have with his own fears. How difficult it must be to do something like that, I thought, to pick yourself up and just go on after an experience like his. Probably all three of us were thinking something similar, for we were all silent, watching the waiter in overalls move around from table to table.

Then Nathan broke the stillness. "If it hadn't been for this one here and how stubborn she was," he said, flashing me a grin, "I might never have taken the risk of trying to remove all those fragments of bone. Frank Kelso might not have kept his arm."

"She can be stubborn, but sometimes she can be right," said Father as he finished the last of his coffee. "Now, look, about today. Do you want to keep on with the trip to Long Reach camp, or would you rather just head on back to Grampian?" He looked from me to Nathan and back again. "Considering the circumstances, I'd expect you'd have people to tell, plans to make, and so on. So I can go on by myself if you'd rather."

"Well, actually, Father, we can't really start any official plans until . . . until Nathan hears from his lawyers. Isn't that right, Nathan?"

He nodded and so we agreed to keep on with our

trip as planned. We packed, said our good-byes, and rode through the trees and down the logging road to the river. There we crossed back over the footbridge to the small railroad way station. The eastbound train was just approaching when we arrived, coming toward us on the horizon. We were traveling west, so there was no need to hurry. Father had ordered a westbound train to take us upriver.

But when we came inside the small shed to wait, the young attendant we had seen the day before jumped off his stool. "You're Doctor McKay, aren't you? There's a message come in from Grampian on the telegraph for you just this morning."

He handed Nathan a brown envelope. Nathan opened it with quick fingers. As he read, his face became a mask.

He crumbled the paper and looked at the attendant. "Put up your signal and stop that train right now," he said. "I've got to take it back to Grampian."

As the attendant scrambled out to the tracks to hoist his signal, Nathan turned to us. His face was grim, his eyes showing strain. "I'm sorry. It can't be helped, though."

"Trouble at the clinic?" Father sounded sympathetic.

Nathan shook his head. "I wish it were that simple, but it's not." He looked at me, and suddenly I felt cold.

He hesitated. Behind him, outside, the train was coming to a stop.

Then, wordlessly, he held out the message for me to read. Scrawled in the attendant's smudged pencil were these words:

HAVE COME TO GRAMPIAN TO TALK ABOUT OUR MARRIAGE. MUST SEE YOU AT ONCE.

ELAINE

The rush of feeling welled up inside of me. "You're going back for this? For her? You're . . ."

"You don't understand, Catherine. She can make more trouble with the divorce. And in town she can make a stir that Grampian won't soon forget."

"What does it matter what they think in Grampian?" My indignation was overriding my good judgment, but I felt too unfairly treated to stop now. "You propose marriage to me this very morning, and now, when *she* snaps her fingers and wants to talk about marriage, you go running off."

His eyes hardened. Outside, the trainman was sounding his whistle impatiently, and the engine was beginning to inch forward. The attendant called for us to hurry up if we were coming.

"I haven't time to explain," he said. "But if you're going to take it that way, then maybe you should just forget that this morning ever happened. Maybe that will make it easier."

He turned and was outside in a few swift strides. Through a haze of tears, I saw him climb aboard the train as it gathered speed.

TEN

Two days later I was on a train traveling west. As I gazed through the windows of the railway coach, the forest passed in a constant flickering of bright green and dark shadow. The rattle of the coach wheels was a steady, monotonous background noise to go with the seemingly endless line of hemlocks, maples, oaks, and wooded green underbrush. Somewhere ahead of us, farther up into the wooded mountains, was the lake called Eagles Mere and the new resort hotel that Father had nearly finished building and expected to open within a week or two, out here in its complete isolation from the rest of the civilized world. We were going to give the hotel its final inspection before the first guests arrived.

Normally, I would have been excited at the prospect of seeing the new building and the deep blue lake for the first time. Today I found it difficult to care whether or not our train ride ever ended. Even though the future of this hotel could make or break Father's fortunes, I had no energy, no desire, to get involved. I was still numbed, unable to accept what had happened and how suddenly Nathan had gone.

I had felt this tired, spiritless lethargy ever since Nathan had climbed aboard that train and gone back to his wife. I had tried to rouse myself, tried not to show my grief to Father, tried not to admit my disappointment even to myself. But it had not been possible. I had barely been able to go through the motions at the second lumber camp, where we had spent the night after an hour's train ride upriver and a long journey on horseback up into the mountains, north of the river this time. I had forced myself to smile at the men when we were introduced by the camp foreman. There were only about twenty men in this camp, but they were in good spirits, just as we had hoped. Father had sent around the rest of the imported whiskey and the cigars during the evening meal, so when the time came to introduce the camp's new owner and his daughter, the rough pine-log mess hall was filled with smoke and merry laughter.

The laughter turned suddenly quiet when Father spoke to the men and told them that he had come up here from Grampian because he needed more wood from this camp—nearly twenty percent more than they had been turning out every day. When Father told them he intended to raise their wages by twenty percent, though, the hall erupted with cheers. And when he told them he was going to see that they were fed twice as well, the cheers became even louder.

Then I was introduced. I stood up and smiled, wishing I could feel the happiness I knew I should have felt. Around the tables I recognized a few familiar faces from the clinic—the men who had gotten well and were now back up here on the job. They clapped and whistled their approval, and then at the table to my right I saw the blond, curly haired giant, Billy Joe Walker, get to his feet, holding a small book.

He pointed to the book, which seemed even smaller

in his big hand. "It's Artemus Ward, Miss Rawles. How about just one story?"

There were cheers, and the book was quickly passed along, hand to hand, table to table, until it reached me. Somehow I managed to get through one of the stories, accompanied by the laughter and then the applause of my appreciative audience, but even that did not begin to touch the emptiness I felt. And the next day I felt just as badly. We toured part of the territory that went with the camp, where we saw two men bring down a great pine tree that stood nearly seventy feet tall, using only axes and pikes. As it crashed to the ground, its boughs hissing and crackling, I almost wished I had been under it.

Now, after a night on this private railway coach of Father's, we were on our way to the third and last stop on our journey, the hotel at Eagles Mere, and I found myself already dreading the thought of going back to Grampian. How could I face seeing Nathan again? I had very nearly wept in front of everyone the night before while I was reading Artemus Ward because it reminded me so strongly of the time I spent in the clinic with Nathan. How would I be able to endure seeing him in Grampian, knowing that his wife might appear at any moment?

Father had been very considerate of my feelings, respecting my privacy whenever possible and allowing me to be alone with the sadness he knew I felt. At our meals together, he had carried the conversation, talking of the details of the camp, the hotel, and this new railway he had built to bring the vacationing guests out to Eagles Mere. He had put a great amount of his fortune into building this railway more than fifty miles through the mountain forests up to the lake, and he had borrowed even more. But in time, he said, he knew it was going to pay off handsomely. There was the hotel for now, and then soon there would be other hotels on the lake, or people would want to build their own homes, and then there would be towns along the railway he had built. Before the decade was out, he predicted, just the land he had bought on both sides of the railroad alone would bring him the price it had cost to lay those many miles of wooden ties and steel track.

" 'Course it won't be worth that much until more people start to settle here," he said, seated across from me in one of the plush red velvet lounge chairs he had had specially installed in his private coach. "Right now that land's too wild even for farmin'. Soil's too rocky and there are too many steep slopes. And it's too far from the river to be worth much for lumber"—he paused—"unless I decide to use this fancy coach for a loggin' train. But I think the hotel's gonna be too profitable to bother with timber out here, especially since you're going to have it all shipshape and squared away in the next day or two."

He waited for me to say something, but I was too absorbed in my own unhappiness to respond. I had been so certain! After so long, after so many doubts, I had finally *known* that I wanted Nathan McKay, and then to have him suddenly go back to his wife . . .

"I said, you're going to have the staff all on their toes, isn't that right?" There was an edge in Father's voice now, and I knew he was irritated at my lethargy. The hotel was important; it was crucial, in fact, and here I was acting as though I had nothing to do with it. Yet I could not seem to do anything else.

"I'm sorry, Father." My apology sounded listless. I felt even worse, because I knew I was not going to be able to keep my promise and give the hotel the attention I knew it deserved. I had scarcely been able even to brush my own hair or to eat properly. I had slept poorly, and I knew I must look dreadfully tired. Whoever the staff was at the hotel, they would see that I was not capable of supervising their work. I was going to fail, and I knew it.

"Well, you're going to have to wake up a bit," he was saying. "You said you were going to give me a hand on this trip, remember?"

"I know, I know. I just can't seem to get started anymore."

"Well, you're gonna have to try. I know this business of Nathan McKay has got you . . ."

"I don't care to discuss it, Father."

"He didn't mean what he said there at the train."

"I said I don't care to discuss it!"

"I don't give a damn what you care to discuss! I'm not going to watch you fall apart like this over . . ."

Angry tears were coming to my eyes. "Oh, so I'm falling apart, am I? That's certainly a nice thing to say. That makes me feel a lot better!" I began to cry, ashamed of myself and my own weakness.

"Goddamn it! You don't have to cry over him! He's just gone back to put her away again. Don't you know that?"

The tears came even faster now. It didn't matter why he had gone back to her. He had chosen her instead of me—that was what mattered. She had asked him to come, and I had asked him to stay, and he had gone to her. The reason was not important. He had gone, and that meant he was still hers. I could never be sure of him. Even though I felt my own love for him so strongly, so irrevocably, I could never know that he had the same love for me. If we were to marry, every day I would have to face knowing that Elaine might call him again and make a mockery of our love.

The tears flowed and my shoulders shook as I sobbed out my grief, feeling utterly alone, even though Father was in the coach with me. I thought I would never stop crying. No matter how I looked at what had happened, there was still no hope. I had seen my own heart, and it was even now still set blindly for Nathan McKay. He had broken off our engagement. He had proven he did not care for my feelings at all when they went against what his wife wanted—and even after that humiliation my heart was still unable to give him up. I don't love him, I won't love him, I had thought, had told myself over and over, but it was still no use. I could not stop. . . .

At least no one else was on the train to see me cry besides Father, I thought. And my tears seemed to have softened his annoyance. He was no longer shouting at me. Gradually I was able to respond to his gruff, quiet words of comfort.

By the time the engine had come to a stop, I was feeling better. I felt tired, and still the inner aching despair was present, but I was at least able to keep the hurt under control so that my mind and the rest of my body no longer had that numbing, exhausting lethargy to contend with. I had gone into the luxurious washroom at the rear of the coach and splashed some cold water on my face. I looked at myself in the gilded oval mirror that hung above the gold-enameled washbasin. Was that really me? I looked dreadful. My hair was dull, my eyes were lusterless and red from weeping, and my face was pale. Surely I could make myself look a little better than this!

I filled the basin with cold water. Then, taking a deep breath, I plunged my face under the surface of the water and held it there. I opened my eyes, feeling the chill of the water cool their angry soreness. I let out my breath between my lips, and I felt the little bubbles against my cheeks as they rose to the surface on either side of my face. When I could do without air no longer, I stood up again and briskly toweled my face dry. I unpinned my hair and rubbed it with the cold, damp towel, and then I brushed it vigorously a hundred strokes and pinned it up again, being careful not to look in the mirror. Finally I had finished. I glanced quickly at my reflection as I left the washroom, and I was somewhat pleased to see that I had managed at least some improvement.

"Well, your color's back," said Father when he saw me return. "I knew you'd snap out of it."

I managed a tight-lipped smile, even though I knew he was wrong. I could at least go through the motions as best I could. Thank God that terrible weariness seemed to have passed.

As we stepped down from Father's coach outside the hotel, a tall, stocky man with a slim gray moustache stepped forward to greet us. "Well, Mr. Rawles!" His smile was wide and professional, the eyes set back, only a small glittering part visible behind the thick folds of his eyelids. "So glad you could come to see how far we've . . ."

"Right, Gilbert. We're glad, too, but where's somebody to help with the bags?" Father's tone was brusque.

"Oh, he'll be down shortly, Mr. Rawles. Just attending to some . . ."

"You go up and get him now. And you tell him that the next time this train stops here he'd better be waiting for it if he wants to keep his job—and every time after that. Now, move!"

Gilbert looked crestfallen and irate at the same time, but he turned and walked quickly up the wide flagstone pathway to the hotel entrance.

"You were hard on him," I said.

"Got to be with these older ones. They think they know all there is to know. If you don't jump on 'em right away, they never listen to you again."

We walked slowly up the path. I admired the wide green lawn and the big white, three-story hotel, which was set at the crest of the green hill, its white-columned portico commanding a view of both our train platform and, on the far side, the deep blue lake. Father had told me about his decision to stop the railway here, two hundred feet from the hotel entrance. It was less convenient for the guests than the arrangement in Grampian, where the station was only a few steps away from the Deer Park Hotel. But out here in the wilds Father had decided that an impressive first view of the resort was more important. Especially since there were to be attendants on hand to take the luggage, the walk up the gradual incline was intended to be more of a pleasure than an inconvenience, giving the feeling that we were ascending the steps of a temple in the wilderness. So far, at least, it was plain that Father had succeeded in giving this impression. The newly planted grass in front of the hotel had come up smooth and green, just matching the green of the folded porch awning, which hung ready over the tops of the white columns, waiting for a rain shower or the glaring afternoon sun.

"It looks most attractive," I told Father as we walked. We ignored the rushing figure of the bellhop, who scurried past us, nodding as he tried to fasten his pillbox cap underneath his chin.

Father gave a satisfied nod, but he was not smiling. "Building's good—saw to that myself. Landscaping looks like it's worked out fine. But the staff! If that sorry excuse for a bellhop is any indication, we may have to clear out the lot and train some new ones in a week!"

Gilbert was standing on the porch steps waiting to greet us again. His smile a trifle strained this time, he began: "Well, I think that the boy understands now, sir. Now, if you'll just step this way, we've prepared the Plantation suite."

Father stood stock-still in front of the steps, looking at the empty porch, which was painted a rich forest green. I could see the anger rising within him.

"Goddamn it! Gilbert, where's the porch furniture?"

Gilbert looked nervously toward the rear of the hotel and said, "Well, it only arrived yesterday. We have it in storage now."

"I know it came yesterday. I told them to deliver it yesterday. I had the train sent up here with it yesterday! What I want to know is why it's not on the goddamned porch!"

"Well, the fact is, sir, we've been really too busy to get it set up."

"You got it set up in storage, didn't you? Why the hell didn't you just set it up on the porch, instead?"

Gilbert flushed almost as deeply as Father, who by this time was crimson.

"Well, the paint, sir, the paint was not quite dry."

"Gilbert, that paint was sent up to you two weeks ago! You were supposed to have it *done* two weeks ago!"

Gilbert hung his head. "Well, the fact is, sir, we've had so many other things to attend to. I'm afraid that we've fallen somewhat behind that schedule you set up."

Father's eyes narrowed. "How far behind?" he asked, speaking slowly and distinctly. I sensed that he was about to explode once again, and I touched him lightly on the arm. "Why don't we go inside and see that for ourselves, Father?" I said. "I'm sure Mr. Gilbert has *some* things that he'd like to show us."

Father considered my proposal for a moment and then gave a tight-lipped smile. "All right, we might as well. Lead the way, Gilbert. The first thing I want to see is the reservations book, but that can wait until you've taken us to our rooms."

Inside, however, there was more to see that could not help but arouse Father's fury. The lobby was magnificent, high-ceilinged with light streaming in from the second-story windows. Yet there were several disheveled men playing cards at one of the white wicker tables, and two women, whom I assumed were waitresses or maids, sat gossiping in two of the armchairs. On another table in the corner of the lobby, flies buzzed around the remains of a sandwich. The ashtrays had not been emptied in days, it appeared, and there were footprints on the light blue carpet.

"I've changed my mind," Father said. "Let's go into the office and have a look at those reservations."

We went behind the front desk, on which there were three nearly empty coffee cups, without saucers, and through the connecting door into the small office cubicle. There Gilbert quickly got out a correspondence box and a black leather looseleaf binder.

Father opened the binder and scanned a few of the pages. "Why, there are hardly any bookings here at all! Most of these rooms show vacant, even during the first week!"

Gilbert gave his strained smile and quickly undid the string around the correspondence box. When he opened it, a sheaf of papers in varying sizes burst forth, and he had to grab them quickly with both hands to keep them from spilling over the manager's desk.

"These are some others, sir. We've just not had the time to enter them all, but I'd estimate we'll be running very close to full capacity for nearly every week of the season." He allowed his look to become a trifle more satisfied, as though he were taking part of the credit for the predicted success.

Father was controlling himself. He pointed at the crammed-full correspondence box. "Now, let me get this straight. You've confirmed all these?"

"Oh, yes. I answer all inquiries and requests myself."

"But you haven't entered them in the book here. You haven't filled them in on the room chart."

"Not as yet, sir. I was planning to attend to that sometime next week."

"Well, then tell me, what do you plan to do if you've overbooked? Suppose you've confirmed more reservations for next week than we have rooms?"

"Oh, I've never had to worry about that in the past. If too many actually arrive, we've always simply found them other accommodations. . . ." His confident voice trailed off haltingly as he realized that this hotel was the only accommodation out here in the mountains for fifty miles. "Oh, dear, I see what you mean. I shall have to get around to that first thing and write to anyone who might be displaced. I suppose I should take them in chronological order . . ."

He was talking as if to himself, and Father interrupted him.

"Yes, well, one more question, Gilbert. Who are those people we saw out in the lobby?"

"Why, they're staff members, sir. Jackson's to be the handyman, and Tolliver and Zambrano are waiters, and Mrs. Jackson and Mrs. Tolliver were there, too, if I'm not mistaken; they're going to be in the linen room. Very reliable people."

"And the chef?"

"That would be Otto, sir. He's been in the kitchen since breakfast, preparing supper. I hope it meets with your approval, and, of course, with that of Miss Rawles. I've had them set a table for three in the dining room for tonight. I thought perhaps the three of us might discuss . . ."

Father drew in a breath and let it out through his nose, slowly. Then, lips compressed, he looked Gilbert in the eye. "Gilbert, I want you packed and on the train outside within the next half hour. You're going back to Grampian. Your work here is over."

A look of incomprehension came across Gilbert's face. His hand went to his mouth, fingers touching his gray moustache. "Am I to understand, sir, that I . . . that I am . . ."

"You don't have a job here anymore," Father said. "When you get back to Grampian, stop at the Deer Park Hotel for your wages. And you can fill in as a room clerk there for a month or two while you find some other position. But you're leaving here, now— Within the half hour."

"But, sir! How . . . why, I've only begun . . ."

"Twenty-nine minutes," said Father.

Gilbert stiffened. He glared at us both. Then he turned abruptly and made for the door, only to realize that he still held the bulging correspondence box with both hands. He looked daggers at the box, as if it had bitten him, then slammed it down on the lamp table beside the doorway. "I hope they all *cancel,*" he said, defiant. "I hope it burns down, and you with it!"

"Don't slam the door," said Father dryly. But Gilbert

slammed it, anyway. I felt sorry for him, but I could not help smiling all the same. Even when he was trying to act outraged, Gilbert was ineffectual.

Father shook his head, his eyes half-closed. "Hard to believe how that glib son-of-a-bitch could have fooled me like this. Can you imagine what would have happened if I'd waited until opening week to come up here?" He shook his head again. "But now where do we go?"

An hour earlier I could not have cared. Yet now I found myself being drawn in, wanting to help get the hotel ready for its opening. "Well, you need another manager," I said. "That's obvious. You need somebody you know and can trust."

He gave me a quizzical look. "You volunteering for the job?"

"Oh, no. I could stay a bit to help, but you need someone with real experience. And on such short notice, I suggest that you have only one choice."

"You mean Bill Malory from the Deer Park, I take it."

"I do. The place looked well enough run when . . . I last stayed there. I'd wire him immediately, and then send the train to pick him up."

"What about his family?"

"Triple his salary. Tell him it's only temporary, but that he can stay on and bring his family later if he likes."

A grin spread over Father's face. "You remind me of me, daughter. That's just what I'm going to do."

He went over to the office telegraph key and sat down. In a minute or two he had finished sending the message and stood up. "Told him to bring out a staff, too, hand-picked. It'll leave us a bit shy in town, but they'll make a good backbone for the operation here."

"What about those people in the lobby?"

Father turned up a palm. "We'll take a fast tour now. If it's really bad, we'll have 'em on the train back to Grampian. They can keep old Gilbert company. But if it's not so bad, we might as well give 'em a chance for a day or two." He paused slightly, as if remembering something, and then he said, "At least that's the way I see it. What do you think?"

I could scarcely believe my ears. Father was making quick decisions in his usual way, but now he was remembering to consult me! Perhaps he was simply trying to take my mind off the way things stood with Nathan. Maybe he thought that keeping me busy with the hotel would be a good remedy for my depressed spirits. Or perhaps he really wanted my opinion, really wanted me to share in the business of managing his interests at this critical time. Either way, Father's considerateness gave me a small, but real, amount of comfort. We had fought so bitterly lately. It was a relief that finally we had reached some sort of peace. If I could only manage to keep the pain of Nathan's loss safely locked away, perhaps I could make myself busy, make myself forget. . . .

What had Father asked me? Oh, yes, about the staff. "I agree," I said. "I think we should at least see what else they've been doing. Why don't we start with the kitchen?"

"Good idea. Let's see if this Otto is the paragon he's cracked up to be. While we're at it, we can have him pack some food for the trainmen to eat on the way back."

It was not until after dinner that we finally got settled in the Plantation suite. We had found Otto to be a trifle imperious but wonderfully efficient. He served us a magnificent seven-course dinner—all Pennsylvania Dutch foods—from the sweet and sour relishes to the rich cabbage soup to the sauerbraten and finally to the rich, gooey-sweet shoofly pie. Everything was cooked to perfection. When Father asked Otto why he had chosen Pennsylvania Dutch cuisine for his first menu, he had informed us that he had not been certain of our tastes and wanted to serve something safe. Actually, he said, his specialty was French cooking, and he asked if we would like eggs Benedict for breakfast.

So Otto was to stay on, indisputably. For the others, we were still not sure. We had toured the rooms and found them all in passable condition, though none was ready for a guest. The small things—the lamps, the antimacassars, the overdrapes, and so on—were either not properly placed or missing altogether. And what was worse, we found that most of the staff were living in four of the larger rooms, even though there was a staff dormitory complete and ready for occupancy only fifty feet or so from the rear of the hotel. Otto had moved into a corner room of that dormitory building already, but the rest—the Tollivers and the Jacksons and Zabriskie—had remained in the rooms that were reserved for guests. Mr. Gilbert, they informed us, when we gathered them together in the lobby for explanations, had said they did not have to move out for a few more days.

Father, of course, told them differently. They were to move out now, either to the staff dormitory or onto the train, which they could hear at that moment outside, getting up steam to leave. Not surprisingly, all chose to stay. Father informed them that he would be watching them quite closely during the next few days and that they would be given an opportunity to prove themselves.

After our meeting with the staff, we ate dinner. Then we went outside to have a look at the lake shore before the sun set completely. The lake was splendid. Deep blue, formed in what we had been told was an ancient volcanic crater, Eagles Mere stretched out before us, dark and majestic. The pines along the opposite shore were nearly a mile away, only a tiny green blur. I had to strain my eyes to see them. Here, on our side of the lake, Father had brought in by train tons and tons of white sand so that people could sun themselves beside the lake just the way they did along the New Jersey coast or on any of the other ocean beaches. The sand had stayed clean and sparkling, inviting someone to come into the water and bathe. I took off my shoes and stockings and, hoisting my skirts, ventured in up to my ankles. The lake was shockingly cold, and I shivered. "How can anyone think of *bathing* in this ice water?" I asked.

Father chuckled. "They'll get used to it. It's good for 'em. Gets the blood going. And it's gonna stay cold, too. That lake's two hundred feet deep out there."

I looked again at the dark, smooth surface of the water, nearly all in shadow now that the sun had gone down behind the edge of the pines. The sand felt smooth underfoot, but my toes were growing numb. I shivered again, but this time it was not from the cold. Doubts about the hotel came over me. Father had so much money tied up in this venture. What if all the guests came out here and were as chilled by the lake as I was? Or what if they were dissatisfied with the staff, or with the isolation? It was so silent out here in the wilderness. What if the silence began to get on the nerves of the guests? I began to feel an unpleasant foreboding that the hotel would not succeed. Something was going to happen. I remembered Gilbert and his angry hope that the place would burn down. Suddenly I was shaking and there were tears rolling down my cheeks.

Father saw me crying and came quickly to where I was standing a few feet away from him. He put an arm on my shoulder and handed me a towel I had brought along. "Hey, now, it'll be all right," he said after I had confessed that I was worried. "They're going to like Eagles Mere—you can be sure of that. All we've got to worry about is the staff—and the mosquitoes."

I looked back at the quiet shadows on the lake, breathing in the clean fragrance of the water and the pines along the shore. Father was right, I told myself. He must be. But the feeling of dread did not disappear. I decided to ignore it. I had locked away the hurt I felt for Nathan, and I would do the same to this nagging premonition!

"Foolish of me," I said. "Of course they'll like it here."

So now we were unpacking in the Plantation suite. I was in my bedroom, one of two, each with its own bath. Between my bedroom and Father's, where he was also unpacking, was a spacious central sitting room done in light blue, with comfortable beige sofas and dark blue chairs.

A knock sounded at the door and Father went to answer it. I heard a brief conversation while I put some of my clothes into dresser drawers and hung others in my closet. And I had expected to be going back to Grampian tomorrow! As things stood, it looked as though I would be needed here at the hotel for several days at least, and probably right on through the opening weekend.

When I came out to the sitting room, Father was alone. He was sitting on one of the blue chairs with a leather-bound note pad, making a list. Beside him on the bamboo end table was an unfolded piece of paper.

He looked up. "That was Jackson. He came to report that they've all moved into the staff quarters out back. And he brought this in—came on the telegraph line in the office."

He handed me the unfolded paper and went back to his list. I read that Bill Malory was pleased to accept Father's offer to come up here and manage the hotel. Malory had chosen a small skeleton staff, and they would be arriving here sometime about noon tomorrow.

"Well, that's a relief," I said, putting the paper back on the table.

He grinned, but he did not look up from his writing. "Afraid you'd have to do the job all by yourself, were you?"

Again I felt that comfortable warmth that I had been somehow accepted. Even though we both knew that my lack of experience made it necessary to have someone else in the position, it was nice at least to flirt with the idea that I could manage the hotel on my own. But I laughed it off. "Don't be silly, Father. What are you doing there?"

"Oh, making lists." He was still preoccupied.

"I can see that. What for? The hotel?"

He finished a line and looked up. "Here," he said, and he tore off two of the sheets he had already written on and folded over. "Take a look. They're for the staff —what each one of them should do tomorrow morning until Malory comes. Then we've got to get a list ready for Malory. Look 'em over and see what else we ought to put in."

We discussed the lists and our plans for the hotel for nearly an hour, and when we had finished we had removed some items and added others, arriving at a small, orderly stack of notes that would see us through the next few days, and another longer list that planned for the rest of the season and the next winter. It astonished me how much we could accomplish by simply sitting down and giving the matter our undivided attention. I found that if I concentrated, I could recall details of the hotel I had seen only once, and that I could also plan for future needs that I had never thought of until that very moment. I was pleased with my newly discovered talent, and so was Father.

After he had arranged the notes in a neat stack on the table, he said, "Well, I think we've got ourselves a hotel by now." He took a cigar from his coat pocket and lit it. "And you did all right for yourself, too, even if it was your first time at this sort of thing. Lucky for me I brought you along."

We chatted a moment or two longer and then I felt the fatigue from the day's activity, along with the sorrow I had been trying to keep so well hidden. Thank goodness I had done something worthwhile today so that I had a good feeling to hang onto! We said good night, and I went into my bedroom to get ready to go to sleep.

And then began the long nightmare of events that I have tried for so long to forget. I was sitting in front of the mirror before I undressed, taking the pins out of my hair and brushing it, still thinking of the satisfying work we had accomplished. Perhaps this really was the way I could get through the pain of life without Nathan, I thought, if I could only manage to get something productive done every day. . . . I heard someone outside in the hall knocking on the door to the sitting room. It must be one of the staff, I thought, continuing to brush my hair. In a moment I heard Father unbolting the door.

"'You!" he said, and something in his voice made me catch my breath momentarily in my throat.

"Well, now, Mr. Rawles, ain't you gonna ask me to come in?" The voice was mean, ugly, and insolent.

"Put that thing away, Campbell," said Father. My eyes went tightly shut involuntarily, and every nerve began to vibrate with fear. Campbell! The leering face at the window flooded back into my memory and I had to bite my lip to keep from crying out.

"Oh, now, *Mis*ter Rawles, don't you like lookin' at a gun? I'd o' thought . . ."

"I said to put it away, Campbell." Father sounded strong, sure of himself, and I began to take courage from his voice.

"Oh, but we need to have a talk, you and me. A few things have happened since that last chat we had, out there in your backyard. You remember?"

"If you want to talk, Campbell, you're going to put that gun away first."

I waited, stunned and helpless. Finally I heard Campbell's voice again as he grudgingly gave in. "You are a stubborn son-of-a-bitch, aren't you?"

Their voices came from closer to my door now, so I knew they had come into the sitting room.

"Seems like you done forgot about Red Campbell, *Mis*ter Rawles, so I just come up on the train to pay you a visit. Just thought we oughtta have a . . .

"Spit it out, Campbell. What do you want?"

The voice was greasy, insinuating. "Well, now, I hear there's sheriffs in three counties lookin' for Red Campbell, on account o' some night watchman got hisself killed."

He waited, but Father said nothing. Campbell's voice turned a shade more respectful. "Come on, now, Mr. Rawles. If I hadn't o' got into that deal with Ruch, that half-assed plowboy, I'd o' never even *seen* that night watchman. I figure ya owe me somethin'."

"You're crazy. I never told you to go near that watchman."

"Told me to pay Ruch off, didn't ya? Gave me two hundred, didn't ya? Where else was I supposed to pay him off—Cottor's mill? I had to get into your place to keep out of sight, and then this watchman . . ."

"I don't believe a damned word of this. You're lying, Red."

Again came the insolence. I could imagine Campbell touching the trigger of his gun as he spoke. "Aw, now, we don't wanna get mistrustin' all of a sudden, do we? Tell you what. You call off those sheriffs—buy 'em off or whatever you do—and then Red Campbell won't be talkin' about that two hundred dollars you gave 'im. Get me?"

"That's what you want, is it, Campbell? Well, let me tell you something. If you want help, you ought to go back to Abel Cottor. Tell him you want some more kerosene to burn down my mill, and see how far that gets you."

"There you go, mistrustin' again! I told ya not to go mistrustin'."

"Goddamn it, Campbell! Put that thing away!"

"You're gonna report me, ain't you? You're gonna tell 'em I was here. I can see it. That's just what you're thinkin', ain't it?"

I could hear his voice rising as he worked himself into a rage. Horrified at the danger Father and I were in, I made my way from my dresser to the door and began to ease it open. I had to do something! I could hear an edge creeping into Father's voice.

"You think you'd help yourself by killing me? You dumb bastard. How many men are chasing you now because of a night watchman? How many more would there be if it was Sam Rawles, too? It'd make your head spin. You probably couldn't even count that high."

I had the door open wide enough now to see Campbell, only a few steps away. He was as tall as Father, but not as heavyset, wearing torn, tight-fitting blue jeans and a dirty brown shirt. Behind that curly red hair, unkempt, and that scraggly, untrimmed beard were the eyes, bloodshot and staring. "You're gonna pay me somethin', Rawles. If you wanna live, you're gonna have to pay me somethin'."

"Campbell, I thought you had brains when I made you a foreman. What kind of money do you think you're gonna get from me with a gun? There's no money at all here in the hotel. You think I'm gonna go back to Grampian and send you a check in the mail?"

Father's sarcasm set my nerves on edge. How far could he push this bearded murderer before making him lose all control? I could see the fury, the desperation, in Campbell's expression as he tried to think. As I watched, I calculated the distance between the gun he held and the spot where I stood. Could I rush toward him, catch him off balance, and force his aim away from Father? If only I could do that, I was sure Father could overpower him.

But then, out of the corner of his eye, Campbell saw me. As quick as lightning, he was at the door and had torn it open, and before I could move he had nearly broken my wrist, turning it viciously, twisting my arm behind my back as he pushed me out into the sitting room. The burning, stabbing pain in my wrist and shoulder made me gasp. I staggered and nearly fell, but that excruciating hold on my wrist and arm jerked me upright again so that I cried out, choking back hot tears.

I could feel Campbell's fetid breath against my neck

as he spoke, sneering the words in a tone that made me shudder. "Well, now, Rawles! Didn't know the slut was still around! Looks like you're havin' a bit o' fun on this trip!"

Father's voice was sheer, cold anger, though I could see the anguish and the heartache in his eyes. "She's my daughter, you bastard. You leave her out of this. Let her go right now."

The pain shot through me as Campbell jerked me upright again and forced me closer to him. His smell was nauseating. I felt the hard point of his pistol tap against my temple.

"Daughter, eh? Well, now, suppose I just blow her head off right now. How'd ya like that, Sam Rawles? Hey?" The pistol cracked against my skull again, harder this time, making little white flashes of light before my eyes.

Father's jaw was clenched, his words tight and strained. "All right, what is it you want? Name it."

Through a red haze of pain I heard that hateful, sneering voice. "Changed your tune, hey, Rawles? Well, here's what you're gonna do. I'm gonna take this slut of yours out in the woods somewhere good and safe, where you ain't gonna find her. And you're gonna go back and get two hunnert thousand dollars in cash for ole Red. You're gonna put it out on that beach out there, right out in the open, where I can see it real good. If it's there when I come back mornin' after next at eight, then I'll pick it up and go back and turn this one"—he twisted the point of his pistol behind my ear as he said that—"loose. Then she'll be able to get herself some food and some water and get back to you. If I don't see the money, or if I see a single, solitary person around this whole hotel, I'm gonna just leave her where she is, with the gag in her mouth and the ropes on her hands and feet. Before you find her she'll have long died o' thirst."

Father kept his jaw clamped shut, but he nodded. Behind me, Campbell was caressing my neck with the barrel of the pistol. "Won't look so pretty, then, would ya, hey? Ever see somebody that died o' thirst? Tongue gets all black, yes, ma'am, and the face . . ."

"Get on with it, Campbell," Father said. "They'll get you someday, and every word you say, everything you do to her between now and the time you release her, will make the rest of your life less of a hell or more of one. You just mark my words."

"Shuddup." He jabbed the pistol into my neck again. "Now, we're just gonna mosey on outta here. What you're gonna do now, Rawles, is get down on your hands and knees and crawl under that sofa over there. I don't wanna see your face when we walk out, Rawles. I just wanna see that fat ass of yours stickin' out from under the sofa. Now, move, or I'll shoot both of you right here and now!"

Father stood stock-still, his gray eyes ablaze. "I'll see you in hell first, Campbell." The words were deadly calm.

"On your knees, I said! Crawl!" He brandished the pistol again, striking me a glancing blow across the forehead with the barrel. My head reeled. Through a dizzy haze I saw Father leap toward me, toward the gun, and then I was pushed violently away, staggering and falling down against one of the smaller chairs partway across the room.

Behind me I heard the sounds of the struggle as Father and Campbell crashed against the tables and chairs, knocking over furniture. Their breath came in harsh gasps. I tried to get up to help, but my arm, when I tried to raise myself to a sitting position, collapsed under me and I had to force myself to keep from blacking out from the pain.

Somehow I rolled over where I could see the battle as the two swayed in deathly combat, each man's grip locked on the pistol Campbell held now with both hands. If only I could get to them! There was a vase on the table that would. . . .

But then both men had toppled over with a crash,

and I heard the muffled roar of the pistol. There was an agonized groan, a horrible thumping sound. And then silence prevailed, except for the rasping of Red Campbell's breath as he got slowly to his feet and came toward me.

For a moment I stared at him, uncomprehending, unable to believe what had just happened. Then I was on my feet, running the few steps to Father where he lay, not hearing whatever it was that Campbell was saying. I knelt beside Father's body, weeping uncontrollably now, as I saw the wound in his throat where the bullet had entered and the gaping red opening at the top of his head. The thin wisps of blond hair at the edges were now stained crimson amid the widening pool of blood that now darkened the carpet. Above me Campbell was cursing, threatening, ordering me to get up and go with him, but I could not move as the sobs came, shuddering, bursting forth with the wild grief that possessed me.

And then a thousand bright lights seemed to explode at the back of my head, and for one fleeting moment I thought: *he's killed me too!* Then the great darkness of oblivion engulfed my entire soul.

ELEVEN

I have no idea how long I remained unconscious, mercifully unaware of everything that was going on around me. I have a vague impression of being picked up and jolted, but then I slipped even deeper into that quiet darkness and remained there. Dreamlike, I thought I was at the bottom of a great, dark sea, struggling upward to reach the surface, but the farther up I tried to swim, the darker it became. Then at last I heard the sound of waves crashing, and I began to gasp for air. . . .

I could still hear the water, but I knew that I was awake and not moving. My wrists and ankles ached terribly from the ropes that bound them together. My mouth was gagged. I was lying on my back on something hard and rough that bent my spine painfully. Water was splashing, and there was another sound, a scrape, metallic. . . .

I opened my eyes and realized I was in a rowboat, moving quickly across the lake. Above me I could see the muscular form of Campbell, his bearded face shadowy in the darkness as he worked the oars. There was no moon above, only a few faint stars, cold and unchanging, heedless of the horror that had taken place beneath them. The image of Father's lifeless body came back to me then and I thought I would go mad with my sorrow and fear and my rage at this disgusting creature that now held me powerless. I clenched my muscles and strained against the ropes, but I could not even begin to move either my hands or feet, so tightly were they bound. In my despair, I tried then to roll my body to one side of the boat in order to make it capsize. I would take him down with me, I thought, down to the bottom of this great, dark lake.

I struggled to move and had succeeded in getting my legs bent just slightly when Campbell gave me a vicious kick in the side.

"Hold it there, bitch!" The voice was low, almost a whisper, and I realized then that there must be people looking for us. If I could only scream!

As he talked, his growling manner turned softer. He spoke the way a person would talk to an injured dog. "Ya just lie there and ride. Can't have ya sinkin' yourself out there. Gonna need ya around, yes, ma'am, get me some money for ya. Big money, too. Reckon ya can sing for your supper back to the folks in town, and they'll give ole Red a good-sized piece o' your daddy's pie just to see you back in one piece, yes. But 'fore I'm done with ya, I'm gonna have me a little fun, yes, indeed."

The filth began to pour from his lips then and I shuddered, concentrating on the stars overhead, and then shutting my eyes altogether and listening only to the splash of water made by the oars, counting the strokes, anything to keep from hearing the vile words that issued forth from that horrible man's mouth. After a time he seemed to notice that I was not paying attention, for I felt the toe of his boot prodding me in the side. "You know, I'm gettin' myself so hard for ya that

I just don't think I can wait no longer! What do ya think of that, hey?"

"I think you're disgusting!" I mouthed the words into the gag. The words were unintelligible, but I felt better for having said them.

"Can't wait for it, either, can ya?" Chagrined, I realized that I had only excited him further by making a response. I clenched my teeth around the gag and vowed to be silent, to shut this creature out of my awareness. He went on talking, though, and what he said made me wince.

"I saw ya out there in that cabin the other night, standin' there buck-naked. Ya thought ya had the curtains drawn good and tight, but ya left enough room for ole Red to get hisself a good, good look. And won't be long now 'fore he gets hisself . . ."

There was more, but I forced myself not to listen. This isn't happening, I told myself. It's only a dream; it isn't happening . . . it isn't.

The sound of the oars changed, slowed, and the boat scraped what must have been the shore. Overhead I saw the edges of tree limbs and the silhouettes of a few small leaves. He stood up, got out at the front of the boat, and lifted it at that end, pulling it onto the shore, hardly making a sound. Then he set it down and came back to where I still lay, bound hand and foot. The voice from that dark shape was greasy and low. "Come on up, now. Ain't never did it with one hog-tied before!"

He dragged me up from the rowboat, forcing me to stand on the riverbank. Then he carried me, with one arm around my waist, as if I were a log. My feet were dragging on the ground. Campbell took me a short distance back into the woods until we reached a tiny clearing in the middle of a thicket. There he stood me up again, his grip hard on my arms as he waited behind me. The air around us had a musty, dank smell that I could not place. Above us were the trees. I had caught a glimpse of the lake when he had gotten me up out of

193

the boat, but the lake was empty as far as I could see in the darkness. How clever he had been! If they were using dogs to track us, they would have no luck at all until they reached this part of the shore—if they came around that far. It was more likely they would follow whatever trail Campbell had made when he had wandered around the hotel earlier during the past two days.

He was breathing heavily now, the only sound besides the quiet lapping of the waves on the lake shore and the pounding of my heart.

He forced me to kneel, and then to lie down on my stomach, my bound hands in front of me, making a painfully awkward pillow as I finally was able to loosen my hands enough to cross one wrist over the other. I steeled myself for what I knew was coming, hoping that when he untied my legs I would somehow be able to do something to escape, or at least to work loose the gag now that I could move my fingers slightly, and then I could scream for help.

His weight was over my back and I felt his hot breath whispering at my ear. "Looks like ya got a good mouth for kissin', bitch. Too bad ole Red can't take a chance on your keepin' quiet now, ain't it?"

He sat up and pulled up my skirt and my petticoat. With his breath coming faster, he tore away my cotton and lace drawers and waited. Out of the corner of my eye I could see him kneeling there, gloating over his prize.

Then his body was pressing down on me again. I squeezed my legs together as hard as I could, but still I felt the stabbing hurt that forced itself between them. And I needed every bit of willpower I possessed to concentrate only on the gag in my mouth, the chafing pain of the ropes that bound my wrists, and the revenge, the terrible revenge I vowed I would one day take on this detestable man.

A short while after his hissing and grunting finally subsided, I was hauled roughly to my feet again. He turned me around to face him, the whites of his eyes and his grinning teeth visible in the darkness. With one hand he pawed at my breasts; with the other he gripped my shoulder hard just below my neck, tightening cruelly when I tried to twist away. "Ain't tamed you yet, have I?" There was a low-voiced, sneering laughter in his words. "Guess I had you figgered right at that. *Thought* you was the kind that'd need more than one ridin' 'fore you finally settled down and behaved." He thrust his face close to mine and squeezed my breast hard, making me wince with the pain. "We're gonna have ourselves another go not too long from now when I get back. I got a good safe place to put ya in the meantime. Ya ain't gonna be too happy with it, but it's good and safe."

With that he turned me around again and half-dragged, half-carried me deeper into the thicket. The putrid smell I had noticed earlier grew stronger. When we stopped, it seemed to be all around us, coming from something on the ground.

"Now you just stand right there and don't fall over, you slut, while I locate your new home here. . . ." He took a few steps away from me and bent over as though he were looking for something on the ground. Then he stopped and gave a grunt of satisfaction. "Yeah," he said, "this is it, all ready for ya."

He straightened up and came back, and soon he had taken me over to the spot where he had been standing. It was a dark place, even in that darkened thicket, what seemed to be a hole dug into the rocky earth. The musty, dank odor of the underground was overpowering here, and I realized with horror that this was not a hole, but a fissure in the earth, one of the cracks in the structure of these mountains that penetrated deep beneath the surface.

I had heard about these "drop-caves" when I was a child in school. To the boys, it was a sign of bravery to clamber down the jagged, slippery surface of the rock with a candle as far as they could go and then leave the candle burning behind and climb back up in the darkness. Then the next boy would inch his way down the narrow, twisting crevasse and try to retrieve the candle. Some boys had died, I had heard, when they slipped on the wet, slimy surface and fell, cracking their heads on one of the jagged protrusions that marked the tortuous descent.

Moments later Campbell had pushed me partway down the opening and then as I sat on the edge he climbed down with me. "All right, now," he whispered, "you just let ole Red slide you down here a bit. Don't go wigglin' around none. This here crack goes down a good hunnert thirty feet. Make a nice deep grave if you try anything funny."

A few painful minutes later he had maneuvered both of us down the craggy, muck-covered incline. After the first few yards the descent was not straight down any longer but at an angle, where the crack went, I supposed, zigzag fashion in the earth. After a few more yards of wiggling me along, our two bodies face to face in a horrible parody of lovemaking, he stopped.

"Keep it good and warm for me, bitch, till I get back. If you're lucky, ole Red's gonna have hisself plenty o' money from whoever's lookin' after your pappy's will. Then I'm gonna turn ya loose after only a few good humps on ya."

He squeezed against me, sliding past and up the narrow, sloping passageway in the rocks. Then I heard his voice again. "Listen good, now. You don't wanna go slidin' around down there. Just under your feet there's a straight-down drop of nearly twenty yards. Hear me? You just stay put right there. If I'm more'n a day or two, I'll have somebody take a look in, maybe pull ya up and give ya a drink o' water." He gave a low, nasty laugh. "Reckon he's gonna get hisself mighty excited when he sees ya ain't wearin' no pants."

And with another chuckle he was gone, leaving me alone in complete darkness. Buried alive, I thought to myself. Who would find me here? The stench of the cave would be too strong for a hunting dog to track where we had come. I could not cry out, and even if I could, my voice would be blocked by the yards-thick layers of stone and dirt that separated me from the surface. Down here the silence was complete, except for the noise of my own breathing. I listened as carefully as I could, but I could hear no more than I could see. I was lying on my back, my hands and feet still tied, every muscle aching from my ordeal. The rock was cold, and the dampness was beginning to soak through my dress, making me shiver. I clamped my teeth tightly on the gag and forced myself to think of escape, of what I could do if another man came, what I would do if Campbell returned, but I was so very, very tired.

I awoke I knew not how long later, for I could still see nothing. It might have been day or night outside for all I knew. Had I fainted? I could scarcely believe that I had fallen asleep, even though I had been up all night and had not slept well for days, not since I had come out here on this trip with Father.

And then my memory came back again. Father was murdered, and I was alone. For a moment the hot tears filled my eyes, but, unbidden, something changed within me. Then the grief was dispelled by a newer, stronger feeling that burned deep inside me and spread throughout my body. I was going to win. I was going to beat them all. With a ruthlessness I had never realized was in me before, I vowed I would live from this moment as though I were beyond all passion. I would somehow avenge Father's death and complete the financial empire he had dreamed of. I saw myself on Vallamont again, in that new brick mansion so different from that of the Cottors, and I realized why I had been alone, why Nathan had not been with me the time I had dreamed of that new mansion before. I was going to have to do it myself. I could not indulge myself with a love for Nathan McKay, even though I might still feel it. I would have to use him, manipulate him, just as I would have to manipulate Steven Cottor to get what I wanted. There was no question now whether I "belonged" to Steven or was "engaged" to Nathan—both commitments, *any* commitments, would have to wait. I might *pretend,* I realized, again with that same strange ruthlessness, but in my heart I would have to belong to no one but myself until I had won. Father's death had changed everything. I was left suddenly with an enormous and complex task, one that would be doubly difficult because I was a woman. It would take all my feminine guile and, yes, my body, too, if necessary, but I would one day stand at the top of the real Vallamont, inside a beautiful brick mansion that was no longer only a dream. . . .

With a start, I realized what must be happening at the hotel just across the lake, at the lumber mill in Grampian, at the camps, at the Deer Park Hotel, at the gas company, at the trolley line—every one of Father's investments would be in chaos today when they learned of his death. And the chaos would build every moment I was away, every moment each investment was without a leader. Each day that passed until I could return would make it more and more difficult for me to take command. I had to get back! I had to get out of here!

I fought off the impulse to move quickly, recalling what Campbell had said about the sheer drop beneath my feet. The rocks were slippery; the leather heels of my shoes could not gain any hold. As I tried to push myself up slowly, my two feet simply skidded off the surface of the rock, and for one horrible moment I found myself slipping down, on my back, hands tied in front of me, unable to stop myself. But somehow I was able to twist myself sideways and double up, digging into the side of the rock with my knees and my forearms, so that I brought my slide to a halt. Then I gradually began to work my way upward, using my knees and elbows. I had no idea how far I had to go or how near I had come to a disastrous fall over the precipice Campbell had warned me about. I only knew that I was moving and that some way I would reach the surface and see daylight again.

It was hard, slow going. I knew it was dangerous to try to move like this, for every so often I would slip back and have to press my arms into the jagged rock alongside me to keep from losing all the ground I had gained, or more. Still I kept on, my eyes straining upward against the blackness, hoping to see some sign of daylight begin to appear above.

I paused to rest. The gag in my mouth was hot, and it prevented me from breathing in fresh air. I could hear the sound of my own breathing as I waited. And then above me I heard something move. It was a scraping noise. Only a few yards away something was coming down the passage. I tried to see. Was I imagining things, or was the darkness up ahead more gray than black? The noise grew closer, and suddenly I felt a rush of fear. What if this was not Campbell returning, not someone from a rescue party? What if this was a black bear, or a rattlesnake, or a copperhead? I had forgotten how far away I was from the hotel, which, as far as I knew, was the only building out here for many miles. Lynx or black bears would roam freely in these woods, and so would snakes, and I was powerless to defend myself. If only I could work my hands free!

But as I struggled again to twist my hands across one another and develop a little slack in the rope, I looked up again and saw that the darkness above me was indeed lightening a little. The sound of movement up ahead grew stronger, and the light was starting to flicker, turning from gray to a pale yellow. It had to be a person coming down the passageway and carrying a candle!

I breathed a sigh of relief that at least it was not a wild animal coming into the passageway, but at the same time came the realization that this might also be Campbell, or the man he had said he would send to check on me. Who else would remain silent all this time? If it had been a rescue team, certainly I would have heard their voices by now.

I thought quickly, and then I closed my eyes and pretended to have collapsed in a death-like faint. If Campbell or his partner had come with water to keep me alive, they would obviously try to make me drink down here. The only way I could get up to the surface was by playing unconscious—then they would be forced to bring me up out of this vile, dank pit and out into the fresh air, where they could bring me back to my senses to keep me alive.

Still, even though I knew that what I was doing was perfectly logical, it took all the effort I could muster up to keep from opening my eyes or crying out in terror as the intruder, whoever it was, drew near. I fancied I could feel his presence as he looked at me, and I am certain I felt the warm air from the flame of his candle. Then I heard his breathing, and there was no doubt that he was there, and watching.

He spoke, and I felt relieved that it was not Campbell's voice, even though it sounded familiar. "Goddamn! What did you do here, fall asleep?"

I felt his hand, cold and wet, touch my cheek, and despite all my self-control I shuddered slightly.

He did not seem to notice. "Hey, passed out, did you? Wake up!"

I forced my features to stay rigidly still, and I concentrated on the voice. Where had I heard it before?

"Goddamn it, don't you want no water? You sick or somethin'?" He shook me slightly, and I allowed myself to moan into the cotton kerchiefs that still gagged my mouth. Suddenly I realized how thirsty I was. How long had I been down here?

He made a few more efforts to revive me, but the passageway was so narrow and the light so dim that he was not able to make much of an impression or scrutinize the way I reacted. Finally he gave up, just as I had hoped.

"Can't let you just lay down here. Goddamn, how we

gonna do this?" He made a clumsy effort to drag me
up by my collar, but the material must have slipped
from his fingers. Then he tried to get one arm under
my shoulder, but that gave him too awkward a position
to move me. Finally he reached down for my wrists
and, grasping them by the rope around them, he began
to move me slowly upward, my arms above my head,
pulling me as if I were a fish wiggling out of the water.
The rock was rough in places and cut into my sides,
but I was nearly numb by now and barely noticed. I
was getting out; that was all that mattered.

Finally I felt the warm, fresh air at the top of the
passageway, and in another moment, after a last bone-
wrenching pull, I found myself sitting upright momentarily, and then I gently lowered onto my back amid
what had to be dry leaves and grasses around the mouth
of the crevasse. Though my eyes were still shut, I could
tell that it was daytime. I wondered if I could risk a
look at the man behind me, who was now breathing
hard, getting his wind back after the effort of hauling
me out.

I fluttered my eyelids, as though I were just recovering from a fainting spell, and I gave a moan that had
more real feeling than pretense to it. I was sore all
over, and I knew that when this numbness wore off I
was going to hurt even more. And I felt physically
weak, even though my mind, considering the ordeal
I had been through, felt surprisingly calm and purpose-
ful, ready to go through with what I knew would have
to be a flawless performance.

I opened my eyes, blinking against the mud that had
dried on my eyelashes, and I saw blue sky and green
leaves overhead.

From behind me came the voice. "Wakin' up, ain't
we? I thought a whiff o' some good air'd bring ya
around." Then I remembered where I had heard the
voice—at Vallamont. This was one of Cottor's men,
one of the two who had nearly caught me that first
Saturday afternoon!

The memory made me shiver, which was quite absurd now, I thought. I had been much safer that afternoon than I was today! And yet I somehow had the feeling that I could manipulate this man to my advantage.

Soon he was undoing the gag around my mouth, his dirty fingers moving quickly. I saw him plainly now: it was Parsons, the dark and wiry man who had pushed me against the pine trees.

He pulled out the gag, but then he immediately clamped a grimy palm over my mouth. "We're gonna keep quiet now, ain't we? Try screamin' for help, and I'll put you out again right quick and you won't wake up for a long time, neither. Nod if you understand."

I nodded, sinking back weakly under the weight of his hand. When he took his hand away and I could speak, I was surprised to find that my mouth was too dry to form intelligible syllables at first. Then he held a canteen to my lips briefly and I could manage better. I asked him how long I had been down there, and I was stunned when he told me it had been less than twelve hours. It had seemed like so much longer. But he said Campbell had come by early that morning and told him he'd just left me here. "Didn't want me to come around till this time tomorrow," said Parsons, "but I figgered you wasn't too strong. And you ain't gonna be much use to us dead, the way I see it."

I shivered. "I'm freezing," I said. "This dress is soaked through with that muck from down there. I think I'm coming down with a fever." I looked at my dress and shuddered again. It was almost completely brown with the slime of the passageway and it was torn. Where would I find anything else to wear?

Then I saw the flicker of lust in his eyes as he looked me up and down, and I knew what I had to do. Now was the time that I would have to use my body. I would have to excite Parsons and make him want me. If I could cloud his judgment or win him over somehow, I might be able to escape before Campbell returned.

"I need to get warm somehow," I said, shivering again. "Don't you have a blanket or something warm?"

"Might at that," he said, his teeth showing a quick grin. "What's it worth to you?"

Later, that evening, I reflected on the decision I had made. I was a three-hour ride away from that horrible cave and the lake, inside the rustic hunter's cabin where Craig Parsons had brought me. A fire still burned in the hearth, where Parsons had heated a kettle of water from the nearby creek so that I could take a bath. The mud and that horrible chilled feeling were gone now. My body smelled of the rough brown laundry soap, but I was clean. I had even managed to get my hair to look more presentable. Though I was a long way from being safe, I was certainly better off here in bed with Craig Parsons than I had been in the cave or with Campbell.

Our arrangement had been strangely businesslike, almost friendly, as though Parsons was not accustomed to playing the role of jailer. Certainly he had not been expecting me to be so tolerant of his sexual desires. I knew he considered Sam Rawles's daughter to be far different from the women he was accustomed to—and certainly I continued to act that way in speech and bearing. Yet the fact that I could at the same time know his own wants—which, after all, were not so different from what I had learned in order to please Steven— seemed to make him feel, or act, oddly vulnerable. His dark, saturnine face, not entirely unattractive, began to lose some of its hardness, and at times he seemed self-conscious, even a little proud of the prize he had brought home.

And as he lay beside me on the bed now, dozing peacefully after having exerted himself for the second time since we had come into the cabin, I found it difficult to imagine that this same man was holding me captive, waiting for that hideous Campbell to return with my ransom money.

Yet he had certainly been careful to take precautions against my escape. To begin with, I had no clothes here in the cabin. When I got out of bed I draped myself in a woolen blanket, for my dress, my petticoat, my chemise, and my shoes were all outside—a good deal cleaner after I had scrubbed them in the washtub, to be sure, but still outside. I could hardly make a sudden dash for freedom without them, and even if I had entertained such a foolish notion, Parsons had securely fastened the door with several tight-fitting wedges. It took several minutes of noisy tapping and twisting to get outside, during which time Parsons would be certain to wake up, even from a deep sleep.

And if I were to escape, assuming I was able somehow to make off with his horse, where would I go? I had no idea how far we had come from the lake. From the sun, I thought we had been riding in a northwest direction most of the way, but I had no idea how near was the nearest town or telegraph outpost, let alone where the nearest railway or wagon road was. Certainly we had passed none of these on our way here, none that I had seen. As far as I knew, the nearest habitation was the Eagles Mere hotel, and that was the direction Campbell would be coming from when he returned from Grampian.

Somehow, though, I knew I had to get away before Campbell's return. It was at that point that he would need some proof that I was still alive, if he was going to use proof at all. After he forced me to write whatever letter or signature he intended to use as evidence that I was still able to be ransomed, I would be of no further use to him. At that point any move I made to escape would doubtless be met with death—they might even kill me, anyway, just so I would not be able to identify them.

Beside me Parsons stirred, waking up now. I watched him, his face shadowy in the firelight, trying to look only at the attractive features so as to make what I knew would soon happen again more bearable. Only half-awake, he felt my warmth next to him and reached for me, his hands rough against the smooth but tender surface of my back and thighs.

I smiled, for I knew that the smile would show in my voice, and my performance had to be flawless at all times. Unless I could simply persuade him that it would bring him more profit in the end to release me, which I doubted, I would have to tire him out, lull him into a sense of safety, and then somehow catch him napping at a weak moment and make my escape.

I was glad then for my experience with Steven, because I knew I could not have managed to act as knowing and seductive had it not been for those hours I had shared with him. "Come on over now," I said softly, drawing him close. "You just enjoy it while it's here."

That next morning I woke up strangely rested. Parsons had drawn my body to his once more during the night, but this had been slower, almost languorous in comparison, so that I scarcely had to emerge from my half-sleeping drowsiness. There was never any real feeling involved, of course—nothing like that which Steven had aroused, or which I had felt for Nathan McKay. But I was just as glad. I was not ready to yield my feelings to a man, and I knew that I would not be ready again for a long time.

I had covered myself with a rough wool blanket and was up out of bed, kindling the fire from the night's remaining coals, when I heard Parsons awaken. Clearly his night's entertainment had improved his spirits, for he sounded almost cheerful.

"Damn," he said, appreciatively, "does a man good to see somethin' like yourself first thing in the mornin', even if you're covered up with that there blanket!"

"I think I'd feel considerably more attractive if I had my clothes," I said, a bit more dryly than I had intended.

"I bet you would. Coffee's in that box of gear over

in the corner, if you can keep from burnin' your fingers on the pan."

He pulled on his trousers and busied himself getting the door open while I measured the coffee and dipped water from the stone crock into a tin pot that seemed to be the cabin's sole cooking utensil. I rested it on the hot coals and had the dark mixture boiling by the time he returned.

"Smells like coffee, anyhow," he said as he banged the door behind him. "Here. You want these?"

He tossed my clothes over the table to me and laughed as I reached to catch them before they went into the fire. The blanket slipped down around my waist, saved from falling off completely only by the back of the wooden chair I had been sitting on. I clutched the bundle to my breasts, momentarily blushing with embarrassment, but then I recalled the role I was playing and recovered my poise.

"Thank you," I said, setting the clothes in my lap and unfolding them, one garment at a time, very deliberately, my breasts in full view. The heavy cotton fabric of my dress was matted and stiff from the laundry soap and cold from the morning air outside, but at least it was clean. My chemise, petticoat, and stockings were in the same condition.

He watched me, fascinated as I slipped on my stockings and then stood up to put on my petticoat. By the time I was about to put on my chemise, he had come over beside me. "You're a bewitchin' sight, ya know that?" he said.

"Didn't I tell you?" I began, but already his hands were on my arms and he was drawing me away from the fireplace to the bed. "Don't you ever get enough?" I said and stepped out of the petticoat again. "I'm never going to get dressed at this rate."

He guffawed, holding me up in front of him for a moment before he set me down amid the now-cool sheets. I could see from his eyes that I was making progress, for his look was more relaxed. He still stayed alert, but he was plainly less suspicious now than he had been previously. In another day or two I would have my chance; I was sure of it.

Afterward I finally did get dressed and we drank the now-lukewarm coffee out of two cracked ceramic mugs. The fire was blazing brightly now, and I tried to persuade myself that it made the cabin cheerful. I was not going to think about Father's death, I told myself, even though I knew the full reaction was beginning to set in. I had to keep going; I had to get away from here before Campbell came back.

Parsons propped open one of the board windows and emptied the coffee remains from the battered pot. "Reckon we'll have some beans for breakfast," he said, reaching into the box of supplies, "seein' as how that's all there is." He drew a long knife from his belt sheath, stabbed the point into the tin of beans, and began to pry up the lid.

As he heated the beans over the fire, I asked him how he had come to be out here in this cabin instead of in Grampian, working for Abel Cottor. I was sure he had recognized me from that Saturday afternoon that seemed so long ago. Considering the circumstances, it seemed foolish to pretend that I had not recognized him. "Oh, I quit on Abel," he said, "quit on him right after the old bastard tried to get me to bust up Rawles's —hell, that'd be your pappy, wouldn't it?—your pappy's mill." He shook his head, grimacing. "Too easy to get caught on a job like that. And I know what happens to the poor devils that get caught. Hell, you saw it yourself, didn't you? Wouldn't want your pappy doin' that to me."

"My Father's dead," I said, trying to keep my voice calm.

His jaw dropped open in surprise. "Son-of-a-bitch," he said, "I didn't know that."

"Campbell shot him. I saw it happen."

"If that don't beat all. Campbell told me your pappy

was gonna pay us to get you back." For the first time Parsons sounded awkward, unsure.

"Well, I saw it myself." I tried not to look at him, for I knew I could not bear to have him be sympathetic. I couldn't afford sympathy right now, for if I softened, I knew I would be unable to continue.

"Damn!" he said. "I'm an . . . oh, hell! I wouldn't o' . . . I just didn't know . . ."

"Never mind that," I said. "But if you really want to do something to make up for it, all you have to do is take me back to Grampian. If you do that, I'd say we were even. You wouldn't have the law after you, either. Nobody'd even have to know you had anything to do with me."

He considered this proposal briefly. Then he shook his head. "Nope, can't do it. Might not have the law, but I'd have Red Campbell, and he's a damned sight worse. Wish I hadn't even gotten mixed up with him, to tell you the truth."

I tried not to let my disappointment in Parsons show; I needed to stay on friendly terms with him. "Well, if you hadn't, I'd still be tied up underground, probably dead by now. So I can't say the same. But how *did* you come across Campbell? I thought he was working for my father."

"Yeah, that's why I was watchin' him, waitin' for him to try to pay off another of our men—Abel's man. But when I quit, I'd had a bellyfull of Abel. So I just waited till the next time I saw Campbell and told him he could have a free hand with the place for all I cared. I said I was comin' up here just to fish and hunt for a while."

"What did Campbell say?"

"Oh, not much. Just said he might apply for the job now that it was open—you know, kiddin'-like. Then he said if he got fed up he might come on out here and see how the fishin' was, too. I told him to look me up, but I didn't think any more of it until yesterday morning when he came by with that story of his. Said you were worth all kinds of money and that we'd be sure to get a good-sized hunk of the pie."

Money. Worth all kinds of money. Suddenly, as I heard those words, the realization struck me like a lead weight. What had Father said about money that afternoon in his library when we had been going over his accounts in those leather-bound books? We were overextended. We owed more than the properties were worth, until they could be built up to pay off. Now that Father was dead . . .

I closed my eyes, not wanting to think of the bankers, the loans that would come due out of the estate, and the fuss that all Father's creditors would make to get their money back quickly before someone else beat them to it. Without Father's name and reputation, the poor state of our finances would be quickly brought into the open. In fact, as soon as Campbell made his demand for ransom money, whoever was acting as executor would search the account books for available cash and find none.

And then the word would spread from bank to bank, quietly, of course, discreetly, but rapidly. And then the chaotic scramble would begin in earnest.

"Hey," said Parsons. He had finished heating the beans and was scraping them onto two tin plates with his knife. "Are you all right? Here. Better have some beans."

I automatically accepted the plate and a bent steel spoon. Holding the plate of beans on my lap, I began to eat, trying not to think, but unable to stop. My dream of managing our family holdings, of building up the hotels, the camps, the mills, of starting new industry, of one day reclaiming Vallamont, was about to be smashed before I could even begin. By the time I got back to Grampian, I would be as badly off as if Father had stuck to his promise a week earlier and really disowned me. There would be next to nothing. Mother and I would probably even have to sell the mansion and move to a smaller house once the creditors began to make their demands.

"Hope there ain't no hard feelin's," Parsons was saying, " 'bout not takin' ya back, I mean. That Campbell, he's a son-of-a-bitch. Even if the law caught up with him, I'd not feel safe unless I saw him hanged first and buried after."

I nodded.

And then the realization came that perhaps, if I reached Grampian soon enough, I might be able to stop any disclosure of our shaky financial condition. If I could only get back, there would be no need to look for a ransom and no need for a quick examination of the books until I could make certain that whoever was doing the examination had been carefully prepared for what he would find, and what he would report. . . .

I looked up, trying to keep my emotions in control. I had to escape, and there was not a moment to lose, yet I could not let that show.

I set down my plate, a bit surprised to notice that I had finished the entire serving. "I . . . I need to go outside for a few minutes," I said in my most ladylike manner.

He had enough manners not to question me. In a moment or two he had gotten up and opened the door. He gave me a perfunctory smile as I bent down to put on my shoes, which he had left outside by the doorway.

"Reckon we'll just keep these in here for the time bein'," he said, taking the shoes out of my hands. "Hope ya understand."

"Do you seriously think I'd consider running off through these godforsaken woods on my own?" I tried to sound pouting and indignant.

He gave me an oddly tentative, almost shy, grin, which looked strangely out of place on his swarthy, unshaven features. "Well, let's just say I don't want to take no chances, though ya sure didn't seem to be havin' such a bad time this mornin'."

I blushed. While we had been been making love that

morning, a vision of Nathan McKay and what this would have been like with him had crept into my mind, and despite all my firm intentions to stay controlled and passionless, I had let my emotions carry me away. Parsons was right. I had enjoyed what we had done this morning, though I am sure he would not have appreciated knowing the reason why.

I was at a loss for words, the color rising in my cheeks. He watched me for a moment or two. His narrow-set brown eyes had softened even further.

"Don't know what to say, do ya? Well, hell, neither do I. Got no business gettin' mixed up with rich dames, I guess, a roughneck like me." He coughed to clear his throat. "Aw, hell," he said.

And then to my surprise I found he was pressing the shoes back into my hands. "Take the damned things. Take the horse, too. Get the hell outta here."

I could scarcely believe what I had heard. For a moment I stood dumbfounded, just staring at him. I knew that I ought to run while the chance was here, but I found myself asking questions, against my better judgment. "But what about Campbell? What are you going to tell him?"

"I'll make up somethin'. Shit, I could tell him ya weren't even there when I rode down to the lake to check on ya. Don't worry 'bout it. Just get goin' now before I change my mind."

I remained just long enough to get my shoes on and ask for some simple directions, and then I took him at his word.

TWELVE

I rode Parsons's brown mare nearly a mile through the shadowy forest before the reaction struck. It was only an hour's ride, he had said, until I would reach Father's lumber camp—the one we had visited the day after Nathan had left us. At the camp I would find a way back to Grampian. I would get home quickly and speak with Mother, and with Judge Hawthorne, and somehow we would manage to prevent our financial troubles from becoming public knowledge.

I urged the mare forward on the narrow trail, keeping my head down to avoid the low-hanging branches of the maples that grew out here mixed in with the pines. The woods seemed quiet this morning, and chilly, even though the sun was up. In spots here and there, it managed to break through the leaves overhead and light the ground with small patches of brightness. The forest was not gloomy and damp, I told myself. I was going home. I was free. How lucky I had been that Campbell's choice of an accomplice had been Craig Parsons! I had been able to soften his feelings, partly by luck, of course, but also partly by my own refusal to be broken, by my own ability to use my body for what I had to do. Was it wrong, what I had done? I could not think about it now; I could only keep going forward, keep on with what I was forced to do and be thankful, I told myself, that I was not in worse circumstances. I was free now; that was what mattered. I could go home for the first time since . . .

The pain came back to me then in a rush that made me shudder. All that had happened—to Father, to me, to everything I had planned for—was all so wrong! So unfair! My eyes blurred, even as I tried to shake off the feeling and ride on. I could not see. In a haze of tears, my breath now coming in gasps, I managed to bring the mare to a stop. The sobs burst forth from me then as though I were possessed of strange demons, and for a moment I thought that I would surely faint and fall to the ground. My chest heaving, my body wracked with pain, I gripped the saddle horn as tightly as I could, but still I felt myself swaying dangerously, powerless, it seemed, to stay upright. I flung myself forward in the saddle and clutched the mare's neck with both arms. Breathing the warm animal scent, my cheek against its smooth coat, I clung to the horse for what seemed like hours as the hot tears and sobs flooded through me and swept away all else before them.

Finally the storm of my grief seemed to subside and I was able to calmly draw my breath again. Weeping quietly now, I waited, and soon I could open my eyes and clearly see the rocks and the dead brown leaves on the trail beside the new green ferns. The woods were still there, quiet, just as before.

I lightened my hold on the mare's smooth neck and pushed myself upright in the saddle again. Above me were the trees and the morning sun. I felt tired, not nearly so sure of my strength as I had been this morning. And I was frightened, too, at the intensity of what had just come over me so suddenly. Was this what despair was like? Was this what others felt and had to overcome? Was this something I had escaped up until now due to Father's protectiveness? Well, that did not matter anymore. I was over it now. I had suffered, but I was going to fight back. I would gather my strength again and one day I would see to it that the right punishment fell to Campbell and also to Abel Cottor.

I drew in a deep breath and urged the mare forward. My mind began to clear as I rode, and I was able to see in greater detail what I would have to do. There were the newspapers, of course; the story of Father's death must not be overplayed, for lurid headlines were bound to result in a rush of reservations cancellations. I only hoped that whoever had discovered what had happened had had the good sense to keep his mouth shut until further arrangements could be made. Now, if that man from the Deer Park Hotel—what was his name?—had only arrived in time to take charge. . . .

These and other details were arranging themselves in my thoughts when I felt the mare toss her head and snort, as though she scented something up ahead.

I stopped and waited, wondering if I would have to run. And in a moment or two I could see, riding toward me, the blond-haired, broad-shouldered outline of a man. I let out my breath in relief that at least the newcomer was not Campbell. Then, as the rider came closer on the shadowy trail, I recognized Billy Joe Walker.

I called out to him and he spurred his horse forward with a whoop. "Goddamn! I knew it! I knew it!"

In a moment he was at my side, asking if I was all right and haltingly, almost shyly, offering his sympathy for Father's death. I thanked him. I was well, I said, and wanted to get back to Grampian as quickly as possible. Could he help me?

"That's what I came for, ma'am. Soon as we got the news ya was bein' held, I took off for Parsons's cabin." He hooked his thumbs in the belt loops of his blue denims, faded and tight, and he nearly burst the buttons on his red wool shirt with that huge chest. "Just yesterday mornin' we had a crew out this way, and I saw old Red Campbell come ridin' like a bastard down the trail here. Didn't have no idea what it was, of course, but this mornin' when we got the news I put two and two together and had a pretty strong hunch they was the ones who done it."

He grinned, his big, friendly blue eyes lighting up with pride that his hunch had been right. "So I figgered I'd head straight out here and see if ya was here and needed a hand. Didn't even tell the boss that I was comin'—just took off. Ain't even ate breakfast."

"I know how you feel, Billy Joe. I've scarcely eaten for two days myself."

His face took on a sudden look of concern and the words came out in a rush. "They didn't give you nothin' to eat? How'd ya get away? Goddamn, they better have treated ya right. C'mon, then, ya can tell me about it while we ride if ya want. I know a quick way down to the river, just this side of the train depot. We can get ya on a coach and back to town."

I did not feel much like talking, so we just rode together in silence until the trail took a turn to the right and went uphill. "That's the way to the camp," said Billy Joe. "Here's where we go, though, so let's head down and start to rough it."

The slope was steep and the soil was damp and treacherously soft, with wet leaves and rocks adding to the hazards of our descent. Twice Billy Joe's mount stumbled, and once the mare slipped under me and nearly pitched me forward and out of the saddle completely. My feet came out of the stirrups, but I dug in my knees against the horse's flanks and caught hold of its mane and managed to keep myself from falling.

I was breathing hard when we reached the bottom of the first incline. Ahead of us I could see another sharp descent, this one even steeper than the logging skid I remembered so well from the first camp. The trees grew smaller here, among a number of rotting stumps that bore witness to previous years' work by the logging crews.

"You feelin' all right?" Waiting just to my right, Billy Joe looked at me critically. "You're lookin' kinda tuckered out."

"No, I'm fine." I did feel weak, but there was no point in complaining. "How much farther is the river?"

"Why, it's just down there a ways. Can't you see it?"

I strained to look in the direction he had pointed, but I could see only the trees and more mountains and the sky. I blinked my eyes, trying to fight off the wave of dizziness that seemed to have come upon me so slowly that I had not even noticed it. I felt my grip loosening on the reins, knew that I was swaying . . .

Like a flash he had reached out and caught me before I toppled over. I felt his big hand on my shoulder, felt the strength in that arm that supported me. Then the darkness was just too much for me to ignore any longer and I let myself sink down, slowly, almost luxuriously, into unconsciousness.

I awoke on a hard wooden bench, still feeling weak but at least able to think clearly. I was inside a shed, the walls of rough boards, freshly whitewashed. In front of me I could see Billy Joe talking with a man who had on a railroad cap. We were at the train depot then. How had he managed to bring me all the way down here?

"Billy Joe," I said, surprised that my voice came out so clearly.

He turned around instantly and was at my side in two strides. "You're all right, then," he said. "Had me worried there for a while. I was just tryin' to get us a doctor."

"When does the train come?"

"Looks like there ain't gonna be any train." He explained that a few miles downriver at a siding there had been an accident. A switch had been left open this morning and an engine had been derailed. The tracks would be blocked until it could be moved.

"Well, I've got to get word back to Grampian. Please send a wire, would you? Send it to Mrs. Sam Rawles."

"Wire's down, young lady," said the attendant, his voice maddeningly placid. "Boxcar's snapped off two of them poles like they was saplin's. Haven't sent or received nothin' here since eleven o'clock."

I drew in a deep breath and pushed myself up to a standing position, still leaning heavily on the arm of the bench beside me. "I really must get back, Billy Joe," I said. "I have to get word back, too. There may be considerable money involved. Are the horses outside?"

His blue eyes did nothing to conceal his doubts that I would be able to make the journey. "I wouldn't let you ride fifty yards, considerin' the shape you're in, Miss Catherine. And Grampian's thirty miles. You're just gonna have to . . ." He turned away a moment, his eyes riveted on something outside the window along the river. "Wait, now, just wait a minute. I got me an idea."

He was out the door and then back again in a matter of what seemed only a few moments, just long enough for me to take a pad and pencil from the trainman and write "Well and coming home—Catherine" on a sheet of paper.

"We're takin' a raft," he said, his big frame filling the doorway and his expression proud again. "It's all set. Should make Grampian by sundown."

I nodded and tore the message off the pad and handed it to the trainman. "You send that as soon as they've fixed the telegraph," I said. "Send it to Mrs. Sam Rawles in Grampian."

His eyes widened behind his silver wire spectacles. He looked at my disheveled clothes and hair in obvious perplexity, as though unable to decide whether he could risk not asking me to pay for the message in advance.

"Is there some problem?" I asked, my voice cool. Behind me Billy Joe took a step toward the trainman's desk.

"Why, no, madam. No, no problem, not at all. It'll be sent off just as soon as I have a signal. You can rely on that."

In a few minutes we were on the raft and under way downriver. We moved fairly rapidly, for the river was still high from the late thaw up in the mountains and from the heavy rains of a week before. Billy Joe stood with his long pole toward the front of the raft, which was a small one, only about fifteen feet long, and he kept an eye out for any rocks or debris that might snag us and spin us the wrong way around in the current. I stayed at the back, behind the little shed built in the raft's middle, holding the broad-paddled oar that served as our rudder. When Billy Joe saw the need he would call out, "Now lean right," or "lean left," and I would lower the oar from its hinged stand, where it was attached up close to the handle, down into the water and lean my weight in whatever direction Billy Joe ordered. I had to lean hard, but for some reason I no longer felt tired. Out there on the sunny river I felt warm and safe and relieved that I was at least going back to Grampian as quickly as I could.

Most of the time I rested, just sitting on the straight-backed wooden chair beside the rudder stand, holding the oar lightly to keep the blade up out of the water until it was needed. On either side of me were the steep green slopes of the mountains, these cool forests rising up from the rocky banks of the river. I thought of the wealth represented by the timber in those mountains—it was like gold that was waiting for those with the drive and the will to go in and take it out. Nathan had said the supply wouldn't last, but looking at those miles and miles of green forests as they stretched out behind me and in front of me as far upstream and downstream as the eye could see, it was hard to imagine that this endless forest land would ever run low. There were always new trees, little saplings, and as long as we took only the ones large enough to . . .

"Will ya look at that!" called Billy Joe, pointing to

the railway on the north bank, where a black locomotive lay derailed and helpless on its side. "Gonna take all the mules in the county to move that son-of-a-bitch!"

It certainly seemed that way to me as we drifted past. The downed locomotive had fallen over both tracks, it appeared, dragging the coal car over on its side along with it and pulling some of the other cars off the track, too, making a zigzag formation of boxcars and coaches that blocked the tracks for nearly a quarter of a mile. We could see the telegraph poles that had been knocked over, and the broken wires from the slightly bent poles on either side dangled and swayed in the breeze. No work appeared to be going on to repair them as yet. Just a number of irritated-looking train passengers were standing around in little knots of conversation, no doubt complaining and speculating on how long it would be until an engine was brought out from Grampian to carry them back to civilization.

As we drifted past, several of the passengers hailed us, for we were no more than forty yards away from the north shore. They called for us to put in by the bank and give them a ride into town, some offering as much as two dollars for the trip.

Billy Joe looked at me for instructions. I was really not in the mood for company, but it was impossible not to feel sympathy for these people, stranded as they were out here along the river. "It's all right, Billy Joe," I said. "We can take a few. But make certain they're the ones who need it the most."

I lowered the rudder into the current and we turned toward the shoreline. But we had not gone more than a few yards in that direction when I saw something that nearly made me lose my hold on the rudder.

Behind a group of men in black business suits who were talking in front of the tender, a man leaned casually against the roof of the stricken locomotive. He was dressed in blue jeans and a dark brown work shirt.

And the man had red hair.

I nearly screamed out in fright, but I caught myself

in time. Hardly able to speak without my voice quavering, I said to Billy Joe, "Look—up there next to the engineer's cab. Isn't that Campbell?"

He looked that way and swore softly. "Damned if it ain't," he said quietly. "You want me to sing out and have him arrested?"

I pictured the scene: a scuffle, then testimony required, and questions from the crowd, from the sheriff, or whoever was here representing the law.

It added up to more of a delay and more publicity about the Rawles family and their troubles.

I set the rudder to carry us away from the shore, my eyes all the while on Campbell. He was looking in our direction; in fact, as nearly as I could determine from that distance, he appeared to be asleep on his feet. It served him right to be that tired. And then, after all his activity, he'd have nothing to show for it. Unless he saw me now, he'd have an unpleasant surprise waiting for him when he returned to Eagles Mere Lake and that smelly, dark cave.

"Let's keep on going," I said. "Campbell can wait until we get to the next town and notify the sheriff."

He looked at me open-mouthed and perplexed. "But he's right up there *now!* You want to take a chance on him gettin' away? That don't make no sense!"

I stepped behind the raft's small shed as we passed directly in front of the locomotive. Maybe Campbell wasn't looking our way, but there was no point in making my presence obvious. Then I explained to Billy Joe how it was important that I reach home to comfort Mother as quickly as I could and that to remain here to arrest Campbell would only cause a scene and delay us unnecessarily.

"Besides," I said, "I know exactly where he can be picked up if they miss him here by the train. I'll just give the sheriff directions to that cave on the far shore of the lake, and you can tell him how to reach Parsons's cabin. All they'll have to do is wait for Campbell to walk into their trap."

I could hear Billy Joe's footsteps as he came back to take the rudder. He coughed, and after a moment or two he said, "Damnation, if I had a gun I could shoot the son-of-a-bitch from here. You sure you don't want me to get him now? That son-of-a-bitch don't deserve to draw another breath, if you ask me."

Billy Joe's righteous anger awakened my own, and I very nearly gave in. Only the thought that every second I spent here would allow time for still more of Father's reputation and our financial empire to slip away kept me from running to the other side of the raft and calling out for the bystanders to seize the murderer of my father. But Father's empire was too important to waste on scum like Campbell. Aloud I said, "I want him killed, too, Billy Joe. But I can't afford to have a lot of people asking me questions right now. I've got to get back and start putting our affairs in order. And, besides," I continued, even though I was surprised to hear myself speak this way, "I don't really want the law to have Campbell. They'd be too easy on him after what he's done." The bitterness in my voice seemed to have a life of its own, and I felt the deep burning of anger inside my heart.

His voice was quiet, respectful. "Well, you can count on me, Miss Rawles. I'm your man whenever you want to see it happen. He'll get what he deserves. You can count on it."

I thanked him, recognizing the sincerity in his voice. Billy Joe was loyal, and Father had said often enough that loyalty in a man was more worth paying for than brains were, because you could always do the brainwork yourself. I would remember Billy Joe's loyalty. And I knew that somehow, some way, I would put that loyalty to work in getting me the revenge Red Campbell so much deserved.

In a few minutes we had drifted out of sight of the locomotive and its stranded passengers and cargo.

The rest of the afternoon, except for the time we used in alerting the sheriff of a little river town that there was a wanted criminal about five miles upstream, I spent resting, gazing at the sky and the wonderful green mountains, or asking Billy Joe questions about the lumber business. It was astonishing to me how much he knew about board feet and pricing and grades of wood, about how to "top" the trees and skid the logs down to the river, and about how to manage one of the big rafts during the late-winter and early spring runs, when six crewmen and a cook lived on board one of these rafts and kept control, he said, of hundreds and thousands of board feet of logs as they came roaring down in the current. He told me about log-rustling, where men changed the wooden brands burned into the logs to mark one owner's lumber from another.

"They used to do that a lot just down here a ways," he said, "down here by the boom. A man'd store a couple hundred logs, and then when it came time to get 'em out we couldn't find 'em—just like they disappeared. It'd be there on the company books, and he'd have his receipt and everythin', but there just wasn't any findin' the logs."

He paused for a moment and pushed us away from an uprooted maple tree that had washed away from the riverbank during the spring floods and gotten caught on a rock. The tree, dead branches and all, now rested close to the middle of the river.

"Have to clear that out of here before long," he said. "Gonna block things up a lot worse if we don't tend to it." Then he went on to explain about how they caught the "log-rustlers." They had checked the books—this had been Nathan McKay's idea, he said—and found that some of the entries had been tampered with to give hundreds of additional board feet of lumber to the Sprague mill. "Never did prove nothin' against old Sprague himself," Billy Joe went on, "but after a few nights of watchin' the bookkeeper and two of the guards, they had themselves three rustlers. Yep. Two with hot irons, and one with an ink pen. That was eight months ago, and I guess they're still in jail."

We drifted in silence for a while, and then as we came around a bend Billy Joe said, "Well, up here's the long reach, right straight ahead. You can just see the start of the boom over there in the middle of the bend."

And I could. About two hundred yards away, at the center of the long blue pathway made by the river, now darkening in the shadows of the late afternoon, I could see what looked to be an even darker shadow that stretched from the middle to the left bank, as though someone had built a low wall out of logs halfway across the river.

As we drifted closer, I could see the long diagonal barrier that held the other logs that were in storage from drifting downriver any farther. These barrier logs were set on stone pilings, attached with strong ropes and spikes so that they could be swung open and shut to let the raft men get at a group of logs that was stored there on the outside. Together, the barrier logs acted as a giant trap that funneled everything that came down the north side of the river over toward the north bank. When the boom was full, as it was now, a huge triangular segment of the river nearly half a mile long was packed so thick with logs that a man could walk across it.

There were three "boom rats" doing just that as we went slowly past. Clad in dirty gray woolens and spiked boots, they were prying and turning up the logs with their long pikes. They looked up and waved, and then they went back to their work. From their steady, systematic prodding, Billy Joe explained, it looked as though they were taking inventory of the logs in that particular section of the boom, making certain that the right number of logs with the right brands on them were stored and ready for shipment the next morning. That was when the raft men would come and take them the remaining five miles down to Grampian and the mills.

Billy Joe squinted at the sun, which had now dropped down almost below the crest of the mountains behind us. "Guess we're a mite slower than I thought," he said. "It's sundown already and we've still got five miles to go. Reckon we'll be in town before dark, anyhow."

It seemed hard to believe that I would be back in our family mansion in only an hour or two. After the days with Father and my ordeal in the wilds, and especially this long and peaceful ride downstream with Billy Joe, the everyday comforts of life in town would seem almost strange. But I told myself there would be other ordeals ahead. I would have to be even stronger in the next few weeks than I had been during these last trying days. There was a fortune at stake. Others would be fighting for a piece of Father's empire, and it was up to me alone to protect it. Mother, I knew instinctively, would not have the stomach for a prolonged battle. She would be grieving for the loss of Sam Rawles, as I would be, too—but the difference was that I would have to shed my remaining tears privately and steel myself each day to carry on.

I was thinking what it would be like to give orders to one of the mill foremen when Billy Joe called out, "Hard left now! Hard left!"

Ahead of us I glimpsed something large and shadowy before I turned to the rudder. It was another downed tree, but this one was blocked up with some logs and debris that must have come loose from the boom and drifted here. I lowered the rudder and forced it to the left as hard as I could, holding the long oar against the current until my arms ached.

But then I heard the scraping, hollow clatter as the front of our raft plowed into the branches and logs that blocked our path.

"Wait, now, hard right!" called Billy Joe, even as we slowed and the current began to hiss around the back corners of the raft, splashing up around my feet and wetting my shoes through with the cold river water. I fought off the impulse to panic as the raft tilted backward and the current came up around my ankles. Instead, I gritted my teeth and took as firm a foothold as I could while I forced the rudder to move.

The current against the rudder gradually began to turn us away from the logs and branches that were blocking our way. As I strained at the rudder, Billy Joe leaned all his weight onto his pole and pushed until we had moved around where the current was hitting us sideways, and then we were spinning, traveling rudder first, around the roots of the tree and out into the open river again.

Billy Joe waved and gave me a big grin. "Hey, now, that was some piece of work with that rudder, I want ya to know."

I managed to grin back. "You weren't so bad yourself!" My teeth were chattering, and even though I felt warm inside, my feet were wet and I was shaking with fatigue.

"Hey, now!" Billy Joe came back to where I was standing by the rudder and looked at me hard. "This'll never do. You got wet back here, didn't you? Can't have that."

He ignored my protests and led me into the shed, dragging the chair with him. Inside it was shadowy now that the sun had set, but I could make out the shape of a stove in the corner. Quickly Billy Joe had set me down on the chair, adjusted the wick of the kerosene stove, and gotten it lit.

The flame shone through the grating and gave the little shed a warmer glow. After waiting a moment to be sure the wick was right, Billy Joe brushed off his hands and stood up. "You get your feet close to this here and get dry. We got about a half hour till we reach Grampian, I calculate. Now I gotta get out and steer."

"What about the pole?" I called to him as loudly as I could.

His voice came from only a few feet away, half-laughing. "Hey, I'm just here." And I realized that the board walls of the shed were hardly thick enough to shut out any sounds. "Don't worry. I can see good from here. If I need you back at the rudder, I'll let ya know."

So I waited there in that little shed, smelling the fumes from the kerosene mingle with the cool river air at dusk, and gradually I got warm and dry. I must have dozed off for a moment or two, because it hardly seemed more than ten minutes until I felt the prow of the raft scrape against the rocky bottom of the riverbank and heard Billy Joe sing out, "All right, this is it! Maynard Street landin'!"

We came to a stop and Billy Joe put his head in the doorway of the shed. "We're here. Figgered this is closer to your place than downtown, even if there's nobody to send for your carriage. You just stay right there while I pull us in, and then I'll see that you get home safe."

We were home! I shook my head and tried to blink the sleepiness away from my eyes. Now was the time I would have to really get moving and be at my best. I could not afford to be tired. Maybe it was the fumes from the stove. . . .

I heard a noise from the front end of the raft, where out in the dusk Billy Joe was making us secure with the rope. I got to my feet and was heading for the doorway of the shed when my heart froze.

Stepping onto the raft, his bearded face twisted in an evil smirk, was Red Campbell.

I tried to bolt from the shed, but he grabbed me by the shoulders and shook me so hard that I could scarcely see. "Thought ya had it made, hey, bitch? Didn't even think I'd be smart enough to notice ya up there by the train? Didn't think I'd be able to get myself a horse and follow ya down here?"

Shaking inside, I forced myself to look him straight in the eye and speak in a level voice. "What have you done to Billy Joe? You're not going to get any money from me, I can tell you that right . . ."

"Shuddup!" He pushed me back into the shed roughly, making me stumble and fall onto the rough planks of the raft. "Your boyfriend up there on the bank'll wake up in an hour or two if he's lucky. By then we'll be gone downriver on this here pile o' logs, and I'll think o' some way to make ya earn your keep."

With a nasty laugh that made my stomach crawl, he slammed the door to the shed, and I could hear the sound of the wooden crossbar sliding into place. Even as I stood up and pushed against the door, I realized that I could never get it open by myself. I needed a crowbar, a lever, something to pry loose some of these boards. I looked around the shed, but there was almost nothing, only the chair and the little kerosene stove. There was no way I could begin to pry loose the . . .

And then I thought of it—the stove! It was a gamble, but I knew it was all I had, and even if I failed, I thought anything would be better than the prospect that awaited me now.

Quickly I bent over the stove and opened the grate. Using the folds of my heavy cotton skirt as I would have used hotmats to lift out a pot from the kitchen stove, I lifted out the metal canister of kerosene, burning wick and all, from the inside of that little stove. Then, praying that my hands would remain steady and that I would not get any of the kerosene on the folds of my dress, I slowly unscrewed the cap that held the wick at the top of the canister. It came loose with agonizing difficulty, but finally it was off. The top of the wick still burned over the cap, a bluish-yellow flame, but beneath the cap the wick was dark and wet.

I bent over the floor close to the front of the shed, and ever so gingerly I sloshed a little of the kerosene onto the boards of the wall. Outside, I could hear the front end of the raft begin to scrape over the rocks; Campbell would be pushing us away from the bank and out into the river. There was no time to lose. I sloshed more of the kerosene on the wall, somehow managing to keep my hands steady so that none of it spilled on me or ignited. Then I quickly touched the burning tip of the wick to the kerosene-soaked boards.

Instantly there was a loud rush of hot wind and a wall of yellow flame in front of me. I backed away quickly, still holding the canister, and I began to scream. Suddenly I was afraid that my plan would not work. What if Campbell saw the flames and decided to run away before they attracted a crowd? Would I be trapped here inside this burning box of wood? The heat was stifling now, oppressive. I clutched the chair with one hand and tried to imagine myself knocking away the burning wall to give myself a path to escape, but the flames were growing more treacherous and I doubted I would be able to get near enough.

I had backed as far away from the flames as I could and was trying to decide what to do next when the door was flung open. I could see Campbell's outline through the smoke and flames, and I heard his voice, snarling. "You Goddamned stupid bitch! What the hell did ya do? I'm gonna beat your . . ."

I did not wait to hear more. With all my strength I pitched the contents of the kerosene canister full in his face. There must have been at least a quart left in the can, and I had the satisfaction of seeing most of it splash squarely onto his chest and his neck. He staggered back, choking, clutching at his eyes, and I hurled the burning canister after him.

It struck his chest and clattered to the deck outside the shed, but its fire had done its work. Again there was that sudden roar of hot wind as the new flames took hold, lighting Campbell's shirt and his beard with a horrid yellow glare. I was partly terrified, but at the same time I felt the fierce, wild joy of revenge as he screamed, loud and harsh, as though the fire had penetrated into his very lungs.

He stood stock-still for a moment and the flames spread over his face and hair and down his legs. Why didn't he run for it?, I thought. Why wouldn't he jump into the water and get out of my way? The wall of the shed on my right was completely ablaze, and the wall behind me had started burning. The flames were only a yard away from me. I had to get out!

His scream suddenly turned to a momentary, mocking laugh, and to my horror I saw him begin to come toward me, into the shed, burning arms raised. . . .

Without thinking, I grabbed the chair beside me and held it up, feet first, to fend him off. Gathering all my strength, I rushed at him, lowering my head and jamming one of the chair legs squarely into his groin as hard as I could. He cried out in pain as I drew back the chair and then rushed forward once more, this time striking him in the chest. He staggered back. With a final rush I hit him again in the chest. Then, as he stumbled away from the door, I gave a last shove and pushed past him, out onto the deck of the raft. In another moment I was in the water, fighting the current that swirled around my thighs, praying that Campbell would not have the strength to leap in after me. Finally I stumbled up the rocky slope of the landing.

Only then did I look back. There behind me, the twilight and the dark, wide river were lit up by the strangely beautiful fire that now consumed the entire raft. Shed, deck, and all were brightly illuminated as the raft, rudderless, turned slowly in the current and drifted farther away from the shore, out toward the middle of the dark water. I could see the raft clearly, every burning inch of it, as it turned round. And I could see most of the river, too, in the light of the fire.

But I could not see Red Campbell.

PART THREE

VALLAMONT

THIRTEEN

By nine the next morning I was waiting for Judge Hawthorne in his downtown office, looking out his window
at the market square below. The morning was cloudy.
The carts and wagons I could see from here on the
third floor of the courthouse seemed to crawl at a snail's
pace as one farmer after the other tried to find an ad-
vantageous spot along the edge of the square, either to
load up from one of the stores or to stop and set out
his goods for sale to the shoppers who would soon be
coming by. It was early in the season, so there was not
much in the way of fresh vegetables and fruits; there
were only some asparagus and strawberries, and occasionally a basket or two of wild mushrooms or cherries.
Most of the carts that were setting up to sell had
brought in eggs, poultry, or jars of preserved vegetables.
Others carried loaves of bread and cakes, or quilts and
knitting done by the women of the family, a number of
whom had come along for the day's shopping and selling.

As I watched the crowd beginning to assemble, it

crossed my mind what Mother had said last night when I had told her of my plans. She had been loving and tender, of course, and very glad to have me home safe, even while she was still deeply grieved over the loss of Father. But she could not seem to feel the same determination I had for keeping Father's empire together. "I guess it's the woman in me," she said, folding her hands tightly in her lap, even as her gaze seemed to wander away from me to the portrait of Father that still hung over the mantel in the large parlor, where we were sitting. "I think it would be grand for you to do it, but I just can't picture anyone but your father being able to keep all those enterprises going at one time. Sometimes I couldn't see how even *he* did it! And how you'd be able to at a time like this . . ."

Her voice trailed off, and I could see her wet, glistening eyes as the glow of the table lamp beside her illuminated her face. I held my breath, feeling my own tears begin to come, but I knew at the same time that they would be of no help for the sorrow Mother would have to endure for . . . I did not want to think about how long.

Mother bowed her head for a moment and touched her small pocket kerchief to the corners of her eyes. When she looked up again her face was set in a smile. "Oh, Catherine, don't listen to me. Forget what I said. I'm just a simple girl at heart, and I never really did understand your father and all his business doings. Sometimes I think I'd have been almost as happy if Sam had stayed with the farming and I'd have just spent my time baking pies and knitting and mending his overalls the way I . . ."

Her brave smile broke, and so did mine. Moving to her side, I had wept with her there, quietly, until the tears subsided.

Now, in the judge's office, I wondered if I, too, might be just as happy taking a simpler path than the one I had chosen. Was there really a need to pick up where Father had left off? No one could possibly blame me for simply accepting whatever settlement the banks or the court gave Mother and me after Father's creditors had been satisfied. Judge Hawthorne would see to it that Mother and I were treated fairly and left with enough money to live comfortably. Then I would be free to try my hand at a position in the city or to visit friends. If I wanted money, there were plenty of wealthy men, and I was just as eligible and charming as any of the young women they sought out and married. I could visit friends in the city, enter society during the winter season after a decent period of mourning for Father, and by the next spring I was certain I could have my pick of the eligible men at the society balls—at least those who could appreciate a woman of intelligence, as well as beauty.

Or if I wanted to stay in Grampian, I knew that Steven Cottor would still want me. And, of course, there was Nathan McKay, unless his wife had somehow managed to win him back. As I thought of these two men, so different in all but their fierce independence, I found myself wondering what it would be like to be the wife of either Steven or Nathan. Both of them had tried to dominate me when Father's fortune was still a reality. What would they do, how would they treat me, if they knew I had no fortune left? And what would either of them do once he possessed the powers of a husband over me? It would be a comfortable and easy life, of course, and I would never want for anything in the way of clothes or jewels or entertainment. But would I be able to find happiness in that kind of a marriage?

I was surprised and even a little worried at how dispassionately I was able to consider these two men and the kind of future each of them would offer. Part of me said, quite sensibly, "Of course you'd be happy. You could soon win either of them over, fortune or no fortune. You could do as you pleased." Another part of me seemed to cry out, "Where is your love? What happened to the feelings you had? How can you think so coldly about picking and choosing?"

Oh, if only I really *did* feel differently!

But I knew, even as I berated myself for seeming to have become cold and calculating, that the feelings still smoldered as strongly and as deeply as ever. The shock of Father's death and the way both Steven and Nathan had disappointed me—these pains had numbed me on the surface, but only there. Beneath my calm, rational self, I still longed for the glowing warmth Nathan had aroused. And though I was ashamed to admit it, I knew I would also have to face up to the truth. I still longed for that painful ecstasy I had shared with Steven. Whether it was right or wrong for me to feel that way, the feeling for Steven was still there. Sooner or later I would have to come to terms with it and make my choice. Where was my real love? Or was it possible to really love two men at the same time?

Yet, even as vague, disturbing fantasies of wedding nights and honeymoon suites with Nathan or Steven drifted in and out of my mind and made my throat go dry, I heard Judge Hawthorne now in the outer office. And then I knew there was yet another feeling that burned stronger within me—a tight, solid knot of warmth between my breasts. This feeling I recognized; it was the heat of my own ambition, my will to meet a challenge and prevail. As its familiar warmth spread through me I felt harder, more alert. My mind was made up, had been made up, it seemed, for as long as I could remember. Steven and Nathan would have to wait. I was going to fight with all my strength and determination to keep Father's empire intact. There could be no thought of friends or travel or society. How could I even have imagined otherwise? Nothing was strong enough to keep me from what I had to do.

The heavy wooden door swung open and Judge Hawthorne, his gray hair shining and neatly combed, came directly toward me. There was a second chair by the window, heavy and wooden, like the one on which

I sat, and he drew it forward. His round red face showed his concern and sympathy as he sat down, his knees almost touching mine, and leaned forward.

"My dear Catherine," he began, "this is such a difficult time."

I held up my hand. "Please, Judge Hawthorne, I appreciate your sympathy, but that's the one thing I have no need for just now. I hope you'll understand. I've come in confidence, and I've come to ask for your help."

He leaned back slightly and regarded me for a moment, his fleshy features showing curiosity. "Well, of course, my dear. I'm happy to do whatever I can. Just what sort of help?"

I kept my hands folded primly in my lap. "Well, first I must tell you that I know all about Father's financial situation. Do you? And if you do, how many others know?"

The judge coughed, surprise showing now. "Indeed? He told you the bad news, did he? Well, he told me, too. Now, as for the others . . ." He held his lip between his thumb and forefinger as he thought, or pretended to think, for I suspected that he was just trying to decide what he was going to do if I asked him to cheat on the creditors and save Mother and me more money than we were entitled to by hiding some of our assets. He went on. "As for the others, I think it's safe to say that nearly all of the banks are aware of the situation by now. Your father's account books were found with him at the hotel, you know."

I nodded, chagrined that I had forgotten. Father had packed the books and taken them along with him. Well, there was no point in letting on that this was any surprise. "I'd discussed those books with him on the trip," I said. "I'd thought, however, that perhaps someone with some discretion might have been able to keep Father's affairs private—at least for a while."

His bulky shoulders lifted and then dropped again, but his expression stayed just the same: grave. He was not going to be an easy man to convince. As he sat stolidly silent, I could see he was refusing to accept any responsibility for the predicament Mother and I were in. Well, perhaps he was right. But I had to make him see that he did owe us something.

I shrugged, too, and then I leaned forward, speaking earnestly. "What's done is past," I said. "No sense in worrying about it. But do you have any idea why I've come to see you, Judge Hawthorne?"

He nodded. "You're a knowledgeable young girl. And let me assure you that I'll do all that I can for you and your mother when it comes to the settlement of the claims against your father's estate. Of course, as you know, there isn't going to be much left, and what there is now has come to be fairly common knowledge because those books were left lying around . . ."

I stopped him, touching his arm lightly with my hand. "That's not why I'm here, Judge."

I sat back then and waited for him to collect himself. Then, gathering up my own courage, I came directly to the point. "I'm here, Judge, because I don't want there to be *any* settlement of *any* claims against the estate now. I want things to continue just as they were when Father was alive. I know we have obligations to pay, loans outstanding, and so on. I want to pay them—but only when they're due to be paid! And in the meantime I want to build up our assets so that we'll be worth twice what we owe, instead of the other way around."

He was opening his mouth to speak, but I went on with the one last thing I had to get in just then: "Will you help me, Judge?"

His mouth stayed open for a few seconds. "Do you know what you're asking for, young lady?"

I kept my voice level. "I certainly do. I'm asking for each of Father's creditors to continue their loans—to me. I intend to take full responsibility for the management of Father's . . . of my properties. What I'm asking you is if you're willing to help me convince those bankers that my proposition makes good business sense."

He gave a shake of his head, but he could not keep from smiling. "Now, see here, Catherine, I admire your stand. I'm sure that this is just what Sam Rawles would want you to be doing. But have you looked at this proposition of yours the way the bankers are going to look at it? Why, they'd have to be plumb crazy to take you up on it."

I stiffened. "Are you saying that you don't think I could pay them back, that I couldn't make our properties grow until they were making enough profit to pay it all back? Because if you are . . ."

He shook his head and held up a puffy hand. "Whoa, there, now. What you'd do with those properties has got nothing to do with it. Wouldn't make a bit of difference to a banker, even if you had a fortune stashed away somewhere else and an ironclad guarantee that you'd be able to pay him back right on time. He'd still want a settlement right now."

Now it was my turn to be surprised. "I don't understand. If we settle now, none of the bankers will get his full payment. Why should any of them want only a partial repayment now if he could have a full repayment later?"

"Oh, come on, now, use your head. How would we raise the money for the settlement? Just answer me that."

"Why, we'd sell the properties, of course—the hotels, the mills, the lumber camps, the . . ."

And then I saw it. Oh, but I had been foolishly naïve! What would a bank want with interest when they had a chance to get a piece of my property! My frustration must have shown, but I was too concerned with this new challenge to try to hide it. Why should a banker wait for repayment and make the small amount of interest he had coming on our loan if he could buy one of the properties outright, and cheap, at a settlement auction? He could manage it for a year or two and make ten times what he would with interest.

"I see what you mean. If I could make a property

239

grow and make a big profit, why, so could a banker." I
paused, an idea growing in my mind. "Or at least that's
what he'll think he can do. I'm going to have to convince him that he can't."

The judge chewed his lower lip reflectively. Behind
his heavy eyelids appeared a glimmer of interest.
"You're talking like it could be done, you know that?"

I nodded. I had a plan now, and I was feeling more
confident. "I think I can do it. Can I count on your
help?"

"That depends." The eyelids and the gaze were
steady, motionless.

"It'll all be perfectly legal," I said quickly.

"Well, of course."

"And I'm not going to ask you for any money. I'm
not even going to ask you to release Father's bank accounts. I know the law requires you to prevent me or
Mother from taking the cash out of those accounts.
And, as I said, I don't want to be involved in anything
illegal."

He pursed his lips and looked at me curiously. "You
sure are Sam Rawles's daughter, all right. What is it
you want me to do?"

I cleared my throat, aware that a lot depended on my
reply. "There are six banks, I believe, that hold the
loans. I'd like you to invite their representatives to meet
with me. Tell them it's in connection with the settlement
of Father's estate, and phrase the invitation so that they
understand it would be to their advantage to hear what
I have to say."

He drew in a deep breath and then let it out. "And
then you're going to tell them they ought to let this
chance go by? That they shouldn't exercise their right
to . . ."

"I'm going to tell them why they'll make more money
doing it my way than by trying to pick apart the estate.
And when I finish explaining, they're going to believe
me."

He shook his head. "I can't for the life of me see how

they would. I sure as hell wouldn't. You're asking me to stick my neck out, to get six important men together ..."

"Not together—I'll want to see them separately, one at a time."

He gestured impatiently with the back of his hand. "Together or separately, it's the same thing. After they've listened to you, they're going to come to me and ask what the hell I'm trying to do."

"No, they aren't. They're going to thank you for protecting their interests and for helping them to avoid making a serious mistake. You mark my words. Just see if that doesn't happen."

"Catherine, I like your spirit, but I'm afraid I . . ."

"Before you make up your mind, Judge, just answer me one question." I leaned forward again conscious of the effect I had on him when I drew close, though he tried hard to hide it. "A few moments ago you said that you were sure Sam Rawles would be proud of what I was doing. Now, as I recall, Sam Rawles gave you a good deal of help on a number of occasions. And, no doubt, you helped him, too, so I won't ask you to do anything for me out of respect for his memory." I saw the corners of his mouth tighten and I smiled inwardly, knowing I had hit a nerve. The judge owed Father a number of favors—though I very much doubted that he would think he was obligated to pay them back to me. All I wanted to do now was to prick his conscience a little before I appealed to his self-interest.

"But here's the question I want you to think about, Judge. Sam Rawles knew how to return a favor. Don't you think his daughter will know how to do the same thing?"

There was a long moment of silence. I imagined the judge was weighing in his mind the possible benefits of having me as a rich ally or a poor enemy. Probably he was also dreaming up a way to get the bankers to me without committing himself. But I didn't care how he did it, or why, really. I only needed him to do it.

Finally he nodded. "All right, Catherine, I'll help you. I'll have them call on you in a day or two, after the funeral. Is that what you want?"

"Just as long as they're men with the power to make decisions on the loans. I don't want them to come and then just tell me they're sorry about Father."

His round cheeks dimpled into a wry smile. "Well, maybe that's all they *will* tell you," he said, "but they'll have the power to say more than that. You have my word. Now, tell me what you're going to say to those bankers that's so totally convincing."

Smiling, I stood up. "Well, Judge, I think it's best if you don't know that—just in case they don't see things my way. But you can tell them that I don't intend to just talk. I intend to show them something. And you can assure those bankers that they'll be most interested in what they're going to see."

He looked at me and shook his head in a fond, grandfatherly way. "Well, more power to you. Good luck." He stood up. "Incidentally, we're mighty glad to have you back. You had us worried there for a while."

I picked up my purse. "No more than I was, I can assure you." My voice tightened momentarily. "Tell me, have they found that man's body yet?"

"No, but they're still looking. Sheriff said he'd keep me posted twice a day until they turn something up. We sent word downriver and they're looking there, too. And we've raised the reward money, just in case somebody pulled him out alive. Won't be long before we hear something."

I nodded. "Incidentally, who was going to put up the money for my ransom? And who's putting up the reward money now? Did you take that out of our bank accounts before you froze them?"

Chuckling, he nodded, but I brought him up short. "Then I'll thank you to put the money back in again, Judge. Red Campbell's dead. And I'm not interested in paying anyone to recover his body. He's not worth a nickel. Besides, I'm going to have need of that money."

"For the settlement?"

"There isn't going to be any settlement, Judge. I thought you understood that."

"I hope you're right, for your sake."

"For both our sakes, Judge. Now, please make certain that the money gets back in today. Campbell's not worth losing even a nickel's worth of interest."

I spent the rest of the morning and all afternoon receiving callers and sending messages, keeping my head high and doing my best to make the upper-level men who had worked for Father understand that things were to go on as usual. At times during that whirlwind of a day I thought of Nathan and wondered why I had not heard from him yet. Surely the news would have reached him by now that I was back in Grampian. He could at least have sent a note. Was he away, gone back to Philadelphia, perhaps with his wife? For the first time I realized how little I really knew of Nathan McKay. I had found him so wonderful, so comfortingly *right* in the things he said and did. I had felt the certainty of my own heart, that I wanted this man, wanted to stay with him and share a glorious future. And yet he had taken himself away from me, and now, when I needed his support, he was still away.

That entire afternoon that I was home, my mind kept inventing excuses and explanations for Nathan's behavior. The whole situation had me disturbed and preoccupied. In fact, just before dinner I found myself in the middle of a conversation with a state senator who had called on me to pay his respects, and I was unable to remember a single thing the man had said thus far.

"Pardon me, please, Senator," I said, and excused myself, walking out of the parlor, where Mother and several other visitors were talking quietly. I went across the hall into the dining room, so that I could be alone and collect my thoughts somehow. I could not go on with this worrying about Nathan! It was time to admit it to myself: he had behaved badly toward me, and there was no way around that fact.

My reflection in the glass of the dining room window, even as I looked out at the garden and the trees outside, seemed to mock the certainty of my decision. Was I sure? How could I pass judgment without hearing Nathan's side? How could I . . . No! I knew that this continuous questioning had to stop. *Whatever* Nathan did or had done, I told myself, it did not change what I had to do. I was going to bring the Rawles properties under family control, and I had my work cut out for me. This was *my* task, not something to be shared. Even if Nathan appeared at the door and offered to help, I would have to say no. I was going to win on my terms, under my own control. Until I had gained that victory, there was no point in even reading a note from Nathan, in the event that he found the time in his busy schedule to write one.

So within my mind I closed a lid tightly on all thoughts of Nathan McKay. I found myself staring at the trees outside in the garden, looking at their fresh green leaves as if they were the men I would have to convince during the next few days. Could I back up what I had told the judge? I felt the warm rush of determination, and I knew that I could. It would be a hectic week, but I would get through it. After what I had endured, any life that included warm, soft beds and well-cooked meals was bearable. And now I would go back into the parlor and talk with the many important men whom Father had helped and who would now be useful to me. . . .

Then as I opened the dining room doors I heard a familiar voice from the front of the hallway. For a moment my heart seemed to stop, but then I forced myself to push forward to the vestibule, where he was arguing with Jared over whether or not I was at home. Those smoldering, dark eyes caught sight of me instantly.

"Catherine!" He was dressed for a formal call, a black cape around his shoulders, his ebony cane and white gloves in his hand. As always, he wore no hat.

The black, wavy hair looked slightly tousled. Had he ridden here rather than taking his carriage? Why did it have to be now, of all times? I steeled myself and gathered my strength, for I was going to need it.

"Hello, Steven." I came forward, interrupting him and cutting off the argument. "Thank you, Jared," I said. "You may put Mr. Cottor's things here on the stand. I'll speak with him in the west parlor."

In a moment Jared had withdrawn to open the west parlor doors for us. There I could talk privately with Steven, for I was not quite confident as yet of receiving him in company, especially in the company of those men who were now in the other room paying their respects to Mother.

I felt his hand grip my arm and I saw the concern in his eyes. No, I thought, I would not let Steven soften me. I had put him out of my life, vowed never again to . . .

"I was at the capital when I heard the news last night. I came at . . ."

"I suggest we have our conversation in the parlor, Steven." I pulled away from him and directed him down the hallway. "No doubt we shall both appreciate the privacy. . . . I let my voice trail off. There! Let him imagine what delights awaited him! Let him recall what he had done the last time we had been together! He would find today that he was in a different house with a different woman, whether he realized it now or not!

Once we were safely in the parlor and the doors were closed, I turned to him. "And, now, what news did you hear? That the man your father sent had killed Father? Or that the same man had kidnapped me and was holding me for ransom?"

"Don't go taking that tone with me, Catherine. You know perfectly well my father had nothing to do with it. Or do you? Perhaps you'd better tell me what happened. I didn't come here to argue." His expression

245

had hardened, but the eyes sought mine, probing, as if they could hold me helpless and subdued.

"A man named Campbell. Are you saying he never worked for your father?"

"I . . . simply don't know. But I will find out. And if he did, you will know about it. You have my word."

"Indeed," I said dryly. "You're saying that you'll give me the evidence that would put your father in jail. I shan't hold my breath until you produce it."

I could see that my sarcasm had stung him. His eyes narrowed. "You're talking like Sam Rawles's daughter, Catherine. What happened to the charming woman who wanted to end this family feuding once and for all? Where did all those noble intentions . . ."

"Don't talk to me of noble intentions! *Your* father is still alive!"

"You're talking foolishly, Catherine. If my father had wanted to kill Sam Rawles, he'd have done it long ago. But you're upset. I can see that. Perhaps I ought to wait for a few weeks until you've had time to come to your senses."

I flushed with anger. "Wait for what? If you have something to say, I suggest you say it now. And I'll thank you to keep your opinions about my mental capabilities to yourself! I'm perfectly capable of intelligent conversation, I assure you."

He shook his head. "You're spoiling our reunion, Catherine. I haven't the patience to bicker with you. Perhaps later . . ."

"Oh, you imagine there will be a 'later,' do you? Well, don't. You'll only be wasting your time. I have other things to do, and my future plans have no place in them for Steven Cottor."

His face remained expressionless for a moment, but I saw the flicker of uncertainty in his eyes. Then it vanished. His old mocking self-assurance had returned. "You're being foolish, Catherine. Do you think you can deceive me so easily?"

"My mind is made up." I kept my voice firm, though the emotions were building up inside.

"No, it's not. I could see that the moment you first looked at me today."

"You're imagining things. I have . . . more important matters with which to occupy my time."

"You may wish you did, but you don't. You haven't forgotten me. Stop pretending."

"You're wasting your time, and mine. I have business matters that need my attention, and I . . ."

"Business matters? What are you talking about?"

"You'll find out, anyway, so I suppose there's no harm in telling you now. I'm taking over the management of our family properties—mills, hotels, and all the rest of it. I intend to . . ."

"You?" This was the first time I had ever seen him look startled. "But that's absurd. Everyone knows by now that there won't be any properties left in the Rawles estate after all the claims have been satisfied. And, besides, what in the world makes you think you could . . ."

"I've heard enough!" I moved to open the door, but he blocked my path, grasping me by both arms, his eyes burning into mine.

"Oh, no, Catherine." His tone betrayed no emotion, but I could see from his look that his passions were beginning to get the better of him. Very well! I thought to myself. Let him explode! The more angry he gets, the more I shall be calm and controlled!

". . . not heard nearly enough," he was saying. "If you think I'm going to stand by idly and watch you make a fool of yourself! This isn't something you know, Catherine. It's a different world entirely. It's dangerous. Whether you're right or wrong makes no difference. Unless you know where the right bribes and threats have to go, and unless you're prepared to back the threats with . . ." He stopped and looked away for a moment.

"With murder—is that what you're saying? I think I

know about that well enough from experience, thank you." I tried to keep my tone cold, but despite myself I was beginning to feel the softening of desire amidst my anger at his superior air.

"Catherine, Catherine." He shook his head, and I found myself being drawn closer to him. "We both know it's a dirty business. What you've got to see is that you don't really want to be a part of it."

"Oh, don't I? You'd like to think that, wouldn't you? You'd like me to always be available for no one but you, always be ready the moment you wanted a bed partner. Well, I'm not your whore, and I don't intend to be. I'm afraid you'll have to . . ."

His grip tightened on my arms and I had to stop talking for fear that my voice would break. He said nothing, but he drew me closer so that I could feel the pressure of his thighs. I tried to stifle the warmth of desire that spread inexorably through my body. This could not be happening! I had to break away from him! I tried to look away, at the pale blue velvet sofa and chairs that stood mutely behind him on the carpet. I breathed in the scent of his cologne and hated myself for the longing that went through me then. I wanted his embrace, yearned for the fierce, demanding pressure, the touch of his cheek, the light warmth of his breath against my face. I tried to concentrate on something else, tried to listen for the other people I knew were in the house, but I could hear nothing here in this quiet, closed parlor except my own breathing and his, and the tempestuous beating of my heart. . . .

"Look at yourself. You know what you really want."

"That's not true. I . . . I'm going back to our guests. There are men I must speak to . . ."

"You're staying here," he said. His voice was soft with passion, and as he drew me to him the force of his own excitement added to mine and overpowered whatever resistance I tried to offer. Soon I could feel the wonderful sweetness of his lips, and as I closed my eyes the sensations swept away all other awareness before them. I could hold back my own passions no longer. I clasped him to me, feeling the warmth of him as he parted my lips and made me tremble. Helpless, I tried no more to control those desires that surged so powerfully. I moved against him recklessly, and for a long time we seemed suspended from the world.

At last he released me, letting me catch my breath and noting with satisfaction how the flush of passion had burned my cheeks scarlet. With his hands now locked behind the small of my back, he moved me toward him and then slightly away again, as if to prove how he could have done with me anything that he wanted to. He was smiling that same half-smile I knew so well. His eyes were pleased, victorious, but when he spoke he sounded strangely subdued.

"You see it now, don't you? I had to make you see, had to show you. You can't change it any more than I can."

My voice shook and I could feel the tears starting to come. "You haven't! You won't do this to me again!"

"I will, and you know it. We want each other. It's senseless to pretend that we don't. And it's even more senseless for you to set yourself up to be ruined, trying to keep your father's estate . . ."

"No!" I struck him across the face as the tears streamed down my cheeks. "That has nothing to do with it! You can't change what I'm going to do, even if"—somehow I knew I had to say the words—"even if you spend every night in bed with me. That's a part of me, too, and it can't be changed any more than . . ."

I realized what I had just admitted, both to Steven and to myself, and I could not go on. I tried to compose myself. But there he was, talking to me in that deliberate, yet strangely tender, voice, and the tears would not stop.

"I'm going to leave now, Catherine. I don't want to upset you any further just now. But don't try to pretend to yourself that I won't be back."

"I won't allow . . ."

"And don't get yourself involved in the lumber business. The fighting's too rough for you. This isn't a child's game."

"I'm not a child. And I can fight. I can fight Abel Cottor, and I can fight you, too, if it's necessary. You won't . . ."

"All right, be stubborn. You'll see how soon it is before you'll need help. I don't know how you're planning to save your father's property, but I do know that you're in a town full of 'friends' who are looking to get it for themselves. You're going to need help, and when you do, I want you to know where to come."

"Steven, you're insufferable! Do you really think . . ."

But he pressed me to him once again, brushing aside my protests, and when he finally let me go, I was too full of emotion to speak.

"I'll be in touch, Catherine." Then he opened the parlor doors into the hallway and was gone. Through the open doorway I could hear him casually greeting a congressman and his wife who evidently had just come in. I closed the door again and tried to quiet the storm that raged inside me. But even as I studied my reflection in the wall mirror and carefully wiped away the traces of my tears, I knew—Steven had regained his hold. Perhaps he had never really lost it.

It took me more time than I wanted to admit before I was finally ready to go back into the east parlor to gain the support of those important men whose help I so greatly needed.

FOURTEEN

When the first of the bankers appeared at our front door several days after Father's funeral, I was prepared to meet him. I had pinned up my hair and dressed in a black cambric with a very narrow white floral border. The dress set off my narrow waistline and full breasts to their best advantage, yet the lines were crisp and authoritative rather than suggestive, which was precisely the reason I had selected it. With the dress, a few deft touches of powder and rouge, and the quietly elegant aura of my coiffure, I hoped to conceal any traces of the fatigue I felt from the funeral and my two days of railway travel to and from New York City.

I studied my reflection in the mirror of the east parlor and was satisfied. My auburn hair shone in the morning light. My eyes sparkled with anticipation, though not, I noticed, in a way as youthful or as naïve as they once had. I looked alert, businesslike . . . or at least I hoped I did.

Behind me I could see Billy Joe Walker, fully recovered from Campbell's attack, looking appreciatively at my reflection in the glass. Billy Joe made a rather imposing figure himself this morning. When we were in New York City, I had had him barbered and fitted for several suits in a summerweight fabric. At my special request, and for a hefty fee, Brooks' had made up one of the suits in time for Billy Joe to bring it back to Grampian with him. Now his new white starched collar and tie set off his rugged, masculine good looks, and particularly his curly blond hair, which was now neatly parted and held in place with brilliantine. With his arms folded across his massive torso, a heavy .45-caliber pistol belted to his hip, Billy Joe cut an imposing figure, indeed.

From the way he was admiring me, though, it was plain that Billy Joe found my own appearance more fascinating than his new clothes or even the treasure that he now guarded in this room. Of course, he had tried to keep his desires hidden. Billy Joe had been brought up to respect a lady of property, and I was his employer now, able to command a certain distance. Still, I had felt him watching me longingly during the New York trip and again this morning. Billy Joe needed a woman. I would have to make certain he was paid for the week soon so that he had the money and the time off to relieve his frustrations in town. There were certainly plenty of women in town who would be only too happy to entertain such a strapping specimen of manhood.

But I needed him now. His striking appearance and his unswerving loyalty were absolutely essential to my plans.

"How do I look?" I asked, inspecting my reflection in the mirror. He blushed, taken by surprise, so I covered his embarrassment with another question. "Do I look like a hard-bargaining businesswoman? A difficult customer?"

He grinned. "I tell you, ma'am, I feel sorry for those poor bankers. They don't know what they're gettin' into here. You're gonna have 'em eatin' out of your hand."

"I hope you're right." I gave a final glance at my reflection and then went over to the carved ebony table where Billy Joe stood beside six large stacks of new fifty-dollar bills. There was nearly forty-five hundred dollars in greenbacks here on the table, divided into shares for each of the six bankers. It represented two years' worth of payments of interest on the loans Father had taken with each of the banks.

The money made an imposing display. The sun's light from the tall French windows behind the table made the stacks of bills seem to take on a luminous quality. Each stack was of a different size, according to the size of the loan. In front of each stack was an envelope with the name of the bank to which the money was to be paid. Inside each envelope was a statement to be signed by that banker, acknowledging receipt of the payment of interest, and extending the loan for another two years. It was up to me to make each of the bankers sign his receipt.

Outside the closed doors of the parlor I could hear Jared in the hallway bringing in the first of them. According to the schedule, that would be a man called Turner, from the Juniata Bank of Harrisburg, to whom we owed seventy-five thousand dollars. My hands seemed to tighten involuntarily and I deliberately relaxed them, feeling at the same time the fluttering of excitement in my stomach. I ought to have eaten breakfast, I thought, but it was too late now to do anything about that. What counted now was getting this man to see that his only choice lay in continuing my loan. If I succeeded with him, a major obstacle would be over. But if I failed with this Turner . . . I did not want to fail, I told myself. I would not fail. Nevertheless, I could not help facing reality: if Turner said no, then the rest would very likely follow his example. And even if they did not, I would still have to sell a crippling proportion of the estate to pay Turner's bank what we owed. And then it would be only a matter of time before . . .

I broke off my thoughts, determined not to show even the slightest lack of nerve. Too much depended on my performance for me to lose confidence now. What I was about to do was nearly all bluff, and unless I carried it off with perfect poise, I would have nothing left when it was over.

Jared opened the doors without knocking, as he had been instructed to do. At this side stood a middle-aged man, gray-suited and quite thin, with large ears and a big nose and a sharply pointed stare. Behind him, standing in the hallway, were several other men. I could not see how many from where I stood.

"Mr. Turner, is it not?" Jared was obviously distressed at having more than one person to deal with, so I thought it would be wiser not to wait for him to announce all the callers. "I am Catherine Rawles. Please come in. Perhaps you would be so kind as to introduce your associates."

The thin man nodded and walked directly to one of the chairs closest to the table. He stopped and gave a glance at Billy Joe and the stack of money as if they had been part of the furniture. His companions followed him into the room and took places in front of the sofa and the other chairs. Then the thin man spoke, gruff and matter-of-factly.

"How do, Miss Rawles. Name's Elliot, from Philadelphia First. Turner's this chap."

He indicated a balding, white-haired man on the other side of the table who looked as though he regularly ate and drank too much. This gentleman nodded at me and offered a perfunctory smile. His pink skin glistened with perspiration, even though the morning was still cool.

I knew what had happened, or I thought I did. They wanted to keep me from playing one against the other. Divided, they would be more easy to persuade, but if they stuck together they could crush me.

Well, if they wanted to play hard, I was certainly not

going to let an old curmudgeon like Elliot act as their spokesman.

I walked over to the round-faced Turner and shook his hand. "Hello, Mr. Turner," I said brightly. "It appears you have invited the others here with you. I count six all together, so I assume I am also speaking to Mr. Ridley, Mr. Otto, Mr. Jacobs, and Mr. Mawson?" I turned to smile at the group. "Please introduce yourselves, gentlemen, as I come around. I find it so much more pleasant"—here I gave a pointed glance at the thin Mr. Elliot and allowed a slight edge to come into my voice—"to know the *names* of my guests when I am speaking to them."

After I had shaken hands all around, I went behind the table where the money was. "This is Mr. Walker, gentlemen. He is here for security purposes, which you can understand are necessary. In a moment or two we should have the coffee and sweet rolls. Ah! Here they are. Please help yourselves."

I waited while Marie, a member of our kitchen staff, wheeled round the silver serving cart. All but Mr. Elliot took coffee and a roll, while Mr. Turner took two rolls.

"Now, gentlemen," I began, "let us get to the point of this meeting. I assume you decided to come as a group, rather than individually, as you had agreed, for reasons that seem good to you. That suits me perfectly, and it saves time. But just let me remind each one of you that if you would like to discuss different terms of arrangements with me privately, I am free for the remainder of the morning."

I paused and looked directly at Mr. Otto, whose bank held the loan with the lowest rate of interest. If he knew what the others were getting, he would likely be the first to want a private discussion.

I was beginning again when Mr. Elliott interrupted me.

"Far as I know, young lady, there won't be any terms to discuss. I promised Hawthorne I'd hear you out, whatever it was you had to say, but you'd better be quick about it. I've got a train to catch."

He sat back, his arms folded, crusty and unpleasant. I detested him, there in his rumpled coat and trousers, which he had not bothered to have pressed this morning, even though they were obviously of expensive fabric and tailoring. Probably he was the sort who would not have changed his socks, either, to save on laundry expenses. What a shame that this wizened little popinjay represented a loan of thirty thousand dollars!

Well, Father had told me that there was no being kind and considerate when you were dealing with a man like this. All they understood was a kick in the backside—or the threat of one. To them polite words were only a sign of weakness.

"Are you quite finished, Mr. Elliot?" I said dryly.

He blinked and then inclined his head a fraction of an inch forward.

"Good. I am sure we all understand now what a very busy and important fellow you are. Let me assure you that you are quite free to go at this moment. If you would like to tell your board of directors that today you refused to continue a thirty-thousand dollar loan with prepaid interest, then you are wasting your time here listening to me. You might just as well go, and I shall send full payment of the loan by the end of the week."

I turned my gaze from Mr. Elliot to the others, and then I smiled again. "You look surprised, gentlemen. Did you expect to find a penniless young waif who would weep and play on your sympathy with sad tales of her poor bereaved mother? Those of you who knew my father, gentlemen, will understand why this is not the case.

"But as for you, Mr. Elliot, I am inclined to judge you lacking in acquaintance with both my father and proper manners. Kindly remember to address me as Miss Rawles, and not 'young lady' if you have occasion to speak to me again."

He tried to retort. When I overrode him, he glared, but he remained in his seat.

"Now, gentlemen, you may be wondering how I can afford to pay Mr. Elliot, and, if I can, why I continue to tolerate his rudeness. Well, there are two answers to that, which I shall explain. No doubt you have already thought of the first yourselves: my father did have the foresight to take out a substantial insurance policy on his life. He neglected to list that policy among his assets in those books that you know about."

I paused. What I said about the insurance policy was quite true. We would have a note for twenty-five thousand dollars from the Lumberman's Mutual within the next two days. Judge Hawthorne had assured me of this. With that, and with the cash I had been preparing to pay as interest to Mr. Elliot, I would be able to pay his loan without selling more than a few shares of the various local companies that we held stock in.

"Of course, if all of you were to demand payment, as you know, that would be quite another matter. I would have no choice but to sell all our family holdings, quickly, and probably for a good deal less than their proper worth. No doubt, also, the banks that you gentlemen represent would be most interested in bidding on those properties, since many of them are of a very substantial value."

I leaned forward and tapped the piles of bills stacked before me. Then I walked around to the front of the table, speaking as I went. "I have asked you to come here today in order to show you why such a course of action would prove costly for your banks, and for your own personal reputations, also, if that course were to be followed on your own advice."

I indicated the money behind me. "Here, gentlemen, is money: fifty-dollar bills, representing two years' interest for each of your loans. If you extend the loans, the money goes to you. Now, with all my bank accounts frozen by law, where did I manage to acquire forty-five hundred dollars in cash? I shall be frank with you. After my father's funeral, I went by train to New York City. There I have a number of friends from my days in college, many of them from families of great wealth. For obvious reasons I shall not be divulging the name of the family that has helped me, but I can tell you that I have spoken to only one of my friends as yet. There are many more, many of whom I am sure would be more than willing to back me."

This was not quite the truth, but it would do. Actually, I had not even mentioned needing money when I had called on Lisa two days earlier. The money had come from a number of hardened jewelers in the narrow dark shops off Broadway. There I had taken Mother's emeralds, with her blessing, of course, and every last piece of the other jewelry we had in the house. We could buy more later, she had said, and in the meantime we could use copies. So in those grimy jewelry shops I had badgered and stood firm, had walked out and been grudgingly called back, and had generally had a full course in the arts of hard bargaining in order to get this money. Well, I was glad for the experience this morning.

"So, you see, you need have no fears that I would be unable to meet regular payments on what is owed you. And you have the added incentive, if you choose to follow my recommendation, of getting your interest money in advance—two years in advance, to be exact. What I am offering you are, of course, better terms now than those that you had from my father."

Mr. Elliot cleared his throat to speak again, but I held up my hand. "Please, Mr. Elliot. As I said, you are free to speak with me later if you wish to discuss terms. But the major question is not about the loan, which would make your banks some profit. You think you can make more profits by snapping up our mills and our lumber camps and hotels and the rest at bargain prices. Probably you have even discussed ways to, shall we say, 'cooperate' on the bidding if there were to be a bankruptcy settlement and sheriff's auction."

I looked at them, one by one, in their seats as I spoke and had the satisfaction of seeing both Mr. Turner and Mr. Otto avoid my gaze with guilty embarrassment.

"Once you bought those properties, though, gentlemen, then what would you do? Run them yourselves? Hire managers to run them for you? That involves great expense, and what I want to show you is that trying to take on a portion of the Rawles properties would be a very expensive proposition for you, indeed."

I opened a drawer of the table and brought out a large leather binder, which I opened to reveal several hundred pieces of paper of varying sizes and shapes. "I want you to look at these notes. As you may be aware, Sam Rawles had a soft spot in his heart when it came to lending money to friends or employees. He hardly ever refused. These are the outstanding notes that you see here, but I can assure you that many more than this have been paid off and returned. Do they amount to much? Not in comparison to the business properties. They're mainly for houses, furnishings, mules, tools—the things people need to get a good foothold. Together they don't amount to more than fifty thousand dollars, and the largest one here is this one for Frank Higschman's house, fifteen hundred dollars.

"But think of the amount of *loyalty* represented here by these notes. Here are nearly three hundred families that my father helped—and more than half of them are working somewhere on Sam Rawles's properties today. Do you suppose they're going to be as happy to work for whomever buys those properties? How do you think they'll react when the sheriff puts the pressure on them to pay what they now owe—as the sheriff must do, according to the law in a bankruptcy case? Think of the public hostility that you'd generate against your own banks. And if you doubt what I'm saying, you might ask any of the six congressmen and two senators who were speaking with me here four days ago. They'll tell you what the public opinion would be, and you can calculate for yourselves what that would do to the number of depositors you now have. I'm sure your competitors would be pleased to see the results."

I set the leather binder down on the table. "But let's suppose you go through with the sheriff's auction, anyway. You'd have one or two pieces of our property and an irate public. You'd also have some key employees who would have a grudge against you, the new owners. Father loaned to the *good* men who worked for him; the slackers didn't get close enough to ask. Those good men can help the operation if they're loyal, and they can hurt it badly if they're not."

I paused and looked each of them straight in the eye again. "I needn't tell you that sabotage in the lumber business is always a threat. And if you think that you could simply fire any man who appears to be loyal to Father's memory, let me just remind you that that man could easily get a place with our competition. And he'd take his knowledge of our weaknesses right along with him."

Mr. Elliot was on his feet, his sour face looking meaner than ever. "I've heard enough. You think you can scare us? Think again." He stepped forward, sneering at me. "I'm calling your bluff, *Miss* Rawles. Philadelphia First will expect full payment by the end of the week, or we will immediately file in the courts for a sheriff's auction and settlement. And I hope every one of you others"—here he turned to look at the rest, who were still sitting—"will have enough sense to follow my example."

With that he turned and walked out of the room, leaving the parlor doors open.

"Well, gentlemen, you heard Mr. Elliot's opinion. Perhaps he does not expect many public repercussions to travel as far as Philadelphia in the event that you all take his advice. But I would urge you to consider your own situations rather than his. Compare your certain profit"—here I placed my hands again on the stacks of bills—"with the risk and expense involved. Knowing the loyalty of Father's men as I do, I should estimate that within six months after you bought one of our properties at auction, the value would have declined even below what you had paid for it."

I looked at each of them again. "So the choice is yours, gentlemen. Do you have any questions?"

A few murmurs and glances were exchanged, and then after a moment or two the pink-faced Mr. Turner stood up. Speaking with more dignity than I had expected, he said, "I think, Miss Rawles, that the Juniata Bank will be pleased to extend your loan under the conditions you have described. As soon as I can arrange for the proper security to transfer the money, I shall be back to sign the receipt."

Despite my determination to remain calm and businesslike, I felt a tightness in my throat. As I stepped forward to shake his outstretched hand, my knees felt a bit unsteady. The relief must have shown in my face, for Mr. Turner's blue eyes began to twinkle in a protective, almost grandfatherly, way. He smiled, clasping my hand in both of his and pumping my arm up and down. "And may I say that I think you've performed brilliantly this morning! I have not the slightest doubt that you will take the Rawles family fortunes to heights . . ."

Mr. Turner was interrupted when Mr. Mawson, tall, gray-haired, and ramrod-straight, came up and good-naturedly put his arm around the smaller man. " 'Scuse me, Jack," he said, giving Turner's shoulder a healthy squeeze, "we can't let you have her all to yourself! Miss Rawles, it will be a pleasure doing business with you, and if you ever want to talk about extending your credit, I hope you'll remember Montour Federated."

And then the rest of them were crowding around me in a pleased and congenial swirl of conversation. Otto would have to confirm with other bank officers, he said, but the others were just as certain as Turner and Mawson had been. I had won! I felt almost light-headed at my sudden success. These formerly cold men were now friendly and jovial, chatting amiably about stocks and dividends and the appreciation in local real estate as though they saw nothing but high hopes and bright promise ahead for the family properties. I had won!

When the last of them had walked down the hall, where Jared was ready with their coats, I still felt exuberant. Behind me stood Billy Joe, relaxed now and smiling broadly. I turned to face him. "We did it, didn't we?" I said. "Lots of work ahead, but we've made a good beginning."

His eyes shone. "Good? Just good? Why, you tore into them stuffed shirts the way a ripsaw cuts pine! I said all along that none of 'em had a chance!"

He clasped his large hands together in delight and then held out his right hand in a gesture of congratulations. "I just want to say, ma'am, that it's been a real pleasure workin' for you. I always knew you were somethin' special, but now I see you're even more'n what I . . ."

"Oh, come now, Billy Joe." I shook his hand, my own feeling absurdly small in comparison. I patted him on his brawny arm. "You're talking as though we were home-free by now. This is only the beginning! We've got a long way to go before we're out of the woods. We can't spend too much time congratulating ourselves, even though I do have to admit that our trip to New York was time well spent."

"Oh, well, I know that's true," he said, looking away. "Just that I guess after today, after those fellas come back for their money, you aren't gonna have too much use for a . . . a security guard anymore around here. So, what I mean to say is, I guess I oughta be gettin' back up the river to the lumber camp, where I belong."

"Wait a minute, Billy Joe. Are you telling me that you don't like working here in Grampian? You'd rather go back to the camp?"

His big forefinger tugged at the inside of his starched collar. "No, ma'am. What I mean to say . . . it's just that . . . I don't want you to think I'm expectin' any more easy work, travelin' and so on, just on account of helpin' you get home last week. I aim to work for my pay."

I thought for a moment. Then I explained that I wanted Bily Joe to help with the security protection around all of the Rawles properties. As soon as the word spread that a woman was running things, I was bound to be tested. And I wanted to be ready. After some discussion, we agreed that Billy Joe would supervise all security arrangements and report directly to me about who was and was not cooperating. He said he would "need some gettin' used to" working in a collar and tie on a regular basis, but he sounded proud to accept the job. I was glad. Just the sight of him as our security chief would be enough to make my competitors think twice before they tried to damage us with any more sabotage.

I was still congratulating myself on this sensible use of Billy Joe's capabilities later that afternoon when I went to see Judge Hawthorne with the signed receipts from the five of our six creditors who had promised to extend our loans.

The judge's face crinkled up in a big smile when he saw what I had brought. "I'll be dad-burned if you didn't do it! What an amazing young woman you are! What in the world did you say to those fellas, and how the devil did you get hold of this much money?"

"Let's just say, Judge, that I have friends, and that I managed to get all but one of those bankers to see reason."

He shook his head, still smiling to himself, as he inspected the receipts. When he came to the one that still remained unsigned, he held it up between his pudgy thumb and forefinger. "I suppose you plan to take care of this one with the life insurance money that's due tomorrow."

I nodded.

"Well, then, having inspected these pertinent documents"—he cleared his throat and his voice took on an official tone—"the court now rules that a settlement in the estate of Samuel C. Rawles is unnecessary, and it will straightaway direct the banks now holding Rawles monies on account to release same on request to either Claire or Catherine Rawles whenever their claim is presented, et cetera." He handed me back the receipts. "That's what you came to hear me say, am I right?"

"More or less. I have to admit that I wanted to see the look on your face, too." I folded the receipts into my purse and stood, smiling.

He gave me a sigh. "Well, I'm glad you did it, Catherine, however you managed to get that money. And I hope I'll be able to give you some help again if you need it. Congratulations. I know your father would be proud."

He stood up, too, and then added, "I just hope it makes you happy."

I descended the marble staircase of the court house with my mind on a hundred things that had to be done: meetings; reports on the Eagles Mere Hotel; procedures for the managers to follow so they would have no doubts that I was in charge now; meetings with the mayor and city officials; an office for me, and a personal secretary. But when I came out through the massive doors and onto the wide courthouse steps, these thoughts were suddenly swept away.

There on the curb beside my carriage stood Steven Cottor. He was talking with Jared, but then his head came up and those dark eyes caught my gaze and held it. I stood stock-still there on the top step between the big stone columns, hating myself for the sudden surge of passion that blocked out all else. How dare he startle me like this! Everything had gone so well, in such good order, and now it was about to be disrupted by Steven Cottor. I knew that he would not be waiting beside my carriage merely to say hello and go off about his business! He would want me to come with him; he would make his demands until his own lusts were satisfied, thinking that I was too caught up in my own desires to resist. I remembered his last kiss, and the warmth that had flooded my body then began to reemerge. Seeing him from a distance, I remembered how well-proportioned his body was, with what easy poise he stood. His light gray suit, the polished black boots, and the lustrous black hair were enough to turn the head of any woman.

Lifting my skirts, I descended the wide stone steps slowly and carefully, telling myself that I had already faced down six men this morning and that I could certainly manage one more if I tried hard enough. For one thing, I could simply say hello and get into the carriage right away. For another . . .

"I recognized Jared," Steven said, coming closer and offering me his arm. His smile of greeting was restrained, cool, somehow. "I've got some good news I think you'll be glad to hear. I want you to come up to Vallamont with me and talk to Abel about something."

"Really, Steven, I . . ." The refusal I had prepared hung on my lips. Had he said Vallamont? A talk with Abel Cottor? Suddenly I felt unsure of my ground.

"Purely a business talk," he said as though he were reading my thoughts. "Some of my work in Harrisburg appears to be paying off. The Cottors may soon be in a position to do you some good—that is, if you're still thinking of becoming a businesswoman. As I said, it's something you should be glad to hear."

We reached the carriage. My head was spinning with emotions and contradictory thoughts. Had I not resolved to make my own way? But hadn't I also vowed to use whomever was necessary to further my plans? Obviously the Cottors did not yet know of my victory this morning. If they thought that I still needed help, they might be less guarded when we talked. Something might slip out. And I did want Vallamont—I *was* going to have Vallamont. And the only way to get it, I reminded myself, was to take it from the Cottors.

But could I trust myself with Steven Cottor? "I don't know, Steven," I said finally. "I really did have a very full afternoon planned. Can we wait until tomorrow morning?"

"I have to leave for Harrisburg tonight. I was hoping to see you this afternoon."

"Intending to call on me, no doubt, when you chanced to notice my carriage," I said, my voice cool and controlled. "How unfortunate that you could not have asked me a bit earlier, before I had made my plans. Then, again, I suppose you still expected me to be always waiting and available. . . ."

His voice hardened with exasperation. "I got the news this morning, and, as a matter of fact, I have already been past your house. Someone told me you had come here—that big redneck you've got all dressed up in a . . ."

"Oh, you mean Billy Joe?" I interrupted, delighted to see signs of jealousy in Steven's flashing glance. "Why, he saved my life! If it hadn't been for him . . ."

"Catherine! I didn't come here to talk about . . ." He stopped suddenly, as though his attention had been caught by something down the street on the next block. When he resumed, his tone was more carefully controlled. "Are you coming with me or not? Make up your mind. My carriage is just around the corner."

I considered the proposal for one more moment, congratulating myself on how well I had managed to keep control of the situation thus far. And I did want to see Vallamont again.

"Very well. Just wait here a moment." I walked over to where Jared was waiting discreetly by the horses. "Jared, tell them at home that I've gone to a business meeting and am to be expected for supper promptly at six. Have Billy Joe go around to Prescott at the mill and Lurie at the hotel to tell them I want to talk with them this evening at eight."

"Sure will, ma'am." Jared quickly swung up into the driver's seat. He might have been a bit stiff with age, but he was certainly doing his best to please his new employer, I thought, as he drove the empty carriage back to the house.

In Steven's carriage I learned what the good news was that he had received this morning. The bill he had been lobbying for was now out of committee in the state legislature. This bill amounted to a re-chartering of the Susquehanna Boom Company as an open corporation rather than a closed-stock concern. In other words, it enabled Abel Cottor, or any of the other Boom Company shareholders, to sell their stock to the public instead of only to each other.

It was a master stroke for Abel. His extensive holdings in the company could now be turned into cash at extremely high prices. This would give the Cottors more than enough money to ward off their creditors during the next few months as their loans came due.

On the other hand, it meant that Vallamont was yet another step away from my reach.

"Congratulations," I told Steven as we rode. "You must have worked wonders in the legislature."

He shook his head, not as pleased as I would have expected. He leaned back against the soft leather of the carriage's interior and folded his arms across his chest. "Money did it. I just planted the idea and saw to it that each little committeeman got his share. Tomorrow I'll be down there seeing that the rest of them are ready to vote for the bill when it comes out on the floor."

"You don't seem pleased."

"Well, in a way I am, I suppose. It's good that those old bastards who own the rest of the Boom Company can't keep Abel from selling his shares at what they're really worth. They wanted to make him practically give those shares away! You should have heard what our kind fellow shareholders were willing to offer when they thought they were the only ones we could sell to. It even made *my* blood boil. But that's the only real satisfaction. Playing the Harrisburg lobbyist doesn't exactly suit my temperament."

"Yet obviously you're good at it."

He cocked his head and looked at me sideways with an ironic smile. "As I live and breathe, that sounded like a compliment! What's come over you, Catherine? Or did you just mean it as an insult?"

I refused to allow myself to be baited. "Merely as a business judgment. I understood that we were going to discuss business matters. What is it that your father wants with me, anyway?"

Instead of replying, he shook his head slightly and glanced out the window. "We're almost there. I think it would be best if Abel tells you that himself."

FIFTEEN

The huge doors at the center of the castle turret closed silently behind us. The light from the turret windows high overhead filtered down, making patches of sun on the gray stones. Inside, the parquet-paneled hall was silent. I remembered that Abel Cottor employed no servants, except for those occasions when he was entertaining. The rest of the time he took his meals in town or ate, they said, with the woman who lived with him as his mistress.

"Let's see where Abel is." Steven led me across the carpet to the middle of the hall, close to the great, wide staircase, where he lifted one of the wooden panels. Behind the hinged parquet there stood a double row of speaking tubes. One by one, Steven removed their stoppers and spoke. "Abel? I'm here with Miss Rawles. Abel? I'm here with Miss Rawles. Abel?"

But one by one the tubes remained silent.

And slowly my suspicions grew stronger.

Steven glanced at the clock standing beside the wall of speaking tubes. "Damnation. It's only two o'clock.

I'd forgotten—he's not expected back until four. Took that woman of his into town to shop. Stupid of me to have forgotten the time. Now here we are with two hours on our hands."

He turned, ready, I knew, to take me into his arms. He was so confident, so certain that his charm would overpower me, as it always did! I felt indignation rising.

"You're wasting your time, Steven. It was a clever trick of yours, and very well done, but I came here to talk business." My voice was controlled, yet even as I spoke came the ache of longing. Oh, why did I have to feel this way? Alone in this house with him, my desire burned stronger than ever. I could feel the pulsating heat begin to flow, feel my senses quicken with excitement.

Steven looked down into my eyes. "It's too bad. I can see what you want. Such a shame, when we both want the same thing. . . ."

His fingers tightened their hold on my arms. "You're beautiful, Catherine. But I can see that same look in your eyes now that you had the first time I saw you. Do you remember? You were hiding something from me then; you weren't going to let on who you were. You didn't trust me. I think you still don't. You're trembling, Catherine. You know what you want, yet you still try to pretend you can go against it."

His voice became softer now, almost whispering with restrained passion. I shuddered. His words seemed to penetrate something vulnerable deep within me. I fought against them. I was hiding, yes, hiding my passion, and hiding my determination, too, my determination to stay independent, to possess Vallamont again. But, oh, how I wanted him, the sweet warmth of his lips, the hardness of his body against mine, the magical abandon I felt when we two moved as one. . . .

"We had to stay apart before, Catherine, but that's finished now. It's all in the past. We're together . . . you and I . . . you're still mine. . . ."

He lifted me to him, and I made no attempt to resist

as he covered my mouth with his, softly at first, then fiercely, making me gasp even as I welcomed his strength against me. My body seemed to glow with sensation, blocking out the small warning voice at the back of my mind. We were together now and the future would have to take care of itself. . . .

His lips stole to my throat, and I pressed him closer to me, burying my fingers in the black waves of his hair, savoring the feel of him all around me. I relaxed, letting his firm hands bear me up and then caress me, so that everywhere he touched seemed to melt, to loosen, to unfold.

Silently he led me up the stairs to a small sunlit room at the back of the mansion, a room that would have likely been a servant's bedroom if Abel Cottor had employed servants. The afternoon light shone brightly on the walls, the single oak chest, and the multicolored soft quilt that covered the simple bed. Steven closed the door behind us and then, with his face illuminated as he stood for a moment at the window, he closed the curtains and changed the atmosphere of the room into a cozy, shadowy softness. Outside I could hear the faint sounds of the forest, and occasionally the fresh-scented breeze would flicker the curtains and let the sunlight glitter all around us as Steven slowly, leisurely, began to undress me. One by one, the fasteners at the back of my dress came undone. Slowly he undid the catch at the back of my lace collar, and then he eased the dress forward and down as I drew my arms out of the sleeves. Then my dress had fallen to my ankles and the curves of my breasts were exposed above my corset. He kissed between them slowly, firmly, his tongue warm and exciting as I held him tightly against me and felt myself tremble with passion.

"I want you, Steven." The words came to my lips as I breathed. Had I said them? The swirl of feelings enveloped all my senses and swept all thoughts away just as a strong wind tosses a single leaf. My petticoats fell, then my corset, and he was cupping my breasts in his palms, his lips pressing on mine, his tongue probing, exploring, touching me in a thousand different ways. I clung to him as he set me down on the warm, smooth softness of the quilt, arching my back to help as he slid away my garter belt, trembling at his touch as he eased off each of my stockings and let them fall softly to rest themselves atop the rest of my clothes.

I knelt before him on the bed, clad only in the thin silk drawers I had put on this morning, when my thoughts had been so far from the power that now held us both. I felt the warm tingle of moisture grow within me as I looked him straight in the eye and began to unfasten his collar. In a moment or two his shirt was unbuttoned and he stood up, taking off his coat and shirt. The muscles played across his torso and his back as he draped the garments across the top of the oak chest and then bent over to remove his shoes and trousers. The scar across his back, the curve of his thighs, the smooth ridges of muscle at his abdomen as he turned, naked, to face me—they were all familiar, yet my breath still caught in my throat and my heart raced faster. There was no turning back. I knew what I wanted, had wanted, would always . . .

"Take them off, Catherine." He stood before me, locking my gaze with his, then savoring his prize as I slid the silk down over my legs and then stretched back, luxuriously naked, reclining on the bed as though I were an artist's model.

"Beautiful."

"For you, Steven."

"From the first."

"Yes, darling, from the first."

I opened my arms and he came to me, our bodies touching in a delicious cool pressure that grew stronger, warmer. We embraced, his tongue finding mine, his arms tight and hard and his hands, smooth and powerful, drawing mine to him. Then he entered me in a slow, sensuous thrust that awoke every dormant nerve and sent currents of sweet fire racing through my veins. I clung, rising, moving with him, every motion more exquisite than the last, wanting only him, the feel of him, the scent of his maleness, the hard roundness of his back, his buttocks under my hands. The tides of passion rose as he quickened, his thrusts driving away all restraint. Soon I moved beneath him, open, abandoned to a pulsating magic that grew ever more forceful, possessing us, bearing us high up to an infinite dark summit where time and sense hung suspended, motionless. Then as Steven cried out, shuddering, a mighty rush of feeling seemed to burst forth from within me, and the two of us plunged headlong down the slope of a great, curling wave that came crashing over us, throbbing, surging, and then slowly, slowly ebbed away.

I felt his muscles soften as the peace enveloped us. The calm, soft emptiness held us together while I pressed him close to me, sighing a little, savoring the warm glow that he had awakened once again. I closed my eyes. It was so lovely here in the quiet protection of his strength. From somewhere halfway between deep sleep and wakefulness, I drifted for what must have been several minutes. Before he stood up, he kissed me lightly on the mouth.

Sometime later, after I had dressed, I came downstairs to find him in the library. Beside his green leather chair on the polished ebony table was a decanter of bourbon. The glass in his hand was half empty.

The dark eyes flickered over me as I entered, then glanced at the mantel clock. "Not a hair out of place," he murmured almost as though to himself. Then he lifted his glass to me and drank.

"Rather early, isn't it?" I crossed over to him, touching his hair lightly with my fingertips.

"Never too early. Want some?"

Something in his manner made me wary, distant. Why was he drinking? After what we had shared, what could . . . and then I remembered that Abel Cottor was coming.

"I think I can face your father without that," I said.
Then something made me say, "Why can't you?"

The remark stung him. I could see he was making an
effort to control his temper. He set the glass down on
the table, then stood up and walked me over to another
leather-upholstered chair. Speaking evenly, he said,
"There are things you don't know yet, Catherine. I have
an idea what Abel is going to say this afternoon; you
don't."

Now it was my turn. My temper began to flare up at
his aloofness, his sudden making of himself into some
sort of stranger from me so soon after what we two had
just shared. "Oh, I don't? Why don't I? Whose fault is
that? Or don't you think you need to be considerate,
now that you ..."

"Stop it, Catherine. This has to do with business. It
has nothing to do with the two of us."

"Except for the fact that you know that I'll be glad
to hear about it. Isn't that what you told me earlier? Or
was that the truth?"

I looked at him, searchingly, while his face remained
impassive. But I could read the answer in his eyes.

"You lied to me, didn't you? What is it that Abel
wants? Tell me!"

He gave a sardonic smile, then a momentary silent
breath of bitter laughter. "Abel's going to speak for
himself. Maybe he's changed his mind, though I doubt
it. In any case, you'll hear him soon enough."

There was the sound of carriage wheels on the gravel
outside.

"What makes you so certain that I won't be pleased
with what he says?"

"Because I know you, Catherine. I know your temper, I know the way you react, I know the way you
feel about your father ..."

"My father? What does this have to do with ..."

"I told you that Abel would speak for himself. But
before he says anything, I want you to know that the
only reason I had anything to do with it was because I

think it could be worth a great deal of money to both of us."

"Is money so important?"

"You seem to think it is. Aren't you the one who's trying to run the Rawles properties and pay off his debts?"

"Why are we quarreling now, Steven? We were so close . . ."

He shook his head slightly, the eyes half shut even as he interrupted. "Can't be helped. That is the way we are. This is the way things are. Maybe when you think about it we'll be together again."

"What are you talking about? What do you mean with this . . ."

But he simply closed his eyes. Voices came from the hallway outside. In a moment the library doors opened wider and there stood Abel Cottor. A tall, exceedingly attractive woman stood just behind him, eyeing me nonchalantly.

"Well, Miss Rawles, glad you're here." Abel turned to the dark-haired woman. "You want to go upstairs now," he said. She shrugged, her painted features seemingly indifferent, though she continued to look at me for a moment before she turned to go. A glance from Abel made her move a bit less slowly, though it was plain that she resented his not having introduced her. I remembered the closed room on the fourth floor the night of the ball, the room where Steven had said she had secluded herself. How painful to have to endure that kind of disrespect from a man! Her life before Abel must have been dreadful, indeed, for her to continue subjecting herself to such indignities—although Steven had said that Abel had taken her shopping in town. . . .

Abel had come expansively into the room, taking off his black wool coat and flinging it over a chair. His close-fitting white shirt brought to mind the first time I had seen him, that Saturday afternoon when he had directed the tormenting of Warren Ruch. I would have to remember that side of his character, whatever his offer was, I thought.

He nodded briefly at Steven as he took the chair behind the polished ebony table. His gaze took in the decanter and Steven's near-empty glass. The teeth showed white as his leathery face creased into a smile. Would Steven look that hardened someday?

"Well, now, Miss Rawles"—he took a long, thick cigar from a leather box on the table—"mighty sad business about your father. Wanted to come to the funeral and all, but I didn't. I knew folks'd start talkin', and I didn't think you'd want that."

I kept my voice neutral. "Yes. I understand from Steven that you have some business you want to discuss."

He lit his cigar and then blew a slow cloud of gray smoke toward the ceiling, as though he were making up his mind about something. "Well, fact is," he said, still looking up into the air, "I wanted to get somethin' else out of the way first. You see, I know that the fella who shot your father used to work for me." He brought his eyes down level with mine and looked straight at me now as he spoke. "But he wasn't workin' for me then. I fired him right after I learned he'd shot up that night watchman at your father's mill."

Was he telling the truth? Instinctively, I glanced over to where Steven was sitting. Arms folded, he gave a barely perceptible nod of agreement. But would Steven be capable of lying to protect his father? I considered the idea, then dropped it. It was unlikely; there was little love lost between the two of them. And even if I could somehow prove it, what good would that do? Abel was not fool enough to have left any evidence that he had ordered Red Campbell to kill my father.

"Instead of just firing him," I replied, "you should have had him arrested. But that doesn't help matters any to say it now. What's your proposition?"

He grimaced, though I could see he was still not about to lose his temper. Whatever he was going to propose, it was clear that Abel wanted it badly enough to stay on my good side.

"I'm trying to make you see the background, Miss Rawles. If you want to remember that I was fightin' your father up to the end, fine. I was. Just don't take it too far. I wanted to beat him; he wanted to beat me. No gettin' around it. But I didn't want him dead."

"I should imagine he felt the same," I said dryly. "The two of you certainly had enough opportunities to kill each other before now. But I don't see why you put so much weight on it."

The tip of his cigar glowed red. "You will. What I'm proposin', Miss Rawles, is a . . . let's call it a workin' alliance between our two families. Now that your . . . that the argument between your father and me is past, I think that's possible. And I also think that you'll agree with me when I say that the Rawles and the Cottor properties together would make the largest single power in the region's industry."

"What sort of alliance are you talking about?"

"Well, for one thing, I understand that you're now in need of help to stave off a few hungry banks that'd like a piece of your holdins'. I could provide some political pressure"—he looked over at an impassive Steven— "and possibly some capital. Steven may have mentioned that we expect to be sellin' our shares in the Boom Company in a short while, and that will generate, as you probably know, considerable revenue."

I nodded, but I said nothing. Abel would have a surprise coming to him when he learned that I no longer needed help with the bankers. There was no point in lying to him, but there was no point in volunteering the information, either.

He raised his large gray eyebrows. "What's your reaction? Would you like that kind of help?"

"Mr. Cottor, my father told me never to comment on part of a proposition without hearing the rest of it first. I've always thought that was good advice, and I intend to follow it."

He nodded. "Most commendable. Well, then, I would also give you the benefit of my experience and guidance in matters concerning the . . . management of what are now the Rawles properties."

"Oh? Are you trying to say that you'd want to run our holdings? Because if you are . . ."

He held up his hand, interrupting. "No, I'm talkin' about somethin' different from that. I want you to keep an open mind now. I'm talkin' about a different kind of relationship between our families, and I'll need your help if it's ever to come about."

"What sort of help?"

"Miss Rawles, let me ask you somethin'. You know that your father and I were enemies." He rubbed under one eye with his forefinger. "But do you know the cause of the quarrel? Do you know what started it all?"

I shook my head no, then waited. No doubt he was going to recount some past injury Father had done him, something I would never be able to prove.

"I see. Well, it goes back twenty years—nearly as far back as you are old. In fact, as I recall, you were not even a year old at the time."

"You seem to have a fairly accurate memory of my age," I said, keeping my voice disinterested. I had to keep reminding myself that this man was not to be trusted, that he was dangerous.

He tapped the ashes from his cigar. "As you will see, I have good reason to remember that detail. Back then in Grampian lumber was not yet the big business it is now. Your father and I were just getting started. We each had our own mill, but we were friendly then. The two of us got the Boom Company started by workin' together, in fact. Each of us knew that there was a lot to be made in lumber."

A pause; he leaned back in the chair, reflective. "In Grampian at that time there was a woman. Let me tell you her story. Her husband was workin' very hard, very long hours, meetin' important people. She was expected to meet them, too, to entertain, to charm them, bring them around to her husband's camp. Well, she was good at it, though she really hadn't been brought up that way. She had a plain-folks charm. Wasn't fancy, didn't put on airs. But she was mighty attractive.

"Well, to make a long story short, she charmed one fellow so well that he fell for her. Couldn't get her off his mind. Seemed like every time he saw her he didn't want to leave. And one day he learned that she felt the same way about him. It didn't matter that they were both married; they still felt that way. And what happened then is what men and women usually do when they . . ."

"Mr. Cottor, are you trying to tell me that my father seduced your wife?"

He shook his head. "That woman was Claire Rawles, Catherine. And I was the man. And after a decent wait, I aim to marry Claire if she's willin'."

He spoke so calmly; That deep, resonant voice made it all seem almost the right thing to do, so sensible, so concerned! It took a moment or two for the statement to register, for the things I had heard Mother and Father say about Abel to come back. "After twenty years," Mother had said. And I thought about that threatening manner Father always took with her whenever Abel's name came up. . . . It had to be true.

But even as I sank down for a moment at the shock of what my mother had done, my anger began to boil. All these years that Abel had fought, hadn't he made Mother suffer, too? Hadn't she cried along with me the night Father told us about losing Vallamont? Hadn't Mother made her choice? And now . . .

I stood up, furious. "You dare to talk about this to me, with my Father hardly even buried? A 'decent wait,' you said. What kind of decency is it to talk about profits and business and then slander my mother . . ."

"Ask her yourself if you don't believe me. I can show you her letters."

"I don't care! What kind of man would marry a woman for profit! What kind of man would walk in to discuss my mother's marriage and flaunt his mistress in my face!"

I strode to the doors and pulled them open. Steven was behind me, his face grim. I would have slapped him if he had come any closer, but instead I fairly shouted. "And what kind of man would say that this was all going to be 'purely business'? Who would let me come up here, *bring* me up here, knowing I was going to have to listen to . . . such insolence! I never want to set eyes on you again! And don't think that I'll be back because I need your help. I don't. I have plenty of money now, and I intend to use it to bur——"

"Your goddamned temper!" His voice cut like a knife. "You're so . . ."

"You told me I'd be glad to hear it!"

". . . blind! You think . . ."

I slammed the doors behind me, and then I was running down the carpeted hall, my skirts swirling around me, barely conscious of the astonished look on the face of Abel's mistress, who had been waiting on the stairs and had probably listened to every word. At the end of the hall, the door to the turret was open. As I pushed at the heavy outside doors I heard Steven's voice, harsh with fury.

"Then go! And be damned if I'll ever . . ."

The voice faded. I was outside. The gravel under my feet, the dark green woods before me, even the blue afternoon sky seemed cold, intrusive, unfeeling. Yet, paradoxically, I welcomed it. The hardness gave me a strange kind of comfort as my own will to fight surged up and gave me strength. If this was the way things were in this wicked world, then so be it! I knew I could fight; I knew I could win. I had been a fool to let Steven tempt me, a fool to give myself to him the way I had!

But I was done with softness now! With a chilling certainty, I knew that I would never give in to Steven Cottter again. I had my empire now. My work would give me satisfaction, comfort . . . and, yes, revenge. At the edge of the clearing, just before the road started its downward slope through the woods, I turned for one last look at Cottor's Castle. The western sun glittered on its leaded glass; the yellow stones of the walls and towers stood awash with light. The polished wood and brass of the huge turret doors shone rich and brilliant. Let them enjoy it while they can, I thought.

Then I set off down the road, determined to reach home before sundown.

The next few days were, if anything, filled with more activity than previous ones. There were the payrolls to be met; the hundreds of buyers and sellers to meet or correspond with; the multitude of small decisions to be made by the managers and to be checked, during this beginning period, by me. My new hard spirit of combat served me well then. Those who were inclined to question orders sensed that I was not about to tolerate insubordination, and those who might have tried to put on condescending airs because I was a woman were soon brought up short. My orders were harsh and to the point when they had to be. More than one man came into my office strutting and insolent, only to leave red-faced and crestfallen.

That first week I made my first major decision, as well. I had sent for Malory to come down from Eagles Mere with a full report on the hotel and how things stood. He was candid. Father's murder, widely reported by the papers, had ruined the opening. Even though Malory had put together a smooth-working staff, only a few guests had come. Most of the reservations for the month of July had been canceled, and there had been only one or two letters to inquire about future visits. Meanwhile, there was the staff to be fed and paid, and we were stuck with the large supplies of food that had been brought in to feed what we had thought would be a multitude of guests.

I decided to close the hotel for this season. We would turn Eagles Mere into a lumber camp instead. We would take some of the best men from each of the two

camps and the mill and send them up on the train to
live in the staff quarters. On either side of the railroad
track, they could cut down whatever looked to be
promising timber. Each day's lumber would be brought
back to Grampian on the train. We would save money
on raftsmen's wages and on boom storage fees—and
we would get the logs sooner. At a time when we were
hard-pressed for lumber to fill our orders; this was an
idea that had to work.

I worked very hard during those early days. I rose
before dawn most mornings so that I could be at the
mill or the hotel or the gas works or wherever I was to
visit before work began. I liked to set an example. The
word quickly spread that there was no telling when or
where I might arrive next, and while this made some of
my managers unhappy, it seemed to do wonders for the
morale of the men in the ranks. They became quite
fond of me, or so it seemed from their manner when I
appeared. Of course, my days where not all spent
simply on tour. Most of the time, in fact, I spent in the
office going over sales and promotional schemes, expenses, orders, and the like. I also talked with my
assistants and local officials about what else Rawles
enterprises could do for the Grampian area. There was
talk of an amusement park out on one of the small
islands in the river, about new gas and water lines to
expand the city limits, and, of course, about Abel Cottor's finances. For a man who had notes coming due
soon, he was spending lavishly, or so they said at the
stock exchange. Rumor had it that Abel had invested
enough for a month's payroll within just the past week.
Evidently he was very sure of himself.

I tried to work hard enough so that I would not think
about Steven. I spent nights poring over figures, dic-
tating instructions, so that when it came time to retire
I was too exhausted to think. But the dreams were
there. Visions of Steven would drift into my mind after
I had closed my eyes, or I would awaken in the morning
with the thought of him still fresh in my mind. I told

myself that I would get over it. I willed him away from my waking hours. For a few days I half-expected that he would make some sort of attempt to talk to me and apologize, so I allowed myself the luxury of imagining how he would act and the harsh and cutting words I would use to reject him.

But after a week had gone by, I still had not heard from Steven. It was then that I began to think seriously of how I would get Vallamont away from the Cottors.

It was also a week to the day after I had last seen Steven that I received a note from Nathan McKay.

His divorce was final now, and he wanted to speak with me.

The note took me by surprise, and I hesitated before making an answer. Was it wise to think of Nathan when I was so completely occupied with business matters? Other than my vague fantasies of how I would reject Steven, I had not permitted myself to think of another man, even though each day seemed to bring yet another suitor who fancied he was talented and charming enough to both captivate me and take care of my business affairs in the bargain.

Well, I thought, as I jotted down a reply, I could take care of myself. I was Sam Rawles's daughter, and I knew how to deal with fortune hunters. And, thank goodness, Nathan had a fortune of his own.

One evening the next week I was at my desk in what had been Father's office, going over some accounts, when Jared brought in the card of Dr. McKay. I held it for a moment, wondering.

"He's in the vestibule, Miss. I told him that you were at work."

"That's all right, Jared." I put the card back onto Jared's silver tray and smiled. "Show him into the east parlor and tell him I'll join him presently."

I looked at the account books and thought for some reason of that terrible afternoon in Nathan's office when I had stood before his desk and heard him say that I was not to come to his clinic again. And now he was waiting for me downstairs. There would be certain satisfaction in letting him wait there for a time, I thought, remembering, too, the abrupt way he had treated me at the train depot. But, then, what would that accomplish? He was here now, and even though I did not like to admit it, I still did not fully know how I felt about Nathan McKay. Nor, really, did I know how he felt about me. There would be nothing gained by waiting any longer to find out.

He was standing at the French windows, watching the twilight fade above the shadows of the garden. When he heard the door open behind him, he turned.

"Catherine." The blue eyes were clear, his lean features open and tranquil. I felt more at ease almost at once.

"I'm glad to see you here, Nathan."

He came to me then and took my hand. "I wanted to be with you sooner. I hope you knew that. In fact, there were times when I wished that I'd not left you at all. I can still remember one morning in Philadelphia when I read in the newspaper about your father."

"Let's not talk of that, all right?" The words came out easily, comfortably. I could say what I felt to Nathan. I began to be even more certain that I had done the right thing in allowing him to call on me.

SIXTEEN

One evening at the end of August Mother came into my room while I was at my dressing table. I was brushing my hair, getting ready after the day's work for a dinner party Mother was giving for Nathan and me. On my left hand glittered a very large diamond. Nathan and I had announced our engagement two days before.

Mother looked well. She had just returned from a month at the home of friends on the beach at Newport, and the salt air and sun had given her cheeks a healthy glow. Tonight she wore a pale green silk dress with a wrapper of white cotton lace. This was the first time she had not worn black since Father's death.

I saw her reflection in the glass as she came in. "You're looking quite well," I said. "I should think we're likely to see a migration to the beaches once the ladies catch sight of what agreeable things the ocean climate does for one's appearance. Did you have a good day?"

She rested her hand lightly on my shoulder for a moment. "It was good to be busy again. I must say the staff in the kitchen has kept on its toes since I left." She fingered the white lace wrapper. "I know there's going to be talk about my coming out of mourning after not even three months. But Sam wouldn't have wanted it tonight. He'd be happy with your choice. He wouldn't want anything to detract from the celebration."

"I'm sure you're right, Mother. He would have approved."

She crossed over to the blue velvet settee, where she could still see my reflection clearly. She was silent for a moment after she had sat down, one hand touching her brown hair lightly, absentmindedly, as though she had forgotten something.

Then abruptly she asked, "Is that why you're doing it, Catherine?"

"I beg your pardon?"

"Because your father would have approved? Is that why you're marrying this Nathan McKay?"

"Why, no, of course not. Whatever would give you that idea?"

"A mother can see things. When I look at you, I don't see a woman in love. Of course, there are other reasons to be married. . . ."

"Oh, nonsense, Mother. Of course I'm in love with Nathan. I've just been working hard. That's why I don't look all starry-eyed. I'm tired, that's all." I could see that easily enough for myself. After more than two months of working twelve or more hours every day but Sunday, my features had certainly lost some of their youthful softness.

"Then I think you ought to have a vacation. Take some time to rest before you make your . . ."

"I'm perfectly well, Mother. I've been making decisions every day, and we're making more of a profit now than we were before. Even with the new Eagles Mere lumber camp, we've got more orders than we have stock to fill them with, and I've already been able to reduce the principal on three of our loans."

Mother raised her eyebrows and shook her head

slightly, her green eyes steady. "That's not the kind of decision I'm talking about, dear, even though you're doing very well, indeed."

"I'm almost ready to get Vallamont back from the Cottors! I can't stop now!"

"But are you happy?"

I spun around to face her. The rather severely cut brown jacket and dress that I was still wearing after the day's work suddenly seemed drab, almost unfeminine, and for a moment so did my success. What nonsense! How foolish even to waste a moment thinking that way! "Of course I'm happy. I'm doing what I set out to do, and I'm succeeding."

"I know that, dear. And I think it's just wonderful. Lord knows I'd not be able to manage things as well as you've done. But I'm wondering is whether it's Nathan McKay who's making you happy. Or would you be just as happy if it were someone else?"

I considered this for a moment, reminding myself at the same time that Mother really had my best interests at heart. It was not like her to meddle; whatever her reason was for questioning me about my engagement, it must have seemed important to her.

But it would not change my feelings for Nathan. I chose my words carefully, trying to think it through for myself even as I told Mother. "We get along well. Of course, we've both been busy, but that seems to help, really. I can see things that he could do with his investments, and he does the same for mine. The way he did so for Vallamont would be a case in point. He knows I want it back for us, so he's helping me break the Cottors. In a few more weeks they're going to have to sell it to me or go bankrupt. And I couldn't have done it without Nathan's help."

Mother's eyes widened with interest. "Do you want to tell me what you've done?"

"Well, it's quite simple, really. The Cottors are counting on a new charter for the Boom Company so that they can make a big profit selling their shares to the public. And the legislature has just passed a bill approving the charter they need."

"Abel must be pleased with himself," Mother said dryly. "He always did like to think he had the knack of bribing those scalawags in Harrisburg. The way he used to talk, he was the one who singlehandedly got the original charter approved."

Something in Mother's tone of voice made me recall what Abel had said about her. It had seemed so true then, but was it? She certainly wasn't talking about Abel as though he was once her lover . . . but it was foolish to waste time speculating about the past. I would never ask her about it; I knew that. I knew she had loved Father very deeply, and I was not going to do anything that would spoil the way she remembered him now.

I brought my attention back to the present. "Abel's going to have a surprise, though. That charter bill isn't law until Governor Hartranft signs it. And it so happens that the governor is an acquaintance of Nathan's."

Mother nodded. "So it won't be long until you've got the Cottors in a fix. I wouldn't look for Abel to give in without a fight, though. He's a treacherous old dog!"

"Don't worry, Mother, we're ahead of him. We've even worked out the details of the sheriff's auction, just in case he refuses to sell Vallamont when we make him the offer. Nathan worked it out, and I've seen to the details myself. Unless something unforeseen happens, I'll be the only bidder when Vallamont comes up."

"Nathan seems to have thought of everything. Is that why you're marrying him? Surely he's more than just a good business partner."

I blushed, indignant. "Of course, we're attracted to one another, if that's what you mean. Even though we're both quite busy, we have our private moments." And this was true, I told myself. Of course, our passion was not the same as that intense compulsion I had known with Steven Cottor. It was not even as intense as the initial way I had felt about Nathan that early morning when the two of us stood beside the stream above the lumber camp. The times we had shared during the past months were more quiet, more comfortable, somehow. And that was good. I had suffered enough from passion, I told myself. I wanted never again to lose myself to Steven Cottor, or to anyone else like him.

But how could I explain that to Mother? Well, there was no reason to. I didn't have to justify myself. It was my choice to make, and I was making it. That was all.

She waited, smoothing the folds of her green silk skirt, as if she expected me to say more. But when I did not elaborate, she nodded as if she understood. "Well, I'm glad for that," she said, smiling. "I just didn't want you to make the same mistake I almost did once, confusing admiration with love. I almost lost your father because of that mistake—and then it turned out that the man I thought was so all-fired admirable wasn't fit to clean your father's boots."

She stood up, her smile more tight-lipped and her gaze far away, her eyes shining. "Sam Rawles made me cry enough after that—and before that, too, Lord knows! But I never was sorry. The love made up for the bad times."

For a moment she seemed lost in reverie as she stood there. But then she drew the white lace wrapper around her more tightly, clearing her throat. "Land sakes, it's only fifteen minutes till they'll be here! I'd better get downstairs and let you have time to get ready. Don't rush. You're the guest of honor; you come down when you want to."

After giving me a friendly pat on my shoulder, she was gone before I could say anything more than "thank you" in reply.

While I dressed, I thought about what Mother had said, congratulating myself that I had not allowed Abel Cottor's proposal to reach her. So it had been true! But it was certainly different from the way Abel had made it sound. What arrogance for him to think that she had been practically waiting for her freedom so that she could rejoin him at last! It was like the way Steven seemed to think of me, as though I were simply marking time until he chose to claim me again! Well, he would have his surprise. Both of them would. Just wait until the governor's office announced thar their precious bill had been vetoed!

As I selected my gown, my thoughts also turned to what Mother had implied about Nathan. Of course he was more than a business partner. The feelings we shared were simply quieter, that was all. And they would grow more intense. I knew they would. I could make him forget that I was in the slightest way connected with business; I was sure of that. I would make him recognize me as a woman.

I had chosen my gown carefully, a light blue silk with long sleeves and a snug-fitting waist, both of which accented the low cut and equally snug bodice. The soft curves of my breasts swelled against the smooth fabric, showing a décolletage that ought to take Nathan's mind away from business matters in short order! I hummed as I applied a few drops of cologne, then put on a single strand of pearls, the one piece of real jewelry I had allowed myself since I had sold the rest in New York. After thinking for a moment, I decided to wear my hair at shoulder length rather than pin it up again. The way it shone, lustrous, in the last rays of the setting sun, it might look even more fascinating in the gaslight later this evening, or in the moonlight, if Nathan and I chose to take some air in the garden. . . .

Finally, with my stiff petticoats rustling, I descended the stairs, savoring the admiring glances and murmers of our guests, who had gathered below. Reverend Scott began the applause, and soon the rest had joined in. I felt the color rising in my cheeks. By the time Nathan stepped forward to take my hand, I was sure I was blushing furiously. "Thank goodness we don't get engaged every week!" I whispered as he drew me to his side.

"You look just lovely tonight," he said easily, giving my hand a squeeze, "just lovely. And remind me to tell you, I've got some good news."

During dinner, while the guests on either side of us were busy with their portions of pheasant cashmere, Nathan told me the news. The veto had come today, late this very afternoon. He had gotten the telegraph message just before he had left to come here tonight. Smiling faintly, Nathan seemed quite satisfied with what we had done. "Shouldn't wonder if Abel himself doesn't have the news by now. He won't even know what hit him."

For some curious reason I felt sad, thinking about the disappointment and shock that the Cottors would feel at having their fortunes so suddenly lost, especially at the very time that their hopes were so high. Now they would have to face the same ordeal I had gone through, but from a much weaker position.

"It cost us eighty-five hundred," Nathan was saying casually, as though he had been talking about the weather. "But I think it's worth it. Whatever we pick up at the auction is bound to be at least double that in value. Just that mountain alone, or even the mansion . . ."

"I think we ought to talk about this some other time," I said, managing to keep my voice calm enough so that Judge Hawthorne, who had begun to listen from his seat across the table, had no idea that I was in any way upset.

After our guests had sampled their fill of the desserts —a giant-sized Charlotte Russe coconut steeples, and apple meringue pie—and after the coffee had been sipped and the toasts were completed, the men remained at the table while Mother and I retired to the west parlor with the rest of the ladies. Now was the time for me to show my ring to those who had not already admired it and to make small talk with those who had until the men had finished their brandy and were ready to join us again. I was feeling impatient to talk with Nathan again, for I had the uncomfortable feeling that he had misunderstood about Vallamont. "We," he had said, but that was not the way it must be. The title to Vallamont would be in the name of Catherine Rawles, and no one else, not even Nathan. This was a family matter; surely I would be able to make Nathan see that.

My thoughts were only half-attending to the smiles and polite talk there in the parlor until Amanda Scott came forward to offer her congratulations. I noted that Amanda had put on weight and looked less animated now. I ought to be charitable now, I told myself. I knew how she had worshipped Nathan, and how hurt she must have been, though she did not show it, when Nathan had politely implied about a month ago that her volunteer services would be better appreciated at the Holt Clinic than at his own. The Holt Clinic was a small local institution where the wealthy with addictions to opium or liquor could go for mineral baths and heat treatments. Every effort was made to keep the names of the "guests," as they were called, confidential. One of the well-guarded names was that of the former Mrs. McKay. As I understood the story, though scarcely lucid, she had insisted on remaining near Nathan after the divorce. Rather than create scenes similar to the one he had endured the day he left us outside the lumber camp, Nathan had decided to put her in the Holt Clinic. Perhaps that was the reason he had suggested the same place for Amanda, I had thought at the time. Perhaps her red hair reminded him of his wife's. I had teased Nathan about that one night, about his not knowing what to do with all his women, and he had smiled a bit. "Well, neither of them will bother us where they are now. So you don't have to be jealous!"

What was Amanda saying? ". . . after you've gone through so much. Now I must confess I had taken a liking to him, but I guess it just wasn't meant to be."

Her smile looked wistful as she took an envelope out of her purse. "But I guess if his first wife can be big-hearted about it, why, then so can I. Do you know that she sent you this note, wishing you all the best, just to make certain you wouldn't feel uncomfortable? Poor thing, she's . . . a bit strange at times, but this letter's as nice as you please. I saw her write it myself. They're not allowed to send anything out that hasn't been looked at first, you see. They might be asking for things they shouldn't have. But, anyway, I do hope you're very happy. And if you haven't chosen all your bridesmaids just yet, I'd be very proud to be one."

I promised her I'd read the letter some other time and said I'd be pleased to have her as a bridesmaid. After all, her father would be performing the ceremony in our church. It would be silly not to give Amanda a place in the wedding party if she wanted one.

Finally I was able to get Nathan outside for a stroll in the summer evening, where we could talk in privacy. Out on the walk in front of the house we went slowly, arm in arm, from one circle of gaslight into the next. We listened to the elm leaves rustle overhead and watched the lamps from the few carriages out on the street as they passed by.

It was easier than I had expected to make Nathan see that Vallamont was important. I had scarcely finished explaining about what the mountain had meant to our family when he interrutped. "I don't see any problem with that, Catherine. The mountain's yours; the house is, too. We'll just have them put in your name, whether we get them directly from Abel or the other way, with the sheriff."

He stopped and turned to face me, ignoring the closed carriage that had stopped at the curb alongside of us. "After all, what would I want with a mountain, or a castle, when I have someone as lovely as . . ."

"McKay!" The voice cut through me, the anger in it catching me completely unprepared. I opened my eyes wide, dazed by what I saw, praying that it would disappear.

In the open doorway of the carriage, his face a harsh, angular mask in the lamplight, was Steven Cottor.

As he stepped down onto the ground, I saw that he had a pistol in his hand.

"No!" I cried out as Nathan turned away from me and waited for Steven to come closer, but he paid no attention to me. In a voice as cold as any I have ever heard, he spoke.

"Cottor, you've lost. Do you intend to go out with a murder?"

Steven snapped the pistol open. There were no bullets in the firing chamber. He gave a short, harsh laugh. "I'm not that big a fool, McKay. I just wanted to see the guilty fear in your eyes when you had to face me. You're not proud of your sneaking work in Harrisburg. I can see that." Steven's anger seemed just beneath the surface, waiting to explode.

Nathan held his ground. "If you're done with looking at me, Cottor, I suggest you leave."

"Not just yet. I want a word with this lady here. You may recall I told you that the two of us—were not strangers to one another."

I stood very still. This was to be my moment of triumph, I thought, but I felt only a saddened concern that Steven was about to do something foolish because his pride was wounded. I knew that I had hurt him as he deserved to be hurt. Why was it that I could only look at him and greet him with, "Yes, Steven?"

"I understand you're planning to marry."

"I am."

"Marry one man to get Vallamont, but not another, is that it?" His cool sarcasm was maddening. "What a shame I hadn't realized what it was you really wanted. I could either have made a deal with Abel or saved myself a lot of wasted effort."

"You've no right to talk that way, Steven. I . . ."

"Money-hungry—that's all you were. Land-hungry, just like Abel, just like your father, and just like this . . ."

"That's not true! You can't . . ."

Nathan stepped forward. "You've said enough, Cottor. Now go on home."

Steven's grin flashed wickedly. "What's the trouble, McKay? Afraid I'm going to take all this property away from you? That nice hotel, those nice profitable mills . . ."

"That's enough," Nathan said. "Now go on. I don't want to have to hurt you."

The words hung in the warm night air. The smile ón Steven's lips seemed to harden. When he finally spoke, his voice dripped with sarcasm. "Well, that's mighty considerate of you, McKay."

Then, slowly, as though he were utterly unconcerned at whatever Nathan might do, Steven drew back his fist and then let fly a savage blow squarely at Nathan's jaw. I gasped, but there was no impact. Nathan turned aside so that Steven's fist missed him by a fraction of an inch. Then, as Steven was off balance, Nathan suddenly brought up his knee and caught Steven hard in the pit of the stomach. The breath went out of Steven in a hoarse, guttural rush. He stumbled, bent over, tried to straighten up, but fell.

Nathan kicked the pistol out of his hand. "Loaded or not, I wouldn't risk your throwing this gun at me, Cottor. Don't worry, impact to the solar plexus causes only a temporary paralysis. You'll be well soon, and able to go home—which I suggest you do the very second you can walk. Now let's go back inside, Catherine, before we begin to attract a crowd."

Steven's coachman had climbed down from his box and was now assisting him to his feet, helping him away from the illuminated circle of the streetlamp.

Nathan took my arm. We turned to go. But then I heard Steven's voice from the shadows at the edge of the lawn shrubbery.

"Catherine!"

I hesitated and then looked back.

Steven had come out under the light again. The dark

eyes, the disheveled hair, the polished boots—all seemed to glitter with an unnatural intensity. But the voice was softer than before. "Do you think you love him, Catherine?"

He said it almost kindly, and the tone caught me off guard so that I hesitated for a moment. Then I recovered my composure. "Really, Mr. Cottor, you are too impertinent," I said.

Taking a firm hold of Nathan's arm, I looked one last time at that strange light in Steven's gaze. Then I turned and walked with Nathan back toward our mansion, where a few guests had come down the front steps from the wide porch and out onto the lawn, wondering what the commotion was about.

Was it my imagination, or did I really hear Steven's voice in the wind behind me? And what was it he said so quietly? "You'll never take it from me, Catherine, never."

"Nathan," I whispered, suddenly afraid, "did you hear that?"

"Of course I did. But don't mind his foolishness, darling. Let's get you inside. A glass of sherry will help you sleep."

For the next day or two, my feelings were still disturbed by the events that had taken place that night. I wondered if Steven would come back to cause yet another unpleasant scene, and on several occasions I caught myself thinking that perhaps the Cottors would find a way to meet their obligations, after all. What if they sold off everything *but* Vallamont? Oh, but that was absurd. How could they live up there without the income from their mill? It would be impossible. And even if it were possible, I knew that Steven would rather starve than live under the same roof as Abel. No, if they had any last-minute hopes of keeping Vallamont from me, those hopes rested on some other plan.

Fortunately, I had more than enough work to keep my mind occupied, so I did not waste much time worrying about Steven Cottor or what he might do. I congratulated myself that I had finally been able to break his hold over me. My engagement seemed to have raised an impassable barrier that cut off all thoughts of that passionate abandon I had fought against only a few months ago. How much more sensible it was not to think of those things that gave only hurt! And when I was married, the barrier would be even stronger. I would be safe, perhaps forever. Steven might be forced to go away and leave me in peace. . . .

Then, three nights after the engagement dinner, I came home to find Emily, the maid, still finishing with the curtains in my room. A small white envelope lay unopened on my nightstand. "I found it in your reticule, ma'am," said Emily, "when we were getting ready to send out your evening clothes to be cleaned. I thought you might have forgotten it."

I opened it and read the barely legible, flowery scrawl of Nathan's first wife. As Amanda had said, Elaine McKay wished me well and wanted me to know that I had her blessings. I shrugged, not certain whether I felt like laughing or weeping at this foolish intrusion. As if this woman still was in a position to give Nathan away! But then, who knew what sort of delusions she might be under as a result of her addiction.

I crumpled the letter and was about to throw it away when I noticed some writing on the *inside* of the envelope. It had been done with the same pen, but the letters were smaller and more precisely formed, as if the writer had been taking pains to print clearly. The message gave me pause:

> Must see you at once. Danger.
> E.M.

Was this more foolishness? The brief note nagged at me all during dinner, so much so that I scarcely spoke to Mother. What could it mean? What danger could this woman possibly know about, shut off from

the world as she was? It had to be one of her delusions.
Yet that small, careful lettering . . .

"Catherine, do you feel well? I don't think you've
heard a thing I've said all this time."

"I'm sorry, Mother. I was distracted. What were you
saying?"

"Well, it's not that important—just that Lem
Sprague's Mississippi stern-wheeler's finally arrived here
on the river. He'll soon have that floating amusement
palace he's been talking about. But that's not any concern of mine, really. What's this that's so much on your
mind tonight?"

"I don't know. It's probably nothing. Nathan's first
wife sent me a note, and hidden on the inside of the
envelope was a message that said she had to see me at
once. That's all she said, except for the word 'danger.'
I haven't known what to make of it."

"Well, why don't you go down and see? Do you want
me to come with you?"

"Oh, I'm not afraid of her, Mother! But what good
could it do? What could she possibly know that would
present any danger to me?"

"Maybe nothing," Mother allowed. "Maybe she's just
trying to get attention. They get like little children, I'm
told, in those places. And from what I've heard of her,
she was certainly enough of a spoiled brat to begin
with."

"So you think it's foolishness, then?" I took the envelope out of my pocket and handed it across the table.

She studied the message for a moment. Then she put
it down. "It's probably nothing. On the other hand, it
might mean something. You'd be surprised how people
talk around places like that. She might have picked up
some gossip about the hotel, or about the mills, or
almost anything. The attendants talk, the visitors talk,
and there are some highly influential people numbered
among those 'guests,' I'm told."

"So you think I should go?"

She smiled broadly, her eyes crinkled at the corners.

"Well, of course! At least it will put your mind at ease, and then you'll be able to listen to me again at mealtimes! We've few enough of these private moments together before the wedding, as it is. I don't want to waste another meal with you off in the clouds with worries of secret notes and other foolishness."

Even though I knew Mother was half-teasing, I had Jared drive me over to the Holt Clinic, anyway. If nothing else, I would see what the first Mrs. McKay looked like.

After a few minutes' delay, during which I helped the matron in charge overcome her guilty feelings for allowing someone in after visiting hours, I was finally shown into an ordinary-looking parlor where several ordinary-looking people were lounging on sofas and chairs, most of them reading, while two men played checkers.

"Visitor, Mrs. McKay," the matron said quietly.

A sharp-featured woman, who looked as if she were in her forties, glanced up from her reading, saw me, and stood up. The matron quietly ushered us into a small room with windows on three sides that were lined with potted plants, as though the area served as a sun porch during the day. She turned up the wall lamp and then left us, closing the two doors—French windows, actually—behind her.

"So they can see anything we do," said Elaine McKay. "They think you're going to bring me in some laudanum or who knows what else, so they keep watch. There, see?" She pointed at a chair midway down the hall, where the matron was now seated, fumbling with some knitting while she watched us out of the corner of her eye. "There's old nursie herself! Yoo-hoo!" And she waved. The matron saw this, of course, and, to my surprise, she waved back.

"Don't look so astonished! At least she treats us as if we were human beings! Do you think we're wild animals in here? Do you think we're crazed lunatics, driven mad by the demons of . . ."

"Mrs. McKay, I believe you sent me this note." I handed it to her. "You did want to see me about something, didn't you? Or did you just . . . well, never mind that. I understood from your note that you felt the matter was urgent."

"Oh, forgive me, Catherine. You don't mind if I call you that, do you? You may call me Elaine if you like. Just let me look at you." Her voice had a breathy, singsong quality that made me uncomfortable. I began to wish that I had simply ignored her note altogether.

"You are just lovely, my dear. How old are you? No, you needn't answer. I know already from Amanda. You're twenty-two. Would you believe that I am only twenty-eight? I can see you don't, but it is God's truth. It's the drug that did it. It burns one's life away faster, Catherine. You live a week in a single night, and ten years in only as many months—at least that's the way it feels, so exciting, so full of so many wonders every moment." She touched her fingers to the loose flesh over her cheeks as she paused. "Then one day you can't get it, and you look into the mirror, and you see that you've really not gained any time at all. You've just grown old sooner than the rest, that's all, and the days ahead seem so dry and long and empty." She bit her lip.

"It must be difficult," I said. "But perhaps after you've had enough rest and treatment here, and with a proper diet . . ."

"I'll go back to it again, just the moment I'm free, that's what I'll do! I've been in places like this before! Don't you understand? They don't work!"

She crossed abruptly to one of the chairs at the small table in the center of the room. "Look at me! I'm twenty-eight years old, and I look as though I were an old woman. I've even had to dye my hair. It used to be red, you know—fiery red. But then there was so much gray mixed in with the red that people thought I was my own mother!" She looked hard at me, tugging at one of the sleeves of her plain black dress. "So I thought that I ought to stay at this place for a while, wherever Nathan was going to be, until he made up his mind."

"Wait a moment. I don't understand."

She spoke patiently, as if she were talking to a child. "I didn't care about the others, mind you. But I thought the wife ought to know. Once I've done that, why, I can go back with a clearer conscience, though I don't suppose for long. I'll probably never even reach thirty."

She stood up and went over to the door. "So there it is. Now you know," she said, about to turn the knob.

"But wait! I'm sure I don't know a thing. I haven't understood more than a few words you've said! Why did you ask me to come here?"

"Why to warn you, of course. You're going to be his next wife, so you ought not to have the same thing happen to you. Let him do what he wants with the others, but don't let him give you any."

She opened the door, giving a prim smile as the matron rose from her chair.

"What shouldn't I let him give me, Elaine?"

"Opium, darling. How do you think I got started?"

She drew back her lips in what had once very likely been a charming smile, nodding her good-bye as though she were on a stage. "Delighted to have met you, Catherine, though I don't suppose you'll be stopping by again. . . ."

She sailed off leaving me vexed with myself for having wasted my time, yet still more vexed at wanting to ask Nathan about her. Outside in the fresh air I tried to shake off the eerie feeling that her lilting, almost mocking, words had left behind. It had to be jealousy at work. She wanted to frighten me away, hoping against hope for a reconciliation with Nathan. All my feminine instincts told me that her story was false.

Yet I still went from this clinic to Nathan's, where I knew he would be working late. I told him exactly what had happened, leaving nothing out, and I waited for his reaction.

He shook his head, bemused, and he leaned back, putting his fingertips together. The blue eyes seemed far away. "That's all she said—that I got her started?"

"That's all. I didn't understand, really, so I thought I'd ask you."

He gave a tight-lipped smile and looked directly into my eyes. "What she says is true. And don't think she hasn't said it before. The courts have heard her complaint long before you did. I'll guarantee you that."

I was suddenly annoyed with the whole business. "I wish you'd just explain, Nathan! I don't care who's heard it before!"

"Don't be upset. I'm sure she'd be only too happy to see that she'd managed to get under your skin this way. Actually, there's nothing to explain. Opium's a very widely used sedative. I gave her a small injection, completely harmless, one morning after she'd been drinking for several days and had driven herself into hysterics. She rested well, but after a month or so I noticed that the supplies I kept in my medicine cabinet had been tampered with. So I had some locks put on and kept the only key in my possession."

He shrugged then and turned up a palm in a gesture of resignation. "And so she began getting it from another source. Do you really want to hear the things she did after that, Catherine?"

I shook my head no.

"If you think I'm to blame in some way, if you think I'm somehow not the kind of man you want to marry, you're free to reconsider. After all, I suppose you owe me a cancellation in return for my leaving you at the train station last June."

He smiled, and I stood up, feeling safe and secure again. "Oh, don't be foolish, Nathan. I could tell she was twisting the truth! I just needed to . . ."

He was holding me in his arms then, and we kissed, and I was glad I had come, after all. He squeezed me tightly before he released me. Then he smiled again.

"So, what do you think of the news of our friends this afternoon? Or have you heard?"

"I heard about Sprague's stern-wheeler on the river."

"Not Sprague. About the Cottors. No? Well, it seems our friend Abel has disappeared."

"Disappeared! Abel Cottor?"

"And he's not likely to come back, either, I'd say. Took almost every dollar he had with him, including the payroll accounts. There'll be a lot of very unhappy men at Cottor's mill when the end of the week comes around. The sheriff's looking out for a riot."

I was thinking of Steven and what he had said about Vallamont. "Could they be planning to use that money to somehow save their property? But that couldn't work, could it? He owes the men for their time . . ."

"No. My guess is that Abel was just looking out for himself. He's probably left the country. He took that woman with him, the sheriff said, but he left Steven high and dry. And now Steven's the one who'll have to face going bankrupt when they've given up the search —unless he runs off, too."

SEVENTEEN

The first Saturday in October dawned crisp and cool. I rose early. Even though I should have felt a special elation, I was tired from a busy week. And I was ravenously hungry. Downstairs in the kitchen, I waited impatiently while Mrs. Jennings, the plump-faced Irish woman who had been our cook from as far back as I could remember, got ready to serve me hot cakes and coffee and set bacon strips to frying on the griddle. The two of us were the only ones up just yet; it was barely light, too early for the rest of the staff to rise on a Saturday. Mother had gone off to New York, partly to visit friends and partly to compare styles for my wedding gown. Nathan and I were to be married in less than a month.

"You've got a good appetite for so early, Miss Catherine." Mrs. Jennings beamed behind her gold spectacles as she watched me at the big center table. "We're going to miss you when you're married. All of us will."

For some reason I felt argumentative that morning. "Oh, come now, Mrs. Jennings, you ought to know better than to think I'd let Nathan pick my staff for me, especially in the kitchen! If anyone ought to be worried about missing anyone, it should be Nathan's cook, not you. All you'll need to think about is how you're going to get used to a new stove—and how you're going to manage getting deliverymen up to Vallamont. As a matter of fact, I may even have you start up there tomorrow. What would you say to that?"

She rested her hands on her ample hips and looked at me, bewildered. "Now, don't you go joshin' an old woman, Miss Cath——"

"Old! Why, you're not even fifty yet!"

One hand went to her bun of graying hair, as though patting it into place. "Humph. That's as it may be. I'm plenty old enough not to take movin' lightly, let me tell you! Here today and somewhere else tomorrow, why, that's just . . ." She broke off and turned to the griddle, where the bacon needed tending, muttering to herself.

"Oh, now you don't have to worry, Mrs. J.," I said, thinking for a moment that I might really have unsettled her. "You'll have plenty of time. But we could start tomorrow if we wanted to. Vallamont's going to be mine this very morning."

"Oh, that's why you're up so early!" She wiped her plump hands on the towel she kept hanging beside the griddle before she picked up the bacon strips with her tongs and set them on a plate. "How big is the kitchen up there? What sort of a stove? And how big is the cold cellar? You don't mind my askin', do you, Miss Catherine? These are things that can make a difference, you know."

She brought me the plate and then started to refill my coffee cup, but she nearly spilled the coffee when I admitted that I had never even seen the kitchen at Vallamont, much less the cold cellar. "Land sakes! You've bought a house and not even . . . why, suppose it ain't a good 'un? How you gonna feed all those folks at your weddin'?"

I patted her arm affectionately. "There, there. I'm

sure the kitchen will serve us very well. Abel Cottor's had banquets and balls up there, and I've never heard any complaints. All the same, though, I promise I'll have a look at it this morning before the auction."

"Auction? You mean you haven't bought it yet? Why, Miss Catherine, then someone else could just as easy outbid you! We might be stayin' here, after all."

I smiled. "Oh, I have my doubts about that. Probably there won't be any other bidders this morning. Most people think the auction's this afternoon, down at the courthouse. That's how the notices read in the paper—that Cottor properties would be auctioned off by the sheriff at two."

"You mean they're havin' a special auction this mornin'? What are the folks this afternoon goin' to say?"

I shrugged. "There's nothing much they can say. This auction was advertised, too, only in a different edition of the paper, and in smaller type, of course. This morning's sale is for the Cottor residence and the land." I smiled inwardly, recalling how willing the sheriff had been to do me this personal favor. It seemed ironic that only a few months earlier the same man had come so very close to selling off *my* properties. And now, instead of going bankrupt, I was about to take back Vallamont after the Cottors had held it for ten years. And the Cottors, instead of "helping" Mother and me, were now in worse financial straits than I had ever been. Abel had not been located since the day he had cleared out his payroll accounts and disappeared. Steven had remained. To his credit, Steven had sold his own mansion in town in order to pay wages to the two hundred men who worked the Cottor mill and camp. He had moved into the Vallamont castle, but he had spent most of his time in the mill, working feverishly. But there was no staving off the inevitable. The income the mill produced after expenses could not match the greater amounts demanded by the creditors. And with Abel gone, those bankers were in no mood to be persuaded

into an extension of credit. Abel had lost in the legislature when the governor's veto had held, and his
running away had only made matters worse for Steven.

So this morning was the Cottors' defeat, and my
victory.

What was Mrs. Jennings saying?

". . . would have been proud to see this day. I never
saw a man so riled up about somethin' as your daddy
was when he had to give up that mountain! And to Abel
Cottor, of all people! Why, your daddy hated that man
ever since you were two years old, and that's a mighty
long time—too long, I thought myself, but that didn't
make a particle of difference to him."

She was busying herself with the day's baking now,
setting out the pans of dough that had risen overnight
and dusting her fingers with flour.

"Actually, I thought it went back even further than
that," I mused, recalling what Abel himself had told me.

"Oh, no." She shook her head firmly, pursing her
lips. "They were good friends right up till your second
birthday—I baked your cake and put on the candles,
so I ought to remember. It wasn't till just after your ma
lost her baby that the trouble started."

"The baby?"

"Yes, ma'am. He would've been a little brother for
you, they said, but he came too soon. Your pa took on
somethin' fierce after it happened, and your ma nearly
died, grievin' the way she did. You wouldn't remember,
though. Most of the time I kept you with me so you
wouldn't hear the fightin'. Lord knows what they
were . . ."

"Yes, well, let's think about the future now, Mrs. J.,
shall we?" I tried to keep my voice steady, but it was
difficult all the same. Had the baby been Abel Cottor's?
How that question must have eaten into Father's soul
over the years! And it must have upset Mother, too,
along with the never-ending doubts of what had brought
on her labor so early. Had it been her anxieties over

her affair, yet unconfessed? And what if the boy had lived?

I brought myself up short. This wasn't the time for the past; I had said that myself. Even though what Mrs. Jennings had inadvertently let slip had awakened a new ache, there was the future to attend to.

I finished my breakfast, determinedly keeping Mrs. Jennings's conversation to the subject of what ought to be served at the wedding. Then, from the carriage house, I led the horse Jared had already saddled for me out onto the driveway and mounted up. I could have taken the carriage, of course, but impulsively I had decided to ride instead. The last time I had come to Vallamont had been in a carriage, and that was a day that I was still trying to forget.

The sun was just clearing the top of the mountains to the southeast. Across the river, the trees had begun to turn shades of red and gold among the green, like the sycamores and the elms here on millionaires' row. There was still a light mist from the early morning that caught the early sun and made the rays sparkle. Up ahead I could hear the chimes of Father's steeple clock strike the hour: six A.M. I would be in plenty of time to meet Billy Joe Walker down at the bank and then ride up to Vallamont by seven with cash for the bidding.

As I rode past the familiar mansions, lawns and hedges now glittering behind the thin gray mist of morning, I couldn't help but think how different my view of these houses was now from what it had been only a few months before. Back then I was noticing the architectural lines, the colors of the garden flowers, and the trim of the shutters. The people inside were only vague presences, friends of Father's whom I might know to say hello to, but nothing more. Now, when I looked at the stately Belmont mansion on the next block from ours, for example, I scarcely looked at the lines of its twin mansard roof towers, which I had previously found dreadfully clumsy. Instead, I thought of the dinner party I was giving for Mr. and Mrs. Belmont a week from today to celebrate their twenty-fifth wedding anniversary. Mr. Belmont owned a sizable bloc of Pennsylvania Railroad shares, and he was very friendly with Pierpont Morgan, Junius Morgan's son, in New York. The right words from him could reduce our railway shipping costs by nearly fifty percent within the state and by at least thirty percent anywhere in the East. Two houses down from the Belmonts' house was the home of the Plaines, newcomers up from Washington. Mr. Plaines was here to supervise the construction of the huge new post office and federal court building, and later he would be in charge of all civil service work in the center of the state. Nathan and I had given them a welcoming party. Nathan had insisted on it as soon as he had learned that Mr. Plaines was a close acquaintance of President Grant. A little farther on was the Wightmans' Italian villa. Mr. Wightman had made a fortune in pharmaceuticals and was now planning to erect an entire city block of offices, stores, and apartments downtown—for which he would naturally need lumber in great quantities. Mrs. Wightman's birthday was in November, and Nathan and I had already let it be known that we would arrange a celebration.

As I rode past Steven's—what had once been Steven's house—I felt an impulse to look away. John Eber's family lived there now. John ran a construction firm and had been ready with cash at the time Steven needed to sell. Steven's loss had been his gain. And now Steven would lose again, and I would win—but why, then, didn't I feel as though I were winning?

I told myself that I really had done nothing to harm Steven. The Cottors would have gone under without me, anyway. Abel had lost at least a half a million dollars lately in the stock market. He had bought some stocks on account, hoping the profits on their sales would give him money to pay; other stocks he had sold short. But Abel had misjudged the market very badly. Two brokers were going bankrupt along with Abel because they had trusted his predictions about stock prices as well as his credit.

So even if Abel had managed to sell his boom shares —which would be bid on this afternoon by other members of the company—it was doubtful that he would have been able to pay off all his obligations. It was all just as Father had predicted months before, I told myself. I really hadn't changed the outcome that much by letting Nathan know of their plans in the Harrisburg legislature. The defeat would have happened without me.

But why did I still feel so responsible?

I forced my thoughts away from such fruitless speculation. The future was falling into place just as I had imagined it. Nathan and I were already entertaining occasionally, whenever we could both afford the time. After we were married we could move up to Vallamont and begin to create that center of social life I had envisioned. We could have neighbors on the lots below the mansion that Abel had surveyed off. Though he could not sell the lots, I knew that I could. All I needed to do was extend the gas line, and immediately those lots would become very desirable residential areas.

Of course, the bank knew this, too. That was why Layton Jacobs was waiting for me now, at this hour of the morning, at the Susquehanna Federated Bank downtown. As soon as Billy Joe Walker arrived, Layton was going to get one hundred thousand-dollar bills out of the vault so that I would have cash enough to outbid whoever might appear on Vallamont at seven o'clock. And if it appeared that more cash might be needed, Layton stood prepared to ride back down for more.

He was standing inside the door when I dismounted, his gray muttonchop sideburns framing a deceptively wolfish face. Layton might look fierce and cynical, but I had always found him charming and cooperative.

We chatted amiably while waiting for Billy Joe. The bank was very glad of this opportunity to be of service to me with this loan. They were certain I would be able to sell the lots for more than I would have to pay for the entire property, and they were pleased I had chosen them. They were still willing to accept the title to the lots as full collateral for the loan.

The clock chimed half-past. Billy Joe was nowhere in sight. I had no idea what might be keeping him; it wasn't like Billy Joe to be late for anything.

But I had to be up at Vallamont at seven for the start of the bidding.

"Layton, you know how much we agreed on. When Billy Joe comes, can you bring it on up? Be there by seven-fifteen at the latest and I think we'll still be all right."

"And if he's not here by seven, Miss Rawles, I'll bring it myself. I'll get one of the sheriff's men to come with me."

"I appreciate your help, Layton." I smiled at him as I went out to the curb and mounted up, before he could offer to help me with that, too. It was money I needed this morning, not patronizing treatment. I took a last look around the square for Billy Joe: nothing. The streets were deserted. Even the farmers would not be in until the growers' market opened at seven-thirty.

Where was Billy Joe? He had done such a good job for me up until now. As I rode up the gradual slope along Market Street, past the last house, past the place where the street became just a carriage-path through a field, then on into the woods at the base of Vallamont, the question tugged at my mind. It was not possible that Billy Joe had forgotten. He had been meticulous in every detail since he had begun work as my chief of security. Two men were now in jail as a result of his alertness in checking a warehouse gate one evening in early September, and I was certain that thousands of dollars' worth of our property had been saved because other local ruffians had learned to fear him. Though they might be for hire to sabotage other mills, they would stay clear of Rawles and Billy Joe.

Well, he would turn up. Nothing was going to get in

the way of my victory here this morning, I told myself.
As I rode along the wooded path and approached the
crest and the clearing, I tried to feel at home again,
here with the familiar clean forest air and the sunlight
dancing through the hemlocks. The maples here and
there were touched with red and gold. In low spots
along the edges of the trail, the fallen leaves and brown
needles were crusted white with last night's frost. My
mare seemed to sense the freshness of the morning, for
she pranced as though glad for the early exercise,
snorting little clouds as we trotted up the mountain.

Yet I still felt a strange anxiety, as though a Christmas morning had come that I did not want to celebrate. Was I feeling sorry for Steven? The thought
popped into my mind unbidden and I quickly rejected
it. I owed him no apology. He had taken me for granted.
He had tried to force me to marry him. He had allowed
his father to insult our family, my father's memory, my
mother's reputation, and my own business ability. He
had taken advantage of the feelings, the attraction we
had for each other. . . . I forced myself not to think of
that. Nathan and I would develop that passion one day.
I could trust Nathan to allow me to be independent, to
make my own business decisions. Could I trust Steven
to do the same? I doubted it. His pride would impel
him to take charge of things. Hadn't he been too proud
to even say hello to me this past month? He was determined to exist without me, so I could certainly well
afford to spare myself the pains and the emotional
storms that he brought into my life.

Besides, Nathan was a much better prospect. He
was growing more and more popular in town, and his
name was beginning to be mentioned for public office.
He had his connections in Philadelphia and Harrisburg,
and he would soon have allies in Washington. Who
knew where the future might take him? And I could be
at his side.

I could see Cottor's Castle ahead of me now. It was
Abel's pride, but Abel was gone now. What a change

from that first Saturday in June when I had ridden up here! Then I had hidden behind the trees so that Abel could not see me, and now I had driven him away. I would buy it this morning, though I had paid for it in many ways months ago. The nightmare at Eagles Mere, the horror of that burning raft—they had brought me here. I had paid for this moment.

But why did I feel apprehension now?

As the mare's hooves clattered onto the gravel path, it came to me that I would very likely have to face Steven this morning. After all, he had been living up here. His pride would not let him accept a defeat gracefully. I was sure of that. He would be here to make a scene of some kind, to show the bidders and those who had come to watch that he was not going to be beaten quietly.

Well, I had been through his temper tantrums before, and a lot worse than that, to get where I was this morning, I told myself. In an hour I would own Vallamont. This tightening that I felt in the pit of my stomach was ridiculous. It would all be over and done with in an hour.

But where was Billy Joe? I thought I heard someone behind me and I looked around. Nothing. The path behind me was quiet, the forest motionless. Maybe a squirrel or a raccoon had stirred up some leaves a moment before, but there were no riders. I would feel a lot better when the money was safely up here and ready to be handed over.

The dew-covered lawn at the front of Cottor's Castle was deserted, so I rode around to the back. There, not far from the rear entrance, a table had been set up at the edge of the grass. About fifteen men stood in small groups close by, watching what looked to be an argument between Sheriff Burnside and Steven Cottor.

One of the sheriff's men stepped forward and took my horse after I dismoutned. Quickly I walked over to the table where the sheriff, a plain man, jug-eared and sandy-haired, who had been a carpenter until two years ago, was speaking with his usual forthright, no-nonsense firmness. ". . . can't see how. The law is the law, and it says that all your father's money's now in the hands of the state."

"But I've just told you that this money is mine. It has nothing to do with him." Steven's face looked drawn, older by years than when I had last seen him. The eyes flickered when he saw me approach, and he nodded a greeting. But the sheriff was holding to his point.

"I know that's what you're tellin' me, but can you prove it? Seems to me this ain't the place to go takin' someone's word, especially in view of the circumstances we got here. If Abel Cottor managed to run off with two hundred thousand dollars that we know about, who's to say that he hasn't managed to get some of it back to you? Seems to me we can't have you biddin' with what might be some of those missin' . . ."

"But you can't prove this is anything but my money! You can't bar me from this sale without any evidence! I've as much right as anyone to be here and to bid as much as I've got."

"I don't agree. I just don't see how I can allow . . ."

"Pardon me, sheriff," I interrupted. "I think I understand the drift of this conversation. Could you tell me how much money is involved here?"

"Why, yes, Miss Rawles, it's sixty-five thous——"

His eyes blazing, Steven cut in. "You can't tell her that! You're giving her an unfair advantage."

"We'd all find out sooner or later, Steven," I replied, surprised at the way I was able to keep my voice under control. "I think it might settle things more rapidly then, sheriff, if I just opened the bidding at sixty-six thousand."

Steven clamped his jaw tightly shut and turned away. How much easier it was, I thought, to deal with him out here, where there were other people around!

Sheriff Burnside let out his breath in a low whistle. "Well, now, I guess that would do it, at that." He tugged at one of his freckled ears, his lips pressed together as he thought some more. "But all the same, Mr. Cottor, I'm going to have to investigate where you got that money. I'll want to see you right after we're through up here."

Surprisingly, Steven simply nodded assent. He remained where he stood while the sheriff went over to the back door to speak with the auctioneer.

I found myself moving toward Steven. "I hope you didn't think there was anything personal involved," I began. "It's just that I'm prepared to pay more than . . ."

"You don't have to apologize. You've always wanted the place, and so have I—not this goddamned castle of Abel's but the mountain. I don't blame you. But I do know this. You're making a mistake." He stared out at the oak tree as he spoke, his features barely moving.

"Mistake?" I had to be careful, I told myself. I was not going to let him come close and try to manipulate me.

"With Nathan McKay. You don't love him. I could see that the night you were with him in front of your house."

I tried to find the right words to say, but the old familiar warmth was beginning to make itself felt! No! I had made my choice. "I don't think that's your concern, Steven. Your opinion . . ."

"Doesn't count, I know. You've tried to make that clear. But you don't believe it. And sooner or later you'll see that Nathan McKay isn't the paragon he pretends to be."

"I'll thank you to keep your . . ."

"Come on, Catherine, you see it yourself, only you won't admit it. Something in you sees it. Why do you think you're holding back from him? You were that night, and I'll wager that you still are. Your own instincts tell you . . ."

"I've heard enough, Steven. You're impossible, and you're wrong."

"We'll see about that," he said laconically. Then he glanced at the crowd that was beginning to form at the

315

rear entrance and around the auctioneer and Sheriff Burnside. "I'm sure you'll pardon me if I don't accompany the inspection tour of the premises. Please feel free to join them if you're tired of my company."

He strode away onto the lawn before I could reply, leaving me to join the inspection party. He still had the same outrageous confidence! As if he were able to read my thoughts! Well, he was not going to change my decision no matter what he said. I would have a look at the house now. That would make Mrs. Jennings happy. Then when we came out for the bidding I would have the house. . . .

I gave a last look around the side of the house for Billy Joe and Layton, but there was still no sign of either one. Well, it was barely seven. Layton had promised to be here at seven-fifteen, regardless. There was no point in worrying.

Inside the house the group moved rapidly from room to room, barely stopping to take in any of the details. I guessed this was to be expected. Those who were about to bid on the entire house and mountain were not likely to be influenced by the furniture or the woodwork. I scanned the faces, trying to decide who was here to bid, who was here out of curiosity, and who, as Billy Joe would have been, had he arrived on time, was here to guard the cash that the bidders had to have available to claim their purchase. There seemed to be only two bidders beside myself, judging from the cut of their clothes and their manner.

But then as we entered the basement, with its stores of preserved food, kerosene, and firewood, I recognized the disagreeable, thin-faced stare of Mr. Elliot, the Philadelphia banker.

"Well, Mr. Elliot, I had thought Philadelphia Federal had given up speculation in Grampian."

"We look for good investments wherever we can find them, Miss Rawles." He returned his gaze to the heavy oak ceiling timbers, clearly indicating that he wished no further conversation.

My sentiments exactly, I thought. But if Elliot liked what he saw, and if he had brought the cash to outbid me . . . I went upstairs to see if Layton had arrived.

With relief I saw both Layton and Billy Joe waiting for me out on the back lawn.

Billy Joe made his apologies for being late. He had been up all night, he said. He had found Red Campbell. Just the mention of that name left me shaken, but quickly I pulled myself together.

"You can tell me all about it after the sale, Billy Joe, because there's no time now. We have to get more cash up here, and quickly." I explained to Layton that a banker was here, a man who had opposed me in the past.

He lofted his eyebrows. "You think we'll need the full hundred fifty?" That was the amount the bank was authorized to lend me.

I nodded. "It's not worth taking the risk. You can leave what you've brought with me."

So down the hill they both went. It was a three-mile ride to the bank. With luck they would be back in less than a half hour.

Fifteen minutes later the small crowd had assembled again in the back and the sheriff was rapping his gavel on the table to bring the group to order. After taking a few more minutes to read the official proclamation of the sale with the terms and conditions of the auction, he turned the gavel over to Ulys Muskie, the local auctioneer. Ulys turned his old bloodhound eyes on us. "Howdy, folks. Remember, raise your hands to bid— no other signals. And I've got a bid of sixty-six thousand to start."

A ripple of surprise went through the crowd when they heard that the starting figure was so high, but Ulys paid them no heed. "So, sixty-six. Now, who'll give me seventy, who'll give me seventy?"

There was silence for a moment. Then to my right, about twenty feet away, I saw Mr. Elliot raise his hand.

At seventy-five, no one was bidding but Elliot and me. We went steadily upward.

"Ninety. Who'll give me ninety-two?"

At one hundred thousand I hesitated, but then I went on. Layton was sure to be back with the rest of the money.

Around us the crowd buzzed each time a new bid was made, especially if the raise was greater or less than the one that had just been made.

At one hundred ten, I saw Layton ride around the corner of the house. He nodded a "yes" to me as he reined to a stop.

"One hundred twenty," I said.

A small cheer went up from the crowd, which by this time had decided that they wanted me to win the contest. Elliot gave them an icy glare.

He held up his hand.

His words were precise, every syllable clipped. "One hundred fifty-five thousand."

I felt as though I had been struck on the back of the head. "No!" I gasped. "He can't have . . . Layton . . ."

Layton looked helplessly at Elliot and then at me as he hurried to my side. "That's five thousand more than what we've got, Miss Rawles. I've got a few hundred of my own with me, and you're welcome to that, but five thousand. . . ." His brow furrowed in concern as he shook his head.

How could this be happening? Absurdly, the thought crossed my mind that one hundred fifty-five thousand was really too much for an out-of-town bank to pay for an investment like this, especially since the bank could not hope to develop it into real estate of any value without my cooperation. No one would build up here these days without a gas line, and I controlled the gas company. I could see to it that a gas line for Vallamont was never put in. But what good did that do me?

"One hundred fifty-five. Who'll give me one sixty?" Ulys was speaking more slowly now, the only hint of reaction he showed to my obvious distress at what had

happened. Around me the crowd murmurs had died
down. I could feel their eyes on me, waiting, expectant,
sensing that the end was near.

"One fifty-five. Who'll give me one fifty-eight?"

"Who *is* that old bastard?" Steven's voice came from
behind me. "What the hell does he want with this
place?"

I whispered the words. "He's a Philadelphia banker.
He tried to stop me before. Philadelphia First was the
only bank that wouldn't continue Father's loans, and
this man's the one who made the refusal. And now he's
doing it again," I said, my voice beginning to break.

"But why?"

"One fifty-eight, gimme fifty-eight. Who'll give me
fifty-eight?"

"I don't *know* why, I tell you! I just don't understand
what he's . . ." The tears came up in a blur and I could
not finish.

"Going once at one fifty-five. Are you all through,
fifty-five? Fifty-eight, do I hear fifty-eight?"

"Bid one sixty." Steven gripped my arm, hard. "Do
you hear me? Bid one sixty."

Disbelief and happiness flooded through me all at once
for a moment. Steven was going to help! But then, just
as suddenly, came the realization that I could not accept. I bit my lip, wanting to cry with frustration.

"Didn't you hear me? Goddamn it, bid! One sixty!"

"I can't, Steven! I haven't got it!" Lord, how it hurt
to do this. "I can't take a gift from you!"

"Goin' twice, now, goin' twice, one fifty-five, are you
done?"

"It's a *loan,* you stubborn fool! I'll be charging you
interest!"

"Steven, it can't change anything! I'm still . . ."

He whirled me around to face him, his dark eyes cold
and intent, his voice low and hard.

"I'm not asking you to change. Go on and bid now.
It's better that you have it than *him!* Don't you see
that? Now *bid!*"

He turned me back to face the auctioneer.

"Goin' three . . ."

My hand went up. God help me, I thought, maybe it is better.

"Is that one fifty-seven, Miss Rawles?"

"It's one sixty, Ulys." I had my voice under control now.

The crowd erupted in a cheer of delight. Besides me, Layton Jacobs patted my hand. "We're still with you, Miss Rawles. We'll just call it a second mortgage, unless Mr. Cottor wants some other . . ."

We looked around for Steven, but he had already disappeared back into the crowd. Over to my right, a grim-faced Elliot stared wordlessly at the trees beyond the auctioneer's table.

"One sixty. Do I hear one sixty-five, one sixty-five?"

Elliot did not move. His arms folded, pointed chin outthrust, he kept staring into space.

"Goin' once . . . one sixty . . ."

"Do you think he'll go another round?" Layton whispered.

Steven answered, behind me again. "He doesn't have it. Ten to one says he can't top one sixty."

From behind a cloud the sun appeared and splashed light onto the eastern side of Cottor's Castle, making it appear half new stucco and half old. Here in the clearing the people were silent. Even Ulys paused in his incantation for a moment.

"Here's your money," Steven said to me, "ten thousand in cash. You won't need more." He pressed a thick fold of bills into my hand.

"Goin' twice . . ."

Elliot gave a brief glance in my direction. Then he turned on his heel and, amid the murmurs of the crowd, walked away to where his carriage stood waiting.

"Goin' three times." Down came the gavel. *"Sold!"* Another cheer went up. "To Miss Catherine Rawles of Grampian, Pennsylvania!"

"Congratulations!" Layton was shaking my hand.

As the crowd pressed closer, I heard Steven's voice. "Well, I'm going now. I'll send you a bill."

"Steven, wait!" Hurriedly I put Steven's money into Layton's hand. "You've got the rest, Layton. You go up and take care of the papers for me, would you? I'll be right back."

Steven was walking away from the crowd, away from the castle, out across the lawn to the large oak. I had to hurry to overtake him, lifting my tan twill riding skirt above my ankles as I went. I knew people would be looking. And they would talk about how quickly Nathan McKay's fiancée ran after Steven Cottor, but I could not help that. Let them talk. I had to set things right with Steven. I had to make him see that I wasn't ungrateful.

He turned when he heard me call out to him. As he waited for me, those dark eyes danced with light and a smile played faintly on his lips.

"So soon?" The easy urbanity of his tone put me on my guard. "I hadn't thought that for a mere ten thousand dollars . . ."

"Steven, don't." I stood still for a moment and caught my breath, trying to find the exact words I wanted. "I don't want you to misunderstand. I just want to say that I do appreciate . . . that I know what Vallamont must mean to you. It must have taken . . ."

He swore softly under his breath. "You really are afraid, aren't you, Catherine?" He shook his head, the look on his face suddenly grim.

"Afraid? I don't . . ."

"You're afraid of me. You're afraid of what you feel. I can see you now, trying to keep it from showing, even to yourself."

I went cold inside, unable to speak. Of course, he was right. But I was still afraid. I could never be open with him.

He was still talking, the voice flat, resigned, only a little sad. "I thought for a while that you'd always held back because it might all come to an end, because of the way our families were. But, no, that's not it. You really are afraid to love me. You want someone who's safe, someone you don't really *have* to love."

"Someone like Nathan McKay." The words slipped out by themselves. I hadn't meant to say them, but it was the truth. Nathan was safer. I might never have the ecstasy, but I would never have the storms. We could live our own lives, pursue our own careers, Nathan and I. Why did that sound so wrong when Steven said it? It was my choice to make, not his!

These thoughts flashed through my mind in an instant, and then I saw that my words had hurt Steven. "And you think that's the good, safe, businesslike thing to do?" he asked, looking away for a moment. "Let me tell you something. At the back of your mind, you're still thinking I'll be here when you want me. You're going to change your mind about McKay. I could see that this morning. And when you do decide, suddenly you'll know what you really want."

He paused, and then looked directly at me, his voice now with a mocking edge. "And then you're going to see Steven Cottor as something shiny and new, something glorious and wonderful. But then it will be too late. In fact, it's too late now."

He touched me under the chin for a moment and then took his hand away. "In fact, it's too late now. Good-bye, Catherine. You won't be seeing me again."

He turned to go, and I recovered my voice. "You'll see *me* again! I'm going to pay you back your money, every cent of it!"

He gave a short, harsh laugh. "That's like you, but don't. There's no need to now."

"That's not true! You're not going to make me feel obligated like that! I'm going to pay!"

"You can't pay me. You won't be able to. And, besides, I'm going to take more than ten thousand dollars' worth of Vallamont away wtih me. Now, good-bye."

"What are talking about? I . . ."

"It's no use talking. Now, don't follow me back into

the house. There'll be gossip enough as it is without your running after me again and making a scene."

I stood watching him stride away. So damnably confident! The way he walked, one would have thought he had just won something!

And the way I felt, I would have thought that I had lost. A cold, numbing fear that I had really made a dreadful mistake began to gnaw at me. But I couldn't think that way! I had made my choice. There was no going back. Vallamont was mine now, every inch of it. The land I was standing on, the grass, the oak tree, the spruce, the forests all around—they were mine.

And I *would* repay Steven—every cent.

He had reached the crowd. After a brief word with the sheriff, he walked up the steps to the back entrance and closed the door behind him without looking back.

From over to the right, Billy Joe was riding toward me, leading my horse behind him.

EIGHTEEN

Boughs of the tall green hemlocks on either side of us lashed the flanks of our horses. Billy Joe and I were riding down the Vallamont carriage path as quickly as was safe, for he had made it plain that speed might be important.

He had found Red Campbell, but the man was dying. "You'd scarcely tell who it was, ma'am," Billy Joe had told me up in the clearing. "Them burns didn't heal right, and I guess he's been on the run till just a few days ago."

"Where is he now?"

"He's at the clinic, ma'am. They don't know it's him, I guess, 'cause he didn't use his real name. That threw me off for a while when I first heard he'd come back to town last night. That's why I had to keep at it till this morning. Finally I got in and had a look at him. He's in a room by himself, under the name of Bell. And he looks like he don't have very long."

"What did you say to him?"

"Asked him what you wanted to know, that's all—

who was he workin' for when he . . . shot Mr. Rawles. But he just grinned. Said he wouldn't tell me, but he'd tell you. He laughed, mean-like, and he got to coughin', so I left. Then I looked at my watch and realized it was past the time for me to meet you at the bank, so I just went straight over there."

So now we were making our way down the trail, headed for town. As long as there was a chance to learn the truth about Father's killer, I knew I could not pass it by. Would Campbell tell the truth? A dying man would have no reason to lie. If only he were still conscious when we arrived!

We came around a bend in the wooded path and suddenly had to rein in our horses. Ahead of us was a carriage that blocked the way. There was not enough room on either side for a rider to get through.

"Hey, speed it up, there!" called Billy Joe. "Comin' through!"

But the carriage kept on at its same sedate pace.

"How far till the end of these trees?" I asked.

" 'Bout half a mile, I think. Can't see the end of 'em from here, that's for sure. Here, come on up close behind him with me. I'll get us along."

We rode up to where we could almost touch the lacquered black wood of the carriage. Then Billy Joe handed me his reins. "Ya just come along and pick me up when we're out of these woods," he said. He quickly dismounted. Then, almost without breaking stride, he leaped up onto the empty brass luggage carrier to the rear of the cab. In another moment he had clambered up onto the roof. I could hear the surprised voice of the coachman, but a few blunt words from Billy Joe—and a look at Billy Joe's massive size, no doubt—soon ended the protest. The carriage began to pick up speed and was soon clattering along at a pace I had trouble matching myself.

Soon I could see the open land ahead. As the coach lurched forward and banged along into the grassy fields where the road widened, I came up alongside. Billy Joe brought the carriage to a stop.

While I waited for him to get down from the cab and mount his horse again, I took a silver dollar from my purse and tossed it up to the startled driver.

"That's for your trouble," I said. "Give our apologies to whoever's in that carriage. I hope we didn't shake them up too . . ."

The carriage door opened and I saw the wizened face of Mr. Elliot. His sharp features looked doubly unpleasant, for he was clearly beside himself with rage. "You . . ." he sputtered, "you . . ."

"On second thought," I called to the driver, "don't apologize. Mr. Elliot probably has a train to catch, and we wouldn't want to keep him waiting!"

And Billy Joe and I were off, leaving behind us the furious Mr. Elliot.

"Serves him right, ma'am," said Billy Joe as we slowed down a bit at the edge of town.

"I know. That's the second time he's deliberately opposed me. Let's hope it's the last." Then I had an idea. "As a matter of fact, Billy Joe, why don't you see what you can find out about Mr. Elliot? See if you can find out something that might give us a way to keep him in check, in case he decides to get in our way again."

Billy Joe flashed me a grin. "Oh, I can tell you that right now, ma'am. I checked up on him right after the first time, soon as you gave me my job. Struck me that a man like that might not be above hirin' a few chaps to see that we had some troubles in the mill. So I looked into things—as much as I could from up here."

"And what did you find?"

"Well, nothin' incriminatin'. But I did find you a good way to keep him in line. Only reason I didn't say anything about it was that I figured you wouldn't need it, now that you're engaged."

"Billy Joe, I don't see . . ."

"If you want to keep Elliot from meddlin', seems to

me all you need to do is have Mr. McKay put in a word or two. He's on the board of directors of Philadelphia First."

"He's what?" I could scarcely believe it. For a moment I was angry. Nathan ought to have known that Elliot was coming. He should have warned me so that I wouldn't have had to go up to the auction unprepared. . . . But it was senseless to expect that of Nathan. He was so busy he scarcely had time to talk to me, much less keep up on the activities of a Philadelphia bank. It was likely he didn't even bother to attend the board meetings, now that he had moved away. Probably that was why he hadn't told me about the connection.

"Saw the name on one of the bank's official reports— Nathan McKay. And it's the same one, too. I wrote the bank, askin' for his address, and they wrote back that he lived in Grampian."

"Well, I shall certainly speak to him about Mr. Elliot. . . ." My voice trailed off. It began to dawn on me that Philadelphia First could hardly have avoided consulting Nathan about any business transactions it planned in Grampian. For a bank to ignore one of its directors . . .

"Billy Joe, did you find out if any of the other directors of Philadelphia First live in Grampian, or anywhere near here?"

"No, ma'am. But none of the other names looked familiar. You want me to check?"

We were stopping in front of Nathan's clinic, where I would have to go in and face Red Campbell. "I don't know yet, Billy Joe," I said, feeling suddenly tired. "I think I've got enough on my mind as it is. Ask me later, would you? Remind me."

I had not been inside the clinic for months, but the familiar reception area had not changed. Behind the desk, Mrs. Martin still had that same dedicated loyalty in her gaze, though her eyes did look a bit less saintly when they recognized me. "Oh, hello, Miss Rawles," she said. "We certainly haven't seen you here in a long time."

"How are you, Mrs. Martin? I'd like to see Dr. McKay, and a patient here named . . ."

I hesitated, but Billy Joe supplied the name. "Bell. He's over there in 1-C."

"Oh, yes. That's the man you were talking to early this morning, isn't it? I'm sorry to tell you that he's not to have any visitors. Those are Dr. McKay's orders. I'd let you speak to Dr. McKay about it, but I'm afraid he's not here just now. Perhaps you'd care to wait?"

At the top of the stairs, a patient in a robe recognized us. "Hey, Billy Joe!" he called. Then, turning away from us for a moment, he called out, "Hey, Pete, guess who's here? You remember Billy Joe and that Miss Rawles, the one who used to come in afternoons?"

I could hear a hubbub of voices upstairs coming from the men's ward. Soon two other familiar faces appeared at the railing overhead and waved down at us, much to the exasperation of Mrs. Martin.

"They're supposed to be *resting!*" she fumed. "Where's that day nurse? Do I have to go quiet them down myself?"

She got up from her desk and headed up the stairs. "Good-bye, ma'am," called Billy Joe. Then, as soon as she was out of sight, he led me quickly to the door of 1-C.

A single wood-frame bed stood in the center of the little room. Behind the headboard, a window with partially opened curtains let in the light, illuminating the hunched figure that lay under the sheets.

I drew in my breath at the sight of him. Billy Joe had understated Campbell's appearance. The red hair and beard had almost completely vanished. All that remained of them were a few tufts, unkempt, on the left side. The right was a mass of scars, barely recognizable as a human face. Only one eye remained; the other was completely encrusted, a depression amid the maze of destroyed tissue.

The one eye opened as we came in. The mouth, a gaping slit, whispered with laughter. "Ya brought her good and quick, didn't ya? Bust your ass to see ole Red now?"

Again, that hideous whistling laugh came forth. I forced myself to come closer to the bed. "You said you had something to say about why you were in Eagles Mere. Who was paying you, Campbell? Who were you working for? Was it Abel Cottor?"

That horrible head, the scars purplish and yellow, barely moved. "Said I'd tell *you,* didn't I?" The voice was a whispered sneer. "But I didn't say I'd tell him. Tell him to go."

"That's absurd. What difference does it make . . ."

"Tell him to go, or ole Red don't say nothin'."

"I'll wait outside, ma'am. And don't worry, I'll keep the desk lady occupied."

The door closed behind him and I was alone in the room with this horribly deformed creature, all that remained of the man on whom I had sworn to get revenge. And in that revenge I had certainly succeeded, I thought. I could scarcely imagine a fate more horrible that what Campbell must have gone through these past months.

I forced myself to speak. I had to get this over with. "All right, Campbell, I've done as you asked."

He remained silent, except for a slight rasping noise that I realized was his breathing.

"Campbell, who was it? Who were you working for?" The voice was petulant whining. "Come closer."

I advanced a few steps and stopped. The head did not move, but the one eye, which faced my side of the bed, opened a bit wider.

"Now, take my hand."

I spoke firmly. "This is as close as I'm coming. Who was it?"

"Take my hand, I said." Beneath the sheet there was movement. Blackened stumps of fingers appeared, groped, and reached out.

I stepped back. "What you have to say doesn't mean that much to me, Campbell."

My harsh words brought a response. "Why, you bitch!" He tried to lift himself up on one elbow. "Did you think I was gonna tell you *anything?* Goddamned dumb bitch! I just wanted to get you in here so I could spit in your eye! I wanted to show you what you done to me!" The hand fumbled with the sheet. "Look at this arm, hey? Ain't it pretty? And my chest—ya wanna see a real . . ."

His words froze in mid-sentence as the door opened behind me. "No!" he yelled, his voice cracking, terrified.

I turned. In the doorway stood Nathan. His face was a mask of cold anger.

And from behind me came that horrid whisper of Campbell's voice. "No, Doc! I didn't tell her! I didn't tell her nothin'!"

And suddenly I knew. And those cool blue eyes of Nathan's looked through me and saw that I knew.

I stood silent for a moment, trying to get over the shock. The thoughts raced through my mind. Nathan had known that I could bid one hundred fifty thousand dollars, and Elliot had come with one hundred fifty-five thousand dollars. Abel Cottor had fired Campbell after Warren Ruch had died. Nathan had taken time out from his busy schedule to come up to the mountains with Father. And that first night we had seen Campbell. And the next day Nathan had gone back to Grampian.

Nathan was closing the door behind him now.

"Billy Joe!" I called. "Come in here!"

Nathan smiled slightly as he turned the key in the lock. "I wouldn't look for him for another hour if I were you, Catherine. Your loyal security man is off doing what he thinks is his duty. We sent in a message that there was trouble at your hotel."

"You knew we were here!"

"I couldn't help overhearing all that commotion up-stairs, could I? Of course, I'd told Mrs. Martin I wasn't available for visitors. She may have been a bit over-zealous, I'm afraid, thinking of my fiancée as a visitor."

Already I had taken off his ring. "Surely you don't still think of me as your fiancée. I . . ."

He interrupted me, the voice impenetrably professional, the doctor to the patient. "You're upset now, Catherine. You think that something terrible has happened, but it hasn't. You'll see that nothing's really changed."

He turned away from me to some bottles on the medicine table beside him as he spoke. "You think that this man killed your father on my orders. Well, that's not true at all. I sent him to look at Eagles Mere, yes, I admit that. But . . ."

"But *why?* How could you . . ."

"He came to me for work. It was the day after his bullet had nearly fractured my skull, but, of course, I didn't recognize him. I thought he might be useful. Your father was concerned about sabotage of his properties, and Campbell said he knew them well."

"You were hiring him to sabotage Father's property?"

"No. I hired him to give me a report. I wanted him to look things over and give me an opinion, in case I wanted to invest. Your father wanted to sell me a percentage of that hotel, you know."

"I didn't know. He never said anything of the kind."

"Well, it's true, all the same. And what Campbell did to you and your father at Eagles Mere was completely his own idea. I told him only to look over the grounds for security. Isn't that right, Campbell?"

The figure on the bed lay silent and still. The sheets were motionless.

"He's dead!" I whispered the words hoarsely, suddenly numb with fear. "Let me out, Nathan! Let me out!"

He was coming closer, the face and blue eyes eerily serene. "Just as soon as you understand, Catherine, that I had nothing to do with your father's death."

"You sent Elliot, though. You told him to go against me, and when that didn't work, you . . ." I looked at the ring in my hand and suddenly the anger rose up inside of me. "You're disgusting!" I flung the ring at him. It bounced off his white shirt and clattered to the floor, but he paid it no attention.

"You're imagining things, Catherine. You've no way to prove that. It's just been a trying time for you to see this man again. Now I'm going to give you something that will quiet your nerves. . . ."

He came toward me with the bottle of brownish fluid in his hand.

"You'll not give me anything! Let me out!"

"It's only a sedative, darling, only a mild sedative to quiet . . ."

"Like the ones you gave Elaine!" The image of that woman's vacant smile and her dazed, semi-conscious manner was suddenly in my mind. Horrified at what this man could do, I made a rush past him for the door. The knob would not turn. I felt Nathan's strong hands grip my shoulders.

"No!" I screamed as loudly as I could. "No!" I kicked frantically at the door and had the satisfaction of hearing the wood crack on one side of the lower panel. If I could break through . . . but he was pulling me away, the power of his tall, lean frame too strong for me.

I screamed again, and then he choked off my cry as the palm of his hand clamped firmly across my mouth, pinching my nostrils shut, so that I could not breathe. "Now, Catherine, you've got to be quiet and listen to me."

I knocked the bottle of opium from his hand, sending it hard against the wall. There was a crash as it hit the floor, and then, as Nathan released me, a pungent, sweet odor of alcohol began to fill the room.

He pushed me aside and was at the medicine table again, opening another bottle. Then from a canister he quickly grabbed a large wad of cotton. I raced to the door and kicked out again with my thin-soled riding boot. I kicked once, then again, until my foot pained me terribly. There was a splintering noise and my boot nearly went through the door. From the other side of the door came the sound of voices. If only the men from upstairs could hear me!

I opened my mouth to cry out again, but before I could utter a sound he was upon me from behind. Cold, wet cotton was clapped across my mouth and nose. The grip of his arm across my chest was like a steel trap. Vaguely I recalled that fluid, that odor that was making me dizzy. The surgeons used ether to put patients to sleep. . . .

And what would Nathan do to me? I held my breath, determined to fight. Fear and anger welled up inside me. In a great, violent outburst of strength I never knew I possessed, I shifted my weight and lashed out savagely with the heel of my boot, catching him across the shin bone with a resounding crack.

He drew in his breath at the pain. And then he tightened his grip. "Why, you little vixen." The voice was low and hard, just behind my ear. "You're a real little fighter, aren't you?"

Then suddenly there was a voice outside the door. "Dr. McKay!" It was a woman's voice—Mrs. Martin's. "Do you need help in there?"

I had to breathe! Desperately I twisted my body to the right, stamping my heel down onto his instep. As he staggered backward, I spun around and dropped down at the same time, still in his arms but with my head below his chest and my face at last free of that hideous, stifling cotton! In one last burst of strength, I hit up at him with my fist as hard as I possibly could, squarely between his legs. He gave a groan and stumbled back toward the bed.

I leaned back against the doorway, gasping for air, watching him bent over as he strained to recover. In a moment or two he would be at me again, I could see that from his eyes.

"Open the door, Mrs. Martin!" I yelled out. "Dr. McKay needs help!"

Before he could take a single step or speak, the lock clicked and the door beside me swung open.

"Go to him," I told the bewildered Mrs. Martin. "He's had some trouble with the patient."

And then I was making my way through the crowd of patients at the reception area. I mouthed greetings and explanations at the same time as I went. The doctor had had trouble, I said, and I was going to get help. Mercifully they let me pass without questions.

Outside there was the October sun and the mountains across the Susquehanna, and the autumn colors shone in the crisp, clear air. The morning out here was calm and natural: a Saturday.

I mounted my horse and set off down the street for home, automatically, simply getting away without thinking. It was not until I had ridden nearly a block from the clinic that I realized how free I felt. The tiredness that had been with me from my awakening this morning, the tiredness that had been with me for so many mornings these past months, had vanished.

You don't love him. Steven's words came suddenly into my mind, and I realized at last that they were true. I was glad to be free. I had thought of Nathan as security, but he had not been what he seemed. He had played me false.

Or had he? I brought my horse to a stop, transfixed by the possibility that Nathan might have been telling the truth, after all. He could have hired Campbell just to look at Eagles Mere. Perhaps he really had wanted to learn the hotel's weak points in the event Father asked him to invest. Also, perhaps he really had not known what the agent of Philadelphia First was doing. . . .

But, with shattering clarity, it finally struck me: right or wrong did not matter. Nathan might have been friend or enemy, and it still did not change what really mattered. I did not love him.

I had loved the ideas he had spoken. I had loved his plans, his ambitions, because I had shared them. He had said that the Rawles family had to stop fighting the Cottors, and I had loved that thought because I had felt the same way. His ideas for different new industries, for expansion, for better schools, and for parks—they were all wonderful ideas.

But they were not the sum of Nathan McKay.

What had Mother said that day when she had so annoyed me with her questions about the way I felt? It was so easy to confuse admiration with love. "Sam Rawles made me cry, but I was never sorry."

Dear God, how close I had come . . .

I took a brief look back at Nathan's clinic, and saw a coach stopping at the front entrance. It was the same coach Billy Joe and I had passed earlier on the road. It was Elliot's coach. I was only a little surprised to find that I felt nothing at all when I saw Elliot get out and go inside. Was he coming to report a defeat, or simply stopping by to say hello? It did not matter. My interest in that question was gone, because my love for Nathan was gone . . . or had never existed.

"You don't love him." As I said these words to myself, the calm emptiness I felt suddenly began to change to a deep, full certainty. "I love Steven." I whispered it once, then again. "I really do." And the warmth, the familiar warmth, began to race through my veins. He was proud, too proud. He wanted to own me, to possess me. I hated that; I was my own woman, and no one could own me. But I had to admit now that I felt the same urge of my own for Steven. I wanted to own him just as much as I had wanted Vallamont, even more. . . .

And I was proud, too, perhaps more so than he. Neither of us was perfect. We would get in each other's way; we would rage at one another. He would make me cry, and I would hurt him, just as we had both done ever since I had come back to Grampian.

But I knew I would never be sorry. And we would have our love.

Then his words from early this morning came back to me, cool, mocking: *And then you're going to see Steven Cottor as something shiny and new, something glorious and wonderful. But then it will be too late. In fact, it's too late now.*

No! Wherever he was going, he wouldn't have gone yet. It had only been an hour or two. I could still catch up with him. I could ride up to Vallamont, talk to him, and make him see reason, make him see love. He didn't look new to me, I thought as I turned my horse around toward Vallamont. He was the same maddening, infuriating Steven.

But I was not afraid to love him anymore.

I came around the corner and turned onto Market Street, the street that led straight up to the Vallamont carriage path. I looked up at the mountain as I always did, to the silhouette of Cottor's Castle at the top. But today the castle was mine. . . .

I saw clouds of black smoke. The smoke was rising into the sky from the top of the mountain.

"I'm going to take more than ten thousand dollars' worth of Vallamont away with me. Oh, Steven! How he had hated his father, hated that castle that Abel had built!

I urged my horse to go faster up toward the mountain and to Steven.

You can't pay me. You won't be able to.

My God, I thought. In my mind's eye I saw Steven as he had been that afternoon in Abel's library, just after we had made love—the glass of bourbon in his hand, that cynical, resigned smile on his lips. . . .

By the time I reached the clearing at the top of the woods, there were flames coming from every window.

My horse froze there at the edge of the gravel. The intense heat came at us in waves. The horse began to neigh in terror.

"Steven!" I yelled. There was no answer, only the crackling and the roar of the great fire. "Steven!" The horse reared up and tried to turn away from the heat, those frightful yellow tongues that glittered so. I steadied my horse, shielding its eyes until I could dismount. Then I sent the horse back down toward Grampian. Whoever was coming up would find the frightened animal and know to look for me.

To enter the front of the house was impossible. The double doors at the tower were open, but behind them was an unbroken wall of yellow fire. The library was to the back; I remembered that.

With my boots slipping awkwardly on the gravel, I dashed around to the rear entrance. "Steven!" The fire had not yet gained a thorough foothold back here. Above the three stone steps, the doorway to the rear hall stood open. "Steven!"

There were flames at the far end of the hall. Could I go in there? The smoke was growing thicker, hurting my throat, burning my lungs, making me choke. . . .

But I knew I could not face tomorrow, or the thousands of tomorrows that would follow, if I had to ask myself: "Why didn't I go in?"

"Steven!" I gave one last call, and amid the roar of the flames and the smoke I thought I heard his voice! "Steven!" I went up the stone steps, feeling their heat already begin to come through the thin soles of my boots. At the open doorway I hesitated, trying to see the library, over at the right side of the hall, trying to get a last breath of clean air before plunging into the smoke. What was it I heard?

And then a sound like a hundred guns came from somewhere within the house, and something—was it the transom of the door?—broke loose and struck me behind my neck and across my shoulders, knocking me down to my knees. As the great darkness swirled around me I prayed for strength, but I only sank deeper and deeper into the clouds of smoke that were so stifling. . . .

NINETEEN

Above me was the blue sky. The black smoke was only one part of that wide expanse, a pillar that rose higher and became ever more diminished, disappearing in wisps and trails as it traveled skyward. The cool green grass touched the back of my neck, my cheek, my hands. . . .

And when I turned, there was Steven. His eyes widened when he saw I was awake. His look of concern deepened as I sat up. The stiffness I felt in my back and shoulders made me wince, and he seemed to feel it, too.

But when he was certain that I was really unhurt, the dark eyes recovered their glitter. And when he spoke it was with his usual offhanded manner, the same bantering smile.

"So you thought I'd have stayed in the flames? Burned myself in despair? My dear, Vallamont wasn't that important. Life may be hard now and again, but it'll suit me just fine until something better comes along."

"Oh, Steven . . ."

"I heard you calling, as though I'd come out when you whistled! And I called back from here, but, I must say, your hearing isn't any better than your judgment."

"Will you be quiet!" I nearly shouted the words, and for the first time I looked around, suddenly conscious that someone else might be nearby. But there was no one. We were out on the back lawn, behind the oak tree. A hundred yards away, the castle had dwindled to a great pile of smoking rubble. The towers were gone. The roof was gone. The shell that remained was barely two stories tall.

"How did you do that?"

He smiled easily, poised, mocking. "Nice to see you taking an interest in what I do for a change. Or are you only wondering about your property?"

"Steven, don't!" I could have slapped him. "I have something to tell you, and I won't be talked to this way!"

"On your own land, is that it?"

And then I did slap him, or tried to. He caught my hand and held me by the wrist.

"Now, don't get excited. You wanted to know how I did it. It wasn't difficult. I used kerosene, and then I packed black powder into the speaking tubes. It's surprising how well that shakes up the interior walls. The whole structure just topples in upon itself."

I recalled the first explosion, and then I seemed to remember others, louder, while he had borne me up in his arms and carried me away from the house.

"So if you and your Nathan decide to go into the demolition business, there's a good . . ."

"Steven!" I was growing angry now. This wasn't the way I had wanted to tell him. Why didn't he let me tell him? Why did he have to be so . . . . "Steven, look at my hand. Can you remember the ring I used to wear there? Nathan's ring?" Why was I shouting?

He glanced at my left hand. The eyes flickered. The face remained mockingly impassive.

"You found out? Thought it might take longer than that till you learned our Dr. McKay has a piece of Elliot's bank. But then you always did have a good head for business, once you got pointed in the right direction."

"Steven, that's not it. I mean, yes, I did find out, but that doesn't matter. I realized I couldn't marry him. I don't love him. I love you."

I'd said it! But he barely moved. A bluejay swooped down from the row of spruce trees behind him and chirped on the lawn for a moment beside Steven's leather suitcase. Then it fluttered and retreated to the forest.

His voice was quieter now. "Not a very businesslike thing to do, is it, Catherine? You'd better think again. Think about what you've been able to do because of Nathan McKay. Think about how he's going to work against you now—all those nice connections in town, all those people who're going to talk behind your back. . . ."

"I'm used to fighting, Steven. I don't care what Nathan does."

"You will, though. When the profits start to slide, when the loans come due again, you're going to say to yourself, 'I gave up what could have been ten million, twenty million, for one cantankerous bastard of a husband who had only fifty thousand dollars to his name.' "

"Sixty!"

"You can't talk it away, Catherine. You want money and land. The desire is in your blood. I've seen it all too often. I even saw it that first day when you came up here, when you were only fourteen!"

"But you loved me then, just the same! And I loved you!"

"And a fine job we did showing it once you'd finished being a schoolgirl and started being a woman! No, Catherine, you're only . . ."

"Damn you!" I flung myself at him, the tears hot and

341

smarting in my eyes. I caught him around the shoulders and bore him down onto the grass beside me. "You said you couldn't change! You said neither of us could change! Do I have to run back into your damned fire again? I'm not afraid anymore. Can't you see that?"

The tears overcame me then and I rested my head on his chest, the white shirt cool and smooth against my cheek. I could hear his heart, feel it under me. And from far away I heard the chimes of Father's clock toll noon.

Steven held me tightly until the last note from the clock had faded away in the mountain wind.

I raised my head and saw there were tears in his eyes. His voice came softly, his lips full and gentle. "Come kiss me, then, my Catherine."

Later, as he helped me onto his horse for the ride back to town, an idea seemed to occur to him.

"What sort of a house," he asked, "do you think we could build up here for fifty thousand dollars?"

The dream that had become so familiar was suddenly a vision in my mind. I was alone at the window of a house on Vallamont. The house was mine, and I was alone, but I was looking out at someone. I was looking out at Steven, and then I was running to the door, flinging it open, welcoming him.

"Federal-style brick would do very well, I should imagine."

FIERY NOVELS of ADVENTURE and UNDYING LOVE!

DIOSA Charles Rigdon
From London to Central America, there was
no woman on Earth like the beautiful Lady
Kate Ashley—the woman chosen by the gods
as their beloved goddess.   #81817 $1.95

FORBIDDEN RITES Joan Bagnel
The passionate story of a woman and two
men—of a savage love that should never have
been, and a hope that could never be con-
quered.   #80944 $1.95

MARILEE Con Sellers
From the post-Civil War South, to the untamed
West, to the riches of Mexico—a big story of
love, embittered passions, and unholy desires in
a time when danger and violence were a way of
life.   #81211 $1.95

Bestselling Novels from POCKET BOOKS